SINCERE LIES

THE LANGFORD BILLIONAIRES
BOOK 2

A.V. ARCHER

DEDICATION

To my girls, may you never read any of my books, lest I die of awkward shame.

Thank you for being my biggest cheerleaders, and for telling anyone who will listen how great my books are, even when you have no idea what they're about. Your unwavering love and support makes the hard days so much better. Never doubt how much you inspire me.
How much stronger you make me.
I love you with all of my soul, and I'm so lucky to call you mine.

1

ASHER

She's so beautiful, even in sleep. The shadows in the room blanket most of her, but faint light sifting through the sheer curtains highlights the curves of her body, the delicate features of her face, painting her beauty in a way that makes the breath catch in my chest. She's never more perfect to me than when she's raw and unfiltered. And I wish more than anything that I had more time with her like this, away from the world, away from all the things that threaten to tear us apart—irrevocably. I can't let that happen.

I take a step closer to her bed, careful not to wake her, even as she shifts fitfully in a restless sleep.

Her brow is slightly furrowed, her full lips are drawn and tight, and I wonder if she dreams of me the way I do of her during the small intervals I do manage to sleep. My pride hopes her trouble sleeping is not from the storm that raged for most of the night, but because she's back in her old bedroom alone, and not downstairs, sleeping with me in our bed.

That has to end.

Ella told me she needed space. I've given her three days.

Some might say that's nothing, but I think I've been more than generous.

Weeks ago, the thought of pining after a woman because of a three-day separation would have been unconceivable. But Ella isn't just any woman. She's the woman who surprised the hell out of me, who glimpsed something in me so few had taken the time to. Before her, I'd never met a woman who saw past my facade. Never known a woman who cared to look at the man behind the money—the person behind the power and prestige. I've never been wanted for anything more than the glittering spectacle of wealth and fame that surround me. Women in droves want Asher Langford—but no woman has ever just wanted Asher.

Until Ella.

But she's so much more than a surprise.

She's the force of nature that burst into my life and obliterated it as it was. Someone whose joy and love and goodness shine like a beacon of warmth in my world of cold indifference. She's the singular person who calls to me like a siren's song, and can't help but fall into her, wholly caught in her spell.

I've never wanted anything as much as I want her.

And yet, here we are, with three days of space between us. I know she's scared. I know she has reservations. With the way our relationship began, and everything that's happened since, how could she not? I understand her fears, truly, I do. But I'm at my wit's end.

I will make her one promise at a time until I can give her everything she wants. Everything she deserves. In the meantime, I need her back to where we were before everything fell apart.

I take one last step toward her sleeping figure, grateful for the lingering drizzle from last night's storm that patters softly against the windows, stifling the sound. I reach into my pocket and grasp the gold ring Ella thought she could take off and leave behind. Holding my breath, I reach for her right hand and gently slip the ring back onto her middle finger.

There. That's better.

Ella does not get to remove parts of me from her. Not anymore. We're too far past that. I gave her space to humor her in a moment when she was incredibly vulnerable—I'm not a complete asshole. But that moment has passed, and I'm done humoring her. Ella is mine.

And when she wakes, she'll be reminded of that.

"Take it easy, asshole," I growl at Declan thirty minutes later as he lands a right hook across my jaw. He gets a little over excited when he's fighting someone who can hang with him, since that doesn't happen often. We're at the VI Club; a gentleman's club my family has belonged to since its inception over two centuries ago. It's where the elite of the elite meet for business, pleasure, and all manner of debauchery. But I'm not here for any of those things, I'm here because they have a state-of-the-art boxing facility that I'm in desperate need of. With everything going on, I feel like I'm about to lose my goddamned mind, and I figure punching Declan in the boxing ring is a better option than punching someone at the office. With the mood I'm in, that could be a real possibility, and with so much on the line, it's not a mistake I can afford to make.

I move my jaw back and forth to work out the pain because even though we're wearing sparring gear, Declan's got a hell of an arm and his hits sting like a bitch.

"Sorry," he grunts through a smile. But I know better. He's not sorry at all. He's enjoying every second of kicking my ass. Declan is the most athletic of the three of us Langford brothers, and if my mother hadn't put up fights about him playing football and boxing, he could have gone far in either of those sports. I barely block his next jab and somehow get in a body shot.

"I take it Ella's still looking for an apartment," Declan says as we dance around one another.

"She is. But unluckily for her, there aren't many vacancies at the moment."

"And you wouldn't have anything to do with that." His tone is mocking.

"It's not my fault the moment Ella sees a listing and calls on it, the realtor lets her know that someone is interested and already put down a deposit."

"Sure, it's not."

"I won't have her anywhere but my penthouse. It's not safe."

"So, she's back to sleeping upstairs."

I get my own right hook in, annoyance buzzing through my veins at his words. "Last night was her last. She wanted space, and I gave it to her, but I'm at the end of my rope."

"Why now? You're leaving for Singapore tomorrow. The ten days you're gone will give her more of that space she wants and time to think."

"That's the last thing I want."

Declan barks out a laugh. "If I recall, this is what you wanted in the beginning. And now you've got it."

"Fuck that," I growl, landing another body shot.

I'm about to lose my fucking mind.

I come at Declan full force. "I was wrong then, and I'm going to fix it now."

"If it makes you feel better, she seems just as miserable as you. I talked to her yesterday when I stopped by your penthouse. She looks like a ghost of herself."

That makes me feel worse. And better. Fuck, this is all a mess.

"You're making this too complicated, Ash. You need to give

in to what you want and just go for it. You're both miserable without each other."

"And the threats over Greenspan? You saw the text."

I can still see the text in my head.

> Unknown: An offer to purchase Greenspan will be delivered to your board next week and it would be in your best interest to accept it. Akio Kobayashi will never walk again, and it would be a shame if you or your pretty little girlfriend came to share that same fate.

AKIO IS our top researcher for Greenspan, a renewable energy company we own. He was injured in an accident on the job that we now know wasn't an accident. Greenspan is being targeted with sabotage to cripple it because it's a major threat to the oil industry. Declan, Sterling, our brother based in London, and I are working to take down the threats from TDC Oil, the company we believe to be behind the sabotage and some of the people responsible for my grandfather's death, but until we take out this threat, Ella is a target, and she's in danger.

And therein lies my problem.

I have to keep her close to keep her safe, but the more I bring her into my life, the more I put her in danger. I want her, and wanting her puts her in danger, so I'm fucked no matter what I do. All I know is I can't lose her the way I lost my grandpa. I won't survive it if I do.

So, I have to be careful about our relationship since our situation is complicated. The problem is, Ella doesn't know that. Not the whole story of it, at least. I've only shared bits and pieces of my past with her because I only just realized that the people who killed my grandfather twenty-five years ago are the same people threating me now. I will tell her, but I don't want to yet. First, because there are still some unknowns I need to puzzle together, and second, because she's just been through hell with her ex. Her fucking ex who pulled a gun on her to extort money from me. The fallout of that situation is a mess— with the media, with the board, and the last thing I want is to burden her with another problem. She needs time to recover first, and I'm determined to give it to her.

Declan dances out of my reach, then stars spark across my vision as he sneaks in a jab that hits me square on the jaw. Shit, that hurt.

"You know as well as I do that the safest place for her is with you. And if you push her away, you'll lose your shares."

I growl and throw a sloppy punch, missing Declan's face by inches. That's the crux of the situation. I was forced into this relationship by my board to improve my image, and now I've unintentionally put Ella in danger. Our relationship may have started as a farce, but it's nothing close to one anymore, and the longer she's with me, the more I fall for her. And the more I know it will gut me if I'm forced let her go.

"As someone who's sworn off relationships, you sure seem keen to push me into one." I don't know why I spit the words at Declan with venom in my voice. This isn't his doing, and I know he's just trying to help, but I can't stop the irrational anger from gushing out of me.

"I'm not pushing you into a relationship for the hell of it. I see the way you look at her. I see the way you two are with one another. She's not just a fling, and you know it."

"You seem a little too invested."

"I'm invested because I care about you, dumbass. I see what a fool you're being, and I'm trying to knock some sense into your head." He does just that, hitting me with another jab that makes my eyes water and my ears ring. "Once upon a time, all I ever wanted was to find love and have a happy little family.

That hasn't worked out for me, and I've accepted that. But you've found the jackpot and you're throwing it away. Don't be an idiot, Asher. You have what none of us ever thought we would, so quit being a bitch, and go for it before you lose her. Because I'll tell you one thing, the minute the world knows she's single and fair game, she'll be hunted like a damn prize. You may have put her on the map, but she's stayed there because she's special—and you're not the only rich and powerful motherfucker to notice it. Every man looks at you with envy when you're with her, and the minute you're out of the picture, men will come swarming like vultures, and you'll lose her forever. Do you really want to live with that?"

Fuck.

Fuck, fuck, fuck.

I haven't thought about that in a while. I've been so caught up in the complications of our situation that I stopped thinking about what the future would look like if I did lose her. This whole situation with Ella was supposed to be an arrangement, and I always knew I'd be letting her go at some point, but somewhere along the way that became unacceptable. And now the thought of her with someone else makes me see red.

"Are you going to be okay watching her move on with her future without you?" Declan continues, hitting me with a quick combination. "Think about how you're going to feel when she moves out—for good. What about when she moves in with another man? What about when she gets engaged, married, has kids with someone else? If you choose not to keep her, someone else will get their happily ever after with her, and you'll regret it for the rest of your life."

Declan's words are like another punch, but instead of wounding me, they incite me. I lay into him, feeding my rage into my arms and hands. I hit him back with my own brutal combination, and he staggers backward into the ropes. When he gets his feet back under him, he shakes his head to clear it, then smirks at me.

"You know you want to fix this."

"I know. And I will, but I need to get this threat taken care of first." I take a few long breaths, trying to calm my racing heart. "Tyrone has some more information for me. I need to hear what he has to say, and then I'll figure out what to do from there."

"And if it's bad news?"

"Then the situation is the same as it was before. I keep Ella close and try to get our relationship back to what it was."

"A fake couple with benefits?"

"Yeah," I huff, still out of breath. "Until Greenspan and TDC are dealt with."

"And once it's over?"

"I'll figure out how to commit to her fully. It's what I want, anyway. I just can't seem to make myself do it while the risks are this high."

"You know this won't be the last threat. Our lives will never be free of them."

I take off my gloves and start removing my headgear. "I know. But this one is bigger than normal—it involves the Russian mafia for Christ's sake."

Declan lets out a long sigh. "Then let's get those fuckers taken care of. You deserve happiness, Ash."

I nod in agreement as I think back to Ella's sleeping form, of the ring I slipped on her finger. I hate that any part of me wavers when it comes to our relationship. I want nothing more than her, and I want to make her mine in every conceivable way. I just have to take it one step at a time until I know she's safe.

The first step is done. The second step will happen when I see her tonight after work.

2

ELLA

I pry my eyes open, blinking against the dull gray light filtering through the rain-spotted windows of my bedroom. Last night's storm looks to be over, though the clouds have yet to clear and make room for the sun. But I don't mind.

I'm in no mood for the sun, anyway.

I rub at my dry, sore eyes, brushing away the salty remains of dried tears and exhaustion. The thunder was so loud, I doubt much of the city slept through that storm. But it wasn't the sounds or the flashes of lightning that kept me awake—it was my mind and heart that wouldn't shut up.

A glint of light catches my attention, and I freeze, my hand an inch away from my eyes.

There's a ring on my finger that definitely wasn't there when I went to sleep.

I drop my hand and take in the sight. It's Asher's ring. Only a part of me is surprised to find it back on my finger. Four days ago, I took it off. Three days ago, I told Asher I needed space. He told me he'd give it to me. But he also told me we weren't over. I should have known he'd take matters into his own hands. Usually I don't mind, but today, I don't know how to feel.

I rub my thumb over the flat top of the ring. AHL. Asher Harrington Langford. The man I'm in love with. There's no question about it. But what I don't know, is if I can trust him.

He's not a cheater, and he's not a liar. It's not the usual worries over trust that I'm struggling with. What I worry about with Asher is the vastness of his life. When you're one of the richest and most powerful men on the planet, you get pulled in a lot of different directions. I'm okay with that. But what I'm not okay with is always taking a backseat to it. If I stay with Asher, will his work always come first? That's what I don't know. That's what I don't trust in the long-term.

I also don't know where we stand in general. We got together as a PR stunt to rehabilitate his image, but we turned into more—how much more is still an unknown. Asher isn't ready for a real relationship, so we've been caught in this scary in-between of not quite a real relationship, but no longer a fake one, either. The only thing we're both sure of is the insane connection we share. We can't keep our hands off each other, and when we're together, we're like fire and gasoline—burning, consuming—out of control.

I love every minute of it. I just don't know if it's something that can last forever.

My phone rings, pulling me from my morose thoughts, and I pick it up, grateful for the distraction. But my stomach immediately coils in dread when I see my boss's name flash across the screen. She's given me as much time as she can, and it looks like my time has run out.

"Hey," I croak, my voice raw and ragged.

"How are you?" Emily asks.

I clear my throat. "I'm okay."

"I'm sure you know why I'm calling. We need to issue a statement." Her tone is soothing, gentle, and I appreciate it, but not for the reason she would assume. "Matthew and I are working on it with the team, but we want you to sign off on it before it's sent out. I'll send it over once we have a draft."

"No need to send it, I'll be in soon." I trust Emily and Matthew, but this is too sensitive to leave in the hands of others.

"I thought you weren't coming into the office for a while."

"That's what Asher assumed, but this isn't going to blow over any time soon. This is my life, my story, so I'm not going to sit back."

"I understand. I'll get to work on it and see you when you get here."

I hang up and let out a long breath.

Four days ago, my ex-boyfriend, Kyle, threatened me at gunpoint to extort money from Asher. The incident has become a major news story that has hit every network around the nation and several around the globe. The media is going crazy with rumors, and nothing has been straightened out— which is just making the situation worse.

I had resisted looking at the stories until last night when I couldn't help myself any longer and got online. I almost lost what little dinner I ate when I saw an article written by RTZ, a trashy gossip website that had planned to release a story about me a few days ago. I got them to agree to shelve the story after some negotiations, but they went back on their word and released a new version of it after what happened with Kyle. Their new article paints the incident as not just extortion, but as a crime of passion, asserting that I cheated on Kyle with Asher, and it almost seems to justify Kyle's actions as the vengeance of a spurned lover.

It's all bullshit.

The only parts of the story that are somewhat controlled are the statements made by the commissioner of the NYPD. He kept the details of the situation as vague as he could since it's an ongoing case, but he divulged enough to send the media into a firestorm of speculation. Needless to say, it's a PR bloodbath, and the world isn't sure if they should paint me as a victim of violence or as a cheater who got what she deserved.

Today, I need to rectify the situation as much as I can.

After a long, hot shower, I step up to the bathroom counter and sigh when I take in my reflection. I'm definitely going to need to wear some full-coverage makeup today. The bruising along my jaw from the punches I took at Kyle's hands are a dark bluish purple, and my under eyes are not much better. I've hardly slept for the past three nights. I've also hardly eaten. And it shows. I look like shit.

In truth, I've been drowning. Surprisingly, not really because of what Kyle did, but because of what I did. After the incident, I pushed Asher away, and it's killing me. It's wrecked me in a way Kyle never could. Kyle's actions hurt me, both emotionally and physically, but at the same time, they didn't really surprise me. The extreme lengths he went to may have surprised me, but the malice behind them didn't.

Now, I just want to move forward. I want to push out my statement, wade through the PR nightmare, and move on until I have to face him in court. Kyle means less than nothing to me, and at this point, I don't care about him or our past. He's just a problem to be resolved.

But losing Asher is a gaping wound that feels like it's shredding me from the inside out.

I miss him.

I ache for him.

And I'm a fucking mess without him.

I wipe away a stray tear and blink like my life depends on it to keep the rest of my tears at bay. No more. No one knows about the distance between Asher and me, and I need to keep it that way. We're still obligated to put on a show for the world as part of restoring his PR image, so I can't let anyone, even my coworkers, see the cracks in my façade. I have to pull myself together and get shit done.

I force myself to think of anything but Asher as I get ready, and with every stroke of makeup, I feel slightly better. I watch the bruises on my face fade. I see my ashen complexion awaken with some color. My eyes finally look less haunted.

I can do this.

I can go into the office and do my job—I just need to avoid Asher while I do so. That way no one will realize I'm broken and half-dead inside, and eventually the pain of pushing Asher away won't feel like a red-hot poker to the chest.

I finish getting ready and head downstairs. The penthouse is empty, and as I make my way to the kitchen, the vastness of the penthouse hits me like a brick, freezing me in place. A shiver of unease slithers down my spine as the silence of the massive, empty space, consumes me. It feels both expansive and oppressive, but mostly, it feels all wrong. Just like the situation with Asher, but the problem is, I don't know how to make it right.

Instead of heading to the empty kitchen, I turn in the opposite direction, toward the security apartment near the gym. I knock on the door.

"Ms. Hale?" Waters asks, opening the door.

"I'm ready to head into the office."

His brows lift in surprise. "I didn't think you were going into the office."

"That's what Asher probably assumed, but I need to go in."

Waters nods. "Give me a minute."

I clench my jaw as he radios to Asher's security to inform them of the change of plans. Of course they'll inform him of this. I won't be surprised if they inform Asher of every move I make for the foreseeable future. I was already heavily monitored by security before the incident, and now it's going to be worse. The only reason Kyle was able to corner me was because

I went out without security, and Asher is still furious over that. I can't blame him exactly, I'm furious with myself too, but now I worry that I won't even be able to take a breath without it being reported back to Asher. He has issues with security from something that happened to him when he was a kid, and I've unintentionally brought up every one of those fears.

"Give us thirty minutes, Jenkins is on his way," Waters says to me as he cuts his call.

I nod and head into the kitchen, deciding to ignore the unease of the quiet and try to eat while I wait, even though my appetite is still practically non-existent. Pierre left some things in the fridge for me. He's diligently cooked all the meals; I just haven't eaten much of them. I settle for some sliced fruit and heat up a small square of quiche in the microwave. I just won't tell Pierre I used the microwave—he'd scold me for sure. But microwaved or not, the quiche is delicious, even though I'm only partially aware of the taste.

Finally, the whole of my security entourage arrives, and we make our way down to the car to head into the office.

As we drive, I start drafting my statement while simultaneously trying to mentally prepare myself to see Asher in the office. *I can do this.* I can work a few doors down from Asher. I just need to focus on my work and find ways to avoid him as much as possible.

He might be the CEO of Langford Holdings, but he doesn't get to call all of the shots. He doesn't get to sneak up into my room and slip a ring on my finger to reclaim me like a prize he lost. I miss him like crazy, but until I have some clarity from him, I will keep my distance. Whether he likes it or not. Whether he agrees to it or not.

And he's going to learn to respect that.

3

ASHER

Declan and I step into a private room in the restaurant on the ground floor of the VI Club, where my American PI, Tyrone, is already waiting. He and my European PI, Oliver, have been working practically around the clock since I got the text that threatened Ella, and they've found some results for me. We decided it would be best to discuss them in person, so Tyrone agreed to meet Declan and me here.

We take our seats at the table just as the restaurant servers finish setting it with a full breakfast spread.

"It's good to meet you," Declan says, shaking Tyrone's hand. Neither Declan nor Sterling have had much to do with the investigation into my grandfather's death since I took it over twelve years ago, but I've decided to change that. Now that his death has been connected to TDC Oil, and the threat has resurfaced, I need them by my side. There's too much at stake to not use their expertise.

Once the dining room is cleared of servers, I call Sterling on a video chat and place my phone on a tripod on the table.

"Oliver and I found another lead," Tyrone says after Sterling answers the call. "As we've already discussed, there's a connection between Greenspan and TDC Oil, but Oliver and I now have strong suspicions that TDC has been quietly attacking Greenspan on and off for almost thirty years. And in the last two years, those attacks have gotten progressively worse."

"How have we not realized TDC was going after Greenspan if it's been happening for thirty years?" Declan muses.

"That's the thing, Oliver and I think it must be an inside job. TDC couldn't have acted alone since they have no access to Greenspan's inner workings. We believe that someone was either planted or an employee was bribed, and that person has been helping TDC sabotage Greenspan from the inside all this time. We don't know who the mole is, but we have a theory. After your grandfather was killed, the division of the company your grandfather oversaw went to his brother, Albert. As soon as Albert took over, he gradually reinstated TDC as the main supplier of oil for Freestone Tires, going directly against your grandfather's wishes."

"Do we think Uncle Albert could have been behind this?" Declan asks.

"Yes," Sterling says without hesitation. "He wasn't exactly quiet about his disdain for Greenspan or his jealousy of Grandfather. I've yet to find any solid links, but I've found some suspicious trails that I'm still researching."

"Then you need to look at Albert's team at the time as well," Declan says. "I highly doubt Albert would have been the one getting his hands dirty, he's more the type to order someone beneath him to do the ugly things."

"Albert headed Research and Development at the time," I say. "He would have had many brilliant minds working beneath him."

We're all quiet as we consider the information. A moment later Declan recites this new information in a clarifying tone. "So, whoever worked with Albert to target Greenspan would most likely have been connected to him through R&D in the mid-nineties, and they are most likely still within the company since the attacks are still happening."

Tyrone nods. "Exactly." He turns to the phone screen. "That should narrow your search down, Sterling."

A glint of malice shines in Sterling's eyes. "I'll have this motherfucker by the balls soon."

TWENTY MINUTES LATER, we climb into the back of the car to head into the office. The streets are crowded and bustling outside the car's windows, but I only partially take in the sights, too caught up in my thoughts. I'm relieved to have some answers, but the fears that haunt the back of my mind seem to rear their ugly heads.

I close my eyes and take a breath, but it doesn't help. With every blink, all I can see is the nightmare that pulled me from sleep far too early this morning. The same one that's been plaguing me since I brought Ella into my life.

THE GUN DIGS into my forehead.

Tears and snot and saliva run down my face as I gag on the tie in my mouth.

Blood runs into my right eye from the gash at my temple. I try to rub it away, but my hands are bound behind my back.

Grandpa lies in front of me, his leg bent at an unnatural angle. The crack of his knee shattering under the force of the hammer still rings through my ears. Blood seeps through his suit pants, pooling on the ground beneath his leg. But I'm not screaming because of the blood around his knee. I'm screaming because of the blood running from his ear. I'm screaming because of his eyes. Grandpa's eyes, the same ice-blue shade as mine, are open. Blank, staring.

Lifeless.

"He's just a boy!" *I can still hear my grandpa's last words play through my head.* "Please, let him go! I don't care what you do to me, but don't hurt him. He's just a boy!"

The hammer moved from his knee, then pounded into his temple. He fell to the ground after that.

He's still on the ground.

I SHAKE my head and try to push away the images of that night, but it doesn't work.

"YOU KILLED HIM, YOU FUCKING IDIOT!" *One of the men in the ski masks yells at the other—his voice strikes me. There's something familiar about it.* "We weren't supposed to kill him! We were ordered to break him until he agreed to the terms, not kill him in the process!"

"What do we do now?" *another masked man shouts, panicked.*

"We have to make it look like an accident! No one can know!"

"What about the kid?" *the third masked man shouts.*

"He has to go, too! No one can know what happened here!"

Grandpa's limp, dead body is hauled from the ground by the first two masked men. They shove him into the back of his car. The third man picks me up and throws me over his shoulder. I fight, kick, scream, but he punches me in the ribs to shut me up and keep me still. My breath is knocked out of my chest.

I'm thrown into the back of the car on top of Grandpa's body. I roll off him, screaming, panicking. What's happening? Where are we going? Why hasn't someone come for us? *Grandpa pressed his alert button when the masked men pulled us from the car. That was a long time ago.* Where is security? Why didn't they come?

. . .

"You okay?" Declan asks, pulling me from my thoughts. He nudges me with his elbow. "You look nervous."

I shake my head and blink away the memory. "I'm fine."

"Don't worry, we'll take these fuckers down."

"I know we will. I just worry what will happen until we do."

History cannot repeat itself. The thought of anything happening to Ella, to my family . . .

"We've got you, Ash. You don't have to do this alone. We won't let anything happen to your girl. She's one of us now."

I lift a sardonic brow.

"Don't deny it," he says with a hard roll of his eyes.

"I'm not."

"Good, because if you need me to beat some sense into you again, I'm more than willing."

I run my hand over my aching jaw. I'm definitely going to have some bruises tomorrow.

"I think I'm good for now. I just need to work some sense into *my girl*, without the boxing ring involved."

Declan shrugs. "Don't knock it before you try it. Could be kinky."

"You're an idiot."

"And you're an idiot who's so far gone for Ella, you're practically a different person since you met her. But don't worry, it's a good different."

I snort. "I'm glad you approve."

"I more than approve. You're a hell of a lot nicer when your balls are getting drained regularly."

I punch his arm. "The fuck?"

He barks out a laugh. "What? It's true. But besides the fact that you're nicer since Ella's been around, you're happy, and that makes me happy for you. And Ella is the best. I couldn't ask for a better sister."

"It would be sister-in-law, and I'd have to be married for that to be true."

He shoots me an unimpressed look. "As if that's not where this is headed. Don't play dumb."

"I'm not playing dumb. I'm being careful. You know what's at stake, what we're up against."

He nods. "And like I said, we'll handle it, and you'll get all the things you want and deserve."

"You make it sound so easy."

"Maybe it will be, or maybe it won't be. It doesn't change the fact that we won't stop until it's done. Just don't fuck up with Ella again in the meantime. And do what you need to do to get back in her good graces."

"Don't worry about that. I've already got a plan underway."

A plan I don't intend to lose.

4

ELLA

The number of paparazzi loitering outside the Langford Holdings building is insane. The sea of them barely parts enough for the driver to pull up to the curb and park, all the while the flashes from their cameras light up the inside of the car even through the morning light. I startle as they bang on the windows, climb on the hood of the car, and swarm us from every angle until it feels like the car is buried under a pile of bodies.

"No one get out yet," Jenkins says. "Robert is bringing additional officers. We need backup to get through this shit."

A minute later, four more security officers arrive. As soon as Waters opens the door, the camera flashes flicker in such quick succession, it's like standing under a strobe light. The security team makes a sort of tunnel, but we're still pushed and jostled by the ravenous paps practically climbing over each other to get a shot. But worse than that is the barrage of questions hurled my way.

"Did you cheat on your boyfriend for a chance at a billionaire?"

"How does it feel to have an ex-lover pull a gun on you?"

"Do you think Asher will stay with you now that you're America's Scarlett Woman?"

And it's not just the paparazzi here, yelling at me. There's a whole crowd of people gathered as well. Three women stand in a huddle alongside the paparazzi, holding up photos of me with red Xs covering my face, chanting, *"Whore! Whore! Whore!"*

It's pandemonium, and I'm beyond relieved when I make it through the glass doors to the building and into the massive lobby. The security officers push out several paps who try to wriggle their way through, and then they are forced to lock the doors to keep everyone out.

My hands shake as I try to calm the adrenaline racing through my body, but I can't quite manage it with the whispers and stares that greet me as soon as I enter the lobby. Today is even worse than it was when my relationship with Asher went public. But this is not the bright attention of a new relationship; this is a scandal bringing chaotic attention to the Langfords, and everyone in this building is all too aware of it.

I keep my head low and do my best to block it out and ignore it. But it's hard. I feel like an animal in a zoo the entire way to the office, and I know I won't even get a reprieve once I'm working. My coworkers knew there was some bad blood in my breakup with Kyle, but only Emily knew how bad things had been. And now I not only have to face that part of the story, but I have to face the fact that Kyle threatened me with a gun to extort money from Asher as part of my job.

I'm just finally calming down when I pass by Asher's office on my way to the conference room, but that changes when he calls out my name. I stop and turn toward him, letting out a frustrated breath as I do. Of course I couldn't sneak by without him noticing.

"I need to see you in my office, Ella," he says, and his voice holds no room for argument.

I internally groan. I don't want to do this right now. The only way I'm going to survive this dating charade is if we go back to what it was supposed to be in the beginning: outward affection for the sake of cameras, a united front in the office, and everything else in our lives stays professional and separate. It's a bit complicated living together, but I moved my things back up into the guest room, so at least there is some distance back in place. But that won't help me here. I may be able to push back against Asher at home, but in the office, that won't work. Reluctantly, I make my way into his office.

He practically lunges at me the second I'm through the door and wraps me in a hug.

"Are you okay? Were you hurt at all? I saw it all from my window."

He's asking about the paparazzi downstairs. Things like that give him major anxiety, and I know it probably stressed him out watching it from the windows and not being able to do anything about it.

"I'm fine. The security team got me through."

I start to pull away, but Asher holds firm. He lowers his head and runs his lips along my jawline. Shivers race up my spine at his touch.

"What are you doing?" I whisper, pushing against him.

"I need to see for myself that you're alright."

"And now you have. I've got to get to work."

He presses his lips to my temple.

"I asked for space, Asher."

"That only counts at home. At work, we're still a couple, remember? And this is how I would react to you nearly being stampeded by paps."

He pulls back and takes my face in his hands. His blue eyes burn with so much emotion it's hard to distinguish what he's thinking. There's a hint of smug victory on his face because he knows he's got me on that point. If this were real, Asher would be doting on me after my run in with the paparazzi downstairs, so if we didn't share this moment, people in the office might question why. But then again, most people that work on this floor know that our relationship is a farce, so I don't know why he feels the need to keep it up. But behind that hint of victory, sadness and pain bleed into his eyes and into the expression on his face. He's trying to mask it, but he isn't fully succeeding. And it guts me. I don't know why, but since first meeting Asher, I've felt drawn to him in a way I've never been drawn to anyone before, and it's like I can sense things inside him as if they were my own. His pain is my pain, and I always want to take it away. But this time I can't. No matter how much I want to, I need to put boundaries back in place between us no matter how much it hurts us both.

I step back, and this time Asher lets me go, but I don't miss the way his hands ball into fists at his sides.

"What are you doing here?" he asks a moment later. "You didn't need to come in. Emily and the team can handle everything."

"I wanted to come. This is too delicate. I trust the team, but I can't sit back and not have a say in what goes out into the world."

"If it's like this tomorrow, I don't want you to come in. I'll send the team to you."

"I don't want to stay stuck in your penthouse anymore. I'll go crazy."

"Just until this situation dies down."

"It's fine, Asher. I'd rather be here at the office. It's too hard to be there . . ." I trail off. I don't want to admit to any more than I already have. I don't want him to know that I hate being there without him. That I hate sleeping in a separate room. That I don't want the space I've demanded between us. I don't *want* any of it. But I need it. It's the only way to protect myself.

Asher's eyes light, and I don't think I've fooled him. He storms toward me, and I back up until I bump into his desk. He grabs me by the waist and lifts me, then sets me down on his desk. He leans down, and I'm forced to lean back on my hands. Still, he moves into my space until there isn't an inch left between us.

"I told you I'd give you space, but remember, I also told you this isn't over."

"You know why it needs to be over."

"You know better than that, Ella," his voice is low, almost menacing. "You know I'm not going to just let you go."

He grabs my left hand. He holds it up and examines it, his eyes narrowing.

"You seem to be missing something on your finger."

"And you seem to have forgotten that you can't just sneak into my room while I'm sleeping."

He chuckles. "You're losing that room, so it's a moot point."

Now I narrow my eyes. "Losing that room?"

"I'm done with you sleeping upstairs, Ella. And I'm done with you pulling away from me. If I have to carry you downstairs and tie you to my bed, I will."

"You wouldn't dare."

He lifts a brow. "Wouldn't I?"

Would he? Sometimes I'm not sure how far Asher would go to get what he wants. And right now, that's me. The thought is both heady and slightly terrifying.

I bite my lip and shake my head, confusion whirring inside me. "Please," I whisper. "Don't make this harder than it already is. You know I feel the same way, but this is all too much. You can't do a real relationship, you've already admitted as much. You're still committed to ending things once the board is satisfied with your image. And I . . . I don't trust myself. I dated Kyle for three years, and he pulled a fucking gun on me. I know now that I ignored a lot of red flags in our relationship, but still, I knew him for years and still didn't see how messed up he was."

"I'm not Kyle," Asher hisses, clearly offended.

"I know that," I say, hurriedly. I move my body forward, and he backs up enough that we're still close, but I'm able to sit up straight. "I know you'd never do anything like that. I'm not comparing you to him. But everything between you and me has happened so fast. In truth we hardly even know each other."

Asher's jaw clenches. "Putting space between us will only make getting to know one another harder."

"Ash—"

"What do you need from me?" he demands. "How can I change your mind?"

"I can't risk falling for you when I know there's only heart-break waiting for me on the other side of this."

He leans his forehead against mine and lets out a long, defeated breath. For once, he has no rebuttal. He knows I'm right. Neither of us knows what the future holds, and the deeper we fall, the harder it will hurt if things end badly.

I press a gentle kiss to his cheek then shift and start to scoot off the desk. Asher reluctantly moves aside, no longer trapping me between his legs, and I'm able to get back on my feet. Without another word, I make my way out of his office, holding back the tears burning in the backs of my eyes.

"Ella," he calls out just as I make it to the door.

I turn, batting away a rogue tear.

"We'll address us later, but I want you to remember one thing today: you have nothing to be ashamed of. I saw you skirting past my office with your head lowered in embarrass-ment, and I won't have that. Not in my building. If anyone gives you a hard time, you let me know. What's going on between us is hard enough, and I want you to be able to put this shit with Kyle behind you. Don't give him or anyone else your worries.

This will blow over. You are my priority, not the story. Don't forget that today."

"Thanks," I squeak, and I practically dart away for fear that if I don't, I'll run into his arms and do what I really want to, which is lose myself in him.

5

ELLA

I head into the conference room the PR team uses as an office, and everyone's eyes land on me. Immediately, it's painfully clear that the team is trying to be quiet and professional, but they aren't succeeding. The vibe in the room is stiff and awkward, and instinctively, I start to shrink into myself, embarrassed.

But then I shake myself out of it, remembering Asher's words. His words make me realize that he's right. I have nothing to be ashamed of. The only thing I'm guilty of is staying with Kyle for too long—of getting caught up in that woman's role as old as time—thinking I could fix him. Thinking that if I just became more of what he wanted, that he would somehow be happier and magically become a better partner. Spoiler alert, it didn't work. And when I broke up with him, all his worst traits seemed to multiply to the point where, months later, he was willing to threaten me at gunpoint. None of that is on me. Those were Kyle's decisions.

I straighten my shoulders as another epiphany hits me: I need to let go and face the fears I was so desperate to protect four days ago. When I found out Kyle was going to release a story with RTZ about our breakup, I wanted to bury it. I wanted to make sure his violent behavior toward me never came to light because I didn't want to face the public scrutiny. I didn't want to be forever labeled as a victim of domestic violence— but now I realize that that was a narrow view. With a little distance and perspective, I now see how lucky I am to have made it out of that situation safely when so many women don't.

It's still difficult to swallow the fact that my private life is being highlighted in the media, but if this story shines a light on domestic abuse, on toxic relationship dynamics, who am I to deny that it might be beneficial to some woman somewhere in the world? This is the price to pay for being with Asher. And in this case, maybe that price helps someone. I can't hate that. So, I will hold my head up high and write my own story, and I will show the world that I may have been a victim, but I refuse to stay one.

"How are you?" Heather asks as I set my bag down on my desk.

"I've been better, but I'm glad to be back in the office."

She gives me a hug. "We're glad to have you back."

I can tell she wants to say more, but she doesn't, though the subtext of her thoughts is clear. If things had gone horribly wrong and I hadn't made it out of that room with Kyle, I wouldn't be here in the office. I'm lucky to be here. I can't forget that today.

Emily directs the team to the table in the corner, and we all head there and take our seats.

"It looks like we have two separate battles to fight," she says, after we're all settled. "One is the cheating, and the other is the domestic violence. We need to prove, concretely, that Ella never cheated on Kyle, because for reasons I don't understand, many men on the internet feel Kyle was justified in his actions. Now, normally I wouldn't worry over some dude-bro trolls and their Neanderthal take on how a man is justified in domestic violence, but this story is a mess, and the more we can clean it up, the better."

"I'll release my videos and texts," I say, firmly. "That will prove everything in one fell swoop."

Emily looks at me with surprise and what also looks like pity. "I thought you were against releasing them."

"I was. But a lot has changed over the last few days. Everyone now knows what Kyle is like, so it's not something I can keep quiet anymore."

"I'm sorry," Emily says after a long pause. "I hate to expose your personal life like this, but I do think it's our best weapon in this case."

I nod in agreement and grab my old phone out of my purse. I forward everything to Emily while the rest of the team discusses more strategies. When I'm done, I reach out to the editor in chief of RTZ and tell him that the deal with the beach and engagement photos I had negotiated with him is off. He may not have released the article that was the catalyst to this entire fiasco as it was, but he still released most of it. And I refuse to make nice and do business with someone who doesn't keep their word.

"Got them," Emily tells me after waiting a bit for the texts to download. Then she turns to address the team. "Josh and Michael, I want you to help me put this timeline of videos and texts together with a narrative of Kyle's past behavior. Daphne and Heather, I want you to put together a statement about domestic violence that we can incorporate into it. Ella and Mr. Langford will have the final say on everything before it goes out, but I want to be well-rounded in our approach. We can't just paint Ella as a victim, we need to also highlight her resiliency and strength. I want to keep Mr. Langford out of the discussion as much as possible, other than to show that once he knew Ella was in trouble, he rushed to help her. We can't disclose the details of what went on in that room as they are under an official investigation, but we can work with what the NYPD already released in their statements."

Everyone nods and gets to work, but since there isn't much for me to do, I head to the bathroom—I need a minute to collect myself. I open the last stall and take some deep breaths. Talking about that night is bringing up flashes of it in my mind, and the shock of having a gun pointed at me is still messing with me, making my heart race and my palms sweat. I can't get over not knowing if Kyle would have pulled that trigger or not. The fear of feeling so blindsided by someone I once trusted is a shock that has yet to wear off, even days later.

After a few minutes, I feel marginally better and I'm about to exit the stall when footsteps *click-clack* against the marble floors.

"I bet Mr. Langford is regretting choosing Ella," Daphne's voice filters from the other side of the bathroom. "This is such a mess. She should have told him about her crazy ex."

I grit my teeth. I did tell Asher about Kyle before we signed the papers for our arrangement. Hell, we broke into Kyle's apartment to get what remained of my things back before we signed the papers. Asher knew what an asshole Kyle was from the beginning; we just both thought Asher's threats would be enough to dissuade him from doing anything else to me. But Kyle is clearly a moron and unstable. When he came forward to RTZ about his farce of a story, I was only partially surprised, considering his past narcissistic and delusional behavior, but even I couldn't have predicted that Kyle would go as crazy as he did. Pulling a gun on someone is not normal.

"If I were you, I'd keep my opinions to myself," Heather's voice says in a warning tone. The water turns on at the sinks, and she raises her voice to speak over it. "Mr. Langford is very protective when it comes to Ella. If he heard you talking like this, he'd probably fire you."

Daphne scoffs. "He's only putting on a show. He's the big

bad boss, so he has to act like a tyrant when it comes to Ella because that's what people expect."

"And how do you know that?"

"It's obvious."

"Is it? Because if I didn't know this was an arrangement, I'd swear he was crazy about her."

"Exactly. He's a good actor. He's been in the spotlight his whole life; he knows how to turn on the charm when he needs to. But there's no way any of it is real. He's *Asher Langford*. He can have any woman he wants. He was forced to take on Ella."

"He was forced into this situation, but he *chose* Ella."

"Yeah, after she clearly set her sights on him. The night we all went to the club, she showed up looking like a slut. Remember how they were just holding hands out of nowhere? She rode in his car that night, and I'd bet anything she sucked him off on the way there."

"Shh! God, Daphne, do you have a death wish? You can't just say shit like that."

"No one can hear me in here."

"Why do you care about this so much? While I highly doubt anything like that happened with Ella, he still chose her."

"I care because this is supposed to be a PR improvement for his image, and it's been nothing but a nightmare."

"That's not true. Their trip to London was one slam dunk after another. Asher even said the executives at Lennox Rose were so taken with Ella that it was a huge factor in their agreement to sign with Langford Holdings. There was also the movie premiere. That was another huge hit."

"What are you, Ella's little bitch? Why are you defending her?"

"Because that's my job, and in case you forgot, it's yours too. Whatever this petty jealousy is you have with Ella, you'd better figure out how to forget it, or it's going to cost you your job."

Daphne scoffs. "I'm not jealous."

"Please. You're so jealous, and you're barely even quiet about it. We can all see it, and I'm sure Emily's about at the end of her rope."

"I'm not jealous, I'm *annoyed*. If Asher had chosen an heiress like he was supposed to, our jobs would be a lot easier."

"Who's to say? All those heiresses had major skeletons in their closets. We would be fighting stories like this no matter what. It comes with the territory of dating Mr. Langford."

"Yeah, well neither of them would have had a psycho ex-boyfriend come for them with a gun. This isn't just PR, this is like a trashy cop show." Her voice is slightly distorted as she speaks, then she finishes with a popping sound, like she's just finished applying lipstick or something.

"No matter what it is, you still need to do your job. And you need to remember that even if Mr. Langford hadn't chosen an heiress, and he hadn't chosen Ella, he still wouldn't have chosen *you*. You need to come back down to earth and stop being salty about the fact that you somehow think he chose Ella over you."

"Fuck you," Daphne hisses.

"See? You're defensive. You've somehow convinced yourself into thinking you were an option when you never were. Ella wasn't supposed to be an option, but she and Mr. Langford clearly have a connection. So, get over it and do your job."

"Ella is nothing but a white-trash slut who somehow got into Mr. Langford's head, and you won't convince me otherwise."

Heels *clack* against the marble again and then a door slams. A few seconds later, a second set of footsteps follows, and the door opens and closes again. God, I can't even escape the ridicule at work. I'll have to thank Heather for standing up for me, but I want to strangle Daphne.

I go to the sink and wash up, then head back to the conference room. I'm so worked up I'm ready to confront Daphne, but

I stop short when I see a delivery man set a massive vase of flowers on my desk. I decide I don't want to confront her in front of the team and create more drama, so I let it go for now and head to my desk.

I try to tip the delivery man, but he waves me off and tells me it's already been taken care of. Emily and Heather come to stand by me, clearly curious and wary.

"Who are they from?" Emily asks as I pluck the card from the arrangement. I open it and groan as I read the note.

I blow out a breath and show her the card. "They're from Blake Covington, Vericom's CEO. He sends his condolences on what transpired and tells me to call him if I need anything or if I need better security measures."

"That was nice of him."

I let out a humorless chuckle. "Nice or not, I need to get rid of these."

"Why?"

"This isn't the first time Blake Covington has sent me flowers, and Asher was less than thrilled the last time."

Emily raises her brows.

"Let's just say Asher has a bit of a jealous side."

Now Emily smirks.

What I can't tell her or Heather is what happened after Asher discovered the flowers and the bracelet Blake sent me. The memory of Asher possessively sliding piece after piece of his family's jewelry onto me and then fucking me senseless makes the heat rise in my cheeks. Thankfully Blake hadn't sent me jewelry this time, but I don't doubt that if Asher knew he'd sent me flowers again that it would hit a nerve. If Asher and I were in a better place I might let him see the flowers, just to see what sort of repeat performance he might stoop to at the office—just the thought of it has my mouth watering. But Asher and I are taking a step back, so that's probably not the best idea.

"I think you're too late," Heather says through a half smile, nodding toward the entrance of the conference room.

I follow her line of sight and grimace. Asher stands in the doorway with his eyes narrowed on me and the flowers.

"I'll just, uh, take these out to the lobby," I stammer before picking up the large arrangement. "There's probably a table I can set them on."

"Good luck with that," Emily says, holding back a laugh.

"What have you got there?" Asher asks as I try to brush past him.

"Just some condolence flowers."

"That's nice. Who are they from?"

I pretend not to hear him and pick up my pace, but seconds later, his footsteps sound behind me. He follows me all the way to the lobby, and as soon as I set the flower arrangement down on an empty table, he snatches the card from my hand before I can toss it into the trash. His jaw flexes as his eyes roam over it.

"Persistent mother fucker seems to think a little too highly of himself."

"Are you talking about you or Blake Covington?" I tease.

"Careful, Ms. Hale. I might be in a mood to punish those who defy me."

I swallow hard.

Asher notices and smirks, then looks down at the card again. "With everything that's happened since we got home from London, I forgot to send Mr. Covington a *thank you* for his gifts. It looks like I need to remedy that."

"What does your *thank you* entail?"

"Nothing you need to worry about."

"Don't burn bridges over something silly like this."

Asher scoffs. "I don't need whatever rickety rope bridge Blake Covington is offering, but I do need him to understand that he isn't welcome to continue sniffing around what's mine."

Asher tosses the card into the trash and grabs me by the

hand. He pulls me after him toward his office, and I have no choice but to follow. I may have pushed for some distance between us, but in the office, we still need to look the part. My mouth dries when Asher ushers me into his office and locks the door behind us. He flips a switch, and the glass windows that face the hallway turn a dark gray opaque.

"You know I have no control over who sends me flowers," I say, my voice a little breathless.

"Oh, I'm aware," he says, leaning down and brushing a ghost of a kiss along my neck. I shiver at the sensation and press my chest against his. Then my brain kicks in, and I pull back.

"What are you doing, Asher?"

He doesn't answer. Instead, he nibbles on my earlobe and runs his hands down over my ass, squeezing it in his large palms.

"There is nothing for you to worry about with Blake."

"Blake, is it?" he growls. "On a first name basis, are we?"

"No. I mean he told me to call him Blake at the launch, but I haven't spoken to him since, and I don't plan to."

"You've got that right."

"What is it about him that sets you off so badly?"

Asher pulls back and looks at me in my eyes. "Because he looks at you and thinks he can have you. Because he doesn't understand that you are *mine*."

"I'm not some toy that belongs to you."

"You are not a toy—but you belong to me just like I belong to you."

"I . . ."

His words hit me. Asher and I haven't really visited that idea, but I can't help it, the thought of it makes me melt. I want him to belong to me.

I want that so much.

I wish we could forget everything that wasn't just the two of us and give in to what feels right. But too many things stand in our path.

My mind is in such a spiral that I don't notice that with a flick of his fingers Asher has popped open the top button of my blouse until he nips at the skin right between the tops of my breasts.

"Asher," I whisper.

"What, baby?"

I groan. Damn him using that word with me. It gets me every time.

"We can't," I somehow choke out.

"Why not?"

"Because we need space."

"I don't recall ever agreeing to needing space."

"Okay, *I* need space."

"And why is it that you need space, Ms. Hale?" His voice is a purr that rumbles against my breasts, making my nipples harden. Damn him again. Asher and I haven't been intimate since before the Kyle situation. And after experiencing something so awful, it's been miserable going without Asher. I've craved his presence and the safety and security he makes me feel. Too many times over the past three days, all I've wanted was to be near him. I've missed him, but I've also missed his physicality. Denying myself of him has felt like dying of thirst and yet refusing to drink the water in front of me.

I feel my resolve crumbling by the second, like a house of cards.

"B-because everything has happened so fast . . . and this is an arrangement." Asher flicks another button open and another, then he runs his tongue over the swell of my breasts. ". . . and this will end . . . and . . . I don't want to get hurt."

God, Asher is a master at making me come undone. I can't think straight when he touches me.

"I believe you owe me some extra credit," he growls against my skin. "And I'm cashing that in now."

"Extra credit?" I say through a confused shiver.

"Remember the night we played our game of truth or dare?"

I nod. I had come up with the game to try to get to know each other better.

"Then you'll recall that I earned extra credit. You agreed to comply with a prize of my choosing at a future date."

"Th-that's not fair."

"It's perfectly fair."

"And what exactly are you choosing for your prize?"

"Your agreement that we can get back to what we were before that article and your ex fucked everything up. I know you want clarity, I want that too, but it can come with time. All I want right now is you. I want us to go back to how we were before. I want you in my room, in my bed. I want us to spend time together and not avoid one another. This space is killing me, and I hate it."

"I don't want to get hurt," I repeat for what feels like the hundredth time, but with the repetition, the phrase is losing its potency.

Asher moves back slightly to look me in the eyes. "Hurt is not a one-way feeling, Ella. If things end between us in the future, you would not be the only one to suffer. This is not a one-sided risk. The thought of how it would feel to lose you keeps me up at night. So, I know you're scared, but I'm scared too. I want all the things you want. I just have to find a way to make them happen while also keeping you safe."

I let out a long breath.

Woah. I hadn't thought about it that way. I've been so caught up in protecting myself and keeping myself safe that I forgot that this is a risk for Asher as well.

"You chose your business before me," I whisper, knowing that this is still one of my hang-ups. "I asked you to trust me that I'd handle the story with Kyle, and you didn't. You asked for something I wasn't willing to give because you were worried about the board and their threats."

I want to trust Asher, but I don't know if I can handle always playing second fiddle to his business. I understand he's a massively successful businessman, and I don't have a problem with that, but I do if it means that his business is always his first and most important priority.

"I know." He brushes his thumb over my chin. "I fucked up. And I'm sorry. I can't change my actions, but I can promise to try to be better in the future."

I sigh, knowing he's got a valid point. The fact that he's willing to try gives me a lot of comfort. Asher doesn't make empty promises, so if he says he'll try, then that's exactly what he'll do.

"So, back to my extra credit." He tugs me to him until I'm flush against his chest. "I'm thinking I want to start on it immediately."

"I didn't agree to it yet."

"Oh, Ms. Hale. You're cute when you think you can win against me."

6

ASHER

I relieve Ella of the last few closed buttons on her blouse, but instead of diving headfirst into cleavage like I want to, I suck in a breath and just take her in. Her eyes are unsure, and I can't blame her. I didn't lie when I said I was scared, too. Every day I spend with this woman is a day I fall harder for her. If this ends, it will destroy me. No question. But I can't budge on the fact that I will destroy myself before I bring her harm.

"We both want the same thing. Don't forget that." I brush my thumb along her full bottom lip. "But we don't have to think about the future today."

And since I can't take another second of looking at those lips and not tasting them, I press my mouth to hers and let out a groan of relief when she kisses me back. A spark burns between us, and I know I shouldn't be pushing this here and now but fuck if I can stop myself. I kiss her like I've been fantasizing about for the last three days, and finally, I feel like a part of my sanity clicks back into place.

And it ignites the beast inside me.

I wrap one arm around her lower back and press so that her

back is slightly arched, then I pull down the cups of her bra, springing her breasts free. I move my mouth from hers and bend down to swipe my tongue over her nipple. She lets out a breathy moan as I suck on one breast while I knead the other in my palm.

"Asher . . . we're in the office." Her voice is breathless, and her paper-thin argument seems to die as her fingers slide into my hair.

"I don't give a fuck," I say as I switch my mouth from one breast to the other.

"I—"

"Extra credit," I growl against her skin. "I earned it fair and square."

To help her make up her mind, I slip my hand up her skirt and brush my fingers over her panties, grinning when I find her wet for me. She groans, but it sounds like it's as much from hesitance as it is from pleasure.

"Please, baby. Don't keep the one thing I want away from me."

"And what's that?" Her voice is barely more than a whisper.

"You."

"Asher," she groans, still trying to put up a fight.

"Ella."

"I . . ."

"Extra. Credit," I growl.

She huffs. "O-okay."

"Good girl."

I grab the elastic of her panties, and when she doesn't protest, I give them a yank and slide them down until they fall to her feet. She steps out of them, and I pick them up and shove them into my pocket. I stand, take her by the hand, and lead her to the couch. As she walks, she wraps one hand around her chest, covering her half-bared breasts.

I sit on the couch and pull her down. I shove her tight skirt up to her waist so she can straddle me, and I reach into her open shirt and unclasp her bra. I don't want anything between me and what I want.

"Asher..." She squirms, trying to cover herself again.

"You don't need to worry, baby, no one can see in."

"But everyone is going to wonder why the glass is suddenly opaque," she hisses. "You know they'll be gossiping about it."

"Again, I don't give a fuck. This is my company, and I'll do whatever the hell I want in my office."

"I care. I'm the one who looks like a whore."

"If anyone says a thing like that, they'll find themselves unemployed."

"Well, some of them already say it."

"Ella, forget about everyone else. This is about you and me. No one else matters." I look at her, really look at her and give her my truth. "I *need* you, Ella."

I kiss her again before she can ask more questions. This, this is where we always find one another. I know it's probably not the healthiest thing, but I can't deny that when we're together physically, everything else fades away. There is nothing I can lose myself in like I can with Ella. And I know she feels the same.

The ache that's been gutting me from the inside since she said she needed space eases as soon as my mouth is on hers again. I take no prisoners, plunging my tongue into her mouth and claiming her. She resists for a handful of seconds before she moans back into my mouth and meets my tongue thrust for thrust.

I kiss her like she's my last meal as I skim my hand up her thigh and through her wet slit. She bucks her hips and moans again, and I plunge two fingers inside her. As she starts to ride my fingers, I use my other hand to unbuckle my belt and undo my pants. When I pull my fingers out of her pussy, she whimpers at the loss of contact.

I free my cock and stroke my hand up and down the length of it, my eyes fixed on Ella's mesmerizing green ones.

"The only way you get to come is on my cock, Ms. Hale."

She bites her lip, debating. But I know I have her. She's too worked up to retreat now, and I know she's missed me as much as I've missed her. Well, maybe not as much, I don't know if that's possible, but I know she's been miserable since the moment I walked out of her bedroom door three days ago. Because I've been the same.

I grab her by the hips and lift her, my eyes still watching hers as I lower her onto my cock.

"*Fuck*," I hiss when she's seated, taking in all of me. Nothing has ever felt as right as when I'm inside her.

Our lips meet again as she starts to move, slowly, tentatively at first. But soon, that same haze of lust and want and need envelops us, blocking out everything else. Her hands tangle in my hair as she rides me, and my hands wrap on either side of her hips, urging her on, grinding her harder on my cock.

Our foreheads meet and it feels like the first real breath I've taken in too many days. Before Ella sliced me open with her request for space, I had already been a mess, worried over her safety and her life after what happened at that hotel. In truth, I don't think I've breathed easily since she stormed out of my office after our argument about the story. But having her here, now, with me, helps to settle that ache in my chest. It's not gone, and it won't be until this impasse between us is resolved. But for now, I'll take this. I'll take any crumb she's willing to give me.

I miss you.

I want you.

Please forgive me.

I swallow back all the words I want to say to her; afraid I'll spook her if I voice them. So, I speak to her the only way I can right now. I glide my lips up the column of her throat, kissing and sucking as I go. I roam my hands over her breasts, stomach, ass, worshiping every inch of her perfect body. I pull her in tight, leaving no room between us, to blot out the echoes of *space* that has plagued me.

I know she's close by her soft moans and quick breaths. I rub her clit with my thumb in a circular motion, with just the right amount of pressure that I know drives her wild, and soon she's coming. Her walls pulse around my cock as she shoves the back of her hand against her mouth to keep from crying out.

A moment later, I come so hard that I see stars. The relief and ecstasy that burns through me hits me, and I bite down on her shoulder to keep from yelling her name for everyone in the goddamn office to hear.

Fuck. Me.

I will never tire of this. I don't think if I fucked her a million times that it would be enough to sate my need for her. I've been with many women, but none of them have felt like this. This connection between Ella and me isn't just a good time or a good fuck—there's something indescribable that burns between us when we're together, both in and out of the bedroom. The gut-wrenching fear I felt both when Ella was threatened by Kyle and then again when she pushed me away, reminds me why I need to get my shit together and give her what she wants. What she deserves. Because if I don't, and I lose her, lose this, it will be the worst mistake of my life.

As I take in the sight of her, drinking her in, I notice a circular object in the small breast pocket of Ella's blouse. How I noticed it, I'm not sure, not when her blouse is hanging open and her perfect tits are right in front of me.

I reach for the pocket and fish out my old ring, a triumphant smile tugging at my mouth. I hold it up between us.

Her eyes move from the ring to my face. "I meant to give that back to you."

"Oh no, baby. There is no giving this back. You should have

realized that this morning when you woke with it on your finger."

"But what if we don't have a future?"

"We do," I say, adamant. But I see the fear and hesitation in her eyes, and I know I need to give her something. "I know I fucked up. I know you asked for me to listen to you and trust you, and I didn't. I had just gotten another threat from the board, and it clouded my judgement. You needed me to be by your side, and I wasn't there."

"I . . . need to know," she whispers, "that you're on my side. If we do have a future together, will I always take a backseat to Langford Holdings? I know your company is a big deal, and I know that it will always take up a lot of your time and energy. I can live with that. But what I can't live with is being pushed aside or disregarded because business always comes first."

I take her hand in mine a press a kiss to her right middle finger, where she wore this ring before. "My father always prioritized my mother and his children. He's given me a good example to follow. So no, that's not something you need to worry about. But it doesn't mean I won't make mistakes. Especially now, in the beginning. I'm not used to sharing my life. I'm not used to basing my decisions on someone else's needs. So be patient with me. I promise you that I am trying. Even when I fuck up. I am trying.

"I want a future with you, Ella. I know that it might not seem that way with my misgivings, but I'm working on those too. I need to deal with the threats being made against my company, because those threats affect you, but I'm doing everything I can to clear them up. And once I do, I'm going to make you mine in every way possible."

The column of her throat bobs as she swallows hard.

I slip the ring back onto her finger and kiss it again.

"Mr. Langford, Mr. Weitzman is here for your nine o'clock

meeting," Haley, one of the receptionists, says over the intercom.

Ella jolts upright. The spell between us is broken, and in an instant, we both remember that we're in the office.

"Thank you," I call out toward my desk. "Let him know I'm running late; I'll be ready in fifteen minutes."

"I'd better get back to work," Ella says, climbing off my lap and heading into the private bathroom in my office to clean up.

I follow her like a puppy, a part of me afraid she'll push me away again if we're separated so quickly after finding our way back to one another.

She yelps in surprise as I open the door.

"Let me help you." I grab a washcloth out of the linen cabinet and turn on the faucet.

"I can do it."

"I know you can, but I want to do it for you."

"Why?"

"Because I'm the one who made a mess of you. It's only fair that I clean you up."

I take the warm washcloth and run it over her pussy, planting a kiss on her nose as I do so.

"You sure know how to work your way back into my good graces, Mr. Langford."

I flash her a knowing grin. "I always strive for excellence, Ms. Hale."

I drop the cloth into a small hamper and button Ella's shirt.

"What about my panties?"

I pull them out of my pocket. "You mean these panties?"

She raises a brow.

"I think I'll keep these." I shove them back into my pocket. "Maybe you can earn them back."

"And how would I do that?"

"I have an unlimited number of ideas."

"You're shameless."

"Always."

She turns and looks at her reflection, straightening her hair, and wiping the smeared lipstick off her face.

I wrap my arms around her from behind and nuzzle into her neck, still unable to get close enough to her, even after fucking her. That connection was like a salve to the possessive beast inside me, but it wasn't enough. Fuck, it's never enough.

"Just so we're clear, that extra-credit I earned has no expiration date."

She scoffs. "You just used it."

"You never said it was a one-time use only."

She clucks her tongue. "That's cheating."

"It's not cheating. There was no rule specified, so I'm not breaking any rules."

"I never agreed to that."

"Again, you never specified a time frame or an amount of uses, so I win by default."

She rolls her eyes.

"But I do promise to use my extra credit to give you orgasms. How about that for a compromise?"

"What am I going to do with you, Mr. Langford?"

"Again, I have an unlimited number of ideas."

She simply shakes her head again.

"So just a reminder, we're back to what we were before. I expect to eat dinner with you tonight. I expect you in my bed, *our* bed. And all these delicious parts of you, your mind, your presence, your tits, your pussy, your ass, they all belong to me."

"And what about my heart?" she says, her voice cracking.

"I think we're both trying to be very careful about how we handle those, baby. Give me some time, and everything will work out." *Hopefully.* "Right now, I'm just counting my lucky fucking stars that I have you here, in my arms again."

She sinks against me, sighing with the same relief I feel. "Me too."

7

ELLA/ASHER

ELLA

A few minutes after I leave Asher's office, my phone rings. I hesitate to answer it. Asher made sure very few people have my new phone number, and with everything that's gone on, I don't know if I can trust it. I answer anyway.

"Hello?" I say hesitantly.

"Ella dear, it's so good to finally speak to you." The voice belongs to a woman, an elegant one with a clear, posh London accent. A voice I've heard on television and in interviews many times. Catherine Rothschild Langford. Asher's mother.

One of the most famous and revered women on the planet.

Holy. Shit.

I swallow hard. "It's . . . uh, nice to speak to you as well."

"I have been pestering my son to meet you, and he hasn't come through, so I thought I would take matters into my own hands. Would you like to come to dinner with Asher tonight at my home?"

My eyes nearly bulge from their sockets. I was enamored by Asher and his fame when I first met him, but the thought of meeting his mother has me starstruck in a whole new way.

"I . . . I would be honored."

"Lovely. Harrington and I are very much looking forward to it. Oh, and Declan will be there as well, I hope that's not a problem."

"Of course not, I love when Declan is around."

"Yes. He is a delightful boy."

I wouldn't describe him as a boy seeing as he's like six-foot-five and built like brick, but then he is her son, so I guess he'll always be a boy to her.

"Thank you for the invitation, I'm very much looking forward to meeting you."

"As am I. It will be delightful to have another woman at the table. I'm always surrounded by my sweet but overwhelming boys."

I chuckle. "I can imagine."

"Dinner is at seven o'clock."

"Thank you. I'll see you then."

After I end the call, I cover my mouth and let out a muffled squeal of delight. *Oh my god, did that just happen?* Did Catherine Rothschild Langford just invite me to dinner? I don't know why it's such a surprise, I've met the rest of Asher's family, but there's something about the grandness surrounding Catherine that has me equal parts excited and nervous.

When I've come back down to earth, I enter the conference room and immediately freeze as I notice the reaction of my coworkers. The call with Catherine distracted me enough that I wasn't thinking about what Asher and I just did in his office. The thought of it comes slamming back into me, full force, as it's clear by the looks on my coworker's faces that Asher and I spending time alone in his office with the windows blacked out was not missed. If they didn't know Asher and I were fucking before, they do now. Or at least they heavily suspect it.

I try my best to ignore their curious looks and make my way to my desk, but as soon as I sit, I want to melt into it. Even

Emily seems to be a bit surprised, and she knows more than most that Asher and I have become . . . close. At first it was out of necessity to pull off this charade, but that necessity turned into a lot more very quickly, and with it all being such a delicate situation, I haven't exactly been up front with everyone about what Asher and I do behind closed doors. It's none of their business, but now it's clear the office gossip has already made the rounds and I'm at the center of it.

With horror, I realize I'm going to be eating dinner at Asher's parents' house, and no doubt Harrington and Declan will have heard what happened in Asher's office, and I'll have to face them at a family dinner. I almost bang my head against my desk. What was I thinking?

I wasn't, that's the thing. Whenever Asher is near, my ability to reason flies out the window. But if there's any consolation I can offer myself, it's that Asher seems to be just as affected by me as I am by him. He still has a ways to go at learning how to be in a relationship, and learning to give and take, but I can't deny how devoted he is when he doesn't feel backed into a corner. When I look back at most of our arguments, or most of the times he's been a dick, it's stemmed from one fear or another. Fear from the board's threats, fear from media attention, and fear from whatever this outside threat is. Take those away, and Asher is practically perfect. So maybe it's not too crazy for me to acquiesce to his little truth or dare extra credit demand. Maybe if I can just hold on while he sorts through this shit, maybe we really will come out on the other side with everything we both want.

The thought gives me some sense of relief, and I push the embarrassment aside. If Asher and I do have a future, my coworkers will have to come to terms with it at some point. And in the meantime, it's none of their business.

I remind myself of why I'm here today and what should be occupying my focus, and I bury myself in work.

Over the next half hour, I tweak the domestic violence statement and finally send it off to Emily. My gut ties itself in knots as everyone else finishes their parts of the story and send them Emily as well. My knee bounces and I drum my nails on my desk, my nerves hitting a crescendo, as I wait for her to put it all together.

"Okay, we're live," she says another twenty minutes later.

As a team, we collectively hold our breath. It will take some time for the story to circulate, but the moment still feels like the first drop on a rollercoaster, where suddenly everything is happening and there's no going back.

For the next little bit, everything will be out of my control. It's a feeling I'm trying to get used to, but it's not easy. I've always been someone who plans, who works hard to make my life what I want it to be. Now my life is like a ship at sea, one day it's calm and perfect, and the next it's a raging storm. It's not something that feels comfortable or natural.

My mother's words from a few weeks ago nag at me. *"Is he worth it?"*

She was asking me if Asher is worth all the trouble with the media. I had said yes when she'd asked, and I still feel that way, but fuck if the media side of this relationship isn't difficult. Hopefully with time I'll grow more used to it. In the meantime, all I can do is keep my chin high and move forward.

Daphne walks past my desk but stops and bends down toward me. She sniffs in my direction. "New cologne?" she sneers. "I mean, *perfume*. Women don't wear cologne. Although, you smell an awful lot like Mr. Langford right now."

I flinch away from her. "First of all, don't sniff me. That's creepy as hell. Second, how would you know what Mr. Langford smells like? Do you go around sniffing him, too?"

Daphne bristles. "Of course not! He wears expensive cologne, the good kind, so you can smell it even when you're near him."

I let out a long breath. "What's the point of this conversation? What is it that you need?"

She narrows her eyes. "I'm just making an observation that the two of you disappeared into his office, he blacked out the windows, and then sometime later the two of you left his office looking a bit disheveled. And now you smell like him."

"What Asher and I do in his office is none of your business."

"So, you admit you did something."

"What do you want, Daphne? You've already jumped to conclusions. I don't understand why you're picking at this."

"I just think it's highly inappropriate to do that sort of thing at work."

I laugh. "I'll report your thoughts to Asher, then. I'm sure as CEO he'll be very interested in your opinion of what he should or shouldn't do in his office."

Daphne pauses and her eyes widen. "That's not what I'm saying, you shouldn't speak about this to Asher."

Asher? Oh, hell no. "It's Mr. Langford to you," I snap. "And why not? You're clearly upset about what you think Asher was doing in his office and you also think it's your place to comment on it. You could bring your complaints to HR, but I have a feeling they would rather eat glass than talk to him about it."

"I'm not upset about what Mr. Langford does in his office."

"So, you're just upset that he did something in his office with *me*. But I suppose if it was *you* he was fucking in his office, you'd be fine with it, right?"

"That's not . . . Ugh." She gives me another glare. "So, you admit to it? That you fucked him in the office?" Her voice is like venom.

I raise my brow. "Again, why do you care?"

She doesn't answer, still waiting for mine. I've had enough of her barbed comments, enough of her petty jealousy, so I lean in close. "Yes. I did fuck him in his office," I say low enough that only she can hear me. "And in our hotel in London, and in his bed, and on many surfaces of his penthouse. Neither Asher nor I planned for our relationship to turn physical, but what can I say, we could only fight the inevitable for so long. And Asher is quite insatiable, because the more he has me, the more he can't get enough of me. But if this is a concern of yours, please bring it to his attention, I'm sure he'll be all ears to your complaints."

A satisfied smirk tugs at my mouth as I stand and turn to leave, having had more than enough of this conversation. Hearing Daphne's blatant jealousy from both earlier in the bathroom and again just now, has me burning. I have no reason to feel jealous myself, Asher probably doesn't even know Daphne's name, but the fact that she so obviously wants him bothers me. It shouldn't, a large portion of the women on planet earth want Asher, and she's no different, but her proximity to him and her knowledge of our situation makes it feel more personal. Now, I kind of see where Asher was coming from with his jealousy toward Blake Covington.

Fuck it.

I'm not feeling any more of the high road today. I know this is stupid. I was literally just chastising myself for this, but right now, I don't care. I'm too raw and vulnerable today, and I need whatever comfort and connection Asher can offer me.

I brush past Daphne and head for Asher's office. I catch her eye and feel a tug of smug satisfaction at her open-mouthed surprise as I knock on his door. I flash her one more smirk before I head in.

He barks an annoyed, "What is it?" since he normally doesn't get many unannounced visitors, but his annoyance morphs into a smile when he sees that it's me.

Before I can second guess myself, I head toward his desk and plant myself in his lap. His hands grab my hips, and I wrap mine around the back of his neck.

"This is a surprise. What can I do for you, Ms. Hale?" he purrs.

"It seems speculations about why your windows were blacked out earlier have made waves around the office."

He raises a brow. "Is that so?"

"Yes. And one of my coworkers thinks that is highly inappropriate work-place behavior."

"Do they now?"

"It seems they're quite concerned about what you do during your workday. Or actually, I think their real concern was that what you were doing during your workday involved me."

"And why would they care about that?"

"I asked the same question and didn't get much of an answer. But I have a theory."

"Call me intrigued."

"I think this coworker doesn't like the fact that I'm the one dating you, and I think she doesn't like that I'm allowed to touch you—and she isn't."

"You think she wants to touch me?"

"I'd bet every cent in my now bloated bank account that she does."

"And how does that make you feel, Ms. Hale?"

"I'm guessing it's similar to what Convington's flowers made you feel."

He flashes me a sinister smile. "Then I guess it's my job to make you feel better." He reaches one hand under his desk and a *click* sounds. Seconds later, the windows of his office turn opaque once again. He sets me down on my feet and stands behind me, then presses me down until my chest is flush against his desk. He hikes up my skirt.

"I guess it's a good thing I kept your panties," he says, running a hand up over my bare ass. "Look at you bent over my desk and spread for me. Fuck, baby."

"I need you inside me, Asher," I practically whine.

He lets out a groan that sounds like a combination of

approval and relief. "You might want to hold on to the edge of the desk," is all he says before plunging inside me.

ASHER

I'M A LUCKY FUCKING MAN.

Ella left my office over an hour ago, and I'm still reeling—in a good way. I can smell her perfume on me, and I swear I can still taste her on my tongue. But it's not just the sex that has me practically floating in my chair, it's the relief of having her back with me. Life suddenly makes sense again, and the overwhelming sense of depression and dread I've been harboring for the last three days has disappeared. It's a euphoric fucking feeling. I still have worries knocking around in the back of my mind, but they're much easier to deal with when I'm not also fighting the pain of being away from Ella.

That blissful high is only slightly dimmed when Haley knocks on my office door, and I give her the go ahead to enter. Ella's remark about Covington reminded me of something I've neglected, and it's time I set a few things straight.

Haley places the box Ms. Graham delivered from my penthouse on my desk. It's the box of watch bands and the diamond bracelet Covington gifted Ella. I shove a not-so-subtle back-the-fuck-off note I wrote for Covington inside.

"Matthew," I say, hitting the speakerphone button on my desk phone. "Come into my office."

"Yes?" he says a moment later as he strolls through my door.

"I have a package I need you to personally deliver to Blake Covington of Vericom. Not his receptionist, not his PA, him. I don't care if you have to storm into a meeting and pull him out by his goddamn collar. Deliver this to him, from me."

"Anything you'd like me to say as I do so?"

"My letter should do the trick. And if it doesn't, I'll grab his company by the balls and break it."

"Did something happen between you and Covington?"

I open the box and show him the contents. "He sent flowers to Ella when we returned from London, as well as jewelry and watch bands as a thanks for the launch."

Matthew tilts his head. "That doesn't seem too out of order. I send gifts to our subsidiaries and partners for things like this all the time for you. Ninety percent of the time, you don't even know."

"He knew," I spit. "He sent her another massive floral arrangement this morning along with his condolences on her situation with Kyle. He also told her to call him if she ever needs anything or if she thinks her security measures are not *adequate*. He's not even trying to play coy. Look at this." I take out the diamond bracelet that had me seeing red back when we returned from London and toss it to him. "Look at the engraving."

He catches and examines it. "Bold."

"I'll fucking say."

"I'll make sure he gets it."

Now that that's out of the way, I take out my phone to text Pierre to make sure everything is set for dinner tonight. Tomorrow, I leave for Singapore for ten days, so I want this last night with Ella to be perfect. I want to remind her again why we're so good together and why we don't need space. I want to give her something to hold onto while I'm gone so that she'll be craving me as much as I crave her by the time I return.

"By the way, your mom called," Matthew says before he leaves my office. "She's beside herself with everything that's happened and is insisting on meeting Ella. Dinner is at seven o'clock at your parents' house."

You've got to be fucking kidding me.

I let out an annoyed breath. "No. This is my last night before I leave, I don't want to spend it at my parents' house. I have a whole plan of a romantic dinner at home with Ella."

"Take that up with Catherine."

My phone vibrates with a text from Ella.

> I've been meaning to ask you, what is the dress code for tonight? Does your family do more formal or casual dinners?

DAMMIT.

"Did you already tell Ella about dinner?" I ask Matthew.

"No. As I said, your mother is full steam ahead on planning this. She must have gotten ahold of Ella herself."

I curse under my breath and text Ella back.

> We don't need to do dinner with my family. We could do a nice dinner at home before I leave tomorrow morning.

> No way. Your mom called me, and there's no way in hell I'm backing out.

I GROAN.

So? What should I plan on as far as clothes go?

Casual dress, I think is what it's called.

You think? I need direction here, Mr. Langford. I'm meeting your mother for the first time. I don't need to remind you who your mother is.

Don't over think it. She'll love you no matter what.

I wish it was that easy.

She already fawns over you to me.

How? She hasn't even met me.

Well, my father and brothers have, and they've told her how amazing you are. And your face and videos have been splashed all over the media, so it's not like you're some enigma. She likes what she's seen and heard so far.

Even with all the Kyle drama?

Even with that.

Then let's hope that continues when she actually meets me.

Don't worry, baby. She'll love you.

AND SHE WILL, I have no doubt about that, but god, I just wanted one more night with Ella to myself before I leave on my business trip. My mother is lucky Ella came into the office today and that I already got my plan back on track. Otherwise, I'd be fighting dirty to keep this little dinner party from happening.

I'll just have to find a way to get Ella to make it up to me.

8

ASHER

Ella's eyes nearly pop from their sockets as we walk up the brick path to my parents' home.

"This is the house you grew up in?"

"Yes. And my father was raised here as well. My grandfather was raised in a similar house on Long Island and bought this one as a second home to be a bit closer to the city."

"Yes, I can see that. Yup. Just a little second home." Her voice drips with sarcasm as she takes in the house.

"I didn't say a small second house. Just a second house."

She snorts.

I reach up and ring the doorbell. Ella runs her hands over her black dress, smoothing an invisible wrinkle.

"You look lovely, stop worrying." Ella could wear rags and look beautiful. She practically did the first day I met her, and even without makeup and wearing a ridiculous outfit, I was still attracted to her. But tonight, in a tight but elegant little black dress? Perfection.

"I just . . . I know you've said your mother is nice, but it's still nerve-wracking meeting someone's mother. And your mother isn't just anyone. She's Catherine Rothschild Langford."

"Yes, that is her name."

Ella gives my bicep a small punch. "You know what I mean. She's a legend. And she's nobility. The fact that she's still known by her maiden name before your father's surname speaks for itself of how big of a deal she was before she married him. She was the 'it girl' of her day, and people are still fascinated by her. It's intimidating."

"Yes, she does draw a lot of attention. She always has. But she isn't the type of person you might expect her to be with her fame. She's still just a person, and most importantly, when it comes to us, she's just my mom. Try not to think about her as the great Catherine Rothschild Langford."

"That is easier said than done. And it's even stranger since we're in this . . . arrangement. What does she know about that?"

Ella's nose is scrunched in that adorable way of hers and I can't help it, I bend down and kiss her below her ear. I wish again that we weren't at my parents' house but that I had her home, naked, in my bed.

"Not here," she breathes, though I can tell by the blush on her cheeks that she's affected. Hmm. Could I convince her to let me have her somewhere while we're here?

"Asher, what does your mother know about all this?" Ella repeats, nudging me away.

I scowl at her. "She knows. And she's supportive."

Ella nods just as the door opens, and Harold, my parents' butler, ushers us inside.

"Welcome, Asher."

"Good evening, Harold. This is my girlfriend, Ella Hale."

"A pleasure, Ms. Hale. Welcome to the Langford residence."

"It's lovely to meet you," she says, holding out her hand and shaking his. Harold looks at me and gives me an impressed wink after he lets go of Ella's hand. Most of the women in our social standings would not have shaken the butler's hand. Our family doesn't operate like that, though. We're not people who separate humans into categories, and so Harold is used to being treated like family in our home, but most of the time, our guests don't extend that same basic courtesy. He's very used to high society guests ignoring him, and he has assured us many times it doesn't bother him, but I know he appreciates it when someone acts with normal human decency.

"Your parents are in the dining room. Have a lovely evening."

"Thank you."

"Residence is a bit of a misleading term," Ella whispers to me as I lead her through the grand foyer. Her eyes are wide as she takes it all in. "Mansion is the word I would use."

I chuckle. "The perks of your family having wealth back when there was still ample land available on the East Coast."

Ella shakes her head in disbelief.

"Asher, darling, welcome," my mother says as we enter the dining room. She hurries toward me and gives me a small kiss on my cheek. Even in my thirties, I cannot escape my mother's affection.

She turns to Ella and grasps her by her hands. "And welcome to you as well, Ella. I've heard so many delightful things about you. I'm so glad I finally get to meet you."

Ella is stiff and clearly nervous. "It's lovely to meet you, Mrs. Langford."

"Please, call me Catherine."

Ella nods shyly.

"Welcome, Asher, Ella," my father says.

"Hey, asshole," Declan says, clapping me on the back.

"Declan!" my mother hisses. "This is dinner! And we have a guest."

"Oh, Ella doesn't mind." Declan waves a dismissive hand. "She's no stranger to our brotherly interactions. She works on the same floor as us. I eat lunch with Ella and Asher at least twice a week."

"Be that as it may, this is dinner in our home, not the office. I expect you to behave like the gentleman I raised you to be."

"I'm afraid your perfect baby, Sterling, is the only one who could pass for a gentleman."

"One out three is better than zero," I tease, winking at my mother.

She scoffs, rolls her eyes, and sits in her seat. But Declan and I can both see the tug at her mouth as she tries not to smile. My mother was raised in high society in England, and she raised us with those same refined manners, but she isn't overly stuffy and controlling like most women of her station. She didn't want to raise us with an iron fist, and she accepted the fact that a house of boys would be rowdy, chaotic, and messy. We're less rowdy, chaotic, and messy now, but we're still her boys, and at home, we don't pretend to be anything but what we are—unless we have guests. But Ella isn't some uptight business associate, so propriety will be damned tonight.

"I apologize for my sons," my mother says to Ella. "I tried. I really did. But they are still a bit feral, even with me, a nanny, and boarding school for their secondary education."

"I'd take feral over boring any day," Ella says with a warm smile, looking like she's growing more comfortable. "And since I know how strong all three of their personalities are, I think it's a miracle your house didn't burn down. I already told Asher you deserve a medal for raising the three of them; I'm sure they didn't make it easy."

My mother laughs and smiles. "I do, don't I?" She turns to my father. "I think we both deserve medals for our efforts. Heaven knows how we made it through without one of them dying or destroying the family name. Although, there were some close calls."

She narrows her eyes at me, while I send her a cheeky smile.

"Indeed. I'm just glad the next set of Langfords will be my

grandchildren," my dad says, "and I can sit back and let the boys do the work of parenting while I spoil the little ones."

"Please, no talk of grandchildren," Declan begs. "We haven't even started eating."

Just as he says that, two servers bring the first course: minestrone soup.

"Well, none of us are getting any younger, dear," my mother says, picking up her spoon. "Your father and I would like grandchildren before we're too old to enjoy them properly."

"And don't forget we have no Langford heir," my father says, pointedly, at me. "By the Langford family traditions, your first born will be the heir."

Ella shifts uncomfortably in her seat and takes a long sip of her wine. I place my hand on her knee and give her what I hope is a *don't worry about any of this*, look.

"I love being the spare," Declan says with a wicked smile. "No pressure to produce the heir."

"You are not the spare. And while we're at it, stop calling Sterling the double spare," my mother snaps.

"You know we're in the works to adjust those traditions with the family trusts," my father says to Declan. "We want all of our sons and grandchildren to inherit their share of the Langford legacy, not just Asher's first born."

"But the first born will get the biggest share," Declan insists. "Or has that changed?"

"No, Asher and his first born will gain the largest inheritances. But we have already cut down the size and assets of that inheritance and divided the excess between you and Sterling."

"And if I don't have children?" Declan asks.

"Then upon your death, your inheritance will be given to Asher's and Sterling's children. But I don't want to hear such things. I want at least two grandchildren from you."

Declan rolls his eyes, and Ella silently eats her soup,

watching the tennis match of my family casually discussing our vast fortune in terms of inheritance.

"Welcome to my family dinner," I whisper with a chuckle in her ear.

AN HOUR LATER, Ella and I stand on the third-floor terrace that overlooks the estate.

"The grounds are incredible," Ella says, taking in the view. "What was it like to grow up here?"

A wave of nostalgia runs through me. "It was the best. We used to imagine all sorts of stories and adventures out in the yard and in all the unused corners of the house. I didn't realize when I was young just how different my life was from other children because all my friends lived in similar houses. It wasn't until I was in my tween years that I discovered there was a world outside manors and estates and household staff members.

"But I'm glad I didn't know any better when I was young. Because what I remember is the magic. I remember playing pirates on a small boat in the pond, running from hissing swans, climbing old trees, begging our cook for sweets, and generally causing chaos throughout the house with Declan and Sterling."

She smiles. "I love that. It does sound magical. Can I see your old room?"

I sigh. "I suppose so. But my parents haven't changed it much since I was a teen. All they did was take down the posters, so no judging."

She smirks. "No promises."

I lead her across the house to the second level of the west wing. Mine and my brothers' old rooms sit down a long corridor along with our old nursery that my mother insisted stay intact. And at the end of the wing is a large room that we turned into a game room as teens.

"Here we are." I step inside and wave my arm at my childhood room. The queen-sized bed is made with its same emerald comforter, the woodwork throughout the room is polished, but still shows signs of scratches and dings, and my same old furniture sits where it always has, holding my trophies, collectibles, and childhood photos.

"It's like a little king's room," Ella muses.

"A little king's room?"

"Yes. It's large enough to have its own sitting room, and you have an en suite bathroom and walk-in closet. The bedroom I grew up in was a fraction of this size and had a tiny closet. But then you are the *heir*, so a little king's room is apt." She winks at me and continues her perusal. Then she suddenly whirls to face me with a glint of mischief in her eyes. "Did you ever sneak a girl in here?"

"A few times when my parents were away."

"Why only a few times?"

"It was hard to get them past Harold. And I had to bribe and threaten Declan and Sterling within an inch of my life to keep it secret."

She laughs. "Were you a ladies' man, even back then?"

"It was hard not to be when women and girls started throwing themselves at me by the time I was fifteen."

"Women?"

I nod. "Women. Money and power can blur many lines of propriety."

"Fucking hell. And did you . . . I mean, were you with any women when you were a boy?"

"No. I was sorely tempted a couple of times, but my bodyguards put a stop to it."

"Thank god for that."

She runs her hand along the dresser and shelves, taking in

all my embarrassing photos and trophies. "I could never have snuck a boy into my bedroom at home," she says, absentmindedly. "It was too close to my parents' room. They would have heard everything, and I would have been grounded until college."

"So, no trysts at home for you?"

"No. Not for me. No trysts until I was an adult and in college."

"Now that we're speaking of trysts, you have my mind working in wicked ways, Ms. Hale."

She stops and turns to look at me again, one brow lifted. "And just what do you mean by that?"

I take three steps and lock the bedroom door, then prowl toward her. "I mean that when I was an idiot teen, I had no idea what the fuck I was doing with girls. My efforts in this room were laughable at best. And you know how much I hate to perform below anything but exceptional standards. I think it's time I remedied that."

"Your parents and brother are downstairs."

"Yes, and they'll stay there. As you said, this is a mansion with plenty of space. No one will hear."

"Asher . . ."

"Ella . . ." I mimic. "Since I've done so well with our games of truth or dare, I would like to start another one."

She bites her lip to hide her smile.

"I gave you a truth. You asked if I brought girls here, and I told you yes. So, it's my turn. And I choose dare. I dare you to hop up on my dresser."

Her breaths quicken, and I know she wants to, but propriety is warring in her mind. Perhaps I'll just help her make up her mind.

I walk toward her, and she steps backward until she bumps into the dresser. Two of my old trophies and a picture tip over, clattering against the wood surface. Ella yelps as I lift her and set her on the dresser, hiking her dress up near her hips. Her green eyes burn with lust, but I can still see the war of indecision in them. I slide my hands up her dress, my palms grazing over her inner thighs. She sucks in a breath when I run my thumb along her center.

I bend down to whisper in her ear. "I dare you to open your legs for me, baby." A beat later, I almost purr with satisfaction when she does. "Good girl. Now lift your hips for me."

She leans back on her hands and lifts her hips, and I slip my hands back beneath her dress and grab her panties. I slide them down her legs, and when I bend down to slip them off her heels, I get the perfect view of her spread legs beneath her dress. I stop for a moment and just enjoy the view. Her pretty pussy is already wet for me. Fuck, yes.

"I could never tire of staring at your pussy open and bared for me," I say as I stand back up. I bend down and nip at her neck. She lets out a little breath that has my already hard cock straining against my pants. Our lips crash together as I unzip the top of her dress and slide the straps down until the top of it sits beneath her bra, then I yank her bra down, baring her tits. I knead them in my palms, growling against her mouth. God, it's only been since this morning that I touched them, since I was inside her, but that's too fucking long.

I pull away from her lips and take each of her tits in my mouth as she leans back on the dresser, wrapping her legs around me.

"Asher," she whimpers.

I unbuckle my belt and unzip my pants. "Now, I dare you to take my cock in your cunt like a good girl, in my childhood room, and make all of my boyhood fantasies come true."

I grab her by the hips and scoot her toward me, pulling her legs open wider. Her dress is now only around her torso, with the top pulled down and the bottom pushed up past her hips. Delicious. I shove inside her in one thrust, and she bites down on my shoulder to keep from crying out. I take deep breaths to calm my over-excited dick because good fucking hell, there is no better feeling than being seated inside her. I could live with my cock inside her and want for nothing else.

"Lean back and let me take you, baby."

She puts her weight back on her arms, and I start moving, using my hands on her hips to help her move. I slam into her over and over, not caring that the wood of the dresser squeaks and groans with our movements. Not caring that my family is in the house a floor below. I'm so lost in the feel of her, at the sight of her tits bouncing as I take her, and the obscene sound of our pounding skin, to care. Ella is everything I want and fucking her in my childhood room is a fantasy come true.

"Asher," she whispers. "Oh, god, yes."

"That's it, baby. Take it. This is why you're perfect for me. A lady on the outside, but a whore in the bedroom. Do you like being my perfect little whore?"

"Yes," she breathes. "For you. Only for you."

"Fucking right. This cunt is mine. And I'll take it when I want. And you'll give it to me like my good little whore."

"Yes."

I'm so fucking turned on, I'm close. I press my thumb to her clit and bite down on her nipple. "Come for me."

"I'm close."

I press harder on her clit. She moans but bites her lip to keep the sound muted. "Come on, Ella. I want to feel you come on my cock."

Seconds later, she comes with a gasp, biting down on her lip again to muffle the sound. I thrust two, three more times before I follow, spilling into her. I bury my face against her shoulder to keep my own cries at bay, and we move together until the last waves of our orgasms fade.

I straighten up and pull back from Ella, watching my cock slide out of her with indecent satisfaction. My cum oozes out of her, running down her thighs and onto my old dresser. Ella gasps softly when she notices it, and when she looks at me, her green eyes still burn with lust and want, then her full lips part as she breathes heavily.

"We should clean that up," she says.

"No. I hope it stains the wood. Nothing in this room has changed in the last seventeen years; it's due for an update."

I lift Ella off the dresser, making sure not to smear the cum, and toss her onto my bed. I grab some tissues that the housekeepers still stock in the room for reasons unknown and clean up Ella's pussy.

"How thoughtful of you, Mr. Langford," Ella purrs, smiling up at me.

"Oh, this isn't altruism, Ms. Hale. This is purely selfish. Although, you'll enjoy it, no doubt."

I drop to my knees and pull Ella to the edge of the bed, wrapping her legs around my shoulders.

"You want to do that now? Your cum is still all over and inside me."

I smile deviously. "I've never been one to want to taste cum. But tasting my own because it's inside your pussy? I can get on board with that."

"You're insatiable."

"You have no idea."

I lower my head, take her cunt in my mouth, and feast on her like she's my own personal goddess.

Because yes, I can fucking get on board with this.

How I'll go without this for ten days on my business trip, I don't know. I'm sorely tempted to kidnap Ella and take her with me. But I don't think that would do me any favors. All I can hope for is that she misses me as much as I'll no doubt miss her. Ella comes with another muffled shout, but her voice is drowned out as loud, furious knocks, bang on the door.

"Asher, you need to get downstairs, now," Declan barks through the door.

Ella's eyes lock with mine and we both freeze for a second, caught off guard to have my brother pounding on the door during such an intimate moment. When the shock wears off, I help her right her clothes, and we both scramble to our feet. Declan no doubt knows exactly what Ella and I have been up to in my room, so for him to interrupt in such an abrupt manner means something is wrong.

"What is it?" I ask Declan as soon I open the door.

"A package was just delivered here. For you."

I clench my jaw. "Me."

"Dad already opened it."

He doesn't elaborate, and Ella and I follow him downstairs to the sitting room off the foyer where my father and mother are seated on a couch, staring down at a box on the coffee table. Their faces are solemn, and my father's eyes are tinged with a deep hurt I rarely see in him.

"Stay right here," I order Ella as I cross the room and look down at the box. A note sits on top.

I do believe these were Edward Langford's favorite

A SMALL JEWELRY box sits open beneath the note. My grandfather's gold Langford cufflinks sit inside. My heart pounds in my chest as I take in a small smattering of blood still on one of them. He'd been wearing these the night he was murdered, but they were not on his clothes when his body was recovered. They've been missing for twenty-five years.

Again, that night comes roaring back to my mind.

. . .

GRANDPA'S LIMP, *dead body is hauled from the ground by the first two masked men. They shove him into the back of his car. The third man picks me up and throws me over his shoulder. I fight, kick, scream, but he punches me in the ribs to shut me up and keep me still. My breath is knocked out of my chest.*

I'm thrown into the back of the car on top of Grandpa's body. I roll off him, screaming, panicking. What's happening? Where are we going? Why hasn't someone come for us? *Grandpa pressed his alert button when the masked men pulled us from the car. That was a long time ago.* Where is security? Why didn't they come?

The door shuts, and the car darts away, tires squealing. Only one of the masked men is in the car. He's driving grandpa's long limo recklessly. The faint lights outside the dark window blur by faster than I've ever seen them as the driver speeds up, swerving, and I fly off the seat, landing on the floor next to Grandpa.

"You must always wear a seatbelt, young Mr. Langford," *my security guard's words ring through my mind. Mr. Henley is always pushy about my seatbelt.*

In a haze, I wriggle my way back up to the seat with my bound hands. I can't reach the over the shoulder seat belts, but the center seat only has a lap belt. I shimmy onto the seat, grab the lap belt, and toss it, trying to throw it over my lap. I try one, two, three, four times before it works. I turn my body and grasp for the buckle with my bound hands, but the driver veers, knocking me onto my side.

I inch my way back up to sitting, frantic. Too fast. We're driving too fast. I look behind me, over my shoulder, trying to get the lap belt into the buckle. My hands shake as I try to fit the buckle together. The two pieces clink against one another, but don't connect. I try again, and again. Each time I'm close, the car hits a bump or swerves. Clink, clink, clink. *No connection, just the two pieces hitting against each other.*

The car engine revs, and we pick up more speed.

The driver starts to shout out a Catholic prayer in a hysterical, manic voice.

I try again. Finally, click. *The seatbelt is fastened! I use my teeth to grab the excess length, and pull it as far as I can, tightening the belt.*

The fabric of the belt barely leaves my mouth before the boom *of the crash.*

Everything goes dark.

ELLA SIDLES UP BESIDE ME. "What's going on, Asher?" she whispers.

I flinch, coming back to myself.

Ella looks down at the package in my hands and gasps.

Lumped in the bottom, beneath the cufflinks, are dozens of photographs. I pluck them out, and my hands begin to shake, ever so slightly. From fear, from rage. The photos are candid shots of me, walking into work with my security, of Declan playing golf, but most of them are of Ella. Of her heading in or out of work, at the Vericom launch, out to dinner with her friends.

I toss them back into the box.

I've hesitated to tell Ella the entirety of the threats levied against me because I didn't want to scare her. I knew I couldn't keep it from her for much longer, but I wanted to give her time to process the fallout of what happened with Kyle first. I didn't want to shove a new problem in her face, but now that's out of my hands.

I set the box down and turn to look at her. "Our family is being threatened. That threat is mostly directed at me, but since you're with me, it's being directed at you as well." My voice is dead, emotionless. I hate to give her this truth. But I know that keeping her in the dark about how dangerous this situation is, is no longer an option. Not when the threat is this overt.

"We need to talk," I say, resigned. Maybe now she'll understand my hesitance about our relationship. It's not about her. It's about this. It's about whether I want to pull her into this for the long term. I have no control over the short term, the board made sure of that. But I don't know how to bring Ella, and maybe someday a family, into my world when this is a part of it. That's what keeps me hesitating. That's what I need to lay out for her, so she understands the truth.

She needs to know that if she stays with me, she'll always be a target.

9

ELLA

"Who delivered that package?" I ask no one in particular as the tension in the air grows thicker by the second. The thought of how that is possible is disconcerting. The Langfords don't live in a neighborhood where you can just saunter up to their front door and drop off a package.

"It was left outside the gates just as we were finishing up dinner," Harrington says. "Security caught footage of a black car with no license plate pull up. A man in a heavy coat and a ski mask exited the car and left the package. My men tested the box to make sure it didn't contain a bomb or a chemical threat, and once they were sure it was somewhat safe to open, they opened it on the grounds. As soon as they saw what was inside, they brought it to me."

Holy fucking hell.

"Even without a license plate to identify the car, this has to be Sergei and Yegor," Asher says to Declan. "What I don't know is if Yegor is still pulling strings from Russia or if he's on US soil."

What the hell?

"Who is Sergei and Yegor? What do they want?"

"I'll explain on the way home," Asher says, resigned.

"Perhaps the two of you should stay the night," Catherine says, worry lacing her tone. "Whoever delivered that threat knew you were here. This was an impromptu family dinner, so your schedule and whereabouts were not known by many people, which means someone followed you here. Who's to say they won't follow you home? You only have Robert and Jenkins with you."

I turn to look at Asher, but his expression gives nothing away.

"You're right," he says after a moment. "If it was just me, I would take my chances, but I won't take that risk with Ella."

"We need to discuss all of this as a family, anyway," Harrington says. "You boys haven't told me all of what you know, and these threats have now made their way onto my doorstep. I will not have your mother or my family in jeopardy like this."

Catherine asks Harold for a tea service, and we all take our seats in the living room. Asher sits so close to me that we're touching, and he rests his hand over my knee as he begins to explain what he, his PIs, Declan, and Sterling have uncovered. I have a hard time following everything since TDC Oil and Greenspan are new to me, but I follow enough to get the gist. TDC Oil is directly threatened by Greenspan, and they've been trying to take out that threat for the past thirty years or so. Asher's grandfather was accidentally murdered by men who kidnapped him to make demands and threaten him, and they covered up the murder by staging a car accident. My stomach nearly bottoms out when Asher divulges that he was with his grandfather that night and was also kidnapped and nearly killed the in the car accident.

And he was only a boy.

"TDC is no longer content to make trouble from the shadows," Asher says, rubbing his palm across his jaw. "They are overtly coming after Greenspan and anyone who gets in their way, which is me, my brothers, and my dad." He lets out a sigh. "But since you're with me, that threat now extends to you.

"TDC's owner, Sergei Antonov, is incredibly connected here in the US, and his cousin Yegor Antonov is one of the heads of the Bratva in Russia," Asher continues. Catherine's lips purse in fear as she takes in his words. "Since Sergei buys most of his oil from Yegor, this affects them both, and they are both willing to do whatever it takes to destroy Greenspan since they know how close its technology is to changing the world."

"Who have you contacted about this?" Harrington asks Asher.

"No one. I don't trust the FBI or the CIA with this. I know Sergei has some deep connections in the government, I just don't know who they are besides Senator Sanders, so until I do, I'm keeping my cards close to my chest."

Harrington fingers his late father's gold cufflinks, and I can see the unshed tears in his eyes. I know from what Asher's told me that Edward was an incredible man, and Harrington loved his father very much. Edward is the Langford who changed the direction of the family. Prior to him, the Langfords were cruel and bloodthirsty, and conquered the business world without conscience or remorse. It was Edward who saw his family's greed for what it was and decided to change that. He implemented more ethical business practices and felt strongly that because he had the power to change the world for the better, that it was his responsibility to do so. Harrington has followed in his footsteps and so have Asher and his brothers. Yes, they're all still ruthless businessmen in many ways, but they truly want to make the world a better place.

It isn't lost on me how rare a man like Edward is. When you're born into incredible wealth and sold the lie that you are inherently better than everyone, it takes a strong character to break out of that mindset and choose a different path. And yet Edward did. I know his death has left its mark on his son and grandsons, not just because of the violent nature of it, but because of the tremendous loss of him as a person.

"There is strong evidence that Uncle Albert was involved with Sergei," Asher tells Harrington.

Harrington merely sighs. "That isn't surprising. His jealousy and bitterness toward his brother were not something he hid well."

"Not unlike Conrad with you. Or Gregory with our boys," Catherine says in a cold voice. She's stiffer than she was just a moment ago, as if speaking about Asher's uncle and cousin is difficult for her. She looks between Harrington and Asher. "You both need to be careful with them."

Asher nods. "We will, but they aren't our main concern right now. Other than the fact that Conrad is all too eager to sell Greenspan. I just don't know if it's because he hates that the company is a money pit or if he has some connection to Sergei."

"Either way, keep away from him. And keep him and his snake of a son away from Ella. You should inform Jenkins that neither of them is to be near her at work."

The fire in her eyes and the tension in her demeanor makes me wonder if there's some sort of history that I'm not aware of. This is somewhat confirmed when both Asher and Harrington agree quickly and assure her it will be done. But I don't ask about it. Whatever that history is, I'll leave it alone unless they volunteer the information. I don't want to pry into something that seems quite personal.

"I'll start keeping a closer watch on Pussory," Declan says. "I've been meaning to, anyway."

"Pussory?" I ask, confused.

"Gregory," Declan says with a smirk. "It's a little nickname I gave him when we were kids."

I hold back a smile. Of course Declan would gift a nickname like that to the cousin he hates.

"What is your plan?" Harrington asks Asher. "We need this taken care of."

"We're working on it now. We've only just had the last bits of information confirmed this morning."

"I want to be kept in the loop, Son. As I said, I won't have this danger threatening my family."

Asher nods.

Harrington's words seem to end the family meeting, and Declan and Asher stand. I follow suit.

Catherine turns to me. "I have something you can wear to bed, Ella."

"No," Asher barks, and then he shudders. "Sorry. That's nice of you to offer, but I don't want Ella in my bed wearing my mother's clothes."

Catherine rolls her eyes. "Don't be dramatic, darling."

"He's got a point, my love," Harrington says with a smirk.

"So what, the poor girl will have nothing to wear . . ." She trails off at Asher's shameless shrug and Declan's sly grin. "Oh, never mind. I unfortunately know what the Langford men are like."

I blush. And then blush even harder as Harrington slaps her ass and shoots her a lascivious grin. "Unfortunate, hmm?"

"Ugh!" Declan groans. "Not again! Keep it in your pants, Dad."

"Oh please, Son. You're all aware of how you were conceived."

Declan makes a dramatic gagging sound. "The sooner my penthouse is finished, the sooner I can get out of this hell."

I shoot Asher a quizzical look.

"Declan just started a remodel on his penthouse, so he's living here with my parents."

"Which means I get a front-row-seat to their disgusting ways," Declan says with a shudder.

Asher snorts. "You act like it's something new, like they haven't been this way in front of us our whole lives."

"Hush, you two," Catherine admonishes. "Be grateful your parents love each other."

"We just wish you'd keep your love a little more private," Declan says with another shudder. Then he turns to Catherine, narrowing his eyes. "Especially you, you're supposed to be proper and stiff like all good Brits. Outward affection isn't supposed to be in your repertoire."

"Well, I didn't defect from the UK for no reason, did I? Your father's charm and flagrant affection won me over. And rubbed off on me."

"That's not the only thing that rubbed off on you," Harrington says, kissing her cheek.

"No!" Declan yells again, covering his ears. "That's it, I'm going to bed before I lose my dinner."

Harrington and Catherine giggle like teenagers as they watch their second son march out of the room with a huff.

"Let's go," Asher says, tugging on my arm. "Before they get even more gross."

"Wait," Catherine says, turning to me again. "I will stay out of the sleepwear situation, but if you'll follow me, I'll get you some toiletries. I don't know what's stocked in Asher's old bedroom."

Asher presses a kiss to my cheek. "I'll meet you back upstairs in my old room." But then he must be thinking about what we were just up to in his old room, because he shoots me his own lascivious grin, and I can't help but agree with Catherine—it seems all the Langford men are insatiable red-blooded males.

I'm a bit nervous as I follow Catherine up the stairs and to the east wing of the house. I've spent most of the evening in her company, but this is the first time I've been alone with her, and the fangirl side of me is activating again. I've had weeks to come to terms with the fact that Asher's mother is Catherine Roth-schild Langford, but I'm still a bit starstruck.

"I do hope Asher is treating you well," she says as we make our way into her and Harrington's massive bedroom, the size of the space making Asher's bedroom in his penthouse look small, which is no easy feat. "I know your relationship had some bumps in the beginning."

"Uh . . . yes, Asher is treating me well. It's just been a little difficult to figure out how to navigate the relationship when it's not a real relationship."

One side of her mouth pulls into a knowing grin. "Ah. Is he still sticking to that?"

"Yes."

"Well, he always was stubborn."

I'm not sure what to say to that, so I remain quiet and try not to gape at the beautiful design of the room as Cathrine leads me into the opulent bathroom. It takes everything in me not to crane my neck to get a better view of the closet beyond the bathroom since Catherine's wardrobe is literally legendary and has been for decades. I know that's a big reason why my fashion makes the headlines it does when I'm photographed out and about. It all stems from her legacy.

"I see the way he looks at you," Catherine says, breaking me from my thoughts as she rifles through her bathroom drawers, pulling out bottles of skincare and shower products. "And whether he has admitted it to himself or not, he cares for you, Ella. A great deal. But I also know that you'll probably have to be patient with him. He's never tried to be in a real relationship. All his previous relationships were barely more than flings. I know you just said the relationship is an arrange-ment, but I have a feeling it won't stay that way, mark my words."

"And you're happy about that?" I blurt out. Then my stomach knots in panic and embarrassment. *Why did I ask that?*

She straightens and smiles warmly. "I am. I want happiness for all my boys, and I fear they've been looking for it in all the wrong places for too long. From everything Asher and Harrington have told me about you, you seem like a perfect fit for my son."

"You're not upset that I have no social standing?" Again, I want to punch myself for my too honest and vulnerable question, but I can't help my morbid curiosity. Catherine is the daughter of a high-ranking noble. Titles and social standing are literally a big deal to the lifestyle she was born and raised in.

"Of course not. Harrington wasn't the only reason I defected from the UK. I hated the pressure and the ruthlessness of the ruling class. Their ways never made sense to me, even though I was raised in them. I want my sons to have partners they love, who love them, and who fit them well. That's it. And grandchildren." She winks at me. "I want a heap of those, too. But I know those will come with time."

I let out a nervous giggle, unsure what to say to that. Again, Asher's family proves how different they are to what people would expect of them. They have ridiculous amounts of wealth and fame, but at the end of the day, they're just a family who want the same basic things as everyone else.

Catherine passes me the bottles. "This should get you through the night, and if you don't want to wear your dress home tomorrow, I can give you something to wear. Maybe since it wouldn't involve a bed, my son wouldn't have a problem with it."

"Thank you," I say with another giggle. "I'll let you know in the morning."

She nods. "Goodnight, Ella dear."

"Goodnight, Catherine."

Ten minutes later, I huff out a sigh in defeat and pull out my phone to text Asher.

> I'm lost. This house is too big, and I can't find my way back to your room. I give up!

> Never fear, fair maiden. I will come rescue you. Where are you?

> If I knew the answer to that, I wouldn't be lost, now would I, good sir?

> Look around you, what do you see?

> A long hallway with stupidly expensive paneling like the rest of the house. But there is a picture of a lady in a pink dress looking out a window.

> Aha! I know right where you are. You're still in the east wing. Stay put, gentle lady, and I will be there shortly to collect you.

> Thank you, kind sir.

A FEW MINUTES LATER, Asher saunters down the hallway toward me still in his suit pants and white shirt, but he's lost his tie, the top few buttons of the shirt are undone, and the sleeves are rolled up. And fuck me. The sight has me practically drooling by the time he reaches me.

"Like what you see?" he purrs as he reaches me. "You're practically eye-fucking me."

"No practically about it. I am absolutely eye-fucking you."

He shoots me his devilish grin that is my favorite. "I like the sound of that."

I nod my chin toward the armful of bottles I'm still holding.

"Well, since I have all these luxury products to use in the shower, maybe you can join me. We can get clean together."

"Only after we get dirty first."

"Oh, I think after three rounds of sex today we're already there."

"We should round it off to an even four then, just to be safe. Or perhaps five. Yeah, five sounds better."

"Whatever you say, Mr. Langford."

"I love it when you say those words, Ms. Hale."

An hour later, after a very naughty shower together, we're lying in his childhood bed, snuggled close. The bubble of happiness we've been in after the tense family meeting has slowly dissipated since we got into bed, and by the stiffness of Asher's body, I can tell there's something on his mind.

I lift my head off his chest to look at him. "Are you okay?"

He tucks a lock of hair behind my ear. "Yes and no."

"Is it about what happened earlier?"

He nods, and I lay my head back down on his chest, hoping to give him a bit of space to collect his thoughts.

"I hope you know," he says after a minute, his breath brushing the top of my head, "that everything we talked about earlier is the reason I've been hesitant to move forward. My reluctance over a real relationship is not about you or us. It's because of this situation. Watching my grandfather's murder so young, and then almost dying myself—it did something to me. I'm reminded of it every time I try to picture my future. It's why I slipped into the role of chronic bachelor. I justified not wanting a real relationship because if I didn't let anyone into my life, then I didn't have to worry about their safety. Maybe if we had solved my grandfather's murder back when it happened, I wouldn't have felt this way. But with the unknown hanging over my head for the last twenty-five years, I've kept my guard up."

I nod in understanding. I get it. I've seen the scars on his back that I now realize must be from the car accident. When we were first together, he would flinch if I accidentally touched them. He doesn't seem bothered by my touch now, but his initial protectiveness over them makes sense. I can't imagine going through something like that as a child, and it's clear that night left him with more than physical scars.

Asher blows out a long breath. "Even now, I don't know if I can bring someone into this mess. But—for the first time in my life—I want to fight that instinct. I want you in my life, but I need to take out this threat before I can fully commit. And even then, I need you to know that things like this will always be a possibility. Your life will always have more risks than the average person if you're with me. I'm trying to come to terms with that, but I still need time." He reaches for my hand and kisses the back of it. "I want this, but I need to take it slow."

"Then we'll take it slow."

"But we'll keep that to ourselves. There's a lot of unrest with the members of my board, and I'm not sure who I can trust. So, as far as the PR team and the board are concerned, this is still a farce for publicity. I don't want anyone to know how much I care for you, at least not yet. But I still need to keep improving my image or I'll risk my shares."

I look up at him, and he brushes his thumb along my lower lip. "I also need you to know that my worries over losing my shares isn't just about the money. It's about the power that it would give the board. They would absorb my shares among them, and none of those snakes deserves an ounce of more power than they already have. My brothers and I are determined to operate as ethically as we can, but the other board members couldn't give a single fuck about that. I don't want my employees, my companies, and a myriad of other people to suffer—and they *will* suffer if the board gains those shares. Given half a chance, the board will slash salaries, benefits, bonuses. You name it, if they can get rid of it to line their pockets with more money, they'll do it."

I take in his words, realizing the gravity of them. This, *this* is why I'm so drawn to this man. Yes, he cares about his shares and his money for personal reasons, but he cares just as deeply about the lives of others. He understands the power he holds, and he takes that responsibility seriously. The world may see the caricature of Asher; they see his money, his reputation, his power and privilege, but I see the real him.

"I'm with you," I breathe. "And we'll take this one step at a time, together."

"Thank you," he says, his words muffled as he buries his face in my hair.

He spends half the night worshiping my body in an almost reverent way, and when we finally drift off to sleep, I feel more at ease than I have in weeks.

10

ASHER

A week later, I sit in a high-rise restaurant overlooking the Central Business District in Singapore for a business dinner. I try my best to listen to Mr. Li across from me, but instead, I sigh quietly into my wine as I think about how long this week has felt, even though it's been jam packed with meetings. I'm running on fumes, ready for the trip to be over, and dreading all the meetings I have over the next three days. I'm homesick—something I never thought I'd experience in adulthood, and I know the exact reason for my homesickness: a certain brunette I'm obsessed with. I can't help but think back to my London trip when Ella was by my side for several of my business meetings, and how her presence made the time away from home much more enjoyable. I'm fairly sure I'm fucked, because after this week, I don't want to go on any more of these trips without Ella.

Some Titan of Business I am.

But if my one Achilles' heel in business is my need for Ella to be by my side? I think I can live with that. I'll just find a way to convince her to follow me around the globe. Declan would laugh and call me codependent if he could hear my thoughts. But I don't care. He doesn't get it.

Mr. Li checks his watch. "I must wrap this up. I have a flight to catch."

Thank God.

"I will put together a final proposal and have it to you within the next two weeks," I say, trying my best to hide my relief. Now I can head back to my hotel and call Ella. It's early in New York, but at this point, I don't care if I wake her up. I need to hear her voice. And I can start planting seeds to convince her to come with me next time. I'm not doing this alone again.

"I'll be waiting for your proposal," Mr. Li says, standing.

I stand as well, and he nods and makes his departure.

"Is there anything else I can get you?" a server asks, making his way to our table.

"Another round of drinks, thank you," a female voice says.

I tilt my head, then almost startle in surprise. Katrina Antonov snakes her way around the server and takes a seat in the chair Mr. Li just vacated.

"What the hell are you doing here?" I snap, both from shock and anger.

"Hello to you too, Asher."

"I didn't say hello. I asked what you're doing in Singapore, at my table in a restaurant."

"I'm here in Singapore on business, like yourself. And I'm here in this restaurant on behalf of my family. My father informed me he sent his offer to your board just moments ago."

I check my watch. It's almost seven a.m. in New York.

"And we have been assured that every member of the board outside of your brothers and your father are going to vote to sell Greenspan."

"What a coincidence that this is going to be put to a vote when I'm halfway across the world."

She smirks. "You don't believe in coincidences, and neither do I."

"And how would you know what I believe in?"

"Our time as a couple may have been short, but it was intense. I learned a lot about you, Asher."

I scoff. "That was what, twelve years ago?"

"You're as stubborn as a mule, I doubt you've changed much."

"Regardless, your family's tactics won't work. The sale won't go through. My family and I are not budging on this."

She takes a sip of the brown liquor the server sets down in front of her, eyeing me over the rim of the glass. "I assume you've received the little gifts from my family."

"I'm glad to hear that putting a man in the hospital and paralyzing him is considered a gift," I practically snarl at her.

She shrugs. "It's better than a sudden disappearance and no trace of a body."

"So, you're finally ready to admit to your mafia ties, then?"

"I'm not admitting to anything."

I take out my phone and text the group chat I have with my brothers, reminding them to do what they must to block the sale and to make sure my father does the same.

"I'm assuming your father sent you to try to convince me because of our history together. It won't work."

She leans on the table, giving me a sultry look. "I told you many times that we could have been great together, you and me. With our families and our names, the world would have been ours."

"The world already is mine. I don't need you."

She quirks a brow and brushes her finger over the back of my hand. I flinch and pull it out of her reach.

"And what about your new little fling? What does she bring to the table? I can't imagine it's much."

I pause, waiting for the desire to throttle Katrina to calm

before I answer. "She brings herself. Nothing more is needed. Just her presence is worth more than all the money and clout you think you bring to a table."

Katrina flinches slightly but tries to hide it with a derisive laugh. "How sentimental. But I wonder. You received your gifts, so you know TDC's position when it comes to your new little fling. It would be such a shame if anything happened to her."

Red flashes across my vision as I try to ascertain what Katrina knows. Her father obviously has an inside with someone on my board if he has intel on how they're all planning to vote. The board thinks that my relationship with Ella is nothing but a farce, but have any of them divulged that to Sergei or Katrina? Or does Katrina think our relationship is real?

Either way, it's best if she thinks Ella is just a fling. However, I can't stop the anger that burns inside me, demanding that I let Katrina know that Ella is not to be touched and what I'll do if she is.

"I see," I growl. "Your father didn't send you because he thought our past might sway me. He sent you because he thought I wouldn't hurt a woman if she's the one making threats against me and my family."

Katrina smirks. "That fling of yours is hardly family, but yes, my father was counting on your chivalry overriding your ruthlessness."

"He was right. I can hardly make a violent move against a woman in a public setting. But let me make myself very clear: you don't know me, Katrina. You know the man I used to be. The man I used to be had a bit more of a black and white view of the world, and he definitely didn't have as much at stake as the one sitting before you. My morals, when it comes to my enemies, have grown much, much looser over the years."

I lean in close so that Katrina doesn't miss a single word. "If your family harms one hair on Ella's head, I will destroy all of you. Not just your father, not just his company, *all* of you. I'll make sure your mother is left a penniless widow. I'll make sure you are blacklisted from the corporate world. I'll ensure your brother's drug habit grows far worse. It's so easy to overdose these days, isn't it?"

Katrina blinks hard but remains silent.

"Your family is not the only one capable of ending lives. It would be extremely unwise to underestimate what I would do to protect the people I care about." I shove away from the table. "I'll be in touch."

I stand and so does Katrina. She blocks my path and brushes a hand over my shoulder. She leans in close and whispers in my ear.

"This doesn't need to turn ugly, Asher. But it will if you continue to be stubborn about this."

She plants a kiss on my cheek before I know what's happening, and I yank my face away from her lips.

"Threaten me again and see what happens," I growl, pushing past her. Fury lashes through my veins as I make my way out of the restaurant.

"Call Jenkins," I bark at Robert as we reach the elevator. "Ella is not to leave the penthouse today, for any reason."

I take my phone back out and call Ella.

"Hey," she answers in a bright voice on the third ring. "I was just about to call you. How was your meeting?"

Any other time I would settle in and enjoy the warmth she exudes, even over the phone, but I don't have time for that, not right now.

"Fine. But that's not why I'm calling. I need to you to listen and do as I say."

She pauses. "What's going on?"

"TDC is pushing for the sale," I say in a clipped tone. "The contract has been sent to the board, and I got a less than subtle threat toward you should I not agree with the sale. I can't sell; it would jeopardize too many things. So, until I have a handle on what's going on, I need you to stay in."

"What about work?"

"I'll inform Emily of the situation. You'll need to work remotely for the time being."

"I hate this," she says through a groan.

"I know, baby. I'm sorry. But I can't risk you."

"What happens after you block the sale?"

"We find out what else TDC has up their sleeve, and we take them out. I'm past negotiations and niceties."

A plan starts to form in my head as a cold, remorseless vengeance takes hold inside me. If Sergei wants a war, I'll give him one.

And I'll destroy everything he holds dear.

11

ELLA

"Again," Waters demands, holding up his gloves. He's taken over my self-defense training since Robert is in Singapore with Asher. After the threat from Katrina, and the attack from Kyle, Asher and the security team are dead set on me becoming as proficient as I can be at self-defense. So far, I think it's going okay. With my years of dance, I can lock on to most of what Waters instructs me to do, but this is a whole different type of movement from what I'm used to. There are times I feel about as coordinated as a newborn giraffe.

I punch again, and this time I hit the pad on his hand closer to its center. Today's focus is on how to land a punch without injuring my own hands or wrists. Last lesson was on the pressure points of an attacker's body and how to inflict pain quickly and get away. Sometime soon, I'll even have handgun training. I won't lie, I'm nervous about that one. I've never even touched a gun, so I'm not sure how I feel about handling or shooting one, but it's apparently something very common in Asher's family. Even his mom knows how to shoot one.

"Remember, keep your elbow slightly bent or you could

hyper-extend it and injure yourself. Your elbow should never fully straighten when you punch."

I try again.

"Better," Waters says. "But try to aim for the center of the target."

I try again and again, determined that what happened with Kyle will never happen again. Asher is right about one thing, if I do stay with him in the long term, my life will never be simple. There will always be potential threats. He's too wealthy, too powerful, and too well-known to have a normal life, and if I'm going to be part of that life, I want to have more control. Yes, I'll always have security officers, but being able to handle myself is something I've realized is non-negotiable.

I get marginally better as the training session progresses, and finally, when sweat is pouring down me in rivulets and my arms feel like they're going to fall off, Waters allows me to stop.

But my relief is only temporary, because the minute I pick up my phone, I see a text from Emily.

> Heads up, a bad headline just hit the press. It's all over the internet. Don't you worry about a thing, though. We'll get it handled.

I HAD my news notifications turned off since I was training, but now I click on the link to the article Emily sent me.

Asher Langford Cheating Scandal

A PHOTO beneath the headline shows Katrina and Asher at a restaurant. She's leaning toward him with a sultry, besotted look on her face, and there's a second photo of the two of them standing and Katrina is kissing his cheek. I knew she surprised him at the restaurant, but I didn't know they were this cozy when it happened.

My gut sinks. I know they have a history together, but I also know Asher hates the Antonovs. The way he described Katrina made me think he didn't like or respect her, but the photos look like he feels quite the opposite. In fact, they look pretty damn incriminating.

A nasty voice in the back of my mind reminds me that you can hate someone and still fuck them.

But Asher would never do that.

Right?

Insecurities and doubts flood me. I've always been a confident person, but I'm certainly not bullet proof. I was cheated on by a past boyfriend. And then there's the whole Kyle debacle. Asher is literally one of the most eligible bachelors on the planet. He can have any woman he wants, whenever he wants —and he's used to that. He's used to sleeping with models, actresses, and any other beautiful woman who catches his eye. He doesn't even have to work for it, they literally throw themselves at him.

I read through the article, my stomach twisting into tighter and tighter knots as I do. The article talks about my meteoric rise to fame but insists that I lack substance to back it. I'm painted as the little PR employee who ensnared Asher, while Katrina is hailed for being an oil heiress well known in New York high society. It also depicts Katrina as Asher's long-lost love, as "the one who got away."

I know it's not true. I know that—I keep telling myself that —but it has a hard time registering. Maybe because of the rollercoaster Asher and I have been on for the last few weeks.

I click out of the article and let out a long breath. *This is part of being with Asher,* I remind myself. Tabloid stories follow him wherever he goes, and the writers of those stories don't give a shit about him or anyone in his life. If I stay with him, I will always have comparisons lobbed at me. I'll be compared to his mom because of her fame, and to any women previously linked to him. I'll always be in the line of fire of having other women compared to me. That's just the way it is. The world just loves to pit women against each other, and I will forever have to deal with it.

I can't let this derail me.

I remind myself of that again and again until I think I believe it.

Two hours later, I'm going stir crazy while texing back and forth with Emily and Matthew as we come up with a plan to combat the article. I'm reading through the article for the third time when an ad for a baking blog pops up on my phone. I click on it. That same nasty voice in the back of my head tells me I must be on the verge of a mental breakdown because I've never had any interest in cooking or baking, but I ignore it. With the Kyle drama, the Langford drama, and now the press drama swirling around me, I'm about one second away from screaming into a pillow, so baking sounds like the perfect distraction. The recipe is for some sort of fancy chocolate chip cookies, so I don't think it can be that hard. Busying myself with baking cookies has to be better than contemplating cutting bangs, right?

I prop my phone on the counter and dig through the massive kitchen and pantry, grabbing the supplies listed. I read through the list twice and think I have it all. I follow the instructions on the blog between answering texts and emails from the team, and it does wonders in distracting me each time I wrap up one of those texts or emails.

I finish with the dough, and then it takes me a solid five

minutes to figure out how to work the fancy industrial-type oven, but I eventually manage to get cookie dough onto a sheet pan and get that pan in the oven. The venture into baking has served as a solid ninety minutes of distraction, so I count it as a win.

My phone rings just as I close the oven door.

"Hi," I say to Asher as I pick up.

"Hi, baby. Emily just sent me the article. Are you okay?"

I sigh. "I'm fine. It's just a very . . . *convincing* article."

"It's all bullshit, I swear to you. If Katrina had been a man, I probably would have punched her right there in the restaurant with how angry I was. But the way the picture was taken, the angle of the photo doesn't show the rage that I know was present on my face."

I think back over the pictures, noting that they were taken from Asher's profile, so it was hard to see the expression on his face.

"She did this on purpose," he growls. "I wouldn't be surprised if she'd planted someone to take the pictures and sell them. At the time I thought she was just playing coy with her advances, trying to soften the blow of the threats she was making so that I wouldn't go ballistic. Now, I realize it was a set up. But I promise you, nothing happened. She surprised me with that kiss, and I pulled away immediately. I don't want that woman anywhere in my vicinity, let alone her lips on my skin. Just thinking about it is making my balls curl up inside me."

I can't help the soft laugh that escapes me. "You promise?"

"I promise. I don't want anyone else, Ella. No woman has ever made me feel a fraction of what I feel for you. This is the Antonovs playing games. I know they have someone on my board in their pockets, and so I can only assume they know, or at least suspect, that our relationship is a PR stunt, and they're playing into that. They know that the more upset the board gets, the more likely I am to lose those shares, and if that happens, they win everything they want."

Some of the knots in my stomach loosen. "I believe you. It's just hard to see. Especially when my shiny newness will fade at any moment, and the articles about me will get worse and worse. The world wants you with another big name. Not a no-name employee."

"Well, the world can go fuck itself, because I don't want a big name. I happen to be stupidly obsessed with my amazing, gorgeous, smart as hell, perfect, no-name employee."

"I'm pretty obsessed with my big-name billionaire, so I guess we're the same in that regard."

Now Asher laughs.

"Are you sure you're okay, baby?"

"I'm fine, mostly. On the plus side of things, since I'm forced to stay in the apartment, I decided to try baking cookies. I think it's going okay."

Pierre enters the kitchen just then carrying two bags of groceries, and freezes. His eyes widen in horror as they scan over the kitchen. I look at it, blushing as I take in the carnage. The island is covered in flour, dirty utensils, baking sheets, bowls, and ingredients. A few chunks of cookie dough that I flung hard to get off my fingers are splattered on the cabinets and floor.

Pierre lets out a slew of words in French that I'm pretty sure are curses.

"Sorry for the mess!" I spurt. "I decided to try baking."

"It sounds like Pierre is enjoying sharing the kitchen with you," Asher says with a chuckle, and I remember that I'm on the phone with him.

I hold the phone close and speak in a low tone. "Yeah, he just got here to prep lunch, and I'm pretty sure he had a mini aneurysm when he saw the state of the kitchen."

"He probably did."

"I think he's cursing in French under his breath."

"He probably is."

"He won't actually kill me, right?"

"Probably not."

I try to start cleaning my mess, but Pierre makes a shooing motion with his hands, and since his left eye is twitching, I back away. I take a seat on a bar stool and focus back on my conversation with Asher.

"So, what are we going to do about this, Mr. Langford?"

"Do about what, Ms. Hale?"

"About the Antonovs and their stupid oil company. I can't live like Rapunzel, locked in a tower for the rest of my days. I mean, your penthouse is one hell of a tower, but still."

"I'm going to start with destroying the Antonovs."

"Sounds good. How can I help?"

He chuckles. "You want to help me take down my enemies?"

"Of course I do. What is that thing where people start to take on the traits and hobbies of their significant other? I have that. Your revenge hobby is now my revenge hobby. Plus, they're threatening me, so it's only fair that I threaten them back."

"You're something else, Ms. Hale."

"I aim for excellence, Mr. Langford. But what I need is a direction to start with. What's your angle with the Antonovs? Whatever it is, I want in."

"I love that you want to help, but you know my answer."

"Asher . . ."

He sighs. "No, baby. There's too much risk and too many unknowns. The best way to help me is to keep doing what you're doing."

"Destroying the kitchen by trying to bake?"

He chuckles again. "No. You can keep creating positive attention about our relationship. The more we're seen together, and the bigger the headlines are, the more ammo we'll have against the board. You let me and my brothers take on the Antonovs, and you take on the media."

"Asher," I say in a groan. "There has to be something I can do."

"Just be you. That's all I need."

"That's very sweet of you to say, but I'm serious."

"And so am I."

"I can do something that doesn't involve risk."

"Absolutely not. I won't take that chance."

"Fine," I huff, knowing I'm not going to win this argument today. I know Asher well enough to know that if I were to put myself in harm's way, he would lose his ever-loving shit. And after what went down with Kyle, I'm in no hurry to put myself at physical risk, so I'm happy to respect that boundary. But I'm not about to sit back and do nothing. I'll just have to find a way to help without alerting Asher.

An acrid, burning smell hits me, and I startle. "Oh, shit! The cookies!"

I drop my phone and race across the kitchen where Pierre is taking a smoking tray of cookies out of the oven.

"I'm sorry, Pierre! Let me help."

He sets the tray down and waves a hand to disperse the smoke in the air.

"No, no. Please, Miss Ella, just let me do the baking for you. You don't need to be in the kitchen. That is what Mr. Langford pays me for."

"Are they ruined?" I don't know why I ask that; they're clearly burnt.

"Miss Ella, these are not cookies. These are rocks. Go, go. Out of the kitchen, please."

"I can clean it up."

"No, Miss Ella. I will clean. I just need you out."

I flush scarlet. "Okay. I'm so sorry I made such a mess."

He waves me off, and I pick up my phone and head into the living room.

"Sorry, I dropped my phone," I say as I get back on the line with Asher.

He barks out a laugh. "It seems like the baking was a success."

"Pierre just kicked me out of the kitchen. But if you hadn't been distracting me, I would have remembered to set the timer on the oven, and then the cookies wouldn't be burnt right now."

Asher snorts. "Somehow I don't think my distractions were the problem."

"Okay, so I'm no domestic goddess. But I don't give up easily. One day I'll bake some delicious cookies."

"You do that, baby. But in the meantime, let's leave the kitchen duties to Pierre and focus on the board."

I can do that. For now.

"You got it, Mr. Langford."

12

ELLA

I'm curled up in Asher's bed three days later, carving my way through a pint of ice-cream at five o'clock, watching an old rom-com. Asher texted me this morning to tell me that his trip had hit a snag and has been extended by four more days. I almost threw my phone across the room. Instead, I put on one of Asher's T-shirts and decided that rotting away and eating my feelings was the only option left for my sanity.

I've been missing Asher like crazy, and it's only been made worse by the fact that I've been holed up in the penthouse by myself. Since he left, I've been living like a stir-crazy ghost, haunting the place. I've mostly been moping around in a state of lonely depression between working from home and my training sessions with Waters. I'm sure that makes me pathetic, but fuck, I didn't realize how much I'd come to want and need Asher's presence. I'd known I was in deep with how much our mini breakup hurt, but this has proven to me that I'm even worse off than I thought. Asher has been gone for ten days, and it feels like ten weeks.

One bit of good news is that I finally got cleared to go back into the office tomorrow, but now the excitement of that is tainted by the fact that I'll have to work for four days without Asher there.

A knock sounds on the bedroom door.

"Ms. Hale," Ms. Graham calls. "You have visitors."

Visitors?

I roll out of bed, wearing only Asher's T-shirt, and pad across the room.

"Who is here?" I ask Ms. Graham through the door.

"Ms. Wilson and Ms. Morozov. Security just let them up, would you like me to invite them in?"

Surprise flows through me. "Yes."

A minute later, Zahra and Lucy, my two best friends, practically burst through the bedroom door and head straight for me.

"This is a surprise," I say, just as Lucy says, "Well, you look like shit."

"Luce," Zahra reprimands. "Take it easy on her."

"That's why we're here, to make her feel less like shit," Lucy says, breezily.

"Get over here, Ella Bella." Lucy opens her arms, and we end up in a three-way hug. A sense of relief surges through me. God, I didn't realize how much I missed my friends until right now. With everything that's happened in the last two weeks, I've been so stuck in my own head that I haven't thought about anything but my situation.

"What are you two doing here?" I ask, happiness bubbling inside me. "I didn't know you were in town, Luce."

"I finally made it in. I've been meaning to come since the incident with Kyle went down. He's lucky your powerful boyfriend made sure he couldn't post bail, otherwise he would have had some of my Morozov cousins here in New York paying him a not-so-friendly visit."

I chuckle. Yep, I'm becoming more and more sure that Lucy's family is highly involved in the mafia, and though her immediate family is based out of Chicago, I know she has some cousins who live here. It was the reason she was allowed to study at NYU in the first place; her father wouldn't have allowed it without knowing she had not only a bodyguard, but also some family members who were always on standby if needed.

"Well, Kyle the asshole is firmly in jail, and we have some time before his case is brought before the courts, so for now, I can put it out of my mind."

"I've been worried about you," Zahra says. "You haven't texted much, and the tone of your texts has become more and more morose. Since Lucy was finally able to make it to town, we thought we'd surprise you."

"You guys are the best. Sorry if I've been a little distant. Things have been crazy here."

"Asher has been gone for a bit on a business trip," Zahra hedges.

I flop down on the bench at the end of the bed, and they sit on either side of me. "Ugh, I'm so pathetic. When did I become this girl? Asher's been gone for ten days, but it feels . . ." I trail off, embarrassed to admit how painful his absence is.

Lucy raises a brow. "You miss him after ten days?"

"Like crazy," I admit after a long pause, knowing I'm not fooling either of them. "And I still have four more to go."

"But I thought this was an arrangement? I thought there were no feelings involved."

"There weren't supposed to be. But . . ." I let out a long breath, not sure what to say. "I feel like a fool in some ways, but I also feel like I can't help it, so why fight it?"

"Are you falling for him?" Zahra asks.

"Fell is more like it," I groan.

"You're in love with him?" Lucy gasps.

I sigh. "Yes." I fall backwards onto the bed and sling my arms over my face, hiding it from view. "I tried not to, I really did. But he's just so much more than people make him out to be. He's nothing like how he's described in the media. At least with me, he's not. He's really sweet and thoughtful, and we just have this insane connection. It's palpable. Resisting it feels like burning myself with hot pokers; it's just not possible."

"Oh, Ella, what are we going to do with you?" Lucy says, half smiling, half grimacing.

"And when it's all over, what happens then?" Zahra asks.

I groan again. "I'm not sure. We're taking it one day at a time with that. We're not sure that there will be an 'over.' But we're also not sure that there won't be. Asher has some issues with the limelight of his life, so we're working through those."

"What kind of issues?"

"Mostly involving safety. Asher is paranoid about how big of a target his family is. He's got me learning self-defense from my bodyguards, and next week I have firearm training."

Lucy nods in approval, which is a bit surprising. She doesn't often give props to people. "You should know how to defend yourself. Look what happened with Kyle."

"That was different."

Lucy raises a sardonic brow. "Not really. He threatened you because he thought he could extort money from Asher. You just happened to know Kyle instead of the extortioner being a stranger."

"Well, shit. You're right."

"I'm not saying you should carry a gun, but knowing how to use one in your situation isn't a bad thing."

Zahra shudders. "Guns freak me out."

I nod wholeheartedly. "Me too."

Lucy ignores both of our misgivings. "If you want to get out of this penthouse and get your mind off how much you miss your not-boyfriend boyfriend, we could head to the range right now. I know everything about guns. I could teach you."

I raise my brows, considering. As of a few hours ago, the security team cleared me to leave the penthouse now that they have tails on several known associates of the Antonovs, but since I was brooding and depressed and had nothing better to do, I decided to stay in.

"It's not like you're doing anything pressing," Lucy says, noting the melting pint of ice cream on the nightstand and the paused movie on the TV.

"I am waiting on Asher's call. He should be leaving for his early morning meeting any time, and he usually calls me while he's in the car."

"Waiting on Asher to call you?" Lucy says through narrowed eyes. "Ella."

"I know, I know. But I can't help it."

On cue, my phone rings, and I smile from ear to ear as I answer it.

"Good morning, baby," Asher says. "Or wait, it's good morning for me. It's good evening for you."

"Hey," I say, practically swooning.

"God, I miss you. How are you?"

My smile widens even more at his words. It's not just me who's suffering at being apart.

"I'm good, but I miss you too. So much."

Lucy rolls her eyes as Zahra herds her out of the room to give me privacy.

"I'm going crazy. I can't wait to be home."

"I can't wait for that, too."

"What have you done to me, Ms. Hale? I never used to struggle with travel like this."

"What have you done to me, Mr. Langford? I never used to sit at home and mope like this."

"It seems the solution is that you should travel with me in the future."

"You want me to go with you on your business trips?"

"I do."

"What about my work?"

"I think I can talk to your boss about being flexible with your schedule and a remote work situation."

I snort.

"You said yourself you haven't seen much of the world. And I've seen so much of it by myself that it's kind of lost its luster. I'd rather see it with you by my side."

"And when you're working? What will I do?"

"You can still work remotely. But besides that, you can tour, shop, go on adventures, whatever you like. And I can plan my trips with some extra time built in to spend time with you."

"That sounds like a dream."

"It's going to be our reality."

I swoon at the thought.

"I almost forgot," Asher says, snapping me back to reality. "Declan will probably be over later this evening. There are some documents I need him to look over, and the only copies are in my home office."

"Okay. Is he going to be here a while? I can have Pierre make enough dinner for him if he'd like to stay."

"I'm sure he'd like that. He told me our mother is having some of her friends over, and I know at least two of them are trying to get Declan to date their daughters."

I chuckle. "I still don't get why Declan doesn't just rent another apartment in the city. It seems like he is constantly trying to evade your parents in some way or another."

"Well, when my parents aren't throwing little get-togethers where he's seen as a prized horse by the guests, he likes it. Declan doesn't do well with solitude. He'd rather live in chaos than quiet."

"What will he do when his apartment is finished being remodeled and he's back to living alone?"

"He'll do what he always does; throw parties and surround himself with people."

"That still sounds lonely, unless he really cares about the people at the parties."

"Which he doesn't. So, yes, he'll still be lonely. But I didn't call you to talk about the grim realities of my brother's life. I called because I'm going crazy without you."

"Is that so?"

"Absolutely. And I see you're wearing my T-shirt," he purrs. "What do you have on under it?"

My stomach flip flops, remembering the cameras in the room.

"Do you want to see, Mr. Langford?"

I can hear the quiet motorized sound of the partition closing in his car.

"Show me everything."

"OH GOD. I don't even want to know what you just got up to in that room," Lucy hisses twenty minutes later when I walk out into the living room. I'm back in Asher's T-shirt, and my hair is probably a disheveled mess. My cheeks are definitely flushed.

Zahra shoots me a disturbed look.

"Like you two have any room to talk," I say, smoothing my hair. I look at Zahra. "I've heard you and Alec fuck more times than I can count. Back in undergrad and again when I lived with you. You two are like bunnies."

Zahra bursts out laughing. "Let's hope we don't replicate like them. At least not for a few more years."

"And you leave a string of broken-hearted men wherever you go," I say to Lucy. "I swear you could have men agreeing to sell their souls to Satan himself for a second date and a second fuck with you. But no. You tap them, and then you ghost them."

Lucy smirks. "It's not my fault if they're not interesting enough for a second date."

"So, let's not get all judgy about our sex drives. The four of us have always been horny bitches." Maya, my sister, is no exception to our friend group in this regard.

"Well, now that you're *satiated*, shall we go shooting?" Lucy asks.

"It couldn't hurt to get out of here for a bit," Zahra agrees. "But we don't have to go shooting guns." She shudders again.

"Nonsense. Ella needs to learn how to shoot. No time like the present."

I weigh it over in my mind. "That actually sounds good. I'm intimidated by the fact that I've never even touched a gun, and I'll probably have some master marksman teaching me if I go with the security team. I'm already embarrassed, and I haven't even started training."

"Good. There's an indoor range not too far from here."

Zahra groans.

"Bend your elbows a bit," Lucy yells, and I can barely hear her through the massive noise-blocking headphones I'm wearing. She stands behind me and is trying to help me with my hold. It's not going well, and I'm literally sweating from nerves. I can't help but picture this same type of gun held in Kyle's hand, aimed at me. The fear I felt in that moment reemerges, curdling in my gut.

"I don't know if I can do this."

"This is important."

"I . . . the last time I saw a gun was when Kyle attacked me. He threatened me with it, and then the thing went off in his hands when I tased him. I wasn't hit, but I'll never forget that sound or that fear."

Lucy gently pries the handgun away from my sweaty palms.

"Take a breath. There's no rush. We'll go at your pace, okay?"

I nod, swallowing hard. I've put Kyle and his bullshit behind me, but sometimes I still flash back to the moment he pulled the gun on me. I still struggle to understand how someone I loved could do such a thing, no matter how desperate they were.

But I also never want to feel helpless again like I had in that moment.

I do as Lucy says and let out a long breath. "Okay. Show me what to do."

Lucy comes to stand behind me again and helps me with my grip. She adjusts the gun in my hands and lightly tugs on my arms to unlock my stiffened elbows.

"If your elbows are locked, you won't be able to absorb the kick back effectively."

"What's a kick back?"

"It's the reaction the gun will have when it fires. You can't expect a gun to stay still when it's launching a bullet out of its barrel."

"It moves?" I say with a gasp. "But it doesn't move in the movies."

Lucy snorts. "That's the movies, babe, this is real life. Just brace your arms a bit. You're shooting a small handgun, not a shotgun, you'll be fine."

I swallow hard, questioning my sanity for coming here, wondering if I should stop while I'm ahead and go sit with Zahra, who refused to participate and chose to watch us through the windows above the range.

"Just watch again," Lucy says, and I slowly let go of the gun as she takes it in her hand. She lifts it and holds it like a pro.

Bang, bang, bang.

Three holes appear through the target. Three holes straight through the head of the outlined body.

"Holy shit. How did you do that?"

"I got my first gun when I was eight."

"What?"

She shrugs. "It was a BB gun. But I've had tactical training since I was twelve. My father may be a backwards misogynistic bastard, but he always wanted me to be able to protect myself."

Damn.

Lucy stands behind me and again helps me to grip the gun. I try paying attention to her words as she explains how to aim, but I'm so nervous that I miss half of it. I finally pull the trigger, but in glorious fashion, I scream when the gun fires, jump in shock when it kicks back, and nearly drop it.

"For the love of god," Lucy snarls, prying the gun out of my hands. "You waved that gun in ten different directions after you fired it. That is the *opposite* of gun safety, Ella."

"I hate this," I say, shuddering. "I don't think I want to learn how to use a gun."

Lucy shoots me a pitying look and pats my shoulder. "You fired one shot. Try again."

I raise the gun, determined to push through my discomfort. I flinch and cry out again as I pull the trigger. Thirty minutes later, I'm barely able to point and shoot without startling and screaming. It's progress, I guess. But I never even hit the target once. Normally, I'm someone who can push past being uncomfortable, but with this, I just can't.

"Well, congratulations, Ells, we've found something else you're terrible at. You can't cook or shoot for shit," Lucy teases, trying to lighten the mood as we exit the range.

I chuckle, not remotely offended. My friends teased me for years that I was a jane-of-all-trades type of girl. Not necessarily an expert at anything, but pretty good at lots of things. They used to take bets when I would try new things to see if I would be okay at whatever it was or if I would be terrible at it. And more often than not, I was decent.

Too bad my friends didn't take bets on my shooting skills.

Lucy exchanges a knowing look with Jenkins, who oversaw the entire thing, as we meet up with Zahra in the waiting area.

"Keep your training up, Jenkins," Lucy says to him. "Because this one might just be hopeless when it comes to firearms."

Jenkins fights back a smile.

"This is not for me," I grumble, still shuddering at the memory of the gun in my hands. I turn and look at my trusty bodyguard. "Don't delude yourself into thinking I'll be able to protect myself with a gun, Jenkins. You're really stuck with me now."

"It's all good, Ms. Hale. I'll handle the weaponry. You just learn some basic self-defense and don't ever evade your security detail again." He gives me a stern look, and I flush with more embarrassment. So yeah, I wouldn't have gotten into that trouble with Kyle if I hadn't skirted my security. "We're here to protect you, and we will."

"Who's going to tell Asher how bad I am at this?" I muse. "Should I?"

Jenkins winces slightly. "That might be best. But I'll back you up."

"You mean you'll tell him I'm the worst shot you've ever seen."

"And that you scream like a little girl every time the gun fires," he says with a wink.

I bury my face in my hands. "At least it was only the two of you who saw it," I say, my voice muffled.

"Oh, I saw it too through the window," Zahra snickers, joining us as we make our way out of the building. "Girl, I don't even know what to say."

I let out a chagrined laugh. "I don't think there's anything to say. I tried. I failed. And now we pray I never need to use a gun."

13

ELLA

Five minutes after we step inside Asher's penthouse, the front door opens and closes.

"Declan!" I say, excited to see him.

"What's up, future-sister-in-law," he says, giving me a squeeze. I bat at his shoulder playfully. Declan is always teasing me about how obsessed Asher is with me and how he knows we'll end up married one day.

"Asher said you'd be here tonight. I told Pierre to make extra dinner if you'd like to stay."

"Hell yeah. I have work to do in Asher's office, but I'm also avoiding my mother's guests for the night, if that's okay with you."

"Definitely."

"Avoiding your mother's guests?" Lucy asks from behind me.

Declan notices her and stiffens.

"I didn't know the shrew would be here tonight," he mutters in a low voice so only I can hear.

"Be nice," I warn.

"Only if she is."

Declan looks at Lucy and nods a hello to Zahra. "My mother is throwing a little dinner party this evening, and too many of her guests have 'available' daughters they'd love for me to meet. I'm not exactly interested, so when that happens, I usually take refuge at Asher's."

Lucy arches a brow. "Asher isn't here."

"It's fine, Lucy. Declan is more than welcome."

Declan drapes an arm over my shoulder. "Yeah. The office hasn't been the same without you there. I've missed you."

"Me too, Dec."

"I didn't realize the two of you were so close," Lucy says, her narrowed eyes still assessing Declan and me.

"We are," Declan says without hesitation. "Ella is practically family now."

"Practically family?" Zahra gasps, half choking on the words.

"Yep."

I roll my eyes. "He's exaggerating."

"Pshaw. Am not. I know my brother. You're going to be my little sister soon enough. You should hear my mother prattle on about it. Though maybe you shouldn't because the woman can't wait to be a grandmother, so she also prattles on about that, too."

"Holy shit," Zahra mutters. "Catherine Rothschild Langford is prattling on about Ella marrying Asher and having his babies?"

"She sure does. So does my father. Our family adores Ella."

"What happened to this being an arrangement?" Lucy snaps.

Declan shrugs. "It still is, technically. But we know Asher, and we know he's done for. The man can barely function without Ella now. I told him it's become unhealthy; he told me to fuck off."

"You are too much," I tell him.

"This is moving quite fast," Lucy says. "You don't want to get in over your head, Ella."

"It's fine. Declan is just joking."

"I'm really not."

I pinch his arm.

"Asher and I are taking this one day at a time."

"To the altar."

"Declan!"

"What, Mrs. Langford?"

I roll my eyes.

"This isn't a joke, you oaf," Lucy snaps at him. "This is Ella's life. And getting tangled up with Asher has made it a chaotic mess."

"That's not true," I say, unable to help myself when it comes to defending Asher.

Lucy arches her brow again.

"Okay, so it's a little true. But it's fine. I knew what I was getting into when I signed that contract."

"This has blown up so much more than you expected. You've admitted that much."

I let out a long breath. "It has. But there's no going back now. It is what it is."

"We're protecting her," Declan says to Lucy. "We know our lives are crazy, but we're doing everything we can to keep Ella safe. We won't let anyone hurt her."

"Her ex already did."

I wince. "Well . . . I kind of ran away from my security, and that's how Kyle got to me."

Now Lucy's hot glare lands on me. "You did not."

I nod, grimacing.

"Why the hell would you do that?"

"It's a long story."

"What are we going to do with you, Ella?" Zahra asks, exasperated.

I hold up my hands as if in surrender. "I learned my lesson. I'll never do it again."

"You'd better not," Lucy and Declan say in unison.

"Hey, at least you two agree on one thing."

They both shoot me unamused looks.

At that moment, Pierre announces dinner, and I let out a relieved sigh. Saved by the chef.

TWO HOURS LATER, Zahra and Lucy make their goodbyes, and I head into the office to see if Declan needs anything. Dinner was a stiff affair with Declan and Lucy shooting barbs at one another and Zahra and me trying to referee the two of them. As soon as dessert was finished, Declan practically ran to Asher's office, and I haven't seen him since.

I knock on the office door and crack it open.

"Dec?" I ask, using his nickname, a habit I've fallen into recently.

"Yeah, come in."

"The girls just left. I thought I'd see how you're doing. Do you need anything?"

Declan sets down a paper and rubs his eyes. "I'm good. I was just finishing up, anyway."

"Can I ask you something?"

His brows raise. "Of course, what's up?"

"I've been hesitant to ask Asher since he's been gone, but what is Asher's plan to deal with the Antonovs? He keeps telling me I don't need to worry about it, but how can I not?"

Declan frowns, looking like he's debating his answer. "It's complicated. We know there must be traitors in our company, it's the only logical reason the Antonovs have been able to hit us like they have, but finding them is taking time. Right now, we don't know who we can trust, and you can imagine how Asher is handling that, especially considering you're now in the line of fire. And in truth, the problems are coming from three sides. The Antonovs with TDC, whoever the traitor or traitors are within the company, and the Volkovs. I know you hate to hear this, but Asher is right to be careful. There are too many threats coming from too many directions. All it takes is one misstep, and the consequences could be catastrophic."

"Where exactly do the Volkovs fit in again?"

"They're relatives of the Antonovs and their main supplier of oil out of Russia. The Antonovs need to keep up the appearance of being good, law-abiding citizens, so the Volkovs, being big players in the Russian Bratva, tend to do their dirty work for them. It's how their families operate."

"So, the Volkovs are the ones responsible for your grandfather's death? And Asher's . . . kidnapping and near death?"

Declan nods solemnly. "On behalf of the Antonovs, yes."

"So, how do you take them down?"

"First, we need to find out who is betraying us, then we go after Sergei and Yegor."

"When you say go after them . . ."

Declan holds my stare before letting out a long breath. "I mean eliminate them."

My pulse jackhammers. Not from the clear promise of murder, ironically, but from the risk it poses.

"And just how dangerous is that?"

"I'm not going to lie; there's a lot of risk involved. But we have extensive resources at our disposal, and we'll use them. We're more powerful than they are, but they've remained a threat because of their ability to operate in the shadows. Once we bring them out into the light, it will be over for them."

"And Sterling is working on that?"

"Yes."

"I know you and Asher want to keep me safe, but I want to help. What can I do?"

"Keep doing what you're doing. We need distraction."

I groan. "That's what Asher said."

"And he's right. Think of it like a magician's act. You can't pull off the trick if people are watching you closely, you need their eyes turned in one direction, so you can work in a different direction without them noticing."

"I doubt our publicity is distracting Sergei and Yegor."

"It's not distracting them, but it is distracting the public. This war between our families cannot come to light. If people knew the truth of our grandfather's death, it would show a weakness that others might try to replicate. And if people knew the lengths that we are willing to go to end this, they might not see us so favorably. As a family and a business, we really do try to operate as ethically as possible, but when you have the money and fame we do, people come after you, and sometimes, you have to sink to their level to stay alive and ahead. We don't love it, but it's necessary. And the public can *never* know about it. They mostly turn a blind eye to our playboy, bachelor antics, but they won't turn a blind eye to violence and murder—even if it's justified. So, as much as it may not seem like you're helping, you really are. Your shiny newness brings a lot of attention that feeds the public's curiosity and keeps them looking in the direction we want them to be looking, so we can handle our enemies in the shadows."

I mull his words over, and turn giddy when not one, but two ideas spark to life. I hurry across the office and sit in the seat opposite Declan.

"I just had a thought. I mean, two thoughts."

"Two whole thoughts?" Declan says with a smirk.

I shoot him a friendly glare. "Just hear me out. I think we apply your same logic in two additional ways."

He arches a brow. "Meaning . . ."

"Publicity. We need it to work in our favor, as you just said. I'll keep trying to make big headlines to keep everyone distracted, but in the meantime, we need to do the same for Greenspan. You and Asher both said you've kept Greenspan quiet. But you also said it's on the brink of a major break-through. That's a story the public would be extremely interested in. Not to mention, it would look good for your family if the public knew you are invested in using your own money to fund green-energy technology. If Greenspan becomes a company the world knows about, it's going to be much harder for the Antonovs to buy it and break it without the world finding out. Not that that would deter them, per se, but it might make things more difficult for them."

Declan runs his hand over his jaw, considering. "What do you suggest?"

"I think we bring a major news outlet into Greenspan, and you show the world what you're working on. Not the details exactly, to keep your proprietary technology safe, but you give them the gist. Putting Greenspan on the map just might help to protect it."

"Well damn, Asher was right. You're not just a pretty face." He winks.

I roll my eyes at the joke, but secretly warm at the compliment.

"So, what was your second thought?"

"I think we need to use negative publicity to preemptively strike at the Antonovs. They're not nearly as famous as your family, but they still hold a lot of notoriety. What happens after you take them down? The media is bound to notice the fall of an oil empire, and they'll be salivating over the story. They'll want to know who and what is responsible. It seems like going after the Antonovs' reputation now may prove to work in your favor later. There needs to be a story, a narrative, to explain their downfall. I think planting the seeds of that now will protect your family in the future."

"Hot damn, Ella, I think you're onto something. With both

ideas. Let's have some directions to go in when Asher returns from Singapore."

"I'll start digging."

"Good. But to be clear, Asher has too much on his plate to deal with this, so you'll probably need to work with Sterling and me on it. He can get you the information you need, and you and I can strategize what to do with it. Does that work for you?"

I nod.

Declan shoots me a mischievous smile that reminds me of Asher and raises his tumbler of Asher's expensive as hell whiskey. "I think you and I are going to have a lot of fun together, future-sister-in-law."

A smile tugs at my lips. "I think we are, too."

14

ASHER

I loosen my tie and groan as I slump into a chair in my hotel suite after a long day of meetings.

Only one more meeting to go.

I can't wait to get home. This entire trip has been mediocre at best as far as business pursuits, and it's only been made worse by the fact that I feel like I can't breathe without Ella. All I want is to get home to her.

"I got an interesting call from Jenkins," Robert says, entering the common space of the suite.

I sit up, my back rigid. "What happened?"

Robert waves a reassuring hand. "Nothing. It's not security related, exactly. He told me he accompanied Ella and her friends to a gun range yesterday. Apparently, Ms. Morozov attempted to teach Ella to shoot a gun."

By the smirk on Robert's face, I can tell he's trying not to laugh.

"Ella went shooting with Lucy?"

Robert's smirk cracks into a twitching smile as he nods. "Jenkins reported to me that Ella did not take to shooting well and is not interested in further tactical training."

"She needs to learn for her own safety."

"Jenkins let me know that for her own safety, as well as anyone around her, she should never touch a firearm again."

I raise my brows.

"Apparently Ms. Hale screams and waves the gun around in fear every time she fires it. She could miss a target from a few feet away."

I pinch the bridge of my nose, exhaling heavily, as my worries over Ella's safety go up another notch.

"But Waters reports that she's making very good progress in self-defense, so there's a bit of a silver lining."

"Small mercies."

I stand to make my way to the wet bar when a chemical smell assaults my nose. I freeze, sniffing.

"Do you smell gas?" I ask Robert.

He stands frozen, his eyes wide as his eyes scan the room.

"Fuck! Get down!" he cries out.

Shock flares through me as I notice a white vapor pouring into the room through the vents. I drop to my hands and knees to keep below the vapor, but within seconds, my head swims and I'm coughing and retching so hard that I crumple to the floor. I hear Robert yelling in his coms for backup.

And everything turns black.

I WAKE with a cry of shock as freezing water spills over my face. I gasp and splutter, choking as it runs into my mouth and up my nose. I try to sit up, but bands that cross my chest keep me bound to the bed, on my back.

What's going on? Where am I?

I blink, my eyes burning as I glance around, recognizing my hotel room. It's dark, only the dim lights of the city outside provide any light. And then it all comes rushing back. My gut sinks.

Where is Robert? Is he okay?

"Good evening, Mr. Langford," a male voice with a thick Russian accent says near me.

He steps up to the bed, and with the dimness of the room, it's hard to see him clearly as he hovers like a shadow over me. "I hope you'll forgive my intrusion. You are a very difficult man to access. Your security team is quite good at their jobs, so I had to find a way around their protocols."

Tendrils of fear begin to spread through me, but I batter them down before they can overtake me. One mistake could mean the difference between life and death. And I refuse to die.

I open my mouth to respond, but I only manage a hoarse cough. My throat burns from the chemicals I inhaled along with the water I choked on. As my mind clears more from the fog it was under, I remember my own protocols, and shift against my bonds, bringing my left wrist to touch my leg. I push the crown of my watch against my thigh and hold it down for five seconds. I hide my sigh of relief when the light buzz of vibration lets me know it's activated.

The man bends slightly, smiling down at me. "I think you know why I am here, but just in case there is any confusion, let me speak plainly. My cousin Sergei tells me you are still being stubborn. His offer to your board was shot down because of you ... yet again."

"Sergei and his offer can fuck right off," I croak out.

The man, who I can only assume is Yegor Volkov in the fucking flesh, laughs.

"I have heard you have a fiery spirit. I'm glad to see it doesn't evade you even when your life is threatened. But let me be very clear, Mr. Langford, I am growing tired. Your grandfather tried to make things difficult for Sergei almost thirty years ago. And now, you're proving to be difficult as well. When Sergei's business suffers, my business suffers. And I do not like it when my business suffers.

"Your green energy business has been a threat to Sergei and me for many years now. But it was a threat we could keep small by poking at it from time to time. A little damage here and there was all that was needed to keep it from growing into a real problem. But those days are over. Your green energy business is no longer a little threat. It is a major threat, and I am done playing quietly."

My breaths quicken as the cold steel of his Glock presses into my forehead.

"We tried the diplomatic route. We tried to buy the company from you legally, through all the correct channels. Wasn't that nice of us? We even offered you a fair deal. And you couldn't be persuaded. So now, we're done being nice. I have the paperwork ready to go. You sign Greenspan over to Sergei and me, at a fraction of the price we initially offered, or I put a bullet through your skull."

He lifts a packet of papers for me to see in the dim light and waves them, a smirk of triumph tugging at his lips.

With a *snap*, the band holding my wrists to the bed retracts. Yegor removes the bite of his Glock, but keeps it pointed at me as he steps back to flick on the bedside lamp. I wince at the sudden brightness, and my head thrums in pain. I take a deep breath. And another, as I push the pain of my head and body down and focus on the man standing over me. He's non-descript in every way. His height and build are average. His face is neither handsome nor ugly. His light brown hair is graying at the temples, and there's more gray spotted throughout his short beard. His eyes are a bland hazel. He's the type of man you would pass on the street without a second thought, a second glance. No wonder he's been so hard to track down all these years. Not only is he a master at keeping his businesses' finances hidden in various illegal accounts scattered throughout the world, but he's also used his appearance to blend in. His suit is clearly well-made, but it's a classic cut—nothing flashy or ostentatious. Nothing about this man speaks of a powerful mobster at first glance.

But now that I've seen his face, I'll never forget it.

And I'll make sure he pays for this in blood.

Yegor sets the paperwork in front of me, holding it upright, then he places a pen in my right hand.

"Sign, and I'll let you live."

I press the crown of my watch into my thigh again, this time in a specific patterned rhythm, until it buzzes twice in confirmation. I lift my hands, holding the paperwork in my left hand, and pressing the pen to the signature line with my right. But before I scrawl my signature over the page, I drop the pen, unclasp my watch, and toss it at Yegor's feet.

Then I roll as far onto my right side as I can and close my eyes.

"What the fuck?" Yegor growls right before a low *boom* rumbles through the room.

I hiss and cry out as small slices tear across my back. Yegor screams and lands heavily a few feet away. Debris clatters like confetti down on top of me, but I take the small reprieve of time to yank off the bonds tying me to the bed.

"You son of a bitch!" Yegor yells, his voice ringing with agony.

Serves him fucking right.

I scramble off the bed and search for the gun, but just as I make it to my feet, Yegor gingerly stands as well. We face one another, both injured, but he's much worse for wear. Cuts crisscross his hands, arms, and legs. Blood oozes from his abdomen and from his temple, and the right half of his face is shredded. I rush at him and slam my fist into his jaw, and he crumples to the floor again. The door slams open, and half a dozen of Yegor's men flood into the room.

Fuck!

I race to the bathroom and slam the door shut. I'm out of options until my security gets here. I have no more weapons since my gun was stripped off me and I already used my watch. I can't take on six armed men while weaponless.

The men shout at one another in Russian and bang around the room, but thirty seconds later, everything falls silent. I wait another minute to be certain, but when nothing but silence stretches through the room, I crack the door open and peek out. I let out a sigh of relief at the empty room. It seems Yegor's men prioritized getting him medical attention over apprehending me.

Thank god for that.

Just as I exit the bathroom, the door to the suite opens with a bang. I rush over to the bedroom door and cautiously look out. Relief floods me again when this time it's my men rushing into the suite. Seconds later, Robert bursts out of his bedroom, opposite mine, stumbling and bleeding from his wrists and temple.

"Fuck!" he yells when he sees me. He slams into me with a hug and claps me on the back.

"What happened to you?" I ask, my voice laced with concern.

"I woke up tied to a chair in my room. I only just got myself loose."

"Dammit," I growl, taking in his hands and wrists, which are littered with rope burns and slashing cuts. "You about took off your hands to get free."

He shrugs. "I had to do what was necessary."

"Yegor just left with his men," I tell my security team.

"They're gone," Sorenson says, pressing the com at his ear. "The front desk just confirmed it."

"What the fuck happened?" Robert growls at his team. "Why didn't you guys get here as soon as I called?"

"Sorry, boss. We tried," Sorenson rasps, out of breath. "All the elevators were shut down and the stairwells were barricaded."

"They clearly planned this well," I say to Robert with a sigh. "They hit us when they knew the rest of the team wouldn't be in the room."

"How long were we out?" Robert asks.

"It's only been fifteen minutes since you were gassed," Sorenson answers. "We got your message and tried to get up here, but as I said, Yegor's team shut down the elevators and stairwells. We had to get hotel security and maintenance to break down the stairwell doors. And the elevators just became operational as Yegor's men fled with him."

"Call a doctor," I order Sorenson through a pained sigh. "Both Robert and I need medical attention, and I'm not about to head out to a hospital."

"Yes, sir."

"And someone call Jenkins. I don't know where my phone has ended up, but Ella needs to be put on another lockdown."

"Yes, sir," the other security officers say, almost in unison.

The suite door beeps, and everyone tenses as it opens again. But we all relax when we see it's just Matthew.

"Holy Mother of God," he says, his eyes wide as he takes in the scene. Like Robert, he makes his way toward me and gives me stiff hug. "What the fuck happened? The hotel security is freaking out downstairs, and people are yelling, saying a bomb went off."

I sigh. "I had to use my watch."

His eyes nearly burst out of his head, and I settle onto the couch and recount the last fifteen minutes, suddenly grateful that I sent Matthew out on a small errand after dinner so that he wasn't here when all the shit went down. I don't know what

I'd do if I lost Matthew. Or Robert for that matter. After my family and Ella, they're the two people in the world I'm closest to.

"Call the pilot," I order Matthew. "I want to leave as soon as possible. I'm done with this fucking city and this fucking trip." *And I need to get home to Ella.* "Then call and cancel my meeting for tomorrow. But don't divulge to anyone what happened. No one can know." I sigh as I look at the half-destroyed bedroom of the suite. "Let's pack up and leave before the police get here. I'm not in the mood to deal with them. And let the front desk know you'll be in touch for the damages."

My hands shake as I scramble to pack, and I soon become useless at it as the enormity of the situation hits me. I sit on the half-destroyed bed, reeling in my thoughts.

That was too close.

Too motherfucking close.

Yegor and Sergei have gone too far, and this situation has now shifted to life or death.

I run my hands through my hair as a heaviness washes over me and I make my peace with what needs to be done. Because I know in my gut that to beat Yegor and Sergei, I'll have to go just as far as they're willing to go.

Despite my acceptance of it, the thought sobers me.

Because I've been there before.

My hands, unfortunately, are not bloodless. Three times I've watched the life drain from someone's eyes because I stole it.

The first time, I was in college when one of my mother's stalkers somehow breeched our home's walls and made it into my parents' bedroom. My father was gone on business, and I happened to be home for the weekend.

I can still hear my mother's scream.

Declan and I raced into the room. Declan pulled the man off her before he did anything, but the scene snapped something inside me. A rage I've never known existed swept over me, and Declan and I went rabid. We beat the stalker to literal death in what must have been less than two minutes.

The second time was only a couple of years later. Sterling was eighteen, but still in high school, when the idiot decided to sleep with one of his teachers. Her husband caught them in bed and attacked Sterling. Being caught so off guard and not as big or bulky as he is now, Sterling didn't defend himself well. When the man finished, he dumped Sterling in the woods near the boarding school's grounds and left him for dead.

Sterling had paid his security officer to fuck off for the night so he could sleep with the teacher, and the son-of-a-bitch accepted the bribe, so Sterling was left defenseless. His saving grace was the fact that he managed to send me an alert on his watch before he passed out. I called Declan, and we raced to the school, traced the GPS tracker on his watch, and found him sprawled naked on the forest floor, battered and bloody and barely breathing.

We could have called the police. But we were not about to let our little brother be pulled into a scandal that would have caused irreparable damage. Instead, we handled it ourselves.

We tracked down the husband and the security guard who decided a couple thousand dollars was worth risking our brother's life, and we took them out into the woods.

Robert helped to make sure no one would ever find the bodies.

After it was over, I promised myself I would never do anything like that again.

But now it looks like I'm going to have to break that promise to myself. Now, I need to fulfill the promise I made to Katrina. I warned her that I would come for her family if they came for mine. I warned her that if her father pushed me to the edge, I wouldn't go quietly.

Yegor and Sergei think I'm above getting my hands dirty.

But that's because they don't know what I'm capable of when the people I love are on the line. So, if Yegor and Sergei are only going to listen to violence, then that is exactly what I'll give them.

I'll burn them and their lives to the ground.

And I'll smile while I do it.

15

ELLA

"Thank you," I say as I step into the conference room, wrapping up my call to a major news organization. Declan put me in touch with them since I'm heading up the Greenspan project. We haven't told Asher yet because I'm trying to get a feel for interest before I put the proposal together. So far, it's looking good—but with a caveat. The news organization would love to do a piece on Greenspan, but only if Greenspan is a *part* of the piece. They want the main focus to be on Asher, me, and our relationship. I told them I'd have to get back to them on that. But at this point, I think it's a good idea. It gives us both things we're looking for: positive media attention about our relationship and visibility for Greenspan.

Just as I hang up, Emily lets out a long sigh, peering down at her phone.

"What's up?" I ask her.

"You may want to sit down."

I groan as I take a seat next to her at the small meeting table in the corner of the room.

She drums her fingers on the table, seeming to choose her words carefully.

"More photos were leaked of Asher and Katrina."

My stomach plummets. "What?"

"They're old photos," Emily says, reassuringly. "Taken back when they were in a relationship. But the public won't necessarily know that. And the articles coming out are all painting the story as a reconciliation between the two of them."

Mother*fucker.*

"I want to warn you; while some of the photos are public photos from old stories, others are more intimate photos—personal photos. They must have been released by someone very close to Katrina."

Nope, Katrina herself, I think bitterly.

Emily shows me her phone, and a knot forms in my throat. The photo is a selfie of Asher and Katrina lying in a bed, tangled up in one another, their lips pressed together. As Emily said, it's intimate, personal, *provocative.*

"Heather and I are already putting a statement together. We'll get as far ahead of this as we can."

Now it's me who lets out a long sigh. This will be hard to get in front of. The initial pushback the team put out against the cheating scandal hasn't had much success, and now the story will grow even bigger. And while it might be obvious to me that Asher is younger in the photo, it may not be obvious to the average person.

The rest of the team joins Emily and me at the table, and they begin to throw out suggestions on how to combat this. We circle around what feels like a million suggestions, but settle on the fact that the easiest, most effective solution is for Asher and me to be seen in public together.

"When does Mr. Langford return from Singapore again?" Michael asks.

"Saturday, and we have an appearance Sunday night at the

symphony. That should help show the world that we're still very much together."

"That's good, but it may not be enough," Heather says. "The articles are all starting to trend. And I'm not going to lie, some of the pictures of the two of them are hot. Asher has had several cheating rumors in the past, so it's not a stretch for the public to believe he's cheating again."

"And people love a second-chance love story," Michael adds, with an uneasy shrug.

"We need something big," Emily says. "To squash these rumors once and for all."

We're all mulling over ideas when the conference room door opens. Haley, one of the receptionists, peaks her head in.

"Ms. Hale, you've been requested by the executives in the other board room."

My stomach clenches, and I shrink as I notice everyone shoot me worried or pitied looks.

"We'll circle back as soon as you're done with them," Emily says, a little too casually.

I only nod in answer.

As I make my way toward the smaller conference room, I mentally try to make a case for myself, assuming this little meeting is about the cheating articles. I also try to tamp down my frustration. Of course the board would bring this up when Asher's not here to defend himself or me. I'm certain they'll try to pin all the blame on me because I'm the much easier target, and that thought only annoys me further because the board knows these types of stories come with the territory of Asher. People flip and flop about whether they want to see someone like Asher happy and in love or in the middle of drama. It changes day to day, and the tabloids use that to their advantage. There is no way to avoid all scandalous or false stories with his level of fame, it's just not possible, and calling me into their conference room to scold me is not going to change anything.

For a moment I debate stopping by Declan's office and begging him to come to the conference room with me. Asher told him to keep an eye on me while he was gone, and if the executives are upset with me about something, Declan will surely have my back. But I decide against it at the last minute. I can do this on my own. I am good at my job, and I have nothing to feel ashamed about. Plus, I need to learn how to handle the suits in the boardroom if Asher and I are going to be together. Asher's world is full of these types of people, and if we stay together, I know I'll be forced to defend myself time and again. It's better that I get used to it now.

Just as I turn the corner near the smaller conference room, I almost run into someone.

"Oh, sorry," I say, catching myself at the last minute. I stop right in front of Daphne, who I just now realized wasn't in our team meeting. But she's not alone. One of the executives stands right next to her. He clears his throat and pushes past Daphne and then me, then disappears behind the corner.

"Did I interrupt something?" I ask, noting Daphne's wide eyes.

"Of course not," she says quickly, her posture stiff. "Mr. Hoffman was just asking me a question. The board is very concerned about this new cheating scandal."

I raise my brows. "And I'm assuming you told him we'd have it in hand."

"Of course I told him we have it in hand. That's our job. I'm not going to get fired because Asher is already bored with you."

I open my mouth to retort but close it just as fast. I'm not going to get into it with Daphne right now, not when I've been summoned to the executives' conference room. I roll my eyes and push past her, bracing myself as I head into the lions' den.

My eyes widen as I step into the room. Most of the members of the board are here, seated and waiting for me. Of course, it's not all the board members since conveniently Asher, Declan,

Sterling, and Harrington aren't here—and two men who only come for official board meetings are also absent, but the rest of the executives who sit on the board are all present. And they're all poised and ready.

"Ms. Hale," one of them says. "Have a seat."

My pulse pounds in my ears as I do. I swallow hard and surreptitiously wipe my sweaty palms on my skirt beneath the table.

"We are here to discuss your abysmal performance in the task you have been given," Janet says. "We have yet another sordid scandal about Mr. Langford in the news. It was your job to make sure this didn't happen."

At least I wasn't wrong in my assumption.

"With all due respect, I can't control what is written about Asher."

"But you are meant to serve as his distraction, and yet he was photographed with another woman."

"Photographs can be misleading, as is the case with this situation. From what Asher told me, Katrina blindsided him."

"Perhaps blinded by her would be a more accurate description. She is exactly the type of woman we wanted for her, but he refused to listen. And now we are stuck with you, a nameless, PR girl who can't even hold his attention for two months. Not to mention, one who was embroiled in her own scandal with a maniac of an ex."

I plaster a fake smile on my face. "I am sorry to have disappointed you all in that regard. I did, however, garner a lot of positive press in London and with other events, and plan to continue to do so in the future. Asher and I will be attending the symphony this Sunday, and our team is meeting right now to discuss strategies to boost positive press for the event."

"This is your last chance," Janet snaps. "We gave you a contract, and we expect you to pull through. If this appearance is anything less than exemplary, we will move forward with stripping Mr. Langford of his shares."

I sit up straight. "Have you told him that? Or are you telling me here and now because there are no Langfords present?"

Conrad and Gregory both scoff. "No Langfords present?"

"Sorry, I meant *relevant* Langfords present," I bite out.

"You'd better watch your tongue, girl," Conrad growls. "You are not in a position to be smart."

Because Asher isn't here. Because if he were, no one would dare to be this bold. But that's okay, I don't need to hide behind Asher. I can handle these assholes on my own.

I straighten my shoulders. "I am in the position to speak truthfully. And truthfully, the rise in interest and revenue in Asher and many of the businesses that Langford Holdings owns is up since our relationship became public. I don't have the exact metrics in front of me since that is Emily's area of expertise, but I know she's happy with the numbers. So, how about you look at those before you go around slinging threats. We all know how well Asher responds to threats."

"You've grown quite brave in your speech since clawing your way up to this position," Alan, the man I almost ran into with Daphne, says. He's one of Janet's lackeys who always agrees with her and always backs her against Asher. I can't stand him. "We will remember it when this all comes crashing down. You'll be lucky if any company in New York will hire you when it's all over."

My gut clenches at the thought. These people aren't Asher, but they still hold a lot of damn power. And they're actively trying to strip Asher of as much of his as they can.

"I am confident that when this is over, Asher will hold all his current shares—that is the point of this whole endeavor, after all. And while we have had some rough waters recently, I can assure you that I will turn those around and give you exactly what you want."

"And what is it you think we want?"

To destroy Asher.

But they don't know that I know that. So, I give them the answer they think I know.

"You want good publicity for Asher. His sordid history and indiscretions made many investors and CEOs of your subsidiaries nervous. You need to appease them, and so far, we have. As I said, Asher and I have received a lot of positive publicity, minus a couple of snags along the way, which is to be expected with someone of Asher's level of wealth and fame."

"Then this is your last warning. Deliver, or you will not only lose your job, but you will also lose everything you value. As I said, we can make sure that you never work in this city again."

It takes all my strength to keep from rolling my eyes. These walking corpses have no idea how the world works anymore. I know the world of the rich and powerful moves more slowly than for the rest of us, and I know these people still have a lot of power and influence, but they forget that social media is the new media, and they can't control it. At least not completely. They only have an idea of how powerful social media is and how much I can use it to my advantage.

An idea springs to my mind. Something big. Something that is exactly what the team is looking for, and something that the board won't be able to turn their noses up to.

"Okay," I say agreeably. "I have kept things somewhat toned down since I didn't want to come out aggressively swinging with Asher's and my relationship, but if you want a spectacle, I can give you one. That's literally what I'm best at."

Conrad raises a brow. "A spectacle?"

I give him a saccharine smile. "A spectacle. I'll make sure everyone falls in love with Asher and me and our love story."

"You say that like it's easy, like you can just manipulate public opinion."

"That's literally my job."

"That you've been failing at."

"As I said, I have gone for a soft-launch type of approach, but if aggressive is what you want, I'll give it to you."

"Fine. Do it. And if you fail, we'll ruin you."

"I won't fail."

I stand and turn on my heel, then waltz out of the room with my shoulders back and my head held high. I wasn't bull-shitting them. The team and I have held back with my exposure to a degree. Yes, we have had quite a few public appearances already, but we've tried to make them look like Asher's normal appearances, only with a girlfriend in tow. There is an ace up Asher's sleeve we haven't played yet, and if the board is making threats, I'm going to play it.

Instead of heading toward the conference room, I make my way to Declan's office.

I knock lightly and he barks the same annoyed answer Asher does when he doesn't know who's on the other side of the door. I peek my head in and his whole demeanor changes from surly to happily surprised.

"What's up, Ella?" he asks as I enter the room.

"I need a little favor."

"What is it? You look nervous."

"Oh, I just had a lovely little meeting with most of the board."

"The fuck? Why wasn't I informed of this meeting?"

"Because I'm sure they didn't want you there. They know all too well that your loyalty is to Asher."

"And what was this little meeting about?"

"They're breathing down my neck about this Asher and Katrina debacle."

"That dirty bitch. I always hated her."

"Yeah well, I've got to bury this story. And I have a plan, but I want to run it by you first since Asher isn't here."

Just as I'm about to tell him my plan, his phone rings.

"Hang on, it's Asher." He picks up his phone. "Hey, big brother. You'll never guess who's in my office with me."

Declan's teasing smile fades, and a second later he shoots out of his seat. His eyes bulge, and his face drains of color.

"Fuck. Are you okay?" he rasps out.

My stomach damn near bottoms out.

"What's going on?" I whisper-shout.

"Of course. Yes. I'll handle it personally. I've got you, brother. And I've got her. Be safe."

Declan ends the call, and his wide, fear-filled eyes meet mine.

"Asher was attacked."

My head swims.

"What?" I rasp out. "Is he . . . oh my god."

"He's okay," Declan reassures me. "He's getting on the jet now and heading home, but he wants you back under lockdown."

Shit.

"What happened?"

"He didn't give me all the details since he was in a hurry. But Jenkins and I are to escort you back to the penthouse immediately."

My thoughts jumble together in a heap of fear and frustration.

"I . . ."

No!

"I just got out of the damn penthouse."

Today is my first day back in the office. Not that it's going all that well, but at least I get to interact with humans.

"I'm sorry, Ells. We can't risk you."

I groan.

"Asher is not going to back down on this. Whatever happened was serious."

Fuck.

I shake my head lightly to clear my thoughts. I may hate heading back to the penthouse, but that pales in comparison to the gut-wrenching fear inside me knowing Asher was attacked. *What happened? Who attacked him?* He's alive and okay, apparently, but still. I can't bear the thought of something happening to him.

Which is why I know I need to calm my racing thoughts and not fight this. Asher will be out of his mind with worry. And if he was attacked, I could be attacked as well, so it's a justified concern.

"This PR shit about Katrina is not important, Ella. Your safety is," Declan says as he gently takes me by the elbow to help me stand.

"O-okay," I say, still in a bit of a daze. I turn to look at Declan. "You're sure Asher is okay?"

"He's got some cuts and scrapes, but otherwise he's fine. Right now, he's focused on getting home and getting you to safety."

"We have to end this," I say, my voice quavering. "Whatever it takes, Declan. I can't stand the thought of something happening to Asher."

"We will, Ella. You have my word."

16

ELLA

My nerves churn in my gut as I pace the floors of the penthouse. Eighteen hours is too long to wait for a flight, and I hardly slept last night. I haven't spoken to Asher since yesterday at noon when his flight took off. He was only able to give me a quick call before takeoff, and with the security concerns, his team decided to keep communication off unless necessary. To make matters worse, I got a text at four a.m. from Asher telling me they hit a bad storm and their flight had been rerouted. He couldn't send any more texts, and I haven't heard a word since. It's been two hours since then, and in those two hours, I've been restlessly pacing, waiting for any news.

All I've been able to think about is the text I read over Declan's shoulder when he dropped me off at home. Asher gave a quick synopsis of the attack, and with every line I read, my stomach sank further. Hotel room gassed, security blocked, Asher and Robert tied up and unconscious in their hotel, Yegor Volkov holding a gun to Asher's head. I hyperventilated near to passing out at the last bit of information.

I've been so foolish, I think, berating myself over how I

pushed Asher away a few weeks ago. I know how fragile life is. I know what it's like to lose someone so important to you that they're irreplaceable. The process of losing my father was slow and painful as he battled cancer for a few years, but even though we had accepted his fate in the end, it didn't diminish the pain. It didn't change the fact that all we wanted, all we craved as his family, was more time with him. Especially the time before the diagnosis. I'd heard my father speak his regrets dozens and dozens of times about how he'd wished he had done things differently. If he'd known he only had a few more years to live, he would have changed his life. He would have cut back at work, he would have spent more time with his wife and daughters, he would have given himself more freedom to spend time on hobbies and on the things that brought him joy. He wouldn't have given so much of himself to a job that hired his replacement the same week he started chemotherapy.

It seems I've forgotten my father's words. I've forgotten that I can't take life for granted. I can't take people and relationships for granted, and I can't move through life only half living because of fear. That's no way to live. It would be a tragedy to wake up one day and realize I didn't live because I was afraid. Pain and loss are a part of life, and buffering and hiding myself away to avoid them won't save me.

I've let my fear of being hurt keep me from giving my all, at least to an extent, to Asher—but that ends tonight. No more holding back. I'll let go and do what feels so natural—being with him. And if things end between us, then I'll deal with the pain that comes with it. I'm going to love Asher, and if he's afraid of committing all the way to me, then I guess I'll just have to live with that until he's ready. I can be brave enough for the two of us.

Finally, after hours of waiting, my phone rings.

I answer it before even looking at the name.

"We made it," Asher's voice says. He lets out a long breath.

"We didn't have to reroute after all, we just ended up circling over the ocean for a bit. And now we're on the tarmac safe and sound."

"Thank god," I rasp, barely able to get the words out. I collapse onto the sofa.

Asher gives a ghost of a chuckle. "Anxious to see me, Ms. Hale?"

"You have no fucking idea. I almost had a heart attack when Declan told me what happened to you."

"You and me both."

"God. Sorry. I've been so caught up in my own fear, I haven't even asked how you're doing. That must have been terrifying."

"It was scary for a minute."

"But you're okay? Truly? I'm so worried about you."

"I'm fine. I can't wait to be home. It's been too long without you."

"Hurry back to me, Asher. Please." I don't think anything will feel okay until I see him and touch him and make sure he's real.

"I will, baby."

We hang up, but I still can't calm my racing mind. Unable to stand another minute of pacing between the living room or our bedroom, I walk out of the front door and stand in the foyer that divides the front door from the elevator entrance. I want to see Asher the second he's home.

A round white table is the only piece of furniture in the space, and a large floral arrangement sits atop it, changed weekly by Ms. Graham. She always chooses something extraordinarily beautiful. This week it's pink peonies with greenery and some other white flowers I don't know the name of. I climb onto the table to sit while I wait. I cross my legs and lean forward slightly, trying not to crush the flowers as I watch the minutes tick by on my phone.

I almost manically chuckle to myself as I think about what

Lucy would say if she saw me waiting on a table like this. She would scold me for sure, but it doesn't matter. I meant what I said to her and Zahra: I've fallen for Asher, and there's no going back. I haven't dared to speak the words to him, but it doesn't change how sure I feel them inside my heart. There is no one else for me, and I know now that I have to do everything in my power to keep him. I'll take on the board, the Antonovs, the Volkovs, and anyone else that threatens him. Because I know now that to live without him would be the worst kind of torture imaginable.

Finally, the elevator doors open. Asher's eyes meet mine, and I practically launch myself off the table. I scramble toward him, and he lifts me into his arms. I wrap my legs around his waist, bury my face in his neck, and let out a sob of relief.

"Ella," he breathes.

"Never scare me like that again," I gasp out.

Before he can say another word, I take his face in both my hands and press my lips to his. He kisses me back, fiercely, ignoring the men who enter the foyer behind him.

"I need you," he murmurs against my lips. "I need you so fucking much."

His lips meet mine again and never leave as he carries me into the penthouse and straight toward the bedroom. I'm running on practically no sleep and am exhausted, but a shot of adrenaline races through me at the happiness and relief of being in Asher's arms again.

There are no words spoken as the two of us tear at each other's clothes, as if we both know that nothing will feel right until there's nothing between us—until we can feel one another skin to skin. So many things in our relationship are complicated, but this, this is where everything is clear and simple. When it's just the two of us, everything makes sense, and it's like the outside world doesn't exist.

And right now, that's what I desperately need.

I fall onto my back, and Asher lies on top of me. I welcome the weight of him. I've always loved the feel of his large body pressing down on mine, but after the hell of the last twenty-four hours, this almost feels like an answer to a prayer.

I lace my fingers through his hair as he kisses his way down my jaw, to my neck, and across my chest. But then his lips leave my skin, and he pulls away, hovering above me. He looks at me, his blue eyes filled with fire, but also relief.

"I can't believe I'm here, and you're real," he whispers.

I trace my fingers down his cheek. "I'm real."

He buries his face in my neck as his hands grip my shoulders, almost bruising me with their intensity.

"I missed you so fucking much. And then I thought I may not make it back to you."

"I know," I choke out, my voice quavering. "I can never go through that again."

He nods into my neck and then kisses his way up along my jaw again.

"I need you. I need to be inside you."

Without another word, he thrusts his cock inside me, and I moan at the feel of him stretching me. Filling me. I could live with this man inside me and never tire of it.

He moves slowly at first, but then his thrusts grow faster, almost frantic with need. He sucks my breast into his mouth, teasing my nipple with his tongue, as he kneads my other breast in his hand. I move my hips, meeting him thrust for thrust, lost in the haze of need right along with him. His mouth and hands trace and worship every inch of me as he pounds into me, and I cling to him like my life depends on it. I might be panting and gasping for air, but it feels like I can breathe properly for the first time in two weeks.

Asher reaches down, circling his finger over my clit, and sparks shiver down my spine. Pleasure pools low in my core, and every thrust of his cock hits that perfect spot inside me, over and over again.

"Don't stop," I gasp out. "Please, don't stop."

Asher answers my plea by thrusting harder, deeper, and I can't fight the moans and whimpers that leave me. Nothing compares to this man. Nothing.

I cling to him, digging my fingers into the flesh of his back, but if it hurts him, he doesn't complain. I couldn't lessen my hold if I tried to, anyway, and I'm sure I'll be left with my own marks as Asher's teeth graze my neck, biting and sucking and claiming.

"Are you close?" Asher asks. "Because it's been too long without you, and I can't hold back anymore."

"I'm close."

"Then come for me, baby," Asher demands, thrusting harder.

Seconds later, my inner walls pulse and flutter. Stars pepper my vision, my ears pop and ring, and I scream Asher's name as the most intense orgasm I've ever had rips through me. Asher pounds into me even harder until he stills, spilling himself inside me.

"Fuck!" he gasps. "Fuck, Ella."

Asher collapses on top of me, and for a few moments we just lie there, my arms and legs tangled around him and his face buried again against my neck. Our breathing slows. Our heartbeats quiet. And it's only once the high of our orgasms fade that we allow ourselves to let go and for Asher to pull out of me.

He leans back on his heels and watches with a fevered fascination as his cum leaks out of me, sliding down my thighs. He reaches for me and brushes his thumbs through it, smearing it across my skin, pressing some back into my entrance. He leans down and presses a kiss to the top of my pussy, then leans his forehead against my lower abdomen.

"I don't know what to do," Asher whispers against my skin.

"What do you mean?"

He lifts his body up and sits back against his heels again. "I'm so fucking glad you weren't on that trip with me. Threats from Katrina. Attacked by Yegor. Then my plane hit a storm that slowed us so much we were worried for a moment about running out of fuel. I couldn't have handled it if you had been there for any one of those situations. And yet, all I could think about the entire time was how much I hated being away from you. I want you to travel with me. I want you by my side as much as possible, but I also don't want to put you in harm's way. And right now, that seems to be the way of my life."

"We'll take care of it. You can't keep living this way. Declan and I have a plan we think will help."

Asher furrows his brows. "Ugh. Don't say my brother's name while you're lying naked beneath me with my cum in your pussy."

I giggle. "Then we can talk about it later when I'm fully clothed. But you should know, I want the same as you. I want to be with you. Wherever you go. I know we can't make it work all the time, but I want to be with you as much as I can. You are an addiction I can't seem to kick, Mr. Langford."

"I can't say I hate the sound of that."

Asher's eyes shine with mischief, then he grabs hold of my legs and hauls me off the bed. I yelp in surprise as he slings me over his shoulder.

"What are you doing?" I ask through laughter.

"Shower," he grunts out.

17

ELLA

Beneath the warm water, we touch and kiss and fuck all over again, and after having him inside me again, I finally feel calm. We dry and dress in silence as if we're afraid to burst the bubble, and this turns out to be a dream. I touch Asher often, to be sure he's here, that he's real, and he seems to be of the same mindset. And when we climb into bed, he pulls me close and I lay my head on his chest and wrap my legs around his, tangling us together.

"After you called me, I couldn't stop thinking about something," I say, drawing idle circles across his chest, which is mercifully bare.

"What's that?" His chest vibrates and rumbles against mine with his words.

"About how fleeting life can be. One day my dad was healthy, and the next he was diagnosed with cancer. Everything can change at the drop of a hat. Before my dad died, he made me promise that I wouldn't spend my time on things that don't matter. He wanted me to live. He told me that work and bills and the monotony of life will always be there, and he wanted me to remember that if you let them, those things will overtake your life. They'll take too much time away from the things that truly matter. Family. Love. Friends. Time spent on things you enjoy and value. I don't want to do that anymore. I know our situation is crazy, but I don't want to live in fear. And I don't want to be away from you. What we have matters—even if it started as nothing more than a contract."

"It's a hell of a lot more than a contract now," Asher says, his breath brushing across my forehead.

"Exactly. I know there are no guarantees, and that the future is murky. But I want to help you get past all this so that we can be together for real, without anything hanging over our heads. No outside pressure. No PR stunts. No threats from Sergei or Yegor. Just you and me and a real relationship."

"I want that too, but I need you to know that in the meantime, we have to be very fucking careful. I can't risk you. I won't. So please be patient with me. The thought of anything happening to you scares me in a way I didn't know was possible. I need you by my side, but more than that, I need you safe."

I continue to trace circles over his chest. "I know. But now that we've been together so publicly, I don't know if there's any going back. Sergei and Yegor obviously know who I am at this point, and there's no undoing that."

"What are you getting at?"

"I was speaking to Declan about this."

He grumbles. "Again, with my brother's name while you're in my bed."

I swat lightly at his chest. "Don't be weird, there's nothing but platonic feelings between Declan and me."

"I know that. I'd hang him by his balls if I thought otherwise. I put him on Ella watching duties while I was gone because he's the person I trust the most. I guess I've just never had a situation like this where the person I was seeing was close to my family. It's still a bit strange to me."

"Would you rather I wasn't close to them?"

"No. God no. I'm glad you are. But I've spent most my life keeping different aspects of it in very separate categories. Work and family have always been a mixed bag with being a Langford, but everything outside of that was mine and mine alone. I've never even introduced a girl to my family, so it's still new for me to have someone fit into my family dynamic. I like it. But I'm still just getting used to it."

"Well, keep working on it, because Declan and I are buddies."

"Buddies?"

"Yep. Buddies. And we also have some plans in the works."

"And just what are these plans?"

"For one, I think you need to show Greenspan to the world. Keeping Greenspan quiet is only giving Sergei more power, and Declan agrees. I think if Greenspan had more visibility, it would be harder for Sergei to keep targeting it. Sergei has been operating in the shadows because Greenspan has lived in the shadows. But if we shine a bright light on it, we chase away those shadows, and then Sergei will have to work a lot harder to keep his actions quiet."

"The world can't know about how he's hit our family."

"I agree. But that doesn't mean you have to hide the amazing things you're doing with Greenspan. You said they're close to a breakthrough in green energy, so tell the world that. You don't have to disclose the technology, just acknowledge that you're working on it."

"But that could put an even bigger target on our backs with more oil companies."

"That will happen when the technology hits the market, anyway. Big oil will push back no matter what. But if you have public support and support from government agencies, it could help provide a lot more protection. Use transparency to your advantage."

"You know, Ms. Hale, you still surprise me with your mind,

even though by this point I shouldn't be. I think I'll forever be thanking Emily for insisting she put you on our little team."

I shift my head and smile up at him. "Me too."

"So, what's your other plan with my brother?"

"Basically the same thing, but with us. The board seems to think they need some big production to override the rumors about you and Katrina."

Asher groans. "Definitely don't speak her name while we're in bed. My dick might shrivel up and die."

I chuckle. "Okay, I won't speak about the she-devil. But just so you're aware, I'm planning a spectacle. You don't have to do anything but show up and smile for the cameras."

"I think I can do that."

"Good."

He shoots me his mischievous smile I love so much. "I may or may not have my own spectacle in the works."

My stomach flutters. "Is that so?"

"I can't say for sure. But all you have to do is show up and smile for the cameras."

I chuckle again. "I also think I can do that."

"Then it's settled. By the time we're done, the board will have everything they could ever want from us."

"Good. Then those snakes will leave you alone."

"They'll never leave me alone. They just won't have any leverage over me. But I have to keep my nose clean for three more years to get to that point."

"Why three years?"

"That's when the stipulations on my shares expire. After that, I can do whatever I want without consequences."

"Sounds like you're looking forward to it. Are you dying to go back to your sordid bachelor days?" I tease.

"Fuck no. You've ruined me. Now that I know what it's like to have you, I never want to go back to that."

"So, I guess I'm secure for the next three years."

Asher pinches my side, and I yelp. "At this point, I don't know that I can ever let you go. I think I'm going to have to make you mine in every way possible."

I lift my head and raise my brow at his meaning. "In what kind of ways, Mr. Langford?"

He smirks. "Legally." He lifts my hand to his mouth and nibbles on my finger. *That* finger.

I shake my head in disbelief, butterflies leaping inside me.

"I think I can get behind that."

"But only once we're through this mess. I won't risk it until then."

"Then we'll just have to get through it as quickly as possible."

Asher smirks again. "Are you in a hurry, Ms. Hale?"

"To be yours, and for you to be mine in every way? You bet I am, Mr. Langford."

I gasp in surprise as Asher yanks his T-shirt that I'm wearing off my head.

"I think I need you at least one more time tonight, just to make sure this isn't a dream," he growls, taking my breast in his mouth.

He'll get no arguments from me.

18

ASHER

"Ready?" Robert asks with a tightening of his jaw as Declan and I climb into the back of my car.

"Ready."

We have a visit to pay. I should be heading back to my penthouse after a long day, but what's been set in motion is ready, and I won't lose out on this opportunity. Just as the car takes off Sterling texts me.

I've spotted Yegor.

Where?

He's back in Moscow. I got some photos of him leaving a hospital. His face looks pretty fucked.

It was. Serves the bastard right. I'm only sad it didn't kill him.

Well, the explosives in our watches aren't
made for that. They're made for escape, which
worked, thank fuck.

> I need a team in there ASAP. I want him gone.

That's the thing, he's in Moscow, but he isn't
staying still. He's been in three different
locations in a matter of a week. He knows
you're coming after him, and he's on the run.
We haven't heard the last from him, but he'll
be lying low for the next little bit while he heals
and regroups.

> I don't want him to get the chance to do either
> of those things.

I know, but as I said, he's a slippery fucker.
Even I'm having a hard time tracking him. But
I'll keep on it.

> Do whatever is necessary.

WHILE STERLING WORKS on tracking Yegor, I've got a little present ready for Sergei. He may not have been the one who attacked me, but he and Yegor are working together. Besides, Katrina is Sergei's daughter, and she threatened not only me, but Ella as well.

And that just won't stand.

The car slips into an underground parking garage as Declan, Robert, and I pull on leather gloves and wipe them down. I text Sterling again.

> Cameras are down, correct?

Yes, they're down throughout the entire
building. You're clear.

MY SECURITY TEAM pulls up behind us and Declan, Robert, and I climb out of the car. It will only be the three of us on this little mission, but I brought a few other men as backup. Just in case.

Right on cue, the lights to the building and the rest of the block cut out. Thank you, Sterling. We give it a minute and then climb the stairwells lit by emergency lighting up to the fifteenth floor. Sergei didn't splurge for a high security building or a penthouse for his useless son, and tonight, that makes our job just a little bit easier.

The hallway is mostly empty, though a few concerned tenants roam up and down the hall to ask each other if they've heard any updates from the power company. Thankfully, with the dim emergency lighting overhead, they can't see us well enough to care about us, and we are ignored as we make our way down the hallway of the fifteenth floor.

"Fifteen twenty-three," Declan says, coming to a stop in front of the door. He takes out an electronic key he managed to get a copy of through his connections and opens the door.

The same faint emergency lighting shines at the entrance of the apartment, but otherwise, the space is dark. Voices filter from the bedroom, which doesn't surprise me. Dimitri is a partier. It's the reason Katrina is the one following in her father's footsteps. Dimitri can't stay sober for more than a week, and he certainly can't say no to a good time.

Taking a leaf out of Yegor's book, Declan, Robert, and I pull on gas masks, then I open the door to the bedroom and toss a can of gas into it.

"What the fuck is that?" a male voice asks, heavily slurring his words.

"It looks like a cloud," a female voice says through a fit of giggles.

Heavy footsteps move through the room for a moment before a loud *thud* sounds from the other side of the door. We wait thirty more seconds, just to be sure.

I push the bedroom door open, and through the dim light coming from the windows, I see two women and four men all passed out around the room. I'm sure they were all probably pretty fucked up before we got here, but I'm taking no risks.

Declan grabs each of the men by the hair and inspects their faces until he finds Dimitri. I shine a flashlight in his face just to be sure, then I take what I need out of my suit pocket. I draw up the syringe of narcotics laced with fentanyl. Declan wraps a tourniquet around Dimitri's arm until his vein bulges. His arms are crisscrossed with track marks already, so it's not hard to find where to inject.

I pierce his vein with the needle and press down on the plunger. When it's emptied, I pocket the vial and drop the needle next to Dimitri and watch as his body convulses. I should feel remorse. A small part of me does. But this is the least of what Yegor and Sergei are willing to do to me and mine.

I snap a picture of Dimitri once he takes his last gasping breath, and the three of us leave the apartment, lock up, and head downstairs. When we reach the car, I send the picture to Sterling, who will send it to Sergei, Katrina, and Yegor from an untraceable IP address.

I warned Katrina that I would follow through with my threat, and she of all people should know that I do not issue warnings without being willing to follow through on them. Sergei has targeted my family and our business for nearly thirty years. Yegor is responsible for my grandfather's death. Katrina threatened Ella's life. Yegor threatened mine.

They have fucked with the wrong man. With the wrong family. And I'm done waiting and watching.

Now, they'll all pay for what they've done.

My phone vibrates with a text from Ella as we pull out of the underground garage.

> Are you close?

> > Nearly there, baby. Sorry, traffic is a bitch.

I HATE LYING TO HER, but she doesn't need to know about the little task I just finished. The further she is from all of this, the better.

> The stylists have your tux ready to go, so you'll need to clean up quickly when you get here.

> > Or we could stay home . . . Just kidding.

TONIGHT IS our appearance at the symphony. We had to push it back almost a week since I was not about to make any public appearances after Yegor's attack. Not until I had more protections in place. But in the end, this suited Ella well as she made some big plans for this appearance tonight.

> I wish we could stay in. I'm so nervous that I'm ready to puke. But the board wants their spectacle, so I'm giving it to them.

SHE SURE IS. Ella decided to pull out the big gun for this event —my mother. She and my father are coming to the symphony with Ella and me, and this will be the first time a girlfriend of mine will be photographed with my mother. In fact, none of my brothers have had girlfriends photographed with my mother, either. So it's a huge fucking deal. The world has been following all our love lives since we were teenagers, and tonight is the first time one of Catherine Rothschild Langford's boys will be putting on a show of real commitment. This united outing insinuates that Ella has received my mother's stamp of approval, which she has, and fuck if that won't make headlines all over the world. As crazy as that shit sounds, it's real for our family.

So, I'm sure Ella is sweating right now. We're supposed to arrive at the symphony in ninety minutes, and I'm not even home yet. I've already fielded several calls and texts from my mother as well. She knows what's on the line, and she knows why Ella asked her to accompany us tonight, and she will expect this to be executed flawlessly. Me running an hour behind is not exactly flawless, and she's not above badgering me about it.

At least neither of them knows *why* I'm running an hour behind.

Thirty minutes later, I'm finally home, and a hoard of people are here, camped out in the space between my living room and dining area. But my focus lands on one person and one person only. I cross the room in a few strides and step in front of the makeup chair she's sitting in.

"Asher!" Ella gasps happily. And even though I know it will get me in trouble with the makeup artist, I grab both sides of Ella's face and bring it to mine. I plant a kiss on her before she can say another word. She lets out a soft moan into my mouth, and I slip my tongue inside. I don't care that we have an audience. I can't wait one more second for this. In fact, there's something else I can't wait for.

"Please excuse us," I rasp out when I finally force myself to pull away. The makeup artist and hair stylist both chuckle as I take Ella by the hand and lead her away—toward our bedroom.

"What are you doing?" she asks as I practically drag her along behind me.

"I know we're running behind, but this can't wait."

"What can't wait?" Her nose is scrunched in that cute way of hers when I shut and lock the door behind her.

"You and me. I need you. I won't make it through the night if I can't touch you first."

Maybe it's the adrenaline still pumping through my veins from what I did to Dimitri or the fact that I finally hit back at Sergei in a concrete way. Or maybe it's because I know that this war between us is only going to get worse before it's over, and the thing I'm scared about more than anything is the safety of the woman before me. But I need to feel her, be with her, be inside her. She's my home, and the only thing I have to hold onto. She's the only thing keeping me sane.

"But we need to leave soon."

"And we will. But only after I've been inside you first."

She raises a brow. "We don't have time."

"I fuck you here or I fuck you at the symphony, take your pick, baby, because it's happening either way."

She scoffs and rolls her eyes. "I can only imagine the headlines if we got caught fucking at the symphony."

"Good, then we agree to fucking now."

"What has gotten into you?"

I nip at her neck. "I just need you. I'm literally dying."

She scoffs again. "Dying?"

"Dying."

Shamelessly, I pick her up, and she wraps her legs around

my waist. Thank fuck she's not in her dress yet and the little white silk robe she's wearing doesn't restrict her. I carry her over to the bed and drop her onto it.

"Strip," I command.

She opens her mouth to argue again, but I cut her off. "Don't make me say it again. And don't think I won't fuck you in public if I can't have you now."

Heat flushes her cheeks, and I know I have her. She opens her robe and discards her bra and panties in a flash. I rip my own clothes off in record time then prowl toward her as she scoots back on the bed. I crash my lips to hers again, but as I move to press her to lie back, she surprises me by slipping out from under me and flipping over to straddle me.

"Andre will kill me if I ruin my hair. So I'm on top, Mr. Langford."

"I'll take you any way you'll have me," I say against her lips as I slip a finger inside her. "Fuck, baby, you're already so wet for me."

She grinds against my hand, moaning into my mouth, as I fuck her hard with my fingers. But too soon, I grow impatient and slip them out of her.

"When you come, it's going to be on my cock."

I lift her by the hips and line myself up with her entrance, then practically slam her back down, letting out a hiss of pleasure at the feel of being inside her. I bite down on my fist to keep from biting and marking her skin with the feral need coursing through me. Normally, I'd revel in the sight of my love marks on her body, but since she will be photographed under immense scrutiny tonight, I find a sliver of self-control and keep my teeth to myself.

"I can't get enough of you," I rasp out as I tighten my grip on her hips, reveling in the feel of their softness beneath my palms. Every inch of her is perfection to me, for no other reason than because it's her. She calls to me in a way nothing and no one ever has. "I want to have you every moment of every day. God, I can't get enough of you."

"Me neither," she breathes.

I let out a long sigh of relief. "Thank fuck for that."

She kisses me hard and rides me harder until I'm seconds away from falling over the ledge.

"Come for me, baby."

And she does. She cries out seconds before release tears through me and I spill inside her. My orgasm is so powerful I yell into my fist again, and my body locks up, practically paralyzed from overwhelming sensation.

Holy. Fucking. Shit.

This woman.

Our chests press and release against one another through our panting breaths as we both come back down to earth. I can't say how that felt for her, but if it was a fraction of how it felt for me, then it was fucking mind blowing. And by the slight trembling of her fingers and her quaking thighs, I'd say she's overcome as well.

"I have one last thing to check off before we go," I say, my breaths still stuttered.

"And what's that?"

I hesitate, suddenly nervous. I'm never nervous. "Come with me and I'll show you."

I stand and pull my briefs back on as Ella wraps herself in her little white robe. I take her by the hand and lead her into our closet, once again opening the safe that holds the Langford jewelry I inherited. There's one box I haven't touched yet. One that my mother always said would be a nice touch when I found the woman I wanted to spend my life with. I can't deny that Ella is that woman, so this is fitting for tonight. And yet I find myself nervous at the prospect. The gravity of it.

I open the box and take out three smaller boxes and open each of them. One holds a necklace with a massive rectangular-shaped emerald surrounded by dozens of small white diamonds, one holds matching earrings, and one holds a diamond and emerald bracelet.

"I want you to wear these tonight," I say, fighting back my nerves.

"Is this why you insisted my dress should be emerald green?"

I nod. When I found out Ella's plan, I knew I had to add to it. And if there's a way to make a statement tonight at our first public appearance with my mother, this is it. I let Ella, Matthew, and Katya know that her dress needed to be emerald green, though I didn't tell them why.

"This set of jewelry was my great-grandmother's favorite. And the first time my mom was photographed officially with my dad, she wore these. These jewels are famous in the Langford family, and my dad wanted to show his family and the world that he was serious about her. She was always meant to marry a royal, that's what she was raised to aspire to, but she turned everything upside down when she met my dad and they fell in love. My dad wanted to prove to the world that while he wasn't an official royal, he was American royalty and was just as rich and powerful. He wanted to show that he could give her as much, if not more, than any of the royals of Europe. Call it American arrogance, or just a marking of territory, but my dad draped my mom in Langford family jewels and showed her off to the world.

"So that's where you get your possessive side from, huh?" she asks with a wink.

"Absolutely."

"This is big, Asher."

"I know."

She gnaws on her lip. "But I'm not famous like your mother.

I'm just a woman who works for your company. You don't have to mark your territory and prove yourself like your dad did."

I can practically see her insecurities flashing across her face, and it makes my possessive side rage. She doesn't see herself clearly.

"You're not *just* anything, Ella. I won't lie; you'll always be compared to my mother. I wish it wasn't the truth, but it is. You need to remember that her fame wasn't earned, either. She was born into a noble family, and she was born beautiful. I'm not trying to take away from her other qualities and accomplishments, I think my mom is amazing, but her initial fame came *before* those accomplishments. She garnered attention because she was noble and beautiful, and therefore a prized potential bride for the royals and nobles of Europe. She proved that she was more than a pretty face and a title with time and with her work, and I know it will be the same for you. You may not have been born into fame like she was, but you've proven time and again that you belong in our world and that you can handle it. Don't be ashamed of being a woman who works for my company. You're brilliant and successful in your own right because of what you've achieved on your own. That's nothing to be ashamed of. You should be damn proud. I know I am."

Tears shimmer in her eyes.

"You're pretty perfect sometimes," she whispers.

"I'm not. But for you, I try."

I lift the necklace from its case and clasp it around her neck. Then I follow with the bracelet, and Ella puts the earrings in place.

"Beautiful," I say, taking in the sight. "You're perfect. And now, you get to write your own story—our story—when you're photographed wearing these tonight."

And because I can't stop myself when it comes to this woman, I tug at the tie on her robe, and open it up, baring her perfect, naked body to me. Before she can protest, I grip her by the waist and set her atop the counter at the center of the closet.

"Before I have to share you with the world, I need you one more time, just to myself."

She spreads her legs without a word, and I nearly come undone at the sight of her perfect pussy on display for me. I slam into her, and she gasps, grabbing onto my shoulders for support. I fuck her hard and fast. Claiming her. Reminding her that whatever comes of tonight, we'll always have this. Just the two of us. And in our little bubble, there is no fame. No comparisons. No rules to uphold. We can just be us.

I come seconds after she does, biting down on my fist to keep from screaming her name loud enough for everyone in the penthouse to hear.

And only now am I ready to face what tonight has in store.

A loud knock sounds on the bedroom door.

"We need to leave in five minutes!" Matthew calls out.

Ella laughs. "Shit."

"It was worth it."

Ella swats at me. "Go get in the shower, Mr. Langford, or I'll make you explain to your mother why we're late."

I wink at her. "You know she wouldn't be surprised. I am my father's son after all."

She scrunches her face. "I forgot about how your parents are."

"Well, get used to it. If my brothers and I have to deal with our parents' horny ways, you do too. Welcome to the Langford clan."

"I'm coming in in five seconds!" Matthew calls out again.

We both rush out of the closet, and I race to the bathroom as Ella grabs her bra and panties, frantically pulling them on right as Matthew saunters into the bedroom with Ella's dress slung over his arm.

"I just love how you two couldn't wait until after the

symphony tonight," he says in a snarky tone. "I've created two monsters. Come on, Ella. Katya and I have five minutes to get you dressed and then Andre and Trenton need to fix what Asher did to your hair and makeup."

I chuckle darkly to myself as I take the fastest shower of my life.

19

ELLA

"Are you both ready for this?" Catherine asks as the car approaches the curb.

"Yes," Asher bites out, his jaw clenched.

Tonight is a lot. It's more than a lot. Any appearance Catherine makes is a big deal. But Catherine appearing with her son and his girlfriend? Huge. Worldwide headline huge. And I can see the enormity of it weighing on Asher. It's weighing on me as well.

"I think so," I say through a shaky breath.

"You'll be wonderful, Ella dear," Catherine says to me, her voice warm and reassuring. Her eyes roam over the necklace and earrings I'm wearing, and I swear I see a glimmer of tears gather in her eyes. "You look very beautiful, and the jewelry suits you. I'm not sure if I told you that or not."

I flush under her praise, and the deeper meaning behind her words. "Thank you, Mrs. Langford. You look incredible, yourself."

"No more Mrs. Langford. Call me Catherine."

I nod, doing my best to swallow my nerves.

Flashes from cameras flicker so quickly it feels like we're

pulling up inside a club. But this is no club. This is a veritable onslaught of paparazzi. Once I let it slip to a "source" that Asher's parents, specifically his mother, would be accompanying Asher and me to the symphony, the news spread like wildfire.

Catherine looks at me, her expression serious. "Your life has already been altered quite a lot in these past few weeks, but this will add another layer of insanity. I'm not trying to scare you, dear girl, I just want to give you one last chance to change your mind. If you need to, we can drive away."

My throat bobs on a swallow. "Thank you, Catherine. But I'm okay. I know this comes with the territory, and if this is what is required to be with Asher, then I accept it."

Asher's hand on my thigh squeezes at my words. I turn and catch his gaze, and his eyes are full of fire. I know he's fighting his anxiety, but I can also see the hope and determination in his eyes. If we want to be together, truly be together, this is a necessary step. We have to show the world that Catherine Rothschild Langford approves of me since we can't escape the fascination the world has with her.

"You'll be wonderful, both of you," Harrington says warmly. "This is a big day for our family."

Our conversation is cut off as the car pulls to a stop. Cheers ring as the car door opens and Harrington steps out first, then the cheers blaze to a deafening roar when Catherine follows. Cameras flash like mad, and the energy surrounding the car is unlike anything I've ever experienced. Catherine always draws a massive amount of attention, but adding Asher and me in a relationship to the equation is like pouring gasoline on an already roaring fire.

"Are you okay?" I ask Asher, knowing his anxiety must be off the charts.

He brushes his thumb along my cheek, nodding slowly. "Like you said, this comes with the territory. It still scares the shit out of me, but I know it's necessary. The bigger question is, are you ready?"

I let out a shaky breath. "As ready as I can be."

He lifts my hand to his mouth and places a kiss on it. "You're amazing."

With that, Asher climbs out of the car to another wave of cheers, and the electric buzz of anticipation seems to bubble up in the atmosphere. He turns and holds out a hand for me, and the crowd goes almost as crazy as it did for Catherine. I slide out of the car and stand next to Asher, smiling for the crowd and the cameras—praying this all goes well—knowing these pictures will live on the internet for all time.

At least I'm dressed well for the occasion.

The emerald gown I'm wearing is fitted but elegant, and my hair flows in simple but classic curls. But it's the jewels I'm draped in that will be the real story tomorrow. I'm still in shock that Asher wanted me to wear something with that level of connection to his mother in such a public way, but I guess I shouldn't be. Asher doesn't do things by halves. He's either all in or all out. It's a miracle we made it through the beginning of our relationship when it was merely a PR stunt. His acting skills are atrocious and almost ruined everything before it really began. It was only once we gave in and decided to stop acting that we made positive headlines about our relationship. Because that's the thing; so much of our relationship just feels inevitable. I've never believed in soul mates, but now that I'm with Asher, it's hard to deny that if they exist, he's mine and I'm his.

And now he's proudly displaying that for the world.

Harrington and Catherine come to stand near us, and the four of us walk through the building's entryway together, blinded by the insatiable flashing of cameras. Catherine walks next to me, giving the photographers exactly what they want, a side-by-side photo of Mrs. Catherine Rothschild Langford and what everyone will assume is a possible future Mrs. Langford.

And at this point, I'm hoping for that, too.

AT INTERMISSION, Catherine and I split from the Langford men and head to the bathroom. The line is ridiculously long, and we immediately begin to attract stares and a crowd. Both of our respective security officers decide waiting in line isn't going to work and usher us away.

"You'll have to wait and go once the performance picks back up unless we find a more private bathroom," Jenkins says, apologetically.

"It's fine," I say. "I'd rather not pee with a crowd gawking at me the entire time, anyway."

Catherine chuckles beside me, but her laugh peters out when we arrive back at our box and find the last person I want to see.

Katrina Antonov.

Anger bubbles inside me at the sight of her trying to get close to Asher. His security has blocked her, but not for lack of her trying to get to him.

"What the hell does she want now?" I mutter through clenched teeth.

"I know it was you!" Katrina shrieks, pushing against Robert while screaming at Asher. "I know it was you!"

What was him?

She looks crazed, and an idea sparks to life. I take out my phone and start recording.

"How could you do this?" Katrina shouts. "How dare you, Asher! How dare you!"

Asher stands impassive, looking at Katrina with boredom.

"Why couldn't you just listen? We could have had everything! We could have joined our forces, joined our families, but you just won't listen! We tried to be fair! But you denied us at every turn! And now you've … you've …" She breaks into a sob. "I'll kill you! How dare you!"

At a nod from Asher, Katrina is hauled off her feet and forcibly removed by two security officers.

I stop recording and notice the gathered crowd. Several people around us are also recording Katrina's antics, and I tamp down the smug smile that pulls at my lips. I get to work as security breaks up the crowd and leads me back to our box. I send the video to Emily and Matthew with a text on our group message.

> I need you two to release this ASAP. Put out the story that Katrina is caught up in a jealous rage at the symphony. Include an official statement that Asher is not and has not been involved with Katrina in over twelve years, but his relationship with me has infuriated Katrina to the point where she's been stalking him for the past few weeks to get back with him. Do whatever you have to do to paint her as an unhinged ex.

A MINUTE LATER, Emily texts me back.

> Emily: Damn, she's batshit crazy. What was that all about?

> I don't know yet. Security is de-escalating the situation as we speak, and I haven't talked to Asher about it yet.

Matthew: Hell yes. We'll take this bitch down.

A lot of people were recording, so this is going to hit social media any second. Act fast. And thank you!

I PUT my phone away and head straight for Asher.

"Are you okay? What was all that about?"

He wraps me in his arms, and I try ignoring the people still recording us. I don't love it, but I can't deny that it will help our cause. I have no idea what is going on with Katrina, but I know she just did my job for me. I've been searching for a way to bring her down, and she just handed it to me on a silver platter. Now, painting the rest of her family in a bad light will be easy, and when the Antonovs fall, there will be a narrative to back it up.

Asher leans down to whisper in my ear. "I warned Katrina that if her family threatened me or made a move against me, I'd retaliate."

Katrina's words hit me, and realization strikes.

"What did you do?"

"What I promised I would."

He doesn't elaborate, not now, not here, but I know in my gut he must have done something big. What else would prompt Katrina to make a public spectacle of herself like that? She must have seen enough chatter about Asher's whereabouts tonight to know where he was and decided to ambush him. As if that would work. But it's clear she wasn't in a rational frame of mind.

A sliver of guilt worms through me at my plan. I hate the way the media lies about me and Asher, and yet that's exactly what I've set in motion against Katrina. It's hypocritical. It's dirty; I can't deny that. But then I think of Asher's grandfather. I think of Asher as a boy almost killed in that crash. I think of a week ago when he had a gun pressed to his head. Katrina may not have been the one to do those things, but her family is the architect of it all, and she's playing right alongside them. She's the one who threatened Asher on behalf of her family. She has no problem with the hell the Antonovs and Volkovs have caused Asher. She feels no remorse that one of Asher's employees was paralyzed in the "accident" ordered by her father.

I don't know what Asher's done, but I know what Katrina's family has done. The thought of his life on the line makes me murderous, and any guilt I feel disappears just as quickly as it came. Katrina dug her own grave, and I'll happily toss the first shovel of dirt onto her casket.

Asher takes me by surprise by cupping my cheeks and kissing me. Then he leads us back to our box where his parents take their seats beside us. Asher takes out his phone, clearly typing out a text, and then nods silently to his father.

Whatever is going on will not be revealed right now, but one thing is clear: the four of us will remain a united front until we're out of the public eye. We'll finish this night out as if nothing happened, and we'll show the world that nothing ruffles the Langfords' feathers.

Especially not crazy exes.

20

ELLA

"Do you want to tell me what that was all about?" I ask Asher as we step into our bedroom. He's been quiet and stoic ever since his run-in with Katrina. A heaviness hangs over him that others might not be able to detect, but I can.

He sits on the bed with a long sigh and runs his hands down his face.

"I need to tell you something, but I'm worried about how you'll react."

I tense at his words. Whatever is on his mind is clearly tormenting him, but I hope he knows that no matter what, I'll always be there for him.

I run my fingers through his hair and tip his head up to look at me.

"What is it?"

"I did something tonight. Before I came home. That's why I was late."

"What did you do?"

"I . . . took care of Katrina's brother, Dimitri."

I pause as his words settle over me. "When you say you took care of him, what do you mean?"

"I killed him."

A shock races up my spine and dread curls in my stomach.

"He was a drug addict," Asher rasps out. "Sergei has been trying to get him clean for over a decade. Not that that excuses what I did, but I warned Katrina that I would come after him if her family followed through with their threats. I told her the night she cornered me in the restaurant, and I sent more messages to her and Sergei that I was not bullshitting around. I warned them that if they made any moves against you, me, my family, or Greenspan, that I would retaliate. And Yegor and Sergei didn't listen."

I swallow hard, trying to wrap my mind around Asher's revelation.

"Most people would say I killed him in cold blood. And that's true. But when Dimitri wasn't high, he was his father's puppet just like Katrina. And if anything, he was worse. He has a lot of blood on his own hands from years of taking out his father's enemies. So, it's not like I killed a saint or anything, but I won't lie and say it's justified. I killed him in retaliation and as a warning. Sergei and Yegor have been under the impression that I won't hit back effectively because I won't dirty my hands. And now they know how wrong they are. I don't want to hurt or kill, but I will if it's a matter of protecting my family. And I don't feel an ounce of guilt over it. A heaviness, yes. But not guilt."

Asher finally looks at me. His face is set with determination but also worry. Worry for how I'll react to his truths.

He runs his hands through his hair and almost seems to be holding his breath. "I understand if this is too much for you. I won't ask you to be with me if this is a line you can't abide."

He blinks rapidly, his throat bobbing on a swallow as he hangs his head.

My heart races as I try to sort through everything he's just said.

Is this too much for me? Is this line too far?

I don't know.

I know the answer should be yes.

Does it make me a bad person that it's not an immediate yes?

I pace the room, my breaths coming in shallow, my thoughts fracturing in a million directions. Asher is so quiet, so controlled about his admission, it makes me wonder . . .

"Have you done something like this before?" I whisper, halting my pacing.

He looks at me briefly before giving a guilty nod.

"Once, when a man attacked my mother. Another time, when a man attacked Sterling, back when he was a teenager."

I sit at the table in the corner, needing space to think.

"I don't relish violence, Ella. I really don't. But the money, the fame, and the power our family has makes us targets. Sometimes, I have to use violence against violence to keep my family safe."

"How do you deal with that? How are you not freaking out right now?"

Asher sighs. "As I said, there is a heaviness in taking a life. I won't deny it. But not guilt. Not when those I've killed have hurt my family or were willing to kill me or my family without a second thought. I would never hurt someone without cause. Every bad thing I've done was in the name of protecting those I love."

I can see the truth blazing in his blue eyes, and it helps to stem the tide of confusion inside me.

I know Asher's heart. And I know he is not the type of man who craves blood or violence. I know he wants to do good in the world. And I believe him when he says he's only acted in defense of his family.

Can I live with this?

I don't know what it says about me, but I think I can.

I stand and make my way over to Asher. His face is lined with apprehension, so I reach out and cup his cheek with my hand. I lift it until his eyes meet mine.

"I'm with you, Asher. I may not like this, and if I'm being honest, it scares me. But it doesn't change anything. I can see that this isn't what you want. You've been forced into this, and you're doing what you must to keep yourself, your family, and me safe."

He shakes his head lightly. "Just myself and my family."

I furrow my brows. "What?"

"You said I'm keeping myself, my family, and you safe. But you *are* my family, Ella. Not officially yet. But that doesn't matter. You are my world. And nothing is more important than keeping you safe."

"Just promise me that you'll never cross the line. Don't lose yourself in whatever you do to fight against Sergei and Yegor."

"I promise." He says it with such raw honesty, such conviction, that I know he means it with everything that he is.

"But," he says through a heavy sigh, "this means things will need to tighten up again. Sergei won't let this stand."

"We have the Hamptons coming up this weekend," I remind him. "And there are several engagements you are required to attend with me."

"I'll find a way to make it work, but security will be severe. I'm warning you now. I won't risk you for some bullshit social outings, I don't care what the board says."

I crawl onto Asher's lap, hiking up my dress to my hips so I can straddle him. I take his face in my hands as he grips my hips.

"As long as we're in it together, I'll deal with it. Whatever security needs to do to keep us safe is fine with me. But you're going to be in it with me, Mr. Langford."

Asher brushes his nose along mine. "I wouldn't have it any other way, Ms. Hale."

MONDAY MORNING, we again pull up in a car to a veritable hoard of paparazzi, this time outside the Langford Holdings building.

"Is everything in place?" Asher asks Matthew over speakerphone as the car comes to a stop.

"Yes. All board members except Sterling are here in the conference room, as well as the PR team."

"Good. See you in five."

A crowd of paparazzi and bystanders have gathered outside because the family outing to the symphony did exactly what I wanted it to do—it garnered a shitload of attention. The photos are still amassing millions of clicks, and the paparazzi are trying to ride that out for more. And that's not even taking into account the interaction Asher had with Katrina, which is also breaking headlines.

"Ready?" Asher asks me with a smirk as security steps up to the car.

"I'm ready."

The shouts hit us the second we're out of the car, just like they did at the symphony.

"Asher, is Ella the one!"

"Will there be a wedding in the future!"

"Does Catherine approve!"

"What do you plan to do about Katrina's stalking?"

Asher and I walk hand in hand into the building, ignoring the torrent of questions and shouts hurled our way.

"Are you okay?" I whisper to Asher once we're in the elevator and have a bit of privacy. "I know we talked about it privately, but I don't want the public marriage talk to freak you out."

He taps my nose, and I realize I was scrunching it again. But he's smiling, so I take it as a good sign.

"It doesn't freak me out. I knew it would happen."

I raise my brows. "You did?"

"People have been speculating about my future bride for damn near twenty years, so of course you being photographed with my mother would spark rumors."

"And you're not upset?"

"No, I'm used to it." He leans down to speak in my ear. "And to be honest, I like it."

Butterflies flip inside me. "You like it?"

"If the rumors and stories are about *you* being my future wife, then I like it."

My eyes bulge and I want to respond, but I don't know what the hell to say. The elevator arrives on our floor before I muster a response.

Asher takes me by the hand and leads me into the smaller conference room where the board members are seated around the table and the PR team is sprinkled in chairs along the back wall. Declan and Harrington are the only ones not seated as they stand next to the door as if waiting for Asher and me to arrive.

"Hello, future sister-in-law," Declan booms as soon as he sees me. Then he practically tears me out of Asher's grip and pulls me into a big bear hug, lifting me off the floor. Asher is tall at six-foot-three, but Declan is the biggest of the Langford boys at six-foot-five, so it's quite the lift when he raises me to his level for the hug. "By the way, I'm calling dibs on best man for the wedding, and I already have ideas for the festivities leading up to it."

"Is that so?" I chuckle.

"It's definitely so."

"Put her down, dumbass," Asher growls.

"What?" Declan says once I'm back on my feet. "I've never had a sister before, I'm *excited*. Is that a crime?"

Asher rolls his eyes, and Harrington laughs under his breath.

"We could use another woman's touch in the Langford clan," Declan says. "Fuck knows mom could use an ally."

"Oh, she's already all over it," Asher sighs.

I furrow my brows at him. "What do you mean?"

He flashes me a shy smile. "She's dying to spend more time with you after the symphony. She called me this morning about scheduling a girls' day. She never got to shop for a girl or do girl things, so she's kind of chomping at the bit to do that with you."

My stomach flips in excitement. "Really?"

"Really. But she wasn't sure if you'd want to do that with her since you have your mom, so she called me to see what I thought about it."

"I would love to spend time with her. She's amazing, Asher."

All three Langford men smile widely, and Harrington practically beams at me. "She'd love that, Ella. Thank you."

"No need to thank me. I'm honored she wants to spend time with me."

Harrington pats me gently on the shoulder, blinking rapidly, and I swear I see a faint sheen of tears in his eyes. Asher told me once that Catherine had miscarried a fourth child, a girl, and she was never able to have another child after that. She loves her boys, but there was always a little bit of grief in her heart for the daughter she never got to have. And now, Declan is casually talking about me joining their family and becoming like a daughter to her. The thought is as amazing as it is overwhelming.

"If you are all about done," Janet snaps, pulling us out of our little Langford bubble. "We have a meeting to get to."

Just like that, the good vibes fizzle away and the four of us take our seats.

"We're going to make this short and to the point," Asher says before anyone else can speak. "You wanted more publicity, and you got it. We don't have official numbers yet since the story is still traveling, but there have been millions of clicks on every social media platform, hundreds of news outlets both online and traditional have reported on the story, it's been covered by entertainment news outlets, and it's traveled to almost every corner of the globe. I am no longer being written about as the womanizing playboy, and your love story has boosted both sales and the opinions of the Langford family as well as Langford Holdings. Our PR director, Emily, will have more concrete metrics for you after we return from our Memorial Day vacation to the Hamptons, as per previously agreed upon, but suffice it to say, your goal has been achieved."

"And what of the marriage rumors?" Janet asks.

"What about them?"

"Is there any truth to them? There is a possible marriage clause in the contract. Are you interested in pursuing it?"

"As of now that is a private matter. If it becomes a possibility, I'll let you all know."

"It would make for more great publicity for the company," a man whose name I don't know says. "Perhaps it's worth pursuing."

"Well, we don't want to overwhelm the public," Janet inserts quickly before Asher can respond. "As Mr. Langford said, we'll address that if it comes to it."

I furrow my brows. Overwhelm the public? Janet wanted this. She even pushed for an engagement to be part of the contract and not an additional amendment to it. Why does it feel like she's suddenly trying to pump the breaks?

"And what about the articles about Ms. Antonov?" a man asks. "Is there truth to them?"

Asher smirks. "To a degree, yes. She cornered me in Singapore to try to convince me to accept TDC's deal. She also tried to convince me to get back together with her."

"Well, that would have benefited us in both ways. Exactly what we wanted in the beginning," Janet says, scathingly.

"In your glaring short-sightedness, you forget that selling Greenspan doesn't help Langford Holdings in the long run. The sell *only* benefits TDC. Any money we lose now will be recouped by record-breaking margins in the future. And I'd rather castrate myself than get back together with Katrina Antonov."

Janet lets out a huff but has nothing to say to that.

"As we just explained, the barrage of positive news because of my relationship with Ella is more than any of you could have hoped for. So I want talks of me losing my shares to halt." Asher's tone is low and menacing. "I know this isn't finalized, but I have done all you've asked and more. Any more threats without sufficient evidence to back them will be treated as insubordination, and I will start making threats of my own."

Asher stands without another word, and Declan, Harrington, and I follow suit. The four of us leave the conference room without a backward glance.

"I think that went well," Declan muses as we all step into Asher's office. "But you still need to keep your nose clean, Asher."

"I'm aware. Trust me, I have no plans for any scandals. What happened with Katrina won't happen again."

"How do you plan to avoid it?"

"I'll glue Ella to my fucking side if I have to. I can't be accused of cheating or even having a wandering eye if she's always with me."

"Always with you?" I cough out.

"Yeah. I already told you I don't want to travel for so long without you. If you're with me, it kills two birds with one stone."

"And if I can't be with you?"

Asher's eyes narrow. "Why couldn't you be with me?"

"Work? Other obligations?"

"Everything can be adjusted or rearranged."

"As easy as that?"

Asher smirks. "As easy as that."

Declan barks out a laugh. "I knew it! I'm totally going to be your best man."

"All right, Dec," Harrington says, clapping him on the back. "Let's give these two some privacy." He tugs a grinning Declan out of the office just as Asher pulls me onto his lap as he sits behind his massive desk.

"Some people might call it codependent if I were to be by your side at all times."

"I don't give a fuck what some people might say." He pinches the inside of my thigh playfully, then frowns. "Why are you wearing pants?"

I snort. "Why shouldn't I be wearing pants?"

"Because I can't get to my pussy as easily with pants on."

I raise a brow. "Your pussy?"

He cups me through my pants, and his blue eyes light as he gives me a searing look. "*My* pussy."

"Your very greedy today, Mr. Langford."

"I'm greedy every day; especially when it comes to you."

A knock on the door is followed quickly by the door opening.

"Your morning meeting is ready and waiting," Matthew says, sauntering in. "You'll have to save this for later."

I laugh as Asher shoots Matthew a glare. I lean down. "I'll make it up to you, Mr. Langford," I whisper in his ear.

He turns his attention back to me and gives me a playful nip on my neck. "I expect nothing less than excellence, Ms. Hale," he growls in my ear.

"You'll get it."

He plants a quick but heated kiss on my lips. "I can't fucking wait."

21

ELLA

Four days later, Asher takes my hand in his as we make our way up a walkway to a massive mansion in the Hamptons for Memorial Day weekend. Cameras flash from across the street, and Asher swears under his breath. The publicity hasn't died down yet, and we have been followed more aggressively than normal since the symphony. At least four paparazzi vehicles tailed us from the airport to the Langfords' Hampton home, and now more vehicles follow us as we head to the afternoon garden party at the Vanderholts' summer residence, which like the Langfords', it's a monstrosity of a mansion on the beach. This weekend is one of the biggest draws of New York society, and the who's who of the elite will be here attending each other's parties all weekend. But apparently, paparazzi being present isn't normal, and it's making Asher tense.

"*Ella!*" I hear my name shouted repeatedly.

"*Look this way!*"

"*Give us a smile!*"

"*Asher! Turn and give us a pose with Ella!*"

"Fucking vultures," Asher growls. "Why aren't the police here yet?"

He's called them; we'll see what happens. I have no idea if the paparazzi parking on the street is illegal or not, but it's pissed off Asher enough that he wants the police involved. Other guests attending the party all shoot us loaded looks—as if we invited the paparazzi—as we all head down a path that leads to the back of the house.

I try to push the paparazzi's presence from my mind and mentally run through the list of guests, trying to match it to the people giving me dirty looks. Heather put together a binder for the weekend; a list of the suspected guests along with their photos, companies, positions, and various accomplishments. I've been studying it like crazy for the last two days. And I'm pretty sure Trenton McMillan and his wife Aster are the uptight older couple looking at me like I'm a disease. But I could be wrong. I let out a nervous breath.

"No need to be nervous," Asher says, reading me. He squeezes my hand.

"Easy for you to say, you're used to this. This is the first time I'll be spending more than an evening with the people of your social circle. I need to be on my game, and the paparazzi's attention isn't helping."

"I'll get them taken care of. And don't worry about the people at these parties. They may give you disapproving looks or make their usual thinly veiled insulting comments, but no one will dare say anything outright cruel to you."

"And why is that?"

"Because you're here with me, and I own most of their companies. They may be the CEOs of those companies, and they may run them, but Langford Holdings is the conglomerate that owns *them*. I don't interfere with how they run their companies as long as they're profitable and running well, so it's sometimes easy for them to forget that I'm there, but *I* don't forget. I own almost all of these fuckers, and if they say anything out of line to or about you, they'll be very sorry indeed."

"The Lions of New York," I say, nudging him in the side.

He nods. "The kings."

We make it to the path and follow it around to the back of the home where tents are set up and a quartet plays a lovely Chopin song that I can't remember the name of.

"Welcome, Asher," a woman in what looks to be her early sixties says, greeting us as we enter the grassy tented area. She's impeccably dressed in a linen summer suit and a large-brimmed sun hat. She gives Asher two quick pecking air-kisses along his cheeks. "It's been too long."

"It has. Elaine, let me introduce you to my girlfriend, Ella Hale. Ella, this is Elaine Vanderholt."

"How lovely to meet you," Elaine says, wrapping me in a bony half-hug. "You've been the talk of the town; we're all quite excited to meet the girl who tamed Asher Langford."

"A pleasure," I say, not responding to the taming comment. Why is it that so many of the people I meet with Asher all say something similar? I know he had a reputation for being a raging bachelor and ladies' man, but good hell, they all describe him as some feral mustang that has been broken or something. "Your home is lovely."

"You're too kind. I had hoped the renovations would be completed by now, but we had several delays on materials. So, we'll keep the party on the grounds only this year. Come."

She leads us to the backyard that overlooks the ocean.

"Wow," I breathe, taking it in.

The grounds are immaculate in a way that is gorgeous, but also at odds with the grassy beach beyond them. Brick paths wind through the perfectly cut green grass. The gardens burst with vibrant flowers, bushes, and trees that all work in together in a carefully crafted way. It's beautiful, no doubt. But somehow, at least to me, the natural state of the white sand and the craggy mounds of grass touching the edge of the ocean is much more appealing.

I tear my eyes away from the view as we enter a massive tent set up at the left-hand side of the yard. The cream fabric and honey-colored wood make for a lovely enclosure, and inside, four long tables are set with probably a hundred place settings and decorated with gorgeous summer flower arrangements.

We must be fashionably late because as soon as we're in the tent, Elaine and her husband, Ronald, I remember from my binder, take to the front of the tent and welcome everyone. A few moments later, we're all settled in our seats, and I let out a little breath of relief. We're seated with Asher's family, and even Sterling has flown in for the weekend's festivities, so at least the people directly to the sides and opposite me are people who like me.

Elaine and Ronald give little welcoming speeches, and then the luncheon is served.

"You'll be happy to note that Lennox Rose Group is thrilled with our new business relationship," Sterling says to Asher. "The transition has started smoothly. We have a ways to go of course, but so far, so good. And they're reporting record profits for many of their companies due to the influx of sales from Ella's London tour."

"Excellent," Harrington says.

"Let's not talk business here," Catherine says, rolling her eyes. "You'll all be doing enough of that this weekend."

The rest of the meal is spent in polite, pleasant chitchat, and I can't help but wonder as I carefully watch Asher's family if that wasn't a little show. At the mention of Lennox Rose Group, a gentleman to Sterling's left perked up; he tried to cover it, but I still caught it. Then, he listened intently to Sterling's short declaration, and now he looks to be mulling over something while tuning out now that the Langfords are discussing boring, banal topics.

Did Sterling and Catherine do it on purpose or was it a coincidence?

I lean in close to Asher and whisper in his ear. "Am I crazy, or did your mother and Sterling try to bait the man sitting next to Sterling?"

He turns and gives me an approving smile. "Perceptive. And yes. Well done, baby."

I'll ask him more about it later; now is obviously not the time, but it's got me curious. And it reminds me that this world really is like a jungle, and to stay at the top of the food chain, the Langfords play to win. But what I've come to respect about them is the fact that they play as a family. At least their immediate family does. One thing I learned from the binder Heather put together on the families attending this weekend is that for most of them, money is everything and family is often a distant second or third priority. Which isn't exactly a surprise, but I find it sad that many of the people here married for alliances and power and had children primarily to create heirs to their legacy. Genuine love is not their concern.

Yet with the Langfords, it is, and I can't help but admire them more for it.

I stay quiet throughout the meal, observing how the Langfords interact, and I'm grateful that no one outside of the Langfords makes any attempt to speak to me. After all the craziness of the last few weeks, and the other engagements we have planned for this weekend, it's nice to sit with my thoughts and not have to engage much.

Although Asher whispers sweet dirty nothings into my ear at regular intervals, so that keeps me on my toes.

Toward the end of the meal, I get several texts, one after another. I try to ignore them, but after a while, curiosity gets the better of me, and I pull my phone out of my clutch.

Matthew and Emily have both sent me a string of articles with my name on them. I click on a link and my stomach drops as I read the first headline.

"Ella Hale's Sordid Past as a Stripper"

WHAT?

Below the headline is a picture of me in a cropped black dance top, short dance shorts, and knee-high black boots. My hair is down, but the picture is an action shot, so my hair is frozen in a flipping motion. I skim the article, growing red and frustrated as it describes me as a poor woman struggling in the jungles of New York who turned to stripping to make ends meet. Then it goes on to describe how I've given up my stripping days now that I've landed myself the Lion of New York and will never want for anything—but only if I can keep the shame of my past a secret from Asher.

What a load of shit.

I click on the link in the middle of the article, and it takes me to a video. Ten seconds in, I groan.

Fuck.

The video is indeed of me, and it has an easy explanation that is anything but easy to explain to the public. In the video, I'm attending what's called a "heels" class. It's a style of dance that is primarily focused on a sensual type of movement, much like what is performed in music videos. It's a legitimate style of dance that is taught all over the place since dancers must be trained in all styles so that they can land jobs. One job might ask for Broadway style jazz, and the next could be a music video, so if you've never tried that style, you wouldn't make the cut and/or be hired for that job. In the dance world, there is nothing risqué or questionable about this routine—but that's the dance world—not the rest of the world. In the video, I'm wearing that tiny dance outfit and dancing in knee-high boots, and I'm performing choreography that is very sexy. But it's not a fucking strip routine, and there isn't a pole anywhere in that room. I'm in a dance studio, and there are a dozen dancers around and behind me, all doing the same routine. This was recorded probably five years ago at a dance class.

So how do we explain that to the public?

And who the hell recorded this video and sold it? I grit my teeth and shove my phone back into my purse, then lean into Asher.

"We're headed back to your parents' house after this?"

He nods.

"Good. I have a situation I'm going to need to deal with."

He raises his brows.

"Not now," I shake my head.

"THERE ARE THREE MORE ARTICLES," I seethe, pacing and reading the articles on my phone. Asher and I are in our bedroom in his parents' house between events. I've been texting Emily and my team nonstop since we left the Vander-holts' garden party. We're trying to put together a plan, but we don't know what direction to take yet because the universe is a bitch, and it's like once one article broke, the dam burst, and now there's a flood of negative articles in various tabloids, all aimed at me.

One article has comments and sound bites from all sorts of random people from my past, from college classmates to friends from high school, and anyone else they could find who wanted a minute of fame and a few bucks to talk about me to the sleazy tabloid. I swear a vein bursts in my head when I read a paragraph quoting my old high school boyfriend telling the world I dumped him because he wasn't rich. *You've got to be kidding me.* Yeah, the reason I dumped that asshole couldn't possibly have been the fact that he kept pressuring me to have sex with him when I wasn't ready to and he wouldn't take no for a fucking answer. It was definitely his lack of money. Because that was my concern at seventeen.

But worse than that is an interview with my aunt, my father's estranged sister. I haven't seen her since I was probably twelve years old. She struggled with drug and alcohol addiction for most of her life and stole money from my father and grandparents on several occasions. They tried for years to get her help, which failed over and over again. Finally, they had to keep her away from the family because she was such a mess.

She apparently got sober a few years ago, and I'm glad for that, but it looks like she either reached out to or was contacted by a tabloid for an interview. In her article, she goes on and on about how I was a spoiled brat who constantly tried to manipulate my family and friends, and how I've always said I would be rich and famous one day, no matter what. It's all complete nonsense and lies. I've probably talked to my aunt Cassie five times in my whole life, and that stopped fifteen years ago.

I toss my phone onto the bed, unable to read anymore.

Asher wraps his arms around me from behind. "We'll take care of this. But in the meantime, let's try to enjoy the weekend."

I huff out a breath and tug at the ends of my hair.

"It's hard to enjoy anything when it feels like everyone who's ever known me is lying about me to trashy tabloid magazines."

Asher lets out a long sigh and leans down to rest his chin on my shoulder.

"I know it's hard to hear, but this is a natural part of being in the public eye. The public wants to build you up and set you on a pedestal, but they also want to tear you down and watch that pedestal crumble beneath your feet. I don't know why that is, but I see it with every single person in the public eye. No one is immune. You've had lots of good press since you were photographed with my mom, so it's only natural that it shifts, and people's claws start to come out."

"Yeah, I noticed. I had to stop reading the comments. Did you know that my smile is so fucking annoying? And my hair is hideous. And lots of people are totally sure I'm just a fake-ass bitch gold digger."

He kisses my neck. "I don't know those things. What I do know is that you're beautiful, and intelligent, and too good for me." He pinches my sides, and I yelp in surprise. "And fucking hell, I want you to recreate that dance for me in our bedroom. I practically blew a load in my pants like a goddamn teenager when I watched it."

I groan. "But it apparently makes me a stripper."

"We'll do what we can to mitigate it, but things like this blow over. And I just count myself all the more lucky."

"Why is that?"

"Because I know you're *not* a stripper," he leans down, and I turn my head to see a wicked smile on his face, "but now I know you can move like one. And I am fully expecting my own private lap dances from now on."

I snort.

His hands tighten around my waist.

"And what do I get in return to be your private stripper, Mr. Langford?"

"At this point, whatever the fuck you want."

I let out a dry laugh. "I guess it's a good thing you're paying me a lot of money to live in this insane spotlight."

"It is good. Plus, as I said, it will blow over quickly. I've made sure of it."

"You've made sure of it?"

"I have my lawyers on it already. But I took it a step further and put Sterling on it as well."

I turn around to face him.

"Sterling? What can he do?"

"Don't forget that he's an incredibly talented hacker. I've given him the go ahead to fuck up the tabloids' businesses from the inside. He's hacking into their systems as we speak. They won't know it was us of course, but they will get a taste of my wrath. And my lawyers will hit whatever is left."

"If this was an option, why didn't you do this in the past?"

"I have done it here and there, with larger stories or threats, but I have never given Sterling full license. I kept his skills on a leash because I didn't want to draw attention to Langford Holdings, but after everything that happened with Kyle, RTZ, and Katrina, I've decided I'm done letting tabloids always have the upper hand. I always try to be ethical, but I'm growing more *flexible* in certain areas, and so I cut Sterling's leash."

"Will it work?"

"If Sterling and I have our way, it will."

"You're terrifying when you want to be, Mr. Langford."

He pulls me back into an embrace. "Only to those who wrong me or mine."

"Are you worried about what people will say tonight? What they'll think?"

"What I'm worried about is the men seeing that video and then looking at you and letting their imaginations run wild. That is for my eyes only."

"But it's now immortalized on the internet."

"We'll try to scrub it as best we can."

I eye him suspiciously. "You're taking this remarkably well. I fully expected a raging, jealous, possessive caveman reaction. What's going on in that head of yours, Mr. Langford?"

"Oh, I'm having that reaction, believe me. But this is the internet, and there's only so much we can do. We didn't learn about the video early enough to fully bury it, so at this point it is what it is." He gives me a cocky smile. "And while I'm a jealous bastard, I'm also a smug as fuck one, and this may or may not give me more reason to be called the luckiest man on earth. I have the money, the career, the family, the prestige, and now the fucking hottest woman on the planet. Isn't that what all men want? A lady in the kitchen and a whore in the bedroom?"

I burst out laughing. "I'm no lady in the kitchen."

"Oh, I know. I got an earful from Pierre after the cookie incident. You're not allowed back in the kitchen, per his orders."

I snort.

"But you're everything else, Ella. You have a successful career in your own right, you're now a brand ambassador, you volunteer with charitable efforts, you manage the chaos and fame of being with me with strength and grace. You're everything I've ever wanted in a woman, which includes my perfect, dirty little whore in the bedroom." He kisses at my jaw. "Maybe I'm not entirely put out that the world knows it."

"You're something else."

He skims his lips along my neck. "I'm a man with needs at the moment."

"As much as I would love to be your little whore right now, we have to get ready for the Daltons' party."

Asher groans. "Fuck my life."

"But, since you've done such a good job at cheering me up, maybe we can revisit this after the party."

"I definitely want to revisit the lap dance part."

I turn in his arms and lightly slap a hand on his chest. "Go change, you horny heathen."

"Whatever you say, vixen."

22

ELLA

"Mr. Langford, it's so nice to have you here," Mrs. Dalton greets as we make our way into the ballroom of her mansion. She gives Asher a peck on both cheeks before turning her assessing gaze to me. Her eyes roam up and down my figure dismissively, but she gives me a brief, and very fake smile before turning back to Asher. "Eugene is here somewhere. I know he's looking forward to speaking to you."

Asher barely nods and pushes past her, tugging me along behind him.

"Like that's fucking happening," Asher mutters under his breath.

"Who is Eugene?"

"Her husband, and if she thinks I'll give him one second of my time when she dismissed you like that, she's delusional."

"Asher, we've already been through this. You don't need to burn bridges because of me."

He scoffs. "Anyone who insults you is insulting me, and I won't accept that for a moment. If someone wants my time or my business, they'll learn quickly to treat you with respect."

I sigh, not really knowing where to go with this. On the one hand, I get it. Asher is protective and possessive, so I'm not at all surprised by his reaction. But on the other hand, he has a life outside of me, he has a gigantic business to run, and he can't be making enemies left and right. With the way people are staring at me, it's clear the article and the video have made their rounds, and the people here have cast their judgement. I want to scream out loud to the room that I'm not a freaking stripper, but a lot of good that will do me. Now I not only have to worry about the board and what their reaction will be to the story, but I have to try and ignore the current of disdain and disgust being directed at me from everyone in the room that's so strong it's palpable.

I lower my eyes to avoid the haughty, judgmental stares and let Asher lead me through the room. I feel like a bit of a coward, shrinking in on myself, but it's intimidating as hell to keep my chin up with an entire ballroom of people judging me. Luckily, we come to stand next to Asher's parents and brothers, and I let out a sigh of relief. At least I have a safe space in this little corner of the room.

A few minutes later, a woman who looks to be in her fifties waltzes up to Asher with three younger women in tow.

"Asher, it's been too long," she says in a saccharine voice. She nods and casts her toothy smile to the others. "Declan, Sterling. It's so nice to see you all."

"A pleasure," Sterling says in a low tone.

Asher and Declan both nod, but don't speak.

"And Catherine, it's so lovely to have you back in the Hamptons. You missed the festivities last year."

"A family engagement back in London," Catherine says.

"Yes, the aristocratic duties call from time to time. What fun." She motions to the three younger women beside her who look to be in their mid to late twenties. "You all remember my daughters, Sophie, Kate, and Rose." They're striking women, dressed to the nines, and they all smile and simper toward the Langford men. None of the men respond, and again, just nod their heads in the women's general direction, looking bored.

"I was just speaking to my husband about his excitement in your potential investment in his newest endeavor, Asher, and my girls are also over the moon about the prospect of an alliance between our families. They're such good girls," her gaze flickers over me for a second before dismissing me, "with high morals and good breeding. It would be such a great thing if our families spent more time together."

Asher's jaw clenches and his eyes narrow. He pulls me tighter into his side and presses a kiss to my temple, then he gives the woman a hard glare.

"That's the thing, our family has so many alliances it's hard to know which ones to prioritize. As of now, I'm not sure we could even manage another. Perhaps there are other families you could network with tonight who might meet your needs."

The woman flinches and pales. "M-meet our needs?"

"Yes. Whatever this investment is, I'm no longer interested. And as for the daughters you are so clearly trying to marry off, I for one am taken, and I'm certain my brothers are not interested."

"Asher," Catherine hisses in exasperation.

"No, Asher is right, Mother," Declan says through a roguish smile. "Someone has to uphold the illusive forever bachelor persona now that Asher's off the market, and I'll happily take up that mantle. Sorry ladies."

Sterling says nothing, but his standoffish demeanor turns arctic, and the three daughters now shrink in on themselves just like their mother.

"It was lovely speaking to you, Anna," Catherine says, trying to both salvage the moment and let the woman know that the conversation is over and to retreat before it gets worse.

The woman lets out a shaky and contemptuous huff before

turning and stomping away, her three daughters scurrying behind her.

"Have I taught you two no manners?" Catherine grumbles to Asher and Declan under her breath. "At least Sterling had the good sense to stay silent if he had nothing nice to say."

"The woman insulted Ella in front of me," Asher growls. "I don't care how she tries to spin or veil it, the insult was clear enough to me, and I won't put up with it."

"I wasn't about to spend the night having those three trailing me," Declan says. "Better to let them know it's not an option out of the gate."

"Subtlety, Declan," Catherine sighs.

"I've never been subtle a day in my life. You should have given up on that a long time ago."

Catherine turns to me. "Thank god for you or I'd fear that none of my boys would ever find happiness. I can only hope both my raging bull, she nods at Declan, and my ice-hearted boy, she nods at Sterling, will be so lucky. I've spent a decade trying to find them matches, and it's clearly going abysmally." She rolls her eyes and clucks her tongue. "And their manners are only getting worse with age."

"Thank you," I say it like a question, taken aback at the unexpected compliment. "I'm not sure what to say to that."

Catherine pulls me into a hug. "You don't have to say anything. I see the way my son looks at you, and I see how happy you make him. That's all I've ever wanted for my boys, and now at least one of them has found it."

"You're not upset about the article today?" I can't help but ask. "Everyone here seems to be reacting quite negatively toward me."

"Oh darling, they'd be reacting negatively toward you with or without that article. All of them want Asher for themselves. The fact that he's off the market is a huge blow to many of these families, and they're not happy about it. The article only gave them an excuse to be outwardly terrible instead of somewhat masking their contempt."

"That's both scary and comforting."

She releases me from the hug and looks me in the eye.

"Don't let these people get to you. You're well aware by now that the tide of public opinion can sway at the drop of a hat, so it's best to learn to ignore it. Your relationship with Asher is all that matters, and we Langfords do not let the opinions of others affect us."

"But I-I'm not a Langford."

"Not yet."

My brows shoot up.

"I'm aware of how this situation and relationship began, but I have eyes, Ella darling, and I know my son. I told you before, I can see where this is headed. Asher would not be putting you out into the public arena like this if this was still just a publicity stunt. He wouldn't insist on you wearing jewelry associated with me, and he wouldn't be this outwardly affectionate. You are his person, Ella. Don't doubt that."

I open my mouth to respond but nothing comes out. Catherine smirks then gives me a pat on my arm before Harrington leads her off to speak to some guests.

"My mother adores you," Asher says, sidling back up to me and placing his hand on my lower back.

My stomach flutters at both Catherine's and Asher's words. And for what feels like the hundredth time already this weekend, I realize how different the Langfords are and how lucky I am to be a part of them.

"I'm pretty fond of her too."

"Good. That makes things much easier."

I want to ask him what he means by that, but a man and his wife stop in front of Asher to make small talk. The rest of the night continues in the same fashion. People bombard Asher, Declan, and Sterling, while Harrington and Catherine work the room. I stand quietly by Asher's side, stuck in the middle of the social warfare quietly raging throughout the room. This is like the other events we've attended in the past, but on steroids. Only the very elite of the elite are here, and the preening assholes are masters of propping each other up while simultaneously tearing each other down.

I realize this is a big reason why the board wanted a high-society woman for Asher. Not just for their inherent notoriety and connections, but because a woman from this background would be much more likely to engage with the people in the room—while I don't really care to be a part of it. I'm fine to stand and stay mostly silent. Maybe that makes me a coward, but I don't care. I'll stand by Asher's side, I'll go to bat with him against the board, and I'll be his partner in crime, but in this scenario, I'm more than happy to be a semi-silent partner. At least I'm not the only one. Sterling hardly speaks as well, letting his glares and "fuck you" vibe keep people away.

Asher must read my mood because he doesn't push. He introduces me to people and then talks to them about whatever it is they want from him, all the while keeping me next to him and keeping a comforting hand on my back. I don't feel left out, but I don't feel forced to participate either. And tonight, I decide to take that as a win.

Near the end of the party, I'm about at my limit. No matter how many times Asher scowls or straight on confronts someone for their treatment toward me, I can't seem to escape the withering stares and gossip. Finally, I reach the end of my rope, and I lean in to whisper in Asher's ear.

"How much longer? I don't know how much more I can take."

Asher's head snaps toward me. His eyes take me in as he cups my cheek. He leans down and plants a kiss on my forehead.

"Then we're done. Let's go," he murmurs against my skin.

"We don't have to leave now, now. I was just wondering what the timeline is."

Asher takes my face in both of his hands. "You've already been ridiculously accommodating with this bullshit party. If you're done, then we're out of here. I won't ask you for anymore tonight. Plus, I'm pretty fucking done, myself."

Asher nods at Robert, who then speaks into his cuff, calling the car. Then the rest of our security detail make their way from their posts toward us as we exit the ballroom. Whispers and titters follow us, and I lean into Asher's side, not wanting to deal with any more of it.

"Don't give these fuckers any more of your attention," Asher says, noticing my unease.

"I'm trying not to. But it's embarrassing to be on the receiving end of their gossip and vitriol all night."

"I know, baby. But if it makes you feel any better, they whisper about me and my less than sparkling past as well."

I let out a defeated sigh. "Yeah, they do. But it's different. They may whisper about what a man whore they think you are, but none of them actually care about that as long as one of them gets to 'land' you in the future. It's such a double standard. I am looked at as a slut because of a dance video while you're looked at as a harmless playboy. They whisper about you because you are the *prize*. They whisper about me because I'm the poor girl with no social connections that you're denigrating yourself with. I can't tell you how many times tonight I heard something about how you'll tire of me soon and toss me aside."

"Well, they're dead wrong about that."

We climb into the car, and I sit in the middle seat so I can rest my head on Asher's shoulder while we drive, still needing to be near him.

"I wish I could say that things will be different in the future," Asher says through a sigh, "but I don't know that they will. This particular news cycle will pass, but people will probably always whisper about how I am with someone who isn't from a powerful family. I don't give a fuck. I don't want any of those cold, lifeless, spoiled heiresses. I've been around them my entire fucking life, and none of them hold any appeal for me. I had a list presented to me, remember, and I turned that entire list down."

"I know. But if our relationship continues, you're not going to regret me one day?"

I hate to speak the words out loud, exposing this vulnerable side to my thoughts, but it can't be helped. I dealt with these insecurities when Asher and I first started "dating," but back then, our relationship wasn't real. He wasn't actually choosing me. I wasn't meant to be a real partner with a future. But now, with the things he says, and the actions he keeps showing me, it seems like we're on that path more and more each day. And now those old insecurities are festering. I was not born into this world, and it's clear that I'm not accepted by the people who live in it. Asher says it doesn't bother him, and maybe it doesn't now, but what about in the future?

"Never. I have never subscribed to the classism ideology bullshit of this world. Which I know sounds fucking ironic since I benefit from it every second of every day. But I understand that it's a mirage and nothing more. Most of the people in that party are fucking miserable, and only their money and their status give them the illusion of joy. But that's just not enough for me. What's the point of having all this money if you're miserable? If you have no one in your life who cares about you? I want to enjoy my life, and *you* are what I enjoy.

"I know it sounds hollow to say just ignore them, but unfortunately, that's our only option. We can let their petty actions eat away at our joy or we can let it run off our backs and say fuck them and live on our own terms and be happy. Those people think they matter so goddamn much when in reality, they don't matter at all."

I lift my head and look at him. "How do you always know what to say to make me feel better?"

He smirks. "Because I'm not trying to manufacture words to make you feel better. I'm just speaking the truth. And the truth is that I'm crazy about you, and you're my priority. Everyone and everything else can take a fucking back seat."

"You're pretty perfect, Mr. Langford."

His blue eyes spark with mischief. And *lust?*

"Hmm. Would you reward that perfection with a little something we discussed earlier?" He bends down and nips at my bottom lip. "A little private showing, perhaps?"

"Are you shamelessly asking for a lap dance?"

He nips at me again. "Absolutely. Is it working?"

I let out a breathy laugh. "I could be amenable to that. But only if it's an official dare."

He chuckles as he brushes a featherlight kiss over my lips. "I love that fucking game."

23

ASHER

Back in our bedroom, now that we're finally alone, I bury my face in Ella's neck, inhaling her scent. A light vanilla and amber. It's my favorite smell. I run my hands down over her ass, squeezing. I've been ogling it in this black gown all night, tormented that I couldn't touch it. With all my self-control officially used up for the night, I unzip the back of her dress, unable to wait another second. It flutters down her body, landing in a light heap at her feet. Then I let go and walk past her, pulling my phone out of my pocket.

"What are you doing?" she asks, clearly puzzled that I unburdened her of her dress but then walked away. I ignore her question and pull the chair from the small table in the corner to the center of the room as I thumb through my playlist until I find the perfect, slow, sultry song.

I sit down on the chair and take in the gorgeous siren of a woman standing in front of me. She's perfect. And all mine.

"I officially dare you to give me a lap dance, Ms. Hale."

Her eyes light with a playful glint.

I push play on my phone.

"You think you can handle a lap dance, Mr. Langford?"

"I know I can."

"It's been two days since we had sex," she says, smirking.

I pause the music. "What does that have to do with anything?"

"Well, you must be . . . backed up."

I scoff, rolling my eyes. "That won't be a problem."

"We'll see. If you want a lap dance then you'll need to pay up, and I'm not cheap. What kind of bills are we working with?"

I pull my wallet out of my pants pocket. Then I pull a wad of bills out. "Hundreds."

"How many are in there?"

I thumb through them. "Twenty. But you'll have to work very, very hard to earn all twenty."

She smiles wickedly again. "I don't want to work too hard; it's been a long day after all. But I do have a counteroffer—a raise in the stakes, if you will. You reward me as you see fit with those bills, but if I make you come *prematurely*, I get all of them."

I scoff again. "That won't fucking happen."

"We'll see. Turn that music up."

She stalks toward me in her black lacy bra and thong and her sleek black heels. God, I'm already hard and she's just walking toward me. Walking like a sex goddess, but still just walking. I cough and adjust myself. There's no way I'll let her win. I couldn't give two shits about the money, but it's the principle of the thing. I don't lose. And I certainly don't blow my load in my pants.

She steps up to me, straddling my legs while standing above me. Then she bends and rolls her body into mine, dragging her tits, then her pussy up my chest. Mother*fucker*. I bite down to keep from groaning. Her first move, and I'm already almost panting. I shove the first hundred-dollar bill into her thong.

I may be determined to win, but I always reward exemplary work.

She threads her hands through my hair and yanks my head backward until I'm looking up at her, then she brushes her tits lightly over my face. I now realize I need to pray to God and thank him—her, them?—for blessing her with the hottest, more gorgeous set of tits ever created.

I slide the next bill into her thong.

She flips around and straddles my legs, facing away from me, and I'm frozen, staring at her bare ass cheeks and her slip of a thong directly in front of my face. I flex my jaw, and my groan is reduced to a grunt. She bends down and wraps her hands around her ankles, and it takes everything in me to hold back and not clamp my mouth down and bite her ass. She arches her back and slowly stands up, flipping her hair, and it tumbles down her back.

Then she slowly, so slowly it's almost criminal, lowers herself until she's sitting, straddling my lap, still facing away from me. She reaches behind with one arm and wraps her hand around the back of my neck and rolls her hips, grinding her ass into my cock. *Fuckity fuck.* I'm already hard, and now it's torture keeping my cock in my pants, it's straining so hard. I tuck a third bill into her thong.

Good god, this woman.

I refuse to lose.

But I may have very much underestimated my opponent.

Just as I grab her hips, wishing she was moving like this with my cock inside her, she flips around and slides off, kneeling in front of me. She places both of her hands on my knees, and rolls her body up along mine again, this time brushing her tits over my cock. Her breath grazes my neck before she arches back again, and those perfect tits are once again thrust right in my face as the rest of her arches away.

I shove two more bills into her thong.

She moves away from me, still swaying, moving sinuously to the slow erotic pulse of the music. She turns, facing away from me, and slides her hands up her ass, up her sides, then her arms reach the clasp of her bra. She undoes it then slowly peels the bands away from one another. She turns to the side just slightly. I can't see her tits, she hides them with a slightly raised shoulder, but I watch as the black strap of her bra snakes its way down her arm until it's around her wrist and falls with a soft *thud* to the floor.

When she turns around, both her hands cup her breasts, but her breasts are large enough compared to her hands that ample cleavage spills out in all directions. I adjust my cock again. *The traitor.* My pants feel like a jail, and my cock is begging for freedom.

She walks back toward me, and this time she slowly lowers herself to straddle me while facing me. Then her hands turn inward, and she leans back and with aching slowness, sliding her hands down her breasts then down her stomach. When her hands leave her breasts, I'm rewarded only a partial view of her perfect tits since her hair hangs over them, but as she leans back more, her nipples peak through, and her hair slides out of the way. All I want to do is lean forward and take one of those perfect nipples in my mouth.

Her hands finish their descent, brushing over her pussy, and I hiss as they ghost over my cock. I add three more hundred-dollar bills to her thong. She arches more, with her hands anchored on my knees, and grinds up and down the length of my cock.

Shit. Junior isn't handling this well. It's too sensitive, and the straining against my pants with the perfect, rolling motion of her pussy is sending sparks and blood pumping through it.

Her back straightens from its arch, and she leans forward, placing both hands on the back of my chair and resting her forearms on my shoulders, and then she starts to move again. Now all I can think of is how much I want to be inside her.

Focus, brain.

She rises, rolling her hips in ways that are definitely illegal in some places in the world—I'm sure of it—and again, she lightly drags her tits and then her pussy up my chest. Her tits brush my face, and this time there's no hiding my groan.

Fucking hell, I'm going to lose.

No, I'm not.

Focus, brain. Shut up, cock.

But shut up, it will not. And maybe Ella has a point. Maybe because I haven't been inside her for two days, maybe because I've been near her all day and couldn't touch her, and also maybe because I watched that leaked video of her doing that dance in those fucking heels, like, fifteen times—but my cock is near its end.

I've had an entire day of temptation without release.

An entire day of looking at Ella and imaging all the depraved things I want to do to her.

An entire day of wishing my cock was sheathed inside her because lately that's the only place I want to be and the only place I feel whole.

No matter the reasons, I'm about to lose this little contest. No matter how hard I'm concentrating. No matter how much I hate losing.

And she's not just winning, she's about to fucking destroy me.

And when she leans back and grinds her pussy again along my lap and up my chest, I can smell the dampness between her legs. My last tether slips, and I explode. Like a fourteen-year-old, I bust a nut in my pants, staining my very expensive tux with a load of hot cum.

Ella leans forward again, hearing my shout, and smiles triumphantly. She reaches down and runs her hands over my cock, chuckling darkly when she feels the damp circle on my pants.

"Pay up, Langford."

Now I chuckle and slap the wad of cash into her waiting palm.

I've never enjoyed losing so much.

She surprises me by dropping to her knees in front of me, unbuckling my belt, and unzipping my pants.

"Let's see what we have here," she says, yanking on my pants and underwear. I lift my hips to oblige.

My cock is now half-hard and covered in cum. She brushes her finger over the head, and I hiss.

"Poor thing has been neglected the last two days," she says, giving it a sweet kiss.

I groan. "We're about to rectify that. Get on the bed."

She giggles as she stands and saunters over to the nightstand, dropping her wad of cash onto it. Then she pulls the other bills out of her thong, and they join the others on the nightstand. She starts to step out of her heels, but I practically snarl at her.

"Don't you dare take those off. Between the video and that fucking lap dance, I've watched you dancing like a minx in heels all day, and now I'm going to fuck you in heels."

She laughs and climbs on the bed, and I'm tearing off my clothes and throwing them any which way as I make my way toward her. I practically leap onto the bed and hover over her, then take her thong between my hands and shred it, tearing it off her. With no other preamble, I shove my already re-hardened cock inside her, hissing and groaning at the pleasure.

"This cunt is mine," I remind her in a growl.

"Yes," she breathes.

"Only my cock gets to be inside you."

"Only you, Asher."

"That's fucking right."

And then I fuck her hard and fast, unable to see or think through the lust blinding my mind. Ella is my drug of choice. My addiction. The need to be inside her, to fill her, to come inside her, dominates so many of my thoughts lately. It's overwhelming, consuming. Because as I feel sweet relief at finally being inside her, I realize she is more than my addiction.

She's my home.

24

ELLA

"I have a surprise for you," Asher says, opening the curtains in our room. I hiss at the sudden brightness.

"What time is it?" I ask through a yawn.

"Nine, sleepyhead. So, you need to get up and get ready. Your surprise will be here in an hour."

"It's your fault I'm sleepy. You kept me up half the night."

"And I won't apologize for it." He tosses a floral summer dress at me. "Wear this, and don't cut corners on getting ready. There will be photos involved."

"What kind of surprise is this?"

"It wouldn't be a surprise if I told you. But I promise you're going to love it. At least one part of it."

One part of it? This better be worth getting out of this cozy bed for.

"I'm holding you to that, Langford."

AN HOUR LATER, Asher and I stand at the edge of the massive patio in the back of his parents' house. He reaches from behind me and his hands come up to cover my eyes.

"Just walk forward," Asher says, near my ear.

"What if I trip on something?"

"There's nothing but grass in front of you, and I'll turn you when you need to turn."

"I'm walking blind, in heels, on grass. This may end in catastrophe."

He sighs. "So dramatic. Keep your eyes closed," he orders, then I feel his hand on my ankle. "Lift your foot." He takes both of my heels off and then a moment later, one hand comes back up to cover my eyes. "I promise, I've got you. Now walk, and I'll tell you when to stop. Just trust me."

I finally relent and do what he says. He promised I'd love the surprise, so I can only hope and take his word for it. As we make our way along the ridiculous expanse that is the back lawn, butterflies leap in my stomach. The suspense of whatever this surprise is has been gnawing at me for the last hour.

"Aaaand . . . stop," Asher says after what feels like a couple of minutes. "You ready?"

"Yes."

"Surprise!" he says, but the word is also shouted by two female voices.

My eyes adjust to the warm morning sunlight, and I gasp as I see my mother and Maya in front of me, standing next to a gorgeous table in a garden.

I squeal something that is an incoherent string of words and run to them. My mother wraps me in a hug first. Tears immediately spring to my eyes. I haven't seen her in six months, and god, I've missed her so much. I didn't realize how much until now. The feeling is compounded by the fact that I've wanted nothing more than to talk to her about everything that's happened since I met Asher, but I haven't been able to. It was too risky to call or text her with details, because even with a very private phone line, I'm paranoid that those calls or texts could be accessed for the right price. And since Asher informed me that paparazzi photos of me are going for near a hundred grand a pop, I can't even begin to think what someone might do or what they might pay to access my calls and texts. If I'd said anything about Asher and my relationship being a fake arrangement, it could have potentially been leaked. So, my mother and Maya still have no idea how Asher and my relationship started. I've hated lying to them, but maybe I can come clean now that they're here in person.

"I've missed you so much!" I say, wiping at my tears.

My mom leans back and takes me in. "I've missed you too, sweetie. You look stunning. It seems dating Asher suits you."

Now Maya barrels into me for a hug, and even though we just parted ways a short time ago in London, I'm in tears all over again. I haven't seen enough of her for the past three years, so this feels like a gift. When Maya finally releases me, I turn and give Asher a hug.

"Thank you," I whisper. "This is the best surprise in the whole world."

"You're very welcome . . . but I hope you still think that in a minute. This is a family brunch, so my whole family will be out here soon."

"A family brunch?"

"It's tradition for the entire family to have brunch the morning of the Langford's annual Memorial Day party. Our family has been doing this for a century."

Good god. Just a casual century of the tradition of eating brunch in the garden of the summer mansion. Just like all the other families.

He drops down and helps me back into my heels, then leads me around a large hedge bush, and I see that what looked like a normal sized table from my previous vantage point is actually a mammoth table set with at least three dozen place settings of fancy plates and goblets and is decorated with stunning floral arrangements.

My mother and Maya follow us to the table, and they both gasp.

"This is gorgeous," my mother says.

"Wow," Maya rasps.

"Welcome to our home," Catherine says, from behind us. "I'm so glad you could both join us. I know you both traveled quite far to be here."

"Thank you for having us," my mother says, gushing. "Your home is incredible."

"It's our pleasure."

A photographer snaps a candid photo of our group and then calls for everyone to stand in for a group photo. Soon, all of Asher's extended family gathers, and they are exactly what I expected based on Asher's descriptions. There are about thirty men and women of different ages, all dressed in their couture summer linens and hats, and there's also a handful of children whose parents are trying desperately to keep them grass stain and dirt free while the photographer orders them into a formation.

Many of them glance my way with looks that follow a similar pattern to what I've already received at the other engagements this weekend: curiosity that morphs to distaste, and finally, dismissal.

I sigh and move aside with my mother and Maya as the family prepares to take the picture, but Asher grabs me by the elbow and pulls me back.

"I'm not family," I mutter noting the many eyes watching him while not even attempting to hide their disapproving sneers.

"Nice try. Now smile your pretty smile, this is for posterity."

Conrad's eyes meet mine and a clear look of disdain and anger flash in them.

My stomach sinks as his cruel words from weeks ago about Asher marrying a suitable woman from a proper family slither through my mind. Only Asher and I know how much the dynamic of our relationship has changed. His immediate family suspects, but Asher hasn't even divulged to them where his head is at. My insecurities about our relationship starting as a farce come flooding back, and I worry again about the future. What if Asher really does regret this one day?

"Why do you want me in a photo for posterity?" I whisper as he pulls me to his side. "What if things change? What if you change your mind one day?"

Asher gives me a stern look and his jaw ticks. "Enough of that. I want you by my side."

"But—"

"Relax, baby," Asher whispers in my ear as he pulls me closer. "Don't overthink this."

I shake my head and try push the insecurities away. But I can't totally relax. This arrangement was supposed to be temporary, and even though things have evolved, I can't help but be reminded that photos are forever.

I want to speak to Asher about it, but as soon as the photo is done, Asher takes my hand and turns us toward an elderly woman walking slowly, if a bit hunched, alongside Declan, who is holding onto her arm to assist her. She's wearing a large sun hat, loads of jewelry, and a dated, but very expensive-looking dress.

"Grandmother, it's so good to see you," Asher says as Declan walks her to us. Asher bends down quite far to give her a kiss on her cheek. "This is my girlfriend, Ella," he says, placing his hand on my lower back. "Ella, this is my grandmother, Jane Langford."

"It's a pleasure to meet you," I say, smiling. But her face does not match mine. Her eyes narrow, and her lips thin.

"So, this is the common girl." She eyes me up and down

then clucks her tongue. "No family of importance to speak of and no business alliances to bring to the table."

Asher closes his eyes and sighs through gritted teeth. "No one cares about those things anymore, Grandma."

Jane cackles. "Don't play stupid, boy. It doesn't suit you. And neither does fawning and simpering over a pretty girl. In our world, alliances and families are of the utmost importance. That hasn't changed. Pretty girls like this are a distraction you should keep on the side."

My eyes nearly pop out of my head.

"Grandmother," Asher snaps. "I'll not have you insulting Ella. She is an amazing woman, and I'm lucky to have her."

His grandmother eyes me with a look of contempt. "Ha! You must be good in bed; I'll give you that."

"Grandma!" Declan groans.

A furious blush warms my cheeks and neck, and I've never been more grateful to have olive skin. If I had Maya's creamy complexion, there would be no masking the embarrassment and shame I'm feeling.

Asher takes a long breath, as if searching for patience. "The world has changed, and old families are not all they once were. Ella brings many things to the table."

"No money, no connections."

"And what do I need those for?" he says in a forced calm. "I have more money than almost any person on this planet. And I have the power to connect to almost any person I want to. Any additional money or connections are superfluous."

"There is no such word as superfluous for our kind of people."

"I disagree."

Harrington seems to sense trouble, because he hurriedly ends his conversation and walks toward us with purpose.

"Find a suitable girl, Asher. And if you can't let this one go, keep her on the side. No one will care if you have a mistress."

Now my mouth pops open, and I'm grasping at words. I want to tell her to fuck off, but she's a little old lady and Asher's grandmother, so I bite my tongue.

"That's enough," Asher says firmly.

"Mother," Harrington says, grasping her shoulders and diffusing the tension. He starts to lead her toward the table. "It's getting warm; let's find you a seat before you get heated."

I think my mouth is still bobbing open and closed like fish as I watch them walk away.

What the literal fuck was that?

"I'm so sorry," Asher says, pulling me into a hug. "My grandmother is a different beast. She is old-school, full stop."

"How is your father so nice if that is his mother?"

Asher sighs. "He has a soft soul and is just innately good, but my grandfather was good too. He was nothing like his wife. He and my grandmother married because of connections, not love."

It explains a lot, but the thought makes me sad. I can't imagine spending my life with someone I didn't like, and someone I was so different from. What a waste.

I also wonder what it would be like to be raised in a home like that, and I'm again astounded that Harrington didn't turn out to be a terrible person.

"A soft soul with a shark for a mother?"

Asher gives a sad sigh. "Yes. She tormented him to make him strong, but she also built him up because he was the heir. Being first born is the only reason he survived. I know she was heard on several occasions to say things like she wished my father had been born the spare and that Conrad had been the heir because she thought him better suited. His personality is a carbon copy of his mother's. But thank god it didn't work that way. I shudder to think where the family would be if my uncle had been the heir."

"I can't even imagine."

Asher leans down and presses a kiss to my temple. "Don't listen to a thing my grandmother says. No one listens to her or cares what she thinks. I love my grandmother, don't get me wrong, but I agree on almost nothing with her. She's old and set in her ways, and she won't be changing her mind on anything before she's gone. We do our best to love her and ignore her in equal measure."

I let out a long breath. I'm a bit shaken by her words, but they also aren't unexpected. The rich do have a different set of rules and expectations they live by. Hating those rules and expectations doesn't change that.

Asher and I go to take our seats near his parents, brothers, and my mother and Maya, but we're stopped several times by more family members. They all approach me with intrigue and feigned politeness that they hadn't shown me earlier. It seems that Asher insisting on me being in the family photo has made them take a much closer interest in me.

"Is there a class you're all given to teach you how to give backhanded compliments and veiled insults?" I ask, whispering into Asher's ear when we finally break away and take our seats. "Because your entire extended family is very good at it."

Asher snorts. "No, we learn the tactics of social warfare by watching and doing from a very young age."

"Gross."

Harrington is seated at the head of the table, and rather than sitting across the massive table at the other end, Catherine sits next to him. Asher is across from Catherine, and I sit next to him, then it's my mother and Maya. Sterling and Declan close in our little group next to Catherine. Once again, I'm grateful for our little bubble on our end of the table. It feels like there is a very real line of demarcation past Sterling and Declan, and I do not want to experience the talk and questions on the other side of the line.

Harrington stands and welcomes everyone to the annual Langford family brunch and graciously welcomes me, my mother, and Maya as guests. From the pursed lips and narrowed eyes of the others at the long table, I gather that it's not custom to have guests, and I suddenly feel like an interloper. Maya looks even more uncomfortable and has a fake smile plastered on her face.

"I'm assuming there are never guests at this brunch," I whisper to Asher once his dad is seated and the servers begin setting silver trays of food on the table.

"No, we don't. Typically, someone outside the family isn't invited unless they are engaged to a Langford, at minimum."

"Then why am I here? And my mom and Maya? Everyone is looking at us like we've barged in on their private Christmas mornings demanding they share their presents."

"You're here because I want you to be here."

"But we're not engaged."

He narrows his eyes at me, and I swear he leaves the word *"yet"* unsaid. I know we've talked about our future, but that was always when it was just the two of us alone together. When we're in our own little bubble it's easy to imagine that future, but when we're surrounded by Asher's world, his extended family, and all the other complications of his life, it's hard to feel as secure about that future.

"I don't give a fuck what my family thinks. The elders of our family don't like girlfriends and boyfriends to come to family functions because then there would be different 'hussies of the moment' here each year. My grandmother's words," he says, rolling his eyes. "All of us grandkids and cousins have a long history of dating many hussies of the moment, and our parents and grandparents are well aware of it, but that doesn't mean they want to see it. Out of sight, out of mind, sort of idea. They don't want someone at family functions unless they're someone we're in a very serious relationship with and someone worth marrying."

I'm quiet for a moment, trying to tamp down my insecurities. Being told you're good enough to be a mistress but not good enough to be a wife is not an easy thing to hear. No matter how confident I am. No matter how much I know what Asher and I feel for one another. Asher may consider me someone worth marrying, but it's clear that most of the people here do not.

"I wanted your mother and Maya to come to our family party tonight. Your mother's flight got in late last night, and Maya flew in with Sterling, so it felt only polite to ask them to brunch after they both traveled so far to be here."

"I don't think your family agrees."

"Again, I don't give a fuck what they think. The only family I care about is my parents and brothers. I tolerate the rest of them."

I cling to the surety in his words and do my best to suppress the hurt and insecurities festering inside me. I dish my plate up with fluffy eggs, bacon, diced potatoes, and a lemon pastry. Mimosas are flowing, and I gratefully sip mine, knowing I'll need some liquid courage to get through this meal.

"I hear you're studying at Oxford," Catherine says to Maya. "That's very impressive."

"I am. And thank you."

"What made you choose Oxford?"

"I didn't actually choose, really. Ella and our mother sort of did that for me."

"Really? How so?"

"I never thought graduate school was an option for me, so when I refused to apply because I didn't have the money, Ella and my mom did it for me, behind my back. I'll never tell my chancellor this, but Ella wrote my application essay. I had no idea she had done it until I was accepted."

"That's wonderful. What a gift to give your sister," Catherine says to me.

"Well, she's the brilliant one who had a perfect GPA throughout high school and college. I just did her applications because I wasn't going to let her forget her dreams because of money. In the end, it was her brilliance that earned her acceptance and a big scholarship."

She turns back to Maya. "What is your field of study?"

"History and political science, with an emphasis on preservation. I hope to work in a major museum as a curator."

"She just secured an internship with the British Museum," Sterling says.

"It's just admin work, but it's a start," Maya says, blushing slightly.

"And how do you like living in England?" Harrington asks.

"I love it," Maya gushes. "And I'm not even too bothered by the weather. I don't know why, but I just connect to it. It will be hard to come home next year when I finish school. Although, lately, England has been a little less fun."

"And why is that?"

"The paps are relentless," Sterling answers when Maya looks sheepish. "They've been hounding Maya since she was photographed with Ella at the polo and cricket matches when we did our Lennox Rose campaign through London. They now know she's her sister, so they're trying to get to her."

"What?" I say to Maya. "Why didn't you tell me?"

"I didn't want to worry you because you have enough going on yourself. And there's nothing you can do about it, anyway."

I bite the inside of my cheek, conceding her point. "I still want to know."

"She can't walk to the tube or go to school without being followed and harassed," Sterling says. "At least she quit her job."

"I didn't quit. I was let go because my boss was over-whelmed with the bombardment of paparazzi."

"Why haven't you hired a driver for her?" Asher snaps.

"I've tried. She keeps refusing my offers."

I raise my brow at Maya.

"I can't afford to pay for a driver. I'm on a student's budget."

"You wouldn't be paying," Sterling says, rolling his eyes. "I already explained this."

"Well, it's too much."

"Nonsense," Harrington says. "If you have paparazzi hounding you, you need a safe way to travel."

Sterling turns to Maya and gives her an "I told you so" smile. "See? Here's your proof. My family will not be bothered if I provide a driver for you. And at this point, we may need to discuss security as well."

He leans in and whispers something else in her ear, and Maya turns and glares at him. My eyes bounce back and forth between them. Clearly, they've been in contact quite a bit since I left London.

"Maya, what else is going on? Why would security be need-ed?" I ask.

"Because her neighbors are cunts," Sterling says.

"Sterling!" Catherine hisses.

"Sorry, Mom." He gives her a side-eyed glance. "But it's not like you shouldn't be used to it. That word is thrown around a lot more in the UK than it is here, as you're well aware."

She shoots him an admonishing look. "We're not in the UK at the moment, are we, darling?"

He lifts his hands in surrender and turns back to me. "You got Maya out of the dorms and into a nice flat, but I told her it probably wasn't secure enough and tried to convince her to move somewhere else, but she refused. Within a week of moving, the paparazzi found her flat and contacted her neigh-bors with bribes. Two of her neighbors took those bribes. She's had a hidden camera set up outside her door and microphones recording near it."

"What?" I shout, then I shrink in my seat when family members from the other side of our bubble shoot glares my way.

"Yes. So, I'm trying again to convince her to move to a much more secure location. With no close neighbors."

"You mean your house," Asher says.

Sterling shrugs. "I have plenty of guest rooms to choose from. And security is always on site. As well as a driver. But Maya is being difficult."

"Maya," my mother says. "You didn't tell me your neighbors had agreed to spy on you. That is extremely disturbing. Not to mention unsafe. You're already alone in a foreign country, and now this makes it a hundred times worse. The paparazzi in London are known to be some of the most aggressive in the world."

"They are, believe me," Catherine says in a hard tone. A ghost of vulnerability flashes across her face, and Harrington reaches out and rubs a comforting hand down her back. She leans into the touch for a second before clearing her throat and straightening her shoulders.

"Thank you for backing my case, Mrs. Hale," Sterling says. Then he takes out his phone and begins texting someone while ignoring Maya's weak arguments that she's fine.

"Done," he says after a moment.

"What's done?" Maya asks, giving him a hard look.

"You know."

"Sterling, don't you dare—"

"What's done?" I ask.

"My staff is on their way as we speak to Maya's apartment. She'll be all moved out by nightfall."

"You can't just have your staff go into my apartment and move my things out!"

"I can, and I did."

"How are they going to get in?"

Sterling snorts then chuckles darkly. "If you think I don't have a key to your apartment—"

"What? How long have you had a key? And how did you get it?"

"I've had a key for as long as you've had a key. I was with you and Ella when you signed the lease."

"And you just took one of the keys? How? I have both."

"I paid for a third."

"And you didn't tell me?"

"No."

"That's illegal. And it's also illegal for your staff to enter my apartment without my permission."

"Sue me."

Maya huffs and shoves a bite of eggs into her mouth, chewing angrily.

What the fuck was that? That conversation seemed a lot more charged than it should be for two near strangers. Not to mention that it was eerily similar to several conversations Asher and I had back at the beginning of our arrangement. I peek at Asher, and he looks back at me, surprise and intrigue written on his face just as I'm sure it's written on mine. I'm going to have to get Maya alone and ask what the hell is going on there.

"Maybe it's for the best, love," my mother says to Maya. "The paparazzi are terrifying. I for one would feel better knowing you're living somewhere safe."

Maya glares at our mother while Sterling gives her another glowing smile. "I couldn't agree more."

I take a drink of my mimosa, not sure if I want to laugh or jump to Maya's defense. Because hell, I know exactly how she feels right now. It's completely overwhelming when a Langford man steamrolls over your life and just changes it at the snap of his fingers. It's also absurd, and it should be wrong—but then the logic behind the steamrolling is sound. I thought Asher was being dramatic when he insisted that I move in with him, but now, after seeing the lengths the paparazzi go to access me, I know he was right. I'm fully out of their reach in Asher's penthouse.

But they can get to Maya, and it seems like they have been. I want to stand up for her and tell Sterling to back the fuck off, but I selfishly agree with him. Maya's safety matters to me more than her autonomy. I don't know what that says about me, but the thought of her being in danger because of her association with me wracks me with guilt. If anything happened to her, I wouldn't be able to live with myself.

"I know it's hard, Maya," I say, choosing my words carefully. "It was very overwhelming when I moved into Asher's apartment so quickly into our relationship. It felt far too soon." I clear my throat. "And as much as I fought it and was uncomfortable with it, it was necessary. With how aggressive the paparazzi can be, I know it was the right decision. Now I can't imagine living anywhere else. It would be terrifying."

"You could handle the situation with more delicacy, dear," Catherine says to Sterling.

Now I snort. Everyone's eyes flash to me. "Sorry," I say. "But if there's one thing I've learned about Asher, and Sterling and Declan as well, it's that they do what they want, and they ask questions later."

Harrington gives a dry laugh. "They got that from my father, I'm afraid. And their mother." He turns and gives Catherine a wink.

"Yes, but I don't bulldoze through these matters like a raging bull. You'd think I taught them no subtlety."

"You tried, Mom," Asher says. "We simply don't possess your patience. When we want something, we go after it, and we don't let anything get in our way."

Asher's hand snakes up my thigh as he speaks, dipping beneath my dress. He gives my inner thigh a squeeze, then his fingers trace their way higher. I clamp my legs together, trapping his hand there, and shoot him a *"what are you doing?"* look. He smirks.

He squeezes my thigh again, and I let go of my grip on his hand. It resumes its upward exploration. His finger brushes over my panties. I wriggle in my chair slightly and give the elbow of his roaming arm a pinch.

"You're receiving this attention because you're Ella's sister," Sterling says to Maya. "And Ella receives *her* attention because she's Asher's girlfriend. None of this would have fallen on your head if not for our family's name and wealth, therefore it's our responsibility to keep you safe from it. End of story."

Asher's finger slips under my panties and gives my slit a brush. I squirm again and kick his leg under the table. He finally removes his hand, giving me a sly smile that's definitely a promise.

A thought occurs to me when I can think without Asher distracting me. I turn to my mom.

"Have you had any paparazzi or press hounding you?"

She sighs and nods her head. "They've been parked in front of my house for weeks."

"Why didn't you call me or tell me what was going on?"

"I didn't want to worry you. Like Maya said, what can you do from New York? You're dealing with enough of it on your own. I didn't want to burden you with more."

"We'll look into it and see what we can do," Catherine says. "If there's nothing to be done, you're more than welcome to stay in one of our homes as long as you need. They are all gated and very safe. Sterling is right, all this fire comes from Ella's connection with Asher. Our family will take care of this."

"That won't be—"

"I insist," Catherine says, cutting Mom off.

I hold in a laugh, seeing for myself what Harrington was referring to. Asher and his brothers definitely get their assertiveness from their mother. But I also see a pattern with my mother. She was just scolding Maya for not accepting the Langfords' offer of help, and one minute later she's doing the same thing. And in the beginning, I tried pushing away Asher's help. It seems our family quirks are at odds with one another.

"Now, as for the ball tonight," Catherine continues before my mother can argue more. "We have something very special planned, an old family tradition, which is why we wanted to make sure the two of you could join us here in the Hamptons. There will be press tonight, though. I apologize. I didn't know that you have both been having a hard time with them, so if you'd prefer, you can stay back in the shadows a bit and forgo the pictures. Or, if you don't mind, we'd love for you to be pictured as well. But know that these pictures are likely to gain much attention, on an international scale, so think it over and let me know by the beginning of the ball what you decide."

"What is going on tonight?" I ask Asher.

"It's a surprise."

"Another one?"

"Yes."

"And it's going to get international attention?"

"Yes."

"Your cryptic answers are incredibly annoying right now. What am I walking into tonight?"

"Nothing crazy. Just wear the gown your team picked for you and let me handle the rest."

"Does my team know what's going down tonight?"

He nods.

"And why haven't they told me?"

"Because they're not allowed to, so don't try to worm it out of them," he warns. "Unless you want to be the reason they're fired."

Dammit. He knows me too well.

"I don't want any of them fired." Well, maybe except for Daphne, but I'm not going to play with that fire today.

He leans in and whispers in a voice dripping with promise, in a tone that makes my panties wet. "Then you'll just have to be my good girl and wait until I give you your surprise."

Fuck me. This is going to be a long day.

25

ELLA

"Wow," my mother says, gushing. "You look . . . stunning. More than stunning." Her eyes grow misty, and she dabs them with a tissue.

"You look beautiful, yourself." I give her a careful hug since we're both in gowns. My glam team just finished with me, but they worked on Maya and my mom as well. I haven't seen Maya yet, but they did an amazing job on my mom. She's in a vibrant turquoise gown that makes her blue eyes pop, and her blonde hair hangs to her shoulders in loose curls. "Just like always, you look so hot that no one will believe you're my mother."

It's not a lie. My mom had me young, at twenty-four, and she's aged like a fine wine. So at the age of fifty-one, she looks more like she's forty-one, and too young to have a daughter in her late twenties. We get asked all the time if we're sisters. I hated it when I was a teen, but now I love it. My mom is beyond beautiful and deserves all the attention she gets for it.

Maya walks back into the loft space the glam team has commandeered for the night after changing into her gown, and again we're all bouncing and laughing in excitement.

"Oh my god! Maya, you look insane!" She's a vision. Her red

hair is down in long romantic waves, and she's in a lavender gown that makes her pale skin look like creamy porcelain and her hair stand out but not clash. She looks like a siren or a nymph from a Greek tale.

"Look at both of my girls done up for a fancy party, looking like modern-day princesses," my mom says, dabbing her eyes with the tissue again.

"Don't cry, Mom, you'll ruin your makeup."

"I can't help it. All I can see is the two of you in dress-ups, sneaking into my makeup and perfume, and doing fashion shows in our living room. If your younger selves could see how beautiful you look now . . ."

"I haven't seen my final look yet, hang on." I move to the full-length mirror in the corner where Katya is ready with a steamer to get out a few stubborn wrinkles at the bottom of my dress. As soon as she's satisfied, I look in the mirror.

I'm wearing a creamy pink strapless gown that hugs my curves but flows in layers of chiffon from the knees to the short train. The cut, color, and layers give it a sweet, romantic feel. My hair is pulled up in a gorgeous up-do, and my makeup is a combination of pinks and bronze, almost giving a blushing bride vibe. Overall, it's a soft, romantic look, and if the gown was white instead of pink, I'd think it was perfect for a wedding.

"You almost look like a bride," Maya says from behind me, mirroring my thoughts.

Katya fits us all with jewelry and reminds my mother and Maya that the pieces are in the Langford's collection and must be returned directly to her at the end of the night. Both of their eyes are wide when they realize the diamonds they're wearing are not just large but are real and are decades or centuries old. I blush, noting that I've seen and worn a couple of the pieces. I turn away to hide my smile at the memory.

Katya fits me with a delicate diamond bracelet and earrings, and I'm of course wearing Asher's gold ring on my right hand. She has me wear a large diamond ring on the middle finger of my left hand, but nothing else.

"No necklace?" I ask, touching the empty space beneath my throat. It looks a little bare.

"Mr. Langford gave me very clear instructions. No necklace tonight."

Hmm. "Did he say why?"

She shakes her head. "Your team and Mr. Langford approved this look and every detail of it. This is what they want; I'm sure they have their reasons."

Emily walks in dressed in a peach-colored gown, surprising me. "Hey! I didn't know you were coming to the party tonight," I say, giving her a quick hug. "You look amazing. I love that color on you!" I introduce her to my mom and Maya, telling them what an amazing boss she is.

"The Langford annual ball is a big deal," Emily says when the introductions are over, "so the whole team is here. They'll stay out of the way so as not to be a distraction, but they're here just to make sure things go off without a hitch."

"Isn't that what the event planners are for?"

"The event planners are running the event. We are running the extra things that pertain to you and Asher."

She looks me over with a critical eye. Not in a rude way, but in the, it's her job to make sure I look a specific way for specific events, way. She gives a relieved sigh, clearly happy with what she sees.

"And what things pertain to Asher and me?" I can't help but ask, starting to feel nervous.

"Asher wants it to be a surprise." She rolls her eyes, and it looks like she's genuinely worried and frustrated. "I can't tell you what's in store, but I need to give you some heads up. Tonight is big. Like *big*, big. So you need to be perfect. Remember any reaction of yours will be seen by a room full of people, and all those people have cell phones with cameras. Anything you do or say can be leaked to the press in a matter of seconds."

"You're making me nervous. Is this big thing a bad thing?"

She sighs. "No, it's a good thing. A very good thing from our PR perspective. I just worry about you."

"Oh my god, what is it?" I can't help asking again. My nerves are getting out of hand.

"Just know that tonight's event will be making the news, so be prepared for a barrage of it tomorrow. And you should know that there will also be a professional photographer taking photos that will be given to the press, not leaked. These will be officially released Langford photos." She turns to Trenton. "Her lipstick is kiss-proof?"

"It is, just as ordered."

Emily nods. "You all did your jobs well, she looks perfect." Now she turns back to me. "Good luck tonight, Ella. I'll talk to you tomorrow."

"That wasn't foreboding at all," Maya says, taking my hand. "What the hell is happening tonight?"

I shrug. "With Asher? It could literally be anything."

"I'll try to get something out of Sterling. Maybe he'll tell me, and then I'll let you know."

"I don't know if that will work. If Asher's ordered it to be a secret, it's going to be a fucking secret."

"Don't worry about it. It's going to be spectacular!" Andre says, packing up his station of hair tools.

"You know what it is?"

He gives me a knowing smile. "Of course I do. Everyone on your team but you knows. We've all been prepped, and I can't wait to see it. Trenton and I were invited personally by Mr. Langford! We've never been to a party like this, even with all our rich bitch clients. We can't wait!"

"See you there!" Trenton says, waving for me to get a move on. We're running a few minutes behind.

With that, we make our way down the second story hallway to the grand staircase, and now I really do feel like a princess of old as my mother, Maya, and I start down the stairs.

Asher and his family are all gathered in the grand foyer below, and I try not to blush as they all look up and watch our decent. Asher's eyes meet mine. He looks a little surprised for a moment, and then his surprise morphs into the dazzling smile I rarely see except behind closed doors. His eyes never leave mine until I'm standing before him.

"You are a vision," he whispers.

"Thank you. You look amazing yourself." And he does. All the men are in smart tuxes, and Asher fills his out like some Adonis in the flesh.

"I can't wait to peel that dress off you later," Asher murmurs in my ear.

I laugh, low and quiet. "Same. You better watch yourself tonight, Mr. Langford, or you might find yourself fucked in a broom closet during the party."

He raises his brow. "Is that a threat or a promise?"

"Both."

He kisses my temple. "I knew I liked you."

Asher glances down at his watch, then lets out a relieved sigh when Harold opens the front door. Shock filters through me when Zahra and Lucy walk through, dressed in gowns.

"What are you two doing here?" I gasp, running to them.

"Your boyfriend flew us in for the party," Lucy says.

The three of us hug, and my mom and Maya join us. My mom hasn't seen Zahra or Lucy for a while, so she hugs them furiously and makes them promise to chat with her and update her on their lives before the night is over.

I notice Asher out of the corner of my eye, standing back from our little reunion.

"You did this?"

He shrugs. "Tonight is a special night. I wanted all your most important people to be here."

I hurry over to him and press a kiss to his lips. "Thank you."

"Anything for you, baby."

"It's time," Catherine calls.

Asher takes my hand, and we follow his parents and the rest of our little group as they head toward the ballroom—yes, the summer mansion has a fucking ballroom in the east wing of the house—but before we enter, Asher pulls me to the side and asks his family to give us a moment.

"Tonight is . . . a big deal for my family," Asher says, suddenly uneasy. "And a big deal for me." My stomach drops. *What the hell is happening tonight?* "And I realized after your reaction this morning to our family photo that it's probably going to be a shock for you."

"What is going on, Asher?"

"It's a big step. And now I'm realizing like an idiot that I probably should have talked to you about it, but it's too late now. And it's fast. I know it's fast. But I didn't expect us to be in the place that we are now. I thought everything would be more business, more cut-and-dried."

He's tripping over his words and rambling, and I've never seen him do either of those things. "Asher, please tell me what's happening. You're starting to scare me."

"It's sudden, I know that. Like I said, I didn't think we'd cross the boundaries we crossed, and so now this feels much different than how I thought it would when the idea was first presented to me. But—"

Cheers erupt from the ballroom.

"It's time to go in, darling," Catherine says. "We've been announced."

"Give us a minute."

"Your minute has passed."

Asher groans and takes my hand, and we follow his parents into the ballroom. The guests' cheers grow louder, welcoming the Langfords to their own party. As soon as the applause dies down, the small orchestra in the corner strikes up a new song, and the mingling begins.

My stomach is in knots, and I want more than anything to ask Asher what the fuck is going on, but I can't. We can't catch a breath with all the people who want to speak to Asher. My worries are somewhat assuaged as Asher holds tight to me as we make our rounds—at least I have him to ground me—but the back of my mind cannot stop worrying as I'm introduced to dozens of people, one after another.

They all simper and fawn over Asher, and most are nice to me, if not curious, while a few seem to be genuinely friendly. The vibe is very different from the other events we've attended this weekend, and I'm grateful. Blessedly, there are so many people to get through that the conversations are short and mostly directed toward Asher, so I only fill in answers and questions sparingly.

My curiosity still burns throughout dinner, but I can't get in any words with Asher since his grandmother is at the table. I don't dare speak about what he was so nervous about earlier with her in hearing distance. As it is, she shoots me piercing looks and cuts at her food more viciously than necessary. I can hardly get a few bites of food down I'm so tied in knots.

After dinner, Harrington and Catherine make their way onto a small stage at the front of the ballroom, and a stage tech hands Harrington a microphone.

"Thank you all for joining us tonight at our annual Memorial Day weekend party," he says. "This is a long-standing tradition for our family, and we're honored by your presence."

He passes the microphone to Catherine.

"As a special surprise, I'd like to introduce our entertainment for the evening. Ladies and gentlemen, please join me in welcoming multi-platinum and Grammy award winning artist, Alena!"

My jaw drops, and I gasp. I turn to look at Asher. He smiles and laughs at my reaction. All my worries of the night disappear, and Maya, Zahra, Lucy, and I can barely stay in our seats as Alena takes the stage. She's my favorite artist of all time, and I've always wanted to see her in concert.

"Oh my god!" Lucy yells.

"I can't believe it's Alena!" Maya squeals.

"And she's right in front of us!" Zahra cries.

We are sitting at the host table at the very front of the room and right up close to the stage, so yes, Alena is, like, twenty feet away from us. I want to die.

The band starts her song, and then Alena's opening notes give me chills. I almost start crying. Asher wraps his arms around me and pulls me in toward him.

"Surprise, baby," he says, giving me a kiss on my neck.

"You booked Alena? For me?"

"She's your favorite."

This is the surprise everyone is so worried about?

Why? This is a dream come true!

I turn and face Asher, placing my hands along his jaw. "You are . . . I don't even know! How is this real? How are you real?"

"I'm real."

"I don't even know what to say."

"You don't have to say anything."

I press my lips to his. "Thank you. Thank you for being the worst liar in history."

"What?" he asks with a laugh, confused.

"You told me when this all started that you weren't relationship material and that you'd probably be terrible at this. That was either a gross underestimation or an outright lie. Either way, you were wrong. You're incredible at this, Mr. Langford, and I feel like the luckiest girl in the world."

He leans down and kisses me, slow and sweet, and I don't care that we're in a room full of people. I don't care how this all started. All I can focus on is him and how amazing he is. When we pull away from our kiss, he turns me around and wraps his arms around me. We sway in our seats and sing along to this semi-private concert.

I've never felt so alive in my life.

"THANK YOU! THANK YOU!" Alena says, bowing and smiling to the crowd. Her set was amazing, and the room is buzzing on the high of her concert. She made eye contact with me and smiled at me several times while singing, and I think that if I died tonight, I'd die a happy woman.

Alena brings her microphone back up to her lips, and the crowd quiets as she starts to speak. "It has been an honor to be here tonight, but I have one more order of business, one more song to sing before I go."

"We can talk about everything after the ball," Asher whispers in my ear. "Just trust me."

I look back at him, confused, but turn back when Alena starts speaking again. "For my last song, I'm going to dedicate it to a very special couple. I need Asher Langford and Ella Hale to come up here!"

"What?" I gasp as shock travels through me.

"Let's go, baby," Asher says, grabbing my hand and pulling me after him.

The crowd cheers and looks on as we walk to the stage. Cameras flash from all directions, and just like Emily said, a professional photographer snaps several photos of us climbing the stairs.

As soon as we're on stage, Alena hugs me, and my soul leaves my body. I still can't believe this is real. And I have no idea what Asher and I are doing up here.

"I hear it's a long-standing tradition in the Langford family for the men to present their women with a meaningful gift," Alena says. The crowd quiets to almost a hush for several seconds, then roars, and as I look out over them, I see a room full of shocked and wide-eyed faces.

Butterflies leap inside me as Harrington, carrying a deep blue velvet jewelry box, and Catherine walk onto the stage. Alena hands Harrington the microphone, and cameras continue to flash over and over again.

"Thank you. We're so happy to have you all here for this extraordinary evening," Harrington says to the crowd. "The Langfords have many long and meaningful traditions, but tonight we are excited to celebrate one that has arguably the strongest significance to our family because of what it represents."

The crowd now fully loses it, cheering and clapping, and it seems as though every phone is out and pointed in our direction, recording. So, Alena wasn't the surprise. This is. Whatever this *is*.

Harrington waits for the crowd to settle before speaking again. "I don't want to bore you with a history lesson, but I will give you a little background to this long-standing Langford tradition. This tradition dates all the way back to the late 1700s, to our great ancestor Henry Langford.

"Henry was a man born of moderate means, but he was a man who dreamed of more. He was determined to make something of himself. During his business travels, he met a maiden named Elizabeth, and they fell in love almost immediately. They wanted to marry, but Elizabeth was considered the town jewel, and there were several men after her hand in marriage. There was one suiter in particular that Elizabeth's father favored because of his high standing and wealth, and so when Henry asked her father for her hand in marriage, he was denied. Elizabeth pleaded with her father, and he eventually conceded—to a degree. He told Henry that he couldn't have Elizabeth unless he could provide her with the same life the other suitor could, and Henry vowed to do so. But Henry knew building his fortune would take time, and he feared he might lose Elizabeth in the interim.

"So what did Henry do? He found a way to create an early promise of proposal. He spent what little money he had on a lovely gold pendant he saw in London and presented it to his sweetheart as a promise of a proposal and begged her to wait for him. She accepted the pendant and agreed.

"Elizabeth's father was furious and tried many times to change her mind, but Elizabeth stood firm. Over the following four years, Henry built enough of a fortune to be an acceptable match for Elizabeth and returned to her with a lavish ring and a true proposal. And since that time, all Langford men have presented their future wives with a gold pendant as a promise of their intentions and to ask a promise of them in return. To wear a Langford pendant is to be promised to the Langford man that gives it to her.

"Now, the world has changed quite a bit in the last two and half centuries, but we have kept this tradition alive because of what it means to our family. We consider Henry and Elizabeth to be the founders of our family as it stands today. Their love, their marriage and children, and Henry's business pursuits are what laid the foundation for all the Langfords that have come after him. And so, to honor our ancestors, we continue to this day to present a pendant to the women we love to give them a promise, to give them our protection, and to welcome them into our family."

My heart drops and my ears ring as I watch Harrington open the blue velvet box. A gold, teardrop-shaped pendant hanging from a delicate gold chain sits on a pillow inside.

"This is the original Langford pendant, the very one Henry

gave to Elizabeth. This pendant is only given to the first-born sons of the family." Harrington turns toward us. "Asher, I gave this to your mother thirty-eight years ago, and now we both give it to you to present to your future wife."

My stomach all but bottoms out. *Future wife?*

Holy shit, is this really happening?

Thinking of Emily's warning, I school my features. I know I must look completely in shock. Asher takes the microphone from his father and reaches out for me with his other hand. I place my hand in his, and he gives it a squeeze.

"Ella, from the moment I met you, I was drawn to you. You came into my world and eclipsed everything else, and I've never been so happy. I know that being with me comes with a lot of good and a lot of difficulties, but I would be honored if you would be willing to take on those difficulties and be with me. To be mine."

My heart races as Asher carefully lifts the pendant from the box and holds it up for me. The crowd roars. Asher steps to me, and tears spring to my eyes. This is all so much. It feels so real, and my heart crumbles and soars all at once because I can't deny it—*I want it to be real.* I want it to be real so much it hurts.

And the last pretense in my mind falls.

All I want to do is shred that contract.

I want all of Asher, and I want him to want me, free of obligation, free of the board.

Just him. Just me.

I turn, and he places the pendant on my chest, clasping it around my neck. As soon as the pendant is in place, Asher turns me back around, takes me in his arms, and kisses me. The crowd roars again, but the sound quickly dies in my ears, and all I can hear is my beating heart.

I'm so shocked and overwhelmed that I don't think. I just fall into the kiss, and kiss Asher without walls, without pretense, letting my hope and wishes bleed into it. And for a moment, it's just the two of us. For a moment, there is no contract. There is only the promise of *more*.

I've never wanted *more* like this.

When we separate, Asher leans his forehead onto mine, and we breathe each other in for one more minute before the bubble surrounding us bursts.

Alena is back on the microphone. "How lovely! What a lucky lady! Congratulations to you both!"

My mind somehow reorients itself as Asher and I hug Alena again. The band starts back up and begins to play Alena's most popular love ballad, and I'm a mess as I wipe tears with shaking hands.

"Why don't you two take to the floor. This one is dedicated to you both," Alena says, just before her cue to start singing.

Asher leads me to the dance floor in the middle of the room. The tables have been pulled aside sometime in the last few minutes, and now we are at the center of the room, all eyes on us, dancing as Alena sings to us. Asher rests his cheek to my temple and holds my hand in his, while his other hand rests on my lower back.

My heart is still racing a mile a minute, and I cling to Asher like a lifeline. Although no one would be able to tell that from the outside. Outside, I look like a girl in love. Inside ...

I'm a girl in love.

26

ELLA

Once the song ends, and the endless flashes of photos stop, Catherine announces that there will be fireworks outside to conclude the evening. I want to speak to Asher about what this means, but I can't because we're bombarded with guests congratulating us. I smile and thank everyone, but it's all a bit of a blur.

"I need a second," I whisper to Asher once people start to make their way outside.

"You okay?" he asks, skimming his thumb along my shoulder.

"I'm a bit overwhelmed."

"Did you like your surprise?"

I laugh. "Which one?"

"All of them."

"I loved all of them." Not a lie. "I just need to run to the restroom before the fireworks. I'll be right back."

"I'll wait by the door."

I hurry off toward a bathroom I know won't be in use because it's back in the main portion of the house. As soon as

I'm in, I lock the door and take a deep breath. I need to get myself under control because I'm freaking the fuck out inside. What I really need is to talk to Asher about what all this means, but that's going to have to wait.

I do my business and give myself one more moment alone before I leave the bathroom to rejoin Asher. As I round the corner to head back into the ballroom, I see Conrad, Asher's uncle.

"Ah, the woman of the moment," he says, grabbing onto my elbow as I pass by. "What a night for you."

I yank my arm out of his grasp.

He leans toward me, lowering his voice. "But do remember, Ms. Hale, that this isn't real. That pendant around your neck will need to be returned. One day, it will adorn the neck of Asher's *actual* wife. Someone suitable to his station. I would hate for you to forget that you are merely a PR stunt to keep the press focused on something new and shiny."

My throat feels clogged as every insecurity I've felt today slams into me again at his words. But I refuse to back down to this jerk. He knows nothing of our situation, and neither Asher nor Harrington can stand him. I don't know why he hates me so much, but he seems to have it out for me. And I'm over it. I square my shoulders and lift my chin, meeting his icy gaze head on.

"And yet the Langford name needed someone new and shiny like me to get that good press. So, doesn't that prove that your power has limits? And whose face is the one selling products for Langford Holding's newest acquisition? Whose name is stirring the buzz for this family? Is it yours? Is it Gregory's or Celeste's? No, it's Asher's and mine. Like it or not, I've built my own power. And now my name will be forever attached to this family, even if Asher does end up marrying someone else."

I don't know where my brash, confident words come from,

A.V. ARCHER

but I don't back down after they're said. I still feel like I'm faking it half the time, but I refuse to cower to Conrad. Whatever is real or not real with Asher and me is our business, not his uncle's.

Before he can respond, I storm off, batting away tears that slip free. So much for getting a moment to compose myself.

Asher sees me a second later and straightens when I wipe away a tear. He hurries toward me.

"What's wrong? What happened?"

I want to stand on my own and tell him that nothing happened. I don't care what his stupid uncle thinks or says, but I just don't have much fight left in me. Tonight has been so amazing, but it's also been an emotional roller coaster. This pendant has forced so many worries and questions to the surface, and it's taken a toll.

"Your uncle, Conrad. He stopped me on the way here and was kind enough to remind me that this is all fake and that I'll need to return this pendant when it's over so that you can give it to your actual wife—who will be someone much more suitable to your station."

Asher freezes and blinks at me. His jaw is locked. "He did not fucking say that to you."

"He did."

Asher moves to go after Conrad, but I stop him. "Don't. He's not worth it. But . . ." And I hate myself as my chin starts to wobble. "What I don't know—is if he's wrong or if he's right."

"Ella—"

"There you two are!" Catherine says. "Everyone is outside waiting for the fireworks to start."

"Give us a minute, Mom."

"Asher, everyone is wondering where you are and what is causing the delay."

"I said a minute."

Catherine gives him a hard look. "Whatever this is, handle it quickly. The press is waiting."

"It's okay," I say, my voice quivering. "We can talk about it later."

"We're going to fucking talk about it now. What do you mean you don't know if he's wrong or right?"

"I don't know what to think or feel about our future. This weekend has shown me that the people in your world may never fully accept me, and that scares me. I don't want you to regret me one day. Not to mention the fact that we still have a contract between us so the line of what we are is still confusing. And then you and your parents put on this big display to give me this family heirloom that is this symbol to put on your future wife. It's hard to know exactly what is real and what is fake, and I *need* to know what we are, Asher. I need to know because . . . I'm in love with you."

I gasp, wishing I could snatch the words from the air between us and shove them back down my throat. But I can't. They're out. And now all I can do is wait and see what Asher says.

Asher stares down at me and doesn't say anything for too long.

"You don't have to answer me now," I finally say to break the silence. "Let's just get the night over with."

Asher leans in toward me, and I step backward until I bump into the wall. Both of his arms come up on either side of my head, trapping me there.

"Does this feel fake to you?" he says, wrapping his hand around my throat, dragging his thumb along the length of it. "When I'm inside of you, does it feel like what we have is fake?" He leans down and nips my earlobe. "Does waking up in my bed with my head between your legs feel like something that's forced?

"Let me be very fucking clear, Ella. You're right. Somewhere along the way, things changed. When I called you my family, and I meant it. The connection we share is rare. So fucking rare that it's powerful, and there's no way we can ignore it.

"Tonight has been a lot with the family history and the symbol of the pendant. But I want you to know, I didn't just do this as a PR stunt; I did it to give you protection. This," he brushes his fingers over the pendant, "shows the world that you're mine. And that tells people that if they hurt you or fuck with you, then they fuck with me. And most people won't dare to do that.

"I know it's a lot to hear about futures and husbands and wives, and I should have talked to you about it beforehand, but I selfishly wanted to surprise you. I meant every word I said on that stage. I never expected to have a serious relationship, not for years and years, so this whole situation has caught me off guard. But if I'm going to have a serious relationship with anyone, it's you. I don't want anyone else. I want marriage and kids, all of it, and I want them with you."

His words settle the fear inside me, and I press my lips to his and pull him so close it's like our bodies are fusing.

"I need you," I say, panting between kisses. "Please. I need you inside me. Right now."

Asher chuckles against my lips. "You did promise me a fuck in a broom closet tonight."

He pulls me behind him and into a small sitting room with a couch and bookshelves, then locks the door. "This should do the trick." He practically tosses me onto the couch and rips open his belt and pants, then he shoves my dress up to my hips. He tears my underwear off and slams himself inside me.

We both gasp out in relief as soon as he's inside me. And for the first time since the pendant ceremony, I feel like I can breathe.

"I mean it every time I fucking say it," Asher growls as he

hammers into me. "You're mine. They're not just empty words, Ella. They're a promise."

"Oh my god, Asher. Yes. Please."

"Tell me you're mine."

"I'm yours. And you're mine."

"Yes, baby. I'm yours. I have been for a long time now."

My worries and insecurities melt away with every kiss, every touch, and the raw need that bleeds between us.

"I will never regret you, Ella. Every day with you is a gift, and I'll spend every one of them on my knees, and between your legs, thanking you."

"Fuck," I rasp.

And I don't know if it's the urgency of time, or the sheer relief at Asher's words, but the feel of him inside me is heightened so much that I'm already close.

"Oh god, Asher!" I cry out as my orgasm tears through me. The relief, the joy, the beauty of this night all meld together, and it's the sweetest euphoria.

"Ella!" Asher yells a second later, following me.

He spills into me, and for a minute, neither of us moves. I want to stay like this, with him inside me, forever. Our foreheads meet and we breathe one another in, savoring the stolen moment.

When he finally pulls out of me, I almost cry with joy at the feel of his cum running down my thighs. I want all of him all over me, inside me, and I never want to let him go.

Asher pulls the pocket square from his jacket pocket and wipes my pussy clean, then he stuffs it in his pants pocket along with my discarded panties. He stands and holds out his hand for me and pulls me to my feet. I shimmy my dress back down below my hips and follow him out the door.

The crowd cheers when we make it outside, and then the fireworks begin. Asher holds me from behind, and I lean into him, my head pressed against his shoulder, happier than I've ever been in my entire life.

Again, tears escape my eyes, but this time they're tears of joy. Tears of relief.

Neither of us have definitive answers of when we'll get to our happily ever after, but now I know the pendant around my neck isn't just a piece of jewelry. And it's not just a PR stunt.

It's a promise.

27

ASHER

I'm a selfish man. I know that. But knowing that doesn't stop me. I should let Ella sleep. She's exhausted from the long weekend, and yet I can't help myself. I roll my beautiful sleeping beauty onto her back and gently tug the covers down, exposing her tanned legs in her silky purple sleeping shorts.

Those will have to go. Same with her panties.

Ella murmurs in her sleep as I slip her shorts and panties off, then brush my nose up the inside of her thigh and across her center. The scent of her pussy drives me mad, and any pretense I had of drawing this out evaporates as the need to feast on her barrels through me. She's my favorite morning meal.

I slip my tongue up her center, groaning at the taste of her. Then like an animal, I wrap my arms around her thighs and spread her wide for me, feeling the need to be between her thighs like I need my next breath. I suck her clit into my mouth and then work my way down until my tongue is inside her, exactly where it wants to be.

"Asher?" Ella mumbles, her voice husky with sleep.

I don't answer her. I keep to my task of making sure she wakes up to a blissful orgasm. Even if she doesn't need to wake for another hour.

Ella's hips move lightly, but with every second she wakes further, and every second she feels me eating her like she's my last meal, her movements grow until she's grinding against my face with her fingers laced in my hair.

"Asher," she moans, her voice clearer now.

That's right, baby. Wake with my name on your lips and my head between your legs.

I'm ready the second her orgasm hits her. As soon as she rides it out, my cock is freed, and I plunge it into her like a dying man.

"Good morning to you, too," Ella says breathlessly, rocking her hips to meet my thrusts.

"I couldn't help myself," I say, reaching down to tear her silky pajama top off her head. "It seems I can never help myself when it comes to you."

I lean down to kiss my way up her sternum, pausing at the pendant resting between her breasts. I haven't let her take it off except to shower since I put it on her Saturday night. And I can't help but want to fuck her constantly while she wears nothing but my pendant and my ring. It's my new favorite obsession, and one I'm not ready to give up any time soon.

But it's Tuesday, we'll be back in the office today, and we'll be forced to leave our bubble we lived in for the holiday weekend. I couldn't drag myself out of bed for my early morning meeting and face the reality of the weekend being over—not without one more taste, one more hit from my favorite addiction.

"You can wake me up like this anytime, Mr. Langford," Ella says, breathlessly.

"I'll hold you to that, Ms. Hale."

That promise is solidified in my mind as another orgasm

hits her and I feel the euphoria of her pulsing around my cock. It spurs on my orgasm, and I come, pumping inside her. There is no better way to start my day, and I plan to wake her up just like this every day that I can, for forever.

I STEP into my office an hour later, already missing Ella. I'm both excited for and simultaneously dreading this stupid meeting I had to leave her side early for. I already presented most of this information to the board, but now Emily has our official numbers, so it's time to force the board back in line, once and for all.

Just as I'm about to leave my office and head to the meeting, Sterling calls.

"What's the word?" I ask, in answer. He's back in London, but he's still working on his pet projects for me.

"It's begun. Just little dips here and there. But it should be promising with time."

He's speaking of his sabotage of TDC Oil's finances. To be safe, he's speaking in vague, loose terms, but he's letting me know he's successfully hacked into TDC's systems and has begun sifting, stealing, and rearranging their money to cause chaos. The money he steals is stored in black offshore accounts that are almost impossible to trace. When we're done, we'll donate that money to charities, but in the meantime, I'll enjoy watching TDC start to crumble.

"But that's not the only reason I'm calling. I've found them, finally."

Greenspan. He's found a mole on the inside.

"You should take care of it today."

"We have a board meeting in five minutes."

"I'm aware, and I'll be attending through video. I just texted Matthew to see if he can clear your afternoon because after the meeting . . . you may have something more important to do."

"Done. Text Margret to clear Declan's afternoon as well. I think I'd like to spend some quality time with my little brother today."

"You got it."

"WHERE IS ELLA?" Emily asks as I take a seat next to her in the smaller board room.

"I made sure Matthew didn't inform her of this meeting."

"Why?"

"Because I'm tired of seeing her belittled by the board and sitting in their crosshairs. She is the one who has saved my ass, and I can't stand watching anymore vitriol hurled her way. I'm fucking over it."

"You really do care for her, don't you?"

I nod. "I do."

I probably shouldn't admit that to one of my employees, but I don't know how to stop myself anymore. It's all hit me this weekend; I'm over the charade. I'm over the PR stunts. I'm over the back and forth. I just want Ella. I want to start a life with her, and the first step toward that is to get the board out of my way. Then I can fully focus on TDC, Yegor, and Sergei and remove the threat they pose. But most of all, I'm done denying my feelings.

As soon as everyone is seated, Emily stands and begins her presentation.

"It's been two months since Mr. Langford and Ms. Hale began their relationship, and I now have some clear numbers to present.

"Press attention associated with Mr. Langford or Langford Holdings has been predominantly positive at a seventy-two percent positivity rate, as opposed to forty percent, which was Mr. Langford's pre-relationship average. Both Mr. Asher and Mr. Sterling Langford report the acquisition of Lennox Rose Group as being greatly helped by Ms. Hale's agreement to become a brand ambassador for their luxury companies, and overall public support of the union between Mr. Langford and Ms. Hale has a sixty-four percent approval rating.

"The influx of press since the beginning of the relationship has driven up engagement on all social media platforms, as well as traditional news outlets, podcasts, and various other entertainment vehicles. All these avenues have practically exploded, with a four hundred percent increase from that of this same time last year. This has resulted in a significant increase in revenue for Langford Holdings as well as for its subsidiaries, particularly those directly marketed by Ms. Hale in her London tour, as well as Vericom in their smartwatch launch. Many of these subsidiaries' revenue is up anywhere from twenty-five to sixty percent, depending on the company and their products.

"All in all, the union of Mr. Langford and Ms. Hale has had an incredibly strong impact on Langford Holdings and Mr. Langford himself, and all objectives of the union have been achieved in only two months' time, even allowing for a few instances of bad press. We project this positive impact to continue to improve in the future. We do expect a plateau at some point, but we also predict that increasing the levels of the relationship to an engagement would continue to create strong and positive press, generate revenue, and all in all greatly benefit Langford Holdings."

Fucking hell. I've never thought of my relationship status in such clinical terms. Who knew it had a sixty-four percent approval rating? How did Emily's team even quantify that? I don't even know what the fuck to do with that information. Not that I care; it's not what matters anymore.

"Thank you, Emily," I say, excusing her. The faces of some board members are far from happy, and I can't fathom why since Emily's report was nothing but fantastic news. Whatever beef they have with this report, I want to listen to it head on and I'll circle back to Emily later.

"Why all the glum faces?" Declan asks the members of the board as soon as Emily leaves. It's like he's reading my mind. "You all threatened and forced Asher into this, and he's exceeded every expectation—no, not just exceeded them—he's obliterated them, just like he always does. With all the money this little arrangement has made you, you should all be crying tears of joy, and yet all I see are unhappy faces. I am at a loss to understand why."

"While we can all appreciate the increase in revenue," Janet says, picking her words carefully—something I've never seen her do, "I do wonder if it's too much. If Asher and Ella are now overshadowing everything else."

"Overshadowing what?" I snap.

"Langford Holdings for one, along with our subsidiaries and the other board members and their endeavors."

"What are you talking about?"

She clears her throat. "Well, there's only so much press coverage to go around. I couldn't get any press for my daughter's engagement this weekend because all any outlet was talking about was you and Ms. Hale."

"You've got to be kidding me. You were one of the staunchest supporters of this, Janet, and now you're mad because your daughter didn't get her fifteen minutes of fame?"

Alan, who sits next to Janet, gives her a pat on the back and nods for her to continue. One of her faithful lap dogs offering support. These fucking clowns.

She sits up straighter and squares her shoulders. "It's not about fifteen minutes of fame. It's about getting the type of press someone of my daughter's station is due. She's a New York heiress for god's sake, and almost no one reported on her engagement. Two months ago, she would have been front-page news, now she was relegated to page six."

I laugh out loud now. "This isn't a fucking popularity contest. I can't help that your and your daughter's feelings are hurt because she's not getting enough attention."

"It's not about feelings! It's about the way of things. Before 'dating' you, no one would have cared who *Ella Hale* was," she says Ella's name with dripping disdain. "And now, she's all anyone can talk about."

"Oh, I see. *'The way of things,'*" I hiss. "Ella isn't an heiress, and therefore she doesn't *deserve* attention above that of your precious little heiress."

"Jesus Christ," Declan says with a sigh. "Do you even hear yourself, Janet?"

"All I'm saying is that families like ours are used to a certain way of things. We're used to our way of life, and our way of life includes attention in the press. That attention helps keep families like ours moving forward."

"And you threatened me and my shares to get that press aimed at me and my love life. You got what you wanted."

"It's not just Janet's daughter," Henry butts in. "I just announced that I'm running for lieutenant governor with Senator Sanders, who's now running for governor, and we didn't get the coverage we needed, either. Our announcement fell flat, and all mentions of me as one of the board members of Langford Holdings fell by the wayside in favor of speaking about Asher Langford and his pendant ceremony."

"Again, that's not my fucking problem."

"It's a problem that you're the only one attracting press," Henry seethes.

I can't help it, and I laugh again. "You're a bunch of four-teen-year-old girls who are pissed that the popular girl is getting all the attention. You want press? Be more interesting.

Be more attractive. Be richer—I don't fucking know. I don't ask for the press; it follows me. Literally. Ella didn't ask for the press; you forced her to go after it. We aren't doing anything to purposefully *outshine* all of you. We're making our pre-determined public appearances that you all decided upon, and the press follows. I can't help that. If that hurts your delicate feelings, get the fuck over yourselves. The millions of extra dollars in revenue that Ella and I have generated for you should be enough to soothe your fragile fucking egos."

"Well, I for one am wondering if this arrangement has served its purpose and run its course," Janet says. "We clearly don't need to drag this on for months. I think we should end it now."

"Yes, the longer we drag it out, the bigger the fallout will be over your breakup," Henry says in agreement. "It's probably better to do it early, before people continue to get attached. We can make this easy or we can make this hurt." His words strike me, and I inhale sharply. Something about them makes me uneasy.

"What did you say?"

"I said, we can make this easy or we can make this hurt. The longer you drag it out, the more it will hurt, and the more upset people will be. It's better to end it now."

His words still bother me, and not because of the situation at hand. Yet I can't put my finger on why. I shake away the thought as murmurs break out among the other board members. It's clear most of them don't agree with Janet and Henry. Money talks, and Ella and I are creating a lot more of it lately.

"That's not happening," I say with forced calm.

"Why not?" Henry demands. "You didn't want to enter into this arrangement; you made that clear from the beginning. We're letting you off the hook. Why don't you take the win?"

Now the murmurs break into full dissent. Voices rise as

everyone starts to argue about whether Ella and I should continue dating.

"Enough!" my father shouts, surprising me. He rarely yells. But everyone quiets, still used to acquiescing to my father since he was CEO for twenty-five years. "You have all said enough on the matter. Janet and Henry, your arguments are absurd. You all wanted a flurry of positive press surrounding Asher and Langford Holdings, and you got it. And you've all made substantially more money this quarter because of it. So take that *win*," he glares at Henry, "and get over yourselves. Ella may have been contracted into this, but she has come to mean much to our family, and I won't see her treated like a bartering chip you all can use or toss aside on a whim."

"Surely the fondness you all show toward her is for the cameras," Janet hisses in disbelief. "You can't mean that you actually like the little social climber."

The last of my patience snaps. I shove up from my seat and slam my hands on the table. All eyes dart to me as I lean over the table and slowly take in every board member one at a time, biting my tongue and searching for patience. After a moment of loaded silence, I stand to my full height and let out a long breath. "I will take you up on the offer to shred the contract between Ella and me."

Declan's head whips in my direction, and Sterling's eyes narrow on the TV monitor feed of him on the other side of the room.

I motion to Matthew, and he hurries out of the room.

Everyone is silent again, waiting for what I have to say next. But I won't speak until Matthew is back with the contract. I've had enough of the board's bullshit. They don't deserve my explanations, and they'll take what I give them. Henry is right about one thing—the opportunity to get out of the contract has been dropped in my lap, and I'd be a fool not to take the offer.

I've been meaning to discuss it with Ella, anyway. I want to move forward with her, and I don't know if we fully can with a contract standing between us. What we feel for one another has nothing to do with the contract anymore, and I think it will be in our best interest to have it gone.

My future with her is everything to me.

Matthew returns, plopping the contract down on the desk in front of me. Everyone's eyes fall to it and watch in disbelief as I sign the conclusion article of the contract, effectively ending the arrangement. When I'm done, I set my pen down with a little too much force, and hand the contract back to Matthew.

"Once Ella signs this, she will be free of its obligation," I say to everyone seated around the table. Henry and Janet perk up, and it's clear they're both wondering how they managed to weasel what they wanted out of me so easily. I smirk at them. "But if you think this will make Ella disappear, you're wrong. Our relationship will very much continue, regardless of the contract. And not only that, but it's bound to garner even *more* attention. Because no, my affection for her is not for the cameras. And if you think the pendant ceremony got a lot of attention, just wait until the proposal and the wedding and the children that follow it."

Janet rears back like she's been slapped. Henry scowls. Everyone else stares at me in shock.

"And, Janet, if you ever insult my future wife again, I'll ruin you."

28

ELLA

"Oh my god, let's see it!" Heather says as I walk into the conference room office space.

I wore a fitted cream dress with a high neckline so the pendant could hang on full display today. I didn't want to wear it to work, but Asher and Matthew told me I needed to, at least for today. After today, the pendant will be cleaned and placed back in secure storage, since it's so old it must be treated with a lot of care. Apparently, there were additional pendants made for each male in the Langford line, and those have been passed down over the last two centuries as well, but since mine is the original, I'll only wear it on special occasions from now on. It's all a bit mind-boggling that something like this is a normal part of a family's traditions, but this is the Langfords. Nothing about them is normal.

"The internet has gone wild," Emily says as the whole team gathers around me to get a look at the pendant. "You and Asher really hit it out of the park with this one."

"It's gone viral on a global scale," Josh says. Josh and Heather now manage my social media, and I mostly stay off it. It's hard to deal with the pressure of it, so I don't often see what's going on, but they fill me in. "The story has millions of likes and shares. And congratulations are pouring in from all over. This is wild."

He's not wrong. The press has been having a field day with the news since America doesn't have any royalty and the Langfords are a sort of stand-in. Harrington and Catherine sold the official photos of Asher and me from the pendant ceremony and donated all the money to charities Asher and I favor. Matthew told me this morning that he's been fielding requests from talk-shows and podcasts all over the world with requests to speak to Asher and me. It's insane.

"You did well," Emily says. "Who would have thought when I picked you for this team that this is where you would end up."

"It's . . . crazy. I could have never predicted this."

"What are you going to do when it's all over?" Michael asks.

"Michael," Emily snaps. "That's hardly the question we need to be asking right now. There are still several months planned. We'll cross that bridge when we get there."

I give the team a smile and head to my desk. Part of me wants to tell them that the arrangement has morphed and that Asher and I want more than a contract, but I bite my tongue. What we have and what we discuss behind closed doors is precious to me, and I want to keep it between the two of us. So much of our lives has already been handed to this team to discuss, dissect, plan, and present like a purposefully wrapped bow. I refuse to do that any further. What Asher and I have is powerful, but it's new, and therefore delicate.

"I know one thing," Josh says. "Whenever this is all over, it will be a shame to work back down on the marketing and PR floor. The executive floor is where it's at."

Emily rolls her eyes. "Let's get to work on our June engagements." She turns and looks at me with her back to the rest of the team. *"Are you okay?"* she mouths to me. I nod.

An hour into finalizing the details for each June engagement, we all receive an email notification from Matthew that states "URGENT" in the title. We all drop what we're doing and click into the email.

"Changes in the NDA?" Emily muses, reading through the email.

"Contract has been terminated?" Michael says.

My stomach drops.

What?

Daphne looks smug as she finishes reading the sentence for him. "It says that the contract with Ella is over, effective immediately."

"Do you know what's going on?" Emily asks me.

Blood rushes to my head, and for a moment all I can hear is the *whoosh* of my pulse in my ears. I swallow hard, trying to form words. "I have no idea."

Daphne tosses her hair over her shoulder and straightens. "It looks like Mr. Langford is done with this little charade."

"Wait," Emily says, reading aloud further down the email. "There will still be a need for the PR team for Mr. Langford and Ms. Hale's relationship, but the numbers will be reduced by half." She looks at me, furrowing her brows. "I don't understand. Why have a PR team if the contract has been terminated? I mean, we'll need one to transition you both out of the relationship, but it says nothing about that."

"Sorry!" Matthew says, bursting into the room. "I was a little trigger happy. I wasn't supposed to send that email yet!"

"Wh . . . what's going on, Matthew?" I stammer. I bury my shaking hands in my lap and blink to clear the black spots peppering my vision.

Asher follows him in, and I stand and make my way over to him.

"What is going on?" I ask in a whisper. I still can't use my full voice; it's so clogged with raw fear. "Are . . . are you done with me?"

Asher's head rears back. "No! Of course not."

"Sorry, Ella, this is all my fault!" Matthew says, and one part of my brain wonders if hell is freezing over. Matthew never admits to doing something wrong—probably because he almost never does anything wrong.

"Let me clarify," Asher says, reaching for me. I slink into him, and he wraps his hand around my waist. I let out a shaky breath, finding relief in being near him, but I still burn with fear. He wouldn't break up with me in front of the team, would he? No. He wouldn't. Just last night he was buried inside me and told me he loved me, saying the words almost like a prayer. Then this morning I woke with him between my legs again. He wouldn't hurt me publicly. *But then what the hell is going on?*

Asher turns us to address the team. "We meant to come speak to you first and send the email afterward, but obviously Matthew got a little excited and sent it too soon. There has been a change in the status quo. The board offered me the option to terminate the contract between Ella and me, and I decided to take them up on the offer."

My pulse pounds in my ears again.

Daphne does nothing to hide a self-satisfied smirk.

"However, this does not mean the end of our relationship."

I take a hopeful, tentative breath.

"I agreed to terminate the contract because the nature of my relationship with Ella has changed. As all of you know, our relationship was a farce in the beginning, an arrangement forced upon me by the board. But over these last two months, Ella and I have come to care for one another beyond a professional setting and beyond our contract. Our relationship is no longer something we're being forced into and is something very real."

I exhale in relief, sagging into Asher's side as gasps break out among the team. Emily looks at me, smiling in shock, with her hands pressed to her chest. Daphne's face is stuck some-where between rage and disbelief.

Asher continues. "Since the board offered a termination, I agreed because I want to move forward with Ella without the contract hanging over our heads. So, from here on out, things will be different. We no longer need a team of this size because there is no more agenda in the press. This will now be a tradi-tional PR endeavor. Living in the public eye means both Ella and I require a PR team, so this team will serve both of us. But it will change in the sense that I'm no longer interested in drumming up attention, and if anything, I'd like the attention to die down. I want to live my life with the woman I love in rela-tive privacy."

"Love?" Emily gasps before clapping her hand over her mouth. Everyone else stays still, silent and stunned.

"Yes, love," Asher says, with a hint of a smile. He clears his throat, and his face morphs back into his stern CEO mask.

I lift my head to look at him. "You scared the shit out of me," I whisper-hiss.

A smirk tugs at the corner of his mouth. "You can't think I'd break up with you by team email," he murmurs back.

"I didn't know what to think. Look," I hold up my hand for him to see, "my hands are still shaking."

"Baby, you're mine now. You can't get rid of me so easily." He leans down and kisses my temple.

We turn back to the team, and they're still standing in shocked silence.

"I'll leave it to Ella, Emily, and Matthew to decide who remains on the team and who returns to their former posi-tions," Asher says. "If you have a preference one way or the other, let them know, but as I said, they will be the ones who make the final decisions."

He takes my hand and leads me out of the conference room, and Matthew follows behind. We head into his office where the contract is sitting on Asher's desk, and the same woman who notarized it the first time sits in a chair, waiting.

"We move forward, but on our own terms," Asher says, nodding his head toward the contract.

I lean down and sign my name on the conclusion article, almost dizzy in disbelief. This wasn't supposed to happen for months. And now I know, without a doubt, that everything between us is real. The contract may have been the thing that brought us together, but it isn't what created the feelings between us.

The notary signs and stamps the document, and Asher flashes me his devious grin that I love so much.

It's over.

No more contract. No more board pushing an agenda.

Just him and me. For real this time.

I reach up, wrapping my arms around his neck and his lips meet mine. The weight of expectations and falsehood falls away. Relief and joy burn through the kiss, and it's like we can both truly just be ourselves for the first time in two months.

When we pull away, Asher smacks my ass, and I look around and realize Matthew and the notary woman are both gone.

"As much as I'd love to continue this, I have something urgent to get to," Asher says, checking his watch.

"I have one more quick stipulation."

He quirks a brow. "Yes?"

"I don't want to work on my own PR team anymore."

"I figured as much. Do you have an idea of what you'd like to do?"

I shrug. "Not sure yet. This happened much sooner than expected."

"Whatever you want, it's yours."

He gives me one last kiss before striding out of his office.

I head back to the conference room, practically floating, but the vibe of the room, with everyone clustered into groups and speaking in low tones, instantly brings me back down to earth.

"So, what do we do now?" Heather asks Emily.

Emily sighs. "I'm not entirely sure. I assume Ella and I need to discuss moving forward with the smaller PR team. So, as Mr. Langford instructed, let me know your preference regarding staying on the team or returning to your previous positions. At this point, I don't know what the numbers look like and how many of you would stay on; I'll have to speak to Mr. Langford about that."

"I don't want to go back down to the marketing and PR floor," Daphne complains. "Would the team still work up here on the executive level?"

"I don't know that, either."

"Uh," I inject, hesitantly. "Probably not. I just informed Asher that I won't be part of the new team. I don't want to do my own PR since it's now my real life, and that feels even more weird than this situation already has been. Anyway, the reason we're all up here is because of the . . . unwanted attention I got downstairs. Without me on the team, that's no longer an issue."

Daphne huffs. "So, what are you going to do then?"

"I'm not sure. Asher and I are going to discuss it."

"Must be nice. You just snap your fingers, and your *CEO boyfriend* gives you whatever job you want."

"Daphne," Emily warns.

"I'm not demanding Asher give me a job, I just don't want to work on my own PR team. I'm qualified to work in other positions, plus I'm not even from PR, I'm from marketing."

Daphne's face contorts into anger. "It's just really convenient how well everything worked out for you." She shoves up from her seat, still glaring at me "You weren't even supposed to be on this team, and then Emily *insisted* on adding you. Then you somehow magically become the candidate chosen, and now you're Asher Langford's girlfriend with all the perks. It's not fair!"

Everyone is quiet, looking back and forth between Daphne and me.

"Daphne, I would stop if I were you," Emily warns again.

"I'm getting really tired of the narrative that I somehow wormed my way into this," I say, snapping back at Daphne. "Emily added me onto the team because she respects my work. Matthew suggested me as a candidate to Asher. And the rest just happened because of all that."

"Oh yeah, Matthew just happened to suggest you after you leeched yourself onto him!"

Anger races through me, but I also want to laugh. "Matthew and I became friends organically. That's how friendship works. It sounds to me, Daphne, like you're sore you weren't the one chosen. But if you remember correctly, *none of us* were supposed to be chosen."

"And yet, you were!"

After weeks of putting up with Daphne's snide remarks, I finally let go and tell her everything I've wanted to from the beginning.

"What do you want me to say? Sorry? Sorry that Asher didn't want to choose any of the women the board suggested? Sorry Matthew noticed that Asher and I have a natural chemistry? It's not like Asher's options were limited to the women on his PR team and you were slighted by not being chosen. His options were so vast he could have practically picked any woman in the world. But he chose me. And not that you deserve an explanation, but what Asher and I have, what we are to one another, is not something you can manufacture. It might have started that way, but it didn't stay that way for long."

Someone coughs pointedly from behind me, and I turn around.

"This is an exciting turn of events," Matthew says, wearing a smug grin. Three executives from the board stand behind him: Janet, Henry, and Alan. "As much as I live for drama and want to wholeheartedly grab some popcorn and watch this play out, I can't."

Daphne scowls at him then glares at me again.

"Don't get me wrong, sweetie," Matthew says to Daphne in a condescending tone, "it's not Ella I'm protecting—it's you. I was just in the board meeting where Asher referred to Ella as his future wife and threatened everyone on the board within an inch of their lives if they disrespect her again. If he's willing to toss threats like that at his board members," he tosses a casual thumb in Janet's direction, "what do you think he'll do to some PR girl who disrespects his *future wife*?"

Daphne's nostrils flair, then she swallows hard.

I flinch. *Future wife? Did he really say that in front of the board?*

Everyone looks at me, but I don't know what to say. No matter that I've been with Asher for two months, I'm still not used to constantly being the center of attention. I knew I would get attention from agreeing to date Asher, but I didn't think I would practically have a spotlight shined on me in my everyday life. In my work life. I grew up performing under spotlights on a stage, but this isn't a stage with practiced choreography or a public appearance with pre-determined expectations—this is an awkward spotlight, and I don't really know how to react. You'd think I'd be better at it by now, but I'm not.

Everyone continues to stare at me as if they're expecting an explanation, but I don't know what to tell them. Asher is a bulldozer who gets what he wants and asks questions later. The fact that he referred to me as his future wife at work is not something I could have anticipated.

"I know this turn of events is abrupt," Matthew says, drawing their attention away from me. "It might seem like it's coming out of nowhere, but it was obvious to anyone close to

Asher and Ella that this was an inevitability. So, abrupt or not, you all need to get on board with this. As of today, Ella is no longer your coworker. She is no longer your team member. She is now Mr. Langford's official girlfriend, and *per his words*, his future wife. You'd do well to treat her as such if you value your jobs.

"We have amended your NDAs, which need to be re-signed. If any of you break any part of that NDA, Mr. Langford will send the wrath of his legal team down on you with such force you'll never recover. You'll be so buried in legal fees and woes that your grandchildren will be in debt. So, I suggest you get over any petty jealousy you're harboring and learn to keep your mouths closed—for your own sakes."

"Thank you," I mouth to Matthew. He winks at me. Matthew may not have the overbearing, intimidating presence Asher does, but he can be just as effective at getting people to fall in line. General Matthew, kicking ass and taking names, per usual.

"We expect you all to be cleared out by this afternoon," Janet pipes in. "We need our conference room back."

Matthew rolls his eyes but otherwise ignores Janet. "Ella, Emily, let's meet in Asher's office in fifteen minutes to discuss moving forward." He turns and exits, shooing Janet and the other board members away in the process.

Emily clears her throat. "Everyone, take thirty minutes to collect yourselves and think about your preference. At the end of that thirty minutes, I want you to email me what you decide." She looks at Daphne. "No need on the preference from you. I think we can all agree it's not a good fit. At this point, you'll be lucky to return to your previous position, but only if you can pull yourself together and be professional from this point forward. You might as well pack up your desk and move back downstairs after you've signed the new NDA."

Daphne bursts into tears, and everyone unconsciously moves away from her as if she has a disease. Part of me feels bad for her, blame my always bleeding heart, but part of me is indifferent. She brought this on herself. No one made her lash out with petty jealousy at work. That was her choice.

While everyone is signing their new NDAs and quietly mulling over their decisions, a few men from maintenance show up with boxes and hand them to each of us. I walk to my desk and wonder what to do with my things, but just as I'm about to start packing them, one of the men beats me to it.

"You don't have to do that," I say to him.

"Pardon, miss. I was told to gather your things and take them to Mr. Langford's office. He said you'll be working there for now."

Well, that answers that.

Ten minutes later, Emily and I are in Asher's office with Matthew, and the box of my desk things sits on the table in the corner. Just as we start to sit, a knock sounds at the door. Matthew opens it, and a sullen Daphne stands at the threshold.

"Yes?" he says, not hiding his annoyance.

"I wanted to apologize before I head downstairs."

Matthew moves aside and allows her to enter. Emily and I stand to meet her near the door.

"I'm sorry, Ella. Matthew was right. I was being petty and jealous, and I was out of line. I've enjoyed our time working together on this team, and I wish you the best moving forward." She doesn't sound all that sincere, but I thank her anyway. I don't want any bad blood.

"Here," she says, holding out a stack of papers for me. "These were left on your desk."

I take them and thank her again, then Matthew, Emily, and I return to the couch.

I shuffle through the stack of papers Daphne gave me. It's another batch of fan mail.

"So, who do we think is a good fit for the new team?" Matthew asks Emily.

"Heather," she answers quickly. "And possibly Michael to give us a male perspective. But no one else really stands out."

"I'm good with them, and I think the three of you would be sufficient for what we need," I say to her, still glancing over the mail. I've tried to answer some of the letters I've received in the past. It's still strange that people would want to hear from me, but I also don't want to alienate people who have gone out of their way to write to me, so I do what I can.

"Well, that was easy," Matthew says. "I'll send an email from Asher's account this afternoon so there's no room for complaining."

I open a blank envelope, and my stomach sinks. I haven't seen a letter like this since the first one, back when one of Asher's stalkers sent me a threating letter that called me a whore and warned me to stay away from him. Ever since my mail has been vetted. The page is blank except for one phrase made of magazine clippings pieced together in the middle.

I warned you

"SHIT," I say, reading the line over and over again.

I drop the letter like it burned me.

Emily snatches it up. "What the hell? This isn't supposed to happen! Who let this slip through the cracks?"

She stands, furious, and storms out of Asher's office. Matthew and I follow her as she hurries to security and forensics on the floor beneath us.

She bursts into the office, waving the paper.

"I need to speak to Thompson, *now*," she hisses at the guards sitting and watching a myriad of screens at the cameras all throughout the building feed.

"What's up?" a man, presumably Thompson, says a moment later, walking toward us from a back room.

"What's up is that Ms. Hale received another threatening letter! Your department is supposed to take care of this. So, tell me why this letter ended up on her desk!"

She brandishes the letter, and Thompson looks at it, eyes wide.

"*Fuck*," he hisses.

"Fuck is right. Someone's head will roll when Mr. Langford finds out about this."

The blood drains from Thompson's face.

Emily starts to yell again, but her voice fades, and she sways on her feet. A second later, the letter slips from her hand, and she collapses. Thompson barely manages to catch her before she hits the floor.

"Emily!" I shout. I lean down toward her, but then the room starts to spin. My knees buckle, and I crumple to the ground. I feel a burst of pain as my head slams into the tiled floor.

Everything goes black.

29

ASHER

"Fourth door on your left," Sterling says in my earpiece. Declan and I didn't want to alert anyone to our presence, so we entered Greenspan through a back door on the ground level. Sterling has the schematics of the building, and he's watching the cameras, tracking the asshole we're after. He's been able to lead us through the building without anyone seeing us. It's a new thing for me to creep through one of my companies like a criminal, but I'm not here for a walk-through inspection. Declan and I are here for answers, and we're not leaving until we have them

"Code is four two three six nine."

I punch in the code and open the door, revealing a dimly lit metal stairwell.

"Wait," Sterling says. "Cameras down in three, two, and . . . go."

Declan and I enter the stairwell and climb as silently as possible up three flights.

"On your left. This door requires a badge. Hang on while I override it."

A minute later, the light on the pad next to the door

changes from red to green, and we enter a filing room lined floor to ceiling with shelves of locked cabinets.

"The door to the research room he works in is on the other side of the room. He's in there alone, so move quickly."

The badge entry system panel again lights up green right as Declan and I reach it. I open the door and walk into a lab with metal tables, computers, and research equipment spread throughout. One man, Andrei Gusev, stands at a table, typing away on his computer.

"Hello, Andrei," I say in a bright voice.

He startles and looks at me, his mouth agape.

"Mr. Langford . . ." he nods to Declan, "Mr. Langford." His throat bobs as he swallows hard. "This is unexpected. H-how can I help you?"

"We have some questions, and we heard you were just the man to answer them. Let's go."

Declan grabs him by his bicep and leads him back through the filing room, down the stairwell, and into a small, very private, very soundproof room typically used for risky types of experiments. As soon as we're in the room, the lock *clicks*, seemingly of its own accord, locking us inside with no way out. Thank you, Sterling.

"Wh-what can I help you with?" Andrei stutters.

"We know," I say, cutting straight to the point. "We know TDC Oil is sabotaging Greenspan, and we know you're helping them."

He winces, and then his face fights to morph itself into an anything-but-believable look of surprise. "That's preposterous. Wh-what makes you say that?"

"Cut the bullshit," Declan growls. "We know what TDC's done; you know what they've done. What we want to know is what TDC's next plan is or any other useful information you can give us. How useful you are will determine what state you are in when you leave this room."

Andrei's jaw ticks, and his eyes shift rapidly.

"I . . . don't know what you're talking about."

"Okay," I say, resigned. I reach into my suit and pull out my handgun, then pull the suppressor out of my pocket and screw it onto the end.

"W-wait," Andrei says. "I can tell you some things, but I don't know everything."

"Is it Sergei or Yegor who ordered the hits on Greenspan?"

"I . . . I don't know. I get my orders from a guy named Ivan."

Declan steps forward and gut punches Andrei. Andrei hunches forward and falls to his knees. He's not Russian muscle. He's a Russian scientist, and he's clearly not used to this side of the violent acts he helps to perpetrate.

"Try again."

"Ivan works for Sergei."

"Good. And what is TDC's next move?"

"They want Greenspan destroyed."

"We know that part," Declan says, lifting Andrei back to his feet.

"They want to undercut the power of Langford Holdings."

"That's also not a stretch to figure out. *How* do they plan to do that?"

"I don't know!"

"What *do* you know?"

"I know the hacker they used is called the Ghost."

Sterling hisses in my ear. "Fuck. I've heard of him. He's a goddamn legend. No wonder all their tracks have been well covered. He's a mercenary hacker and doesn't really care what the job is. He just works for the highest bidder."

"What else?" I demand.

"Yegor is putting pressure on Sergei. This was supposed to be done years ago. The research is getting closer, and Yegor wants it shut down before it gets any further."

"Who ordered the questioning of my grandfather?"

Andrei's mouth pops open again, but nothing comes out. "I-I don't know anything about your grandfather. He died before my time here."

"Surely you've heard something."

"No. Nothing. I-I had no idea there was a connection."

I can't tell if the terror on his face is genuine because he doesn't know or if he's trying to hide what he knows.

"For the last fucking time, what is TDC's next plan?" Declan growls.

"Th-they want the company, and they'll do anything to get it. Your board is eager to give it to them. I-I don't know what they'll do to get it, but they have something planned. I don't what, though!"

Declan twists and punches Andrei straight on the nose. Andrei crumples to the floor.

"Try again," Declan says, standing over him.

"The sabotage isn't working," Andrei says through a nasally, wet tone, clutching his bleeding nose. "They're trying for a different tactic. They're planning to hit Asher personally, where it hurts. They can't get control of Greenspan without going after Asher's power." He looks up at me. "You hold too much power, and they want to take it for themselves. That's all I know."

"So, you were nothing more than a mindless minion willing to hurt innocent people. Good to know."

"Please," he pleads.

Declan and I cross the room to put some distance between us, then I raise my pistol and aim it at his head.

"Akio Kobayashi is going to spend the rest of his life in a wheelchair because of you."

"I didn't *want* to hurt Akio. I had to; those were my orders!"

I let out a derisive laugh. "You knew what you were signing up for when you were hired by TDC."

"Please!" he whimpers this time. "You told me that how

much information I gave you would determine how I leave the room. I told you all I know!"

"Like you, I lied."

I shoot him between the eyes.

Robert and Wilkins enter the room a minute later.

"You three take care of the body and make sure everything is cleaned up," I order the guards and Declan. I'm headed back to the office."

I turn to leave, but Sterling yells in my earpiece. "Asher! Wait! Something happened to Ella."

I freeze. "What?"

"The panic button in the security room at Langford Holdings went off a minute ago. I just pulled up the cameras. Ella is in the room, but she's lying on the floor, unconscious. So is another woman. Emergency services are on their way."

"Fuck!"

"Do you need help?" Declan asks, hearing Sterling's words through his own feed.

"No. Take care of this."

Fear like I haven't felt since the night Ella was threatened by Kyle hits me in my core, and I race out the way we came in, desperate to get to her.

30

ASHER

"This way, sir," the nurse says, directing me to the private rooms in the hospital.

"How is she?" I demand.

"She's being treated as we speak."

"What happened?"

"Poisoning. I'm told she and the other woman brought in both touched a letter that had been laced with poison."

Fury rages inside me. *How the fuck did this happen?*

"You'll need to wait outside until the doctor comes to speak with you."

"How long will that be?"

"I don't know. Her team is doing everything they can."

"I want the best team you have working on her."

"They are, sir. She and the other woman are responding to the treatment, but it's still early in the process. I don't have any more information for you at the moment, I'm sorry."

My heart sinks in my chest. Nothing can happen to her. She has to be okay.

I don't know what I'll do if she's not.

"TELL ME YOU HAVE SOMETHING," I demand to Sterling as I answer his call. It's been three hours since Ella was admitted, and I'm losing my goddamn mind. I've heard nothing of use. The nurse has stopped by twice to tell me they're still working to get her stable enough for me to come in.

Cyanide poisoning.

A very low dose, but enough that she was critical for a moment before the doctors administered the antidotes. Her prognosis is good because she got to the hospital quickly, but the doctors are being cautious.

"Forensics just got back to me. The letter is a threat."

"No shit."

"No, you don't understand. It's a blatant threat, written out. The team found a message written on the paper using a black light. The letter is courtesy of Sergei. He targeted Ella in retribution for Dimitri."

"Why the fuck wasn't this vetted? Those types of letters weren't supposed to get to her."

"The team found the original envelope. It's just like the last ones. It came from your stalker lady in Indiana, but she didn't do this. Someone within Langford Holdings had to have known about the stalker's letters and decided to use them as an opportunity to send a threat that wouldn't compromise you but would still send the message. That person had to have intercepted the letter and they either wrote the message and laced it with poison themselves, or they took it to someone to do it."

"Fuck," I hiss under my breath.

"I've gone through the cameras to see when the letter arrived and trace its route, but I couldn't track it. It was covered well."

"So where does that leave us?"

"Don't worry. Not all is lost. In my searches, I found something quite interesting that's been happening up on the executive floor for the past month or so. It looks like Alan has been getting cozy with one of Ella's coworkers. A Daphne Erickson."

"Cozy how?"

"They've been having little trysts all over the floor. Bathrooms, closets, his office. And to think everyone has been gossiping about you fucking Ella in your office."

"Watch it," I growl.

"Hey, no judgement here. If I had a woman like Ella at work with me, I'd be hitting it as often as I could."

"Don't make me loosen your teeth the next time I see you."

"Okay, okay, Mr. Sensitive. Anyway, the point is, Alan has been asking Daphne lots of questions, and Daphne has been feeding the board information about Ella. It hasn't been anything of note since Daphne's information was weak at best, but it looks like Alan has been using Daphne any which way he could—including making sure she was the one to deliver the letter directly to Ella. He sent her a text message with instructions two minutes before she showed up at your office door to hand the papers over."

"Get Declan on it. I want Alan in a dark, soundproof room within the hour. And I want answers."

"Done."

Just as I end the call, a doctor in scrubs walks toward me. He's tall, broad, and young.

"Mr. Langford?" the doctor says, reaching out to shake my hand. "I'm Doctor Williams. Ms. Hale is stable and doing well."

"Thank god," I sigh. "Can I see her?"

"Yes, I'll take you there now."

He fills me in on her condition while we walk. "The antidote protocol worked well, and I don't think she will have any long-term effects from the poisoning, but it's too early to know for sure. She also has a large goose egg on her head and a concussion from her fall, but otherwise, we're very happy with her progress. She'll need to stay in the hospital for a day or two, just to be safe, but as of now, I think we're in the clear."

"Thank you."

"I'm actually a friend of Ella's. I'm sorry that we're meeting under these circumstances."

His words bring me up short. "You know Ella?"

"I'm Alec, Zahra's boyfriend. Ella was living with us before she moved in with you."

I look over him again, and recognition clicks into place. Of course. I've seen a photo of the handsome, African American doctor with Zahra.

"I'm the resident on her case. The head of her case, Dr. Wong, will speak more with you. She's with Ella now."

I rush to Ella's side once we reach the room. She's asleep, hooked up to an IV and monitors, and has oxygen tubes in her nose. I pull a chair next to her bed and sit down, taking her hand in mine. Both relief and dread fill me. Seeing her alive and in recovery is everything I want, but knowing she's been through this because of my enemies chills my blood. Ella, the one thing I've come to care about more than anything else in the world, was targeted and poisoned just to send me a fucking message.

I lift her hand to my mouth and press a kiss to it, wishing the apology in my kiss was enough.

Dr. Wong comes to stand next to me and gives me more details about Ella's treatment and prognosis.

When she's done, she gives me a concerned look. "Do you have any information on how this happened? A poisoning like this is obviously very rare. We had very little to go on when she was brought in."

"It seems some enemies of mine targeted her to get to me," I say before thinking. I probably shouldn't have told her that. But then again, she and Alec are her doctors, they need to know the truth. "A letter addressed to her was laced with the poison.

Needless to say, her mail will be destroyed before it ever gets to her from now on. And I'll be upping her security."

"That is good. I'm very sorry this happened, Mr. Langford."

"How long will she be out for?"

"We're keeping her sedated for the next twenty-four hours to let her organs rest. We'll be checking her labs every few hours to keep tabs on their functions."

I thank Dr. Wong and the other team members for what they've done for Ella. Then all of them but Alec leave.

"Ella doesn't have anyone listed as an emergency contact since she was unconscious when she was brought in," he says, placing a comforting hand on my shoulder, "but I know her mother, Maya, Zahra, and Lucy would be beside themselves if they knew what happened and weren't informed. I can't call them without Ella's permission, but I think they'd all appreciate it if you did."

I nod to him as he leaves. Of course I should inform Ella's loved ones of what happened. I stupidly didn't even think about it until now since all I could think about was her condition. I take out my phone but don't let go of Ella's hand as I dial. Not touching her is unthinkable right now.

I make four fuck-awful phone calls.

BRIGHT LIGHT SLICES across the dark room, stirring me from my half-asleep state in the lounger in the corner of Ella's room.

Robert enters. "Boss, we've got to go, and we've got to get Ella out of here. Now."

"What's going on?" My voice is gruff from lack of sleep.

"I have my eyes and ears out searching for threats, and they've found one. News has quietly traveled that Ella's in the hospital and that you're here with her. I just got a report that Antonov's men are on their way here to corner you while Ella's laid up. It's not safe to stay. We need to get you both back to your penthouse."

"Goddammit. Grab Alec—Dr. Williams."

Five minutes later, Alec enters the room, brows raised.

"What's going on?"

"My team picked up a threat," Robert explains. "There are very dangerous men headed this way to get to Ms. Hale and Mr. Langford while they're vulnerable."

Alec's professional, detached manner drops. "Shit."

"We need to remove Ms. Hale from the hospital for her safety and the safety of every other patient."

"Where will you take her? She's still not out of the woods yet."

"Back to my penthouse," I say. "They can't breach the security there. And you're coming with."

"I . . . still have a few hours on my shift."

"You don't anymore. I'll inform the head of the hospital. I'll call whoever I need to call. I'm taking Ella, and you're coming with to make sure she's okay."

"Yeah, okay. Of course. Give me a minute, I need to grab some portable leads and some supplies."

He hurries out of the room while I untangle Ella from her wires. I wrap her in a robe and tuck her IV bag into it. Just as I pick her up and carry her, Alec returns, and we, along with ten security officers, make our way down a service stairwell to the back, private entrance of the hospital.

I let out a small breath of relief when all three of my town cars are ready and waiting. I get in the middle one with Robert, Jensen, Alec, and two other security guards, while the others file into the two remaining cars. I barely have Ella buckled before we're off.

"I hate to ask, but is this . . . type of situation normal for you?" Alec asks, his brow creased. "First the poisoning and now this."

I cradle Ella into me and brush my fingers through her hair, hating the truth. "It can be." I let out a resigned breath. "It used to be extremely rare for a threat like this to hit my family, but now, it's happening more often."

"Why is that?"

"My family, being what it is, has many enemies. Some old ones have resurfaced."

"And now Ella is a target because she's with you."

I flex my jaw, irritated. "Yes."

"We're putting more security protocols into place," Robert says. "And increasing our numbers. This won't happen again."

Alec runs his hand over his face. "I hope not, for her sake."

A heavy silence settles over the car.

A few minutes later, Andrew speaks from the driver's seat. "There are two cars following us."

Robert cranes his head to look out the windows, then speaks to the other agents through his wrist cuff. "Jenkins, call the building and let them know to shut down entrance to the garage as soon as all three of our cars are inside."

"Shit!" I hiss in surprise as Andrew takes a sharp, unexpected turn at the last second.

"Sorry, Mr. Langford," he calls from the driver's seat. "I'm trying to lose our tail."

For the next thirty minutes, Andrew ducks and weaves through New York traffic, taking a winding, confusing route to the penthouse. We manage to shake one of the cars, but the other stays with us, no matter how skilled Andrew is at shaking them. I grit my teeth and hold Ella close, doing everything I can to keep calm. But my patience and my nerves are shredding by the second. Yegor and Sergei have officially gone too far. It's one thing to attack me. To threaten me. It's another to come after Ella. I thought they might have learned their lesson after the message I sent with Dimitri: they threaten my family, I take out theirs. But I was naïve. I should have expected a retaliation like this.

I can never let it happen again.

"Call the NYPD," I bark at Robert. "I want squad cars surrounding the garage entrance by the time we reach it."

A minute later, sirens wail through the streets as we all near the building of my penthouse. Finally, the black sedan tailing us slows and turns, obviously noting the dozen squad cars with their flashing red and blue lights, gathered around the entrance.

Andrew pulls in and the doors to the garage immediately shut behind us, then heavy locks click into place.

"No one is to come in or out of this garage tonight," I order Robert. "I don't care if they live in the building. It's my building, and they're out of luck until I know Ella is safe."

"I'll make sure it's done, sir."

The ride up the elevator is filled with silence. Everyone is relieved but still anxious. We have been anticipating retaliation and more threats from our enemies, but they blindsided us with this one. I knew there were security risks for Ella at work, but I never could have predicted this. And I certainly never could have predicted that Sergei would dare to infiltrate a hospital.

It seems as though every time I try to anticipate what Sergei or Yegor will do, they surprise me. I feel like I'm always on the defense, always on my back foot, and I hate it. I feel like I'm going crazy trying to stay as cautious as I can to keep Ella safe while also trying to eliminate my enemies. I can't seem to balance the two and it's fucking killing me.

I carry Ella into our bedroom, and Alec gets to work hooking her up to her portable leads as soon as I lay her down on our bed. He sighs in relief when her stats all look good, and he gets her IV bag set back up to hang from the bedpost.

"Since we're not in the hospital and this has turned

personal, I'm going to call Zahra," he says. "She needs to know why I won't make it home tonight."

I nod. "I'm sure she'd welcome an update from you; she was beside herself when I spoke to her earlier. There are three guest rooms upstairs, take your pick."

"I think Ella should be fine, but if any of her monitors sound off, come and get me. I'll be in first thing in the morning to check on her."

"Thank you, Alec. I mean it. I know Ella is important to you, so you would be there for her anyway, but it means a lot to me that you're here."

"You're welcome. But, Mr. Langford?"

"It's Asher. No formalities here."

"Asher? Please take care of her. Whatever is going on, do what you must to protect her from it. We can't lose Ella. She's family."

I swallow thickly. "She's my family now, too."

"Good. I've been worried about her since the two of you started dating. Forgive me, but your reputation wasn't something that gave me a lot of comfort. I've been expecting you to leave her heartbroken, and with the spotlight she's now in . . ."

"That won't happen. I swear it. I know my past isn't anything to be proud of, but it's most definitely behind me. Ella is my future."

"Then your future should be a bright one. And I guess that means we'll be seeing more of each other."

I'm surprised at how much the thought pleases me. "I'd like that."

Alec smiles. "Me, too."

He leaves the room, and I feel just a little bit lighter. I haven't had a friend outside of my brothers in years. Too many men in my social circle just aren't worth spending time with, and I've lost contact with most of my friends from my school years.

The thought of befriending my girlfriend's friend's boyfriend almost makes me laugh. It's something so mundane to normal people, but it's almost exciting to me. It's not something I can typically do. I have to guard myself, always. I can never trust that someone wants to be close to me to be close to *me*. They want the mirage of who and what they think I am. Not me as a person. But maybe that can be different with Alec. I don't know Zahra well, but what I do know of her from Ella leads me to think that she wouldn't have stayed in a relationship with someone for so many years if he wasn't a good man.

I put the thoughts of friendship aside and strip down and get in bed beside Ella. I pull her sleeping body into mine and rest her head on my chest. It's how she usually lays before we go to sleep, and I've grown used to it to the point where I have a hard time falling asleep if I don't have that with her. She's my anchor, my lifeline, and the most important thing in my world. She's the reason my cold heart that was so set on a lifetime of solitude found a reason to beat. She's the reason the very axis of my life has shifted, because a life without her at the center of it isn't a life worth living. Every smile, every laugh, every word that leaves her mouth is a gift I'm unworthy of. And yet I can't stop myself from taking them. From coveting every part of her —mind, body, and soul.

My hand shakes as I brush it over her hair, tucking it behind her ear. Everything that happened today and this evening is almost a blur, it's so surreal. And the fact that it all centered around hurting Ella guts me.

"I'll fix this," I whisper to her. "I promise."

31

ASHER

lood drips from my hands. I wipe them on a towel
Declan hands me, his split knuckles mirroring mine.
Alan sits slumped in a chair, his head hanging low,
lulling in his unconscious state. My last right hook to his face
was a little more than he was able to withstand, and at this
point, I don't know if it's worth bringing him back around. He's
given me fuck all for information, but with what a whimpering
pussy he is, I'm starting to believe it's because he doesn't have it.
All he's told me is that Janet is out for my blood, and she has
allies on the board.

As if I didn't already know that.

"We can't get rid of Janet easily or quickly. She holds too
much sway," Declan murmurs, almost to himself.

"No. I'll let her hang on for a bit. But I need to know who
else she has in her pockets before she's gone. I want all the rats
off my board, and I can't do that if I don't know who they all are.
But I'll start with Alan. He's not leaving this room alive."

Declan shifts, surprised by my words. "And how are we
going to frame this?"

"I'm going to take Ella's advice. She said we needed to create gossip and scandal for Sergei so that when he falls, there is a pattern of behavior to explain it away. If his fall from grace doesn't come out of left field, people are less likely to ask questions and look for answers. So, it looks like Sergei is going to be the prime suspect for Alan's murder."

Declan flashes a sinister smile. "Your girl is brilliant, but you know that already. So, what's Sergei's motive?"

"Revenge. Alan also has a useless son who likes to party. He obviously supplied Dimitri with the drugs that caused the overdose."

I pull out my Glock and put a bullet through Alan's chest. Anyone who hurts or threatens Ella in any way no longer gets to breathe. And Alan is the first to go.

I turn to Declan. "I'm heading back home to check on my girl. You and Sterling make that story happen. Spread it far and wide."

"Will do."

I'M BARELY BACK in my penthouse before the doorbell rings. I groan. I wanted some time to check on Ella without an audience, but it looks like that isn't going to happen. Ella's mother has been beside herself, and she and Lucy flew in to check on Ella.

Before I can even make it to the front door, Lucy barges through, having been let in by security.

"You have some explaining to do, Langford," she sneers. "Where is Ella?"

I've only had the misfortune of speaking to Lucy over the phone, and now I get to see her in person. Oh joy. I had hoped Declan's description of her as a hellcat was hyperbole, but unfortunately, it looks like it's not.

"She's in our room, resting."

"I want to see her."

Natalie, Ella's mother, and Zahra file in after Lucy.

"This way," I say, leading them to our bedroom.

"How could you let this happen?" Lucy demands, hot on my heels. "I thought your family was untouchable. Do I need to send some of my men to help your asses protect her?"

"That won't be necessary. And what do you mean by your men?"

We stop at the door, and Lucy rolls her eyes and clucks her tongue. "Clearly your buffoon of a brother didn't get through to you. I am a Morozov of Chicago. So, yes, I have *men*."

Understanding clicks into place. "You've got to be fucking kidding me," I growl. The Morozovs are one of five major Russian mafia families. They are cousins of the Antonovs.

"I'm not kidding. And I would flay my men alive for allowing harm to come to someone like this."

"I have it handled. Something like this will not happen again."

Lucy huffs and narrows her eyes, clearly not impressed by my answer.

I take her by the elbow and pull her out of earshot of the others. "Maybe instead of grinding my balls about this, you should talk to your goddamn cousins."

"Get your paws off me, Langford," she hisses. "And what's that supposed to mean?"

I pause. Sterling will be pissed when he finds out I told her, but if Lucy has any sway with the Antonovs, it's worth the risk. "The Antonovs are responsible for this."

Lucy's brows shoot up. "Which Antonovs?"

"Sergei."

"TDC Oil, Sergei?"

I nod.

"Fuck. What does he have on you?"

"Nothing. He wants something from me."

"Then you better give it to him."

"Can't do that. But I will do whatever it takes to keep Ella safe."

"You're a fool. Sergei plays the harmless gentleman, but he's a very dangerous man. He doesn't get his own hands dirty often, but that doesn't mean there aren't rivers of blood spilled on his orders."

"Then I'll spill his blood."

She scoffs. "A Langford ordering a hit? I thought your family was too moral for such things."

If only she knew. "We typically are, at least the last couple of generations of us. But you should know as well as anyone that my family's fortune was built on blood. I'm not proud of it, but it doesn't make it any less true. I want to do good in this world, but I'm not above getting my hands dirty if I'm forced to."

"So, what do you plan to do, Langford?"

"I'm not about to reveal my plans to the cousin of my enemy."

Lucy narrows her eyes. "I would never do anything to hurt Ella."

"I may be forced to have you around because you're Ella's friend, but I don't trust you enough to give you any information."

"I would *never* compromise Ella."

"Your last name is Morozov, so I will be keeping my cards close. Nothing you can say will move me on this. I'll tolerate you, but if I find out you're helping your cousins, willingly or not, there won't be a place on earth you can hide from my wrath."

Lucy's brows raise. "Maybe you are worthy of her after all." She pats my shoulder. "Time will tell."

With nothing else to say to the viper, I lead her back to the bedroom where the others are gathered around a sleeping Ella.

Natalie reaches down to stroke her cheek, and Ella stirs. A moment later, she blinks awake.

A sigh of relief rushes through me. Ella's hardly been conscious since Alec took her off the sedation meds, and I haven't even spoken to her about what happened. Alec and Brenda, the nurse, have taken turns to be here around the clock, so I've been assured many times that she's okay, but seeing her awake helps to calm the nonstop anxiety I've felt since Sterling told me she'd collapsed at work.

"Ella!" Natalie rasps, sitting down on the bed next to her. "I've been so worried about you."

Ella blinks slowly. "Mom?"

"Yes, sweetie. It's me."

"Why are you all here?" Ella slurs, her glazed eyes taking in the women standing over her.

"You were in the hospital," Natalie says. "You've . . . been sick."

Ella tries to speak again, but only gibberish comes out. Her eyes roll back into her head, and she dozes back off to sleep.

I stand over her, annoyed that she's being disturbed. "Okay, you've all seen her. She's alive and in one piece, but she obviously needs rest."

"Is she going to be okay?" Zahra asks Alec.

"She's fine," he says in his reassuring, doctor voice. "Her labs all came back normal, and she's doing very well. She's just still very groggy, although I'm not sure why. I took her off her meds last night."

"You know she's a lightweight," Zahra says.

He chuckles. "I forgot just how light, so this isn't abnormal for her. I'm not concerned; she just needs to sleep it off."

"Yes. Come back once she's slept it off," I say. These women's presence is already overwhelming, and they've only been here for five minutes.

"You're in a hurry to push us out. Why?" Lucy demands.

"Because I don't want you all overwhelming her."

"How can she be overwhelmed while she's sleeping?"

"If she wakes and you're all hovering over her, she will be overwhelmed."

"I don't like this," Lucy hisses. "I don't like that she's trapped here with you, and I don't like you lording over her, pushing her family and closest friends away. This is all your fault, Langford. If she weren't with you, this wouldn't have happened."

"Lucy," Zahra grumbles.

"What? I don't like this arrangement, and I think it's time you terminate the contract. This is a nightmare."

"What contract?" Natalie asks.

"The dating contract."

"What?" Natalie looks bewildered.

"Oh, shit. You don't know?" Zahra says.

"For fuck's sake," I mutter under my breath.

"What is going on, Asher?" Natalie asks me.

You can't throttle one of Ella's best friends, I remind myself as I shoot Lucy a glare. I repeat it to myself two more times, just to be sure I remember it.

Resigned, I make a motion to follow me out of the bedroom.

"Ms. Graham?" I call out, and a second later she appears in the living room. "Would you mind setting out some food and drinks for our company? It looks like we're going to be here for a bit."

"Of course, sir."

Five minutes later, we're all sitting on the couch with refreshments set out on the coffee table, and I explain to Natale the beginning of Ella's and my relationship.

Forty minutes after that, we're still here because I've re-explained, and explained for a third time—because Lucy kept interrupting me with questions and comments—everything I can about the situation.

"And the contract is now void?" Lucy asks for the fourth time.

"Yes," I snap. "But Ella and I are not over."

"Why not?"

"Because I'm in love with her!" I shout, my patience finally snapping. "I don't know how to make that any more fucking clear to you Lucya Morozov! Ella and I may have started as some twisted arrangement, but within that arrangement, we fell in love."

"And if that love fades? How will you ensure her protection? Did that idiot brother of yours bring you my terms?"

I close my eyes and pinch the bridge of my nose. "He did. And I not only met them, I exceeded them."

"I want proof."

"*Fucking hell*, woman."

The women all stare silently as I grab Ella's phone out of the kitchen and log into her banking app.

I hold up the phone for all of them. "You can see this is Ella's account, and only Ella's account. I have no access to it."

"But you just logged into it," Lucy argues.

I bite my tongue, and my nostrils flare. *You can't throttle one of Ella's best friends.*

"I'll make sure Ella changes her password when she's feeling better," I growl. I stand over Lucy and thrust the phone in her face. "Satisfied?"

"A hundred million dollars?" she whispers.

I smirk. All those millions are worth it to get this demon of a woman to quiet down.

"What?" Natalie gasps.

Natalie and Zahra stare at me with open mouths when I hold the phone closer for them to see.

"I transferred the money into her account the morning we ended the contract. The money should never be necessary since I plan to marry her and she'll never want for anything ever again, but I also know that my lawyers will push for the fiercest prenup they can. But regardless of any of that, I want Ella to have her own safety net in case anything happens to me or between us to end our relationship. I know you think I'm some incompetent, sadistic monster, Morozov, but I'm not. I love Ella, and I will do anything to make her happy and keep her safe."

"Well then . . . we'll just come back when she's awake," Zahra says, grabbing Lucy by the elbow and hauling her to her feet. "It looks like Ella's in good hands."

Lucy looks like she's going to argue, but Zahra shoots her a look that shuts her up.

Thank the lord.

I promise Natalie that I'll call her as soon as Ella is able to stay awake for visitors and do my best to herd them to the door without looking like I'm rejoicing in their departure. I should probably offer Natalie a room, but I'm a selfish asshole, so I set her up in a five-star hotel instead. I don't want to share Ella once she's awake. Visits will have to be good enough for everyone.

I let out a long breath once the three of them are gone. I'm not used to having to explain myself to people, and I find it fucking tedious. And I find Lucy *beyond* fucking tedious. I'm already thinking of ways to make sure I'm not around when she visits. If I never saw that woman again it would be too soon. I'm glad Ella has family and friends who fiercely protect her, but Lucy just feels like cruel and unusual punishment.

I strip out of my clothes and slide into bed. I hold Ella to me, just like last night, and breathe her in. After a moment, I'm finally able to calm down. Because everything is always better when it's just Ella and me, and she's in my arms. Exactly where she's supposed to be.

I just wish her safety wasn't on the line to be there.

32

ELLA

"It's nice to see your eyes open, Ms. Hale," Asher says, brushing my hair back from my forehead.

I blink and stretch, trying to put my thoughts in order. My brain is mush. Asher is shirtless and in bed with me, but it's light in the room. Definitely too light to be morning.

"What time is it?" I croak.

"Five-thirty. You've been sleeping for almost forty-eight hours."

"What? Why?"

"Do you remember what happened in the security room at work?"

I think back. It takes a minute, but memories click into place. "Emily fainted. And then maybe I fainted too? I'm not sure."

"You did. The stalker letter you received had been tampered with," he says, and quiet anger bleeds through his tone. "It was laced with poison."

It takes a minute to understand his words. Then they hit me. "Laced with poison? Is Emily okay?" She held onto the letter much longer than I did.

"You were both rushed to the hospital, and I made sure you both had the best care available. Her case was more severe than yours, but she has fully recovered as well."

"Thank god," I say through a sigh.

"How is your head? I'm supposed to ask about your pain per Alec's orders. You hit your head pretty hard when you fainted."

"I don't feel anything." But as I notice the IV in my hand, I realize I'm probably on some heavy pain meds. No wonder I've been sleeping constantly. "Wait, Alec? Like, Zahra's Alec?"

"He's your resident doctor."

"Oh god. I wasn't stripped down or anything, was I?"

Asher chuckles. "Yes, you were, to get you in a hospital gown. But Alec is a professional."

I groan. "And my old roommate."

"Who knows if he was even there when you were stripped down. Doctors are usually the last people in the room."

"That's true. Let's hope so."

"Let's focus on what matters: you."

"Me."

"You gave me quite the scare, Ms. Hale."

"How did this all happen? I can't believe the stalker letter was laced with poison. That sounds like a bad movie. And how did it get through the vetting process?"

Asher's jaw ticks and his eyes flash with anger. "The letter came from the stalker, but the poison didn't. It was tampered with after it arrived in the mail."

"I don't understand." My mind is still slushy. "If the letter was tampered with after it arrived at Langford Holdings, does that mean someone inside the company did this?"

"Very good, Ms. Hale. Your mind is not as slurry as your words."

I try to smack his arm, but with how weak I am, it's barely a tap. He snorts.

"Do you know who it was?" I ask.

"Yes."

"And?"

"You don't need to worry about it. I'm taking care of it. You just worry about getting better."

"Nope. I was poisoned, Asher. I deserve to know who did it."

He sighs. "I guess you're right about that. It was Alan from the board, but he didn't work alone. We've learned through surveillance that he and Daphne have been having an affair for about a month now, at least that's what we've been able to catch on the cameras. It could have been going on longer."

"Ew. He's, like, twice her age."

"Par for the fucking course in my line of work."

My brows rise to my hairline. "She helped him?" Holy shit, I knew Daphne didn't like me, but I never would have suspected that she would do anything like that.

"What was their goal? Were they trying to . . . kill me?"

Asher brushes his thumb down my cheek. "No. We don't think so, but we're still trying to put the puzzle pieces together. Alan didn't give much away as far as information, but Daphne is distraught and spilling everything. Though, she doesn't know much, so it still hasn't given us a lot to go on."

"So, what do you know?"

"We know that someone within Langford Holdings has been secretly working with TDC to sabotage Greenspan, and it's been going on for about thirty years. And we know that person must someone high up in the company. Alan certainly fits the bill."

"So, he's the person on the board who's been betraying you and Greenspan?"

"Yes, but I don't think he's the only one. Janet has also had it out for me for years."

"He's always trailing her like a faithful dog."

"So far I can't find anything on Janet, but that doesn't mean she's innocent."

"Okay, so all that aside, why poison me?"

"Because Alan got a call from Sergei. I hurt Dimitri, so Sergei wanted to hurt me, but he can't kill me until I give him what he wants, so he went after the thing that would hurt me the most. You."

He brushes a kiss to my temple.

"Unfortunately, Ms. Hale, you are very much my weakness, and my enemies and my board are now very aware of that. Alan decided to try to use you against me to see if it would work, but he couldn't get close to you without it being noted as strange, so he's been using Daphne. He kept his eyes on the PR team and quickly figured out that Daphne was jealous and held a great deal of animosity toward you, so he exploited that. He introduced himself to her and flattered her—made her feel special —and because he's rich and powerful, it worked. It didn't take much convincing for her to spy on you and report to him.

"When he got his orders from Sergei to find a way to hurt you, he came up with the plan to use the stalker letters so that it couldn't be traced back to him, and he used Daphne to deliver the letter. The last thing we caught on camera is Daphne picking up the pile of fan mail from her desk and delivering it to you. But surprisingly, there's no footage of how it ended up on her desk. The cameras have had an ironic number of glitches from the day and time the mail was initially sifted through to when it ended up on Daphne's desk."

"Did she know it was poisoned?"

"She denies it. She admitted that she knew there was a stalker letter in the stack of mail, but she insists that she had no idea it was poisoned and that Alan didn't divulge that part to her. She said that he told her it would scare you—and scare me —like it had the first time. She was feeling angry and petty after the disastrous meeting beforehand, so she gave you the mail earlier than planned. She was supposed to give it to you later that day."

"Why?"

"There was another meeting scheduled for the afternoon, and I think Alan wanted a spectacle. He wanted you to faint where everyone would see you and it would show the board that I am susceptible to threats which would undermine my power and leverage. He wants to sow more discord between the board and me. He had Sergei's orders, so he decided to use them to his advantage. But he won't be a problem moving forward."

The finality in his tone makes me freeze.

"He won't?"

"No."

I stay still as I process the words Asher isn't saying. "And why is that?"

He leans down and kisses my forehead again. "You know why."

I nod, swallowing hard. The enormity of the situation with Asher and his board, and the threats from TDC, hits me like a ton of bricks. And so does the reality of Asher's ability to be one person with me and another person when he's dealing with his enemies. It's a bit of a mind fuck, and yet it doesn't change the way I feel about him. I still wonder if that makes me a bad person. But whether it does or doesn't, I know that Asher isn't left with many choices in this situation. If he was able to handle these people and these threats like a normal person, I have no doubt he would. But he's not afforded that luxury. Not when his world works with its own set of rules. You either work within those rules or you fail. Simple as that. Such is the way of cutthroat savagery wrapped in the glittering glamor of high society.

"What does this mean moving forward?" I ask, knowing full well that Asher will not risk something like this again.

"Well, first off, I have something for you. It's been in the works since the beginning, but it's finally done."

He reaches across me and grabs something off the nightstand. He holds a red velvet jewelry box toward me.

"Jewelry?" I quirk my brow. This isn't exactly a romantic moment.

"Just open it."

The box opens smoothly and silently, so different from the creaking and groaning of his antique jewelry boxes. A gold watch is inside. "It's beautiful," I say, admiring the delicate band and diamond-encrusted watch face.

"It's not just a watch." He lifts it from the box. "See this button?" He points to a button I probably wouldn't have noticed on the side of the face opposite the crown. "This is a panic button. If you press this and hold it for three seconds, it alerts the entire security team. Or you can hit it three times in quick succession if you can't hold the button down. There's also a feature like my watch has, where you can use it to create a small explosion. But that's to be used only if you need to get away, like I did in Singapore."

I blink at him. "Like a bomb? Is it safe to wear?"

"It is. The propellant is safely housed inside and can only be ignited by clicking the crown with a very specific pattern."

"But it's so small, I can't imagine it doing much damage."

"It will do enough. It looks delicate, but it's damn near indestructible and waterproof. I know this all sounds crazy, but our enemies are not a small matter. Which means you're to wear this watch at all times. I don't care if you're in the shower, at home, or somewhere you think is safe. You will wear this watch."

"So demanding," I tease as he fastens the watch around my left wrist then presses a kiss to the sensitive skin there.

"I'm serious, Ella. I can't . . . what happened to you . . ."

"This watch wouldn't have changed that."

"I know, but I have to do something. Otherwise, I won't be able to function. I worry for you constantly. It's always in the back of my mind. I'm trying to fight my compulsions to . . ." He sighs. "It's getting harder to deal with you being a target, and every day I'm closer to snapping."

My brows furrow. The fear and anguish in his voice is so real, raw. But his words make my stomach coil in apprehension.

"What compulsions?"

His jaw tenses, clearly avoiding the question.

"What compulsions, Asher?"

"In the beginning, they were to run away, to push you away. A terrified voice in the back of my mind keeps screaming at me to do that, and to stay away this time."

My heart stutters in my chest.

"Not because I want you gone, but because if you're not with me, then one day people will forget about you, and then you can live a safe and normal life."

I meet his eyes and hope that the fire in mine can get through to the fear in his. "I don't want a safe and normal life if you're not in it."

He kisses my forehead. "I know."

"What's another compulsion? It sounded like you had more than one."

He hesitates before answering. "I want nothing more than to lock you away until this is over. I know it's fucked up, but I can't help the instinct to hide you where my enemies can't find you. Until they're all dead."

"I am not a princess that can be locked in a tower, Asher."

He sighs. "I know, baby."

I narrow my gaze. "Do you?"

"Yes. Of course I know that."

"You've already had me on a lockdown."

"And I'm about to put you on another one."

"I will not stay in your penthouse again like that. I nearly went crazy last time."

"It's your penthouse too."

I wave my hand, dismissing that.

"It's for your safe—"

"I am aware it's for my safety," I snap. "But we have to find another way."

"I don't want you in the office anymore. It's not safe there, not when I don't know how many traitors I have in my midst."

"What about work?"

"What about it? Your current job is null and void with the dismantling of the contract and PR team. Whatever needs to be overseen will be handled by the smaller team, and I can have them brought here when they need to work directly with you."

"I can agree to the office, but I won't give up my work with the school pantry and some other charities I'm interested in working with. I also have photo shoots and brand deals for Lennox Rose coming up; I can't do those from here, and I'm not backing out of them."

"I'm not asking you to back out of anything besides the office. That's where you're most vulnerable. As far as everything else, we'll make it work by putting more security in place. I've hired an additional personal security guard for you, a female, and she will quite literally go everywhere with you. Jenkins can't always move through female places like restrooms, so Flores will accompany you in those spaces, and then the two of them will be with you at all other times unless you're at home. It's the everyday Langford Holdings that is the problem. We've found some answers, but we're missing others. Something about this isn't adding up and I'm not risking you while we figure it out."

"So, unless I have a planned outing, you want me to stay here all day because something isn't adding up and you don't even know what it is?"

"Yes."

"Asher," I groan. "What am I supposed to do all day?"

"We can find another type of work, but it needs to be remote so you can do it from here."

"And if I don't agree to that?"

"Then I'll fire you and make certain you're not allowed inside the building unless you're with me."

"You would not do that!"

"You underestimate what I would do to keep you safe. Firing you is one of the least sins I would commit."

"You're unbelievable."

"It's not just the poisoning, Ella. I had to remove you from the hospital early. You weren't supposed to be discharged until today, but you've been home for two days."

"Why?"

"There was a threat intercepted by our team. Sergei learned what hospital you were in and knew that I was with you, and he sent a team after the two of us."

"To do what? Kill me? Kill you?"

"No. To corner and intimidate me while you were vulnerable in the hospital. They can't get what they want if I die. I hold all the power and if I die that power passes to my brothers, so it won't help their cause. But they could hurt me and make me watch while they hurt you, to get their point across. Their message was hidden on the stalker letter. They have demanded that I sign Greenspan over to them or they're coming for me. And they're coming to me through you."

Fuck.

"Every part of me wants to give in and give them what they want so that I can keep you safe. But I can't. I can't set that sort of precedent. If it gets out that all someone has to do is threaten you and I'll give them whatever they want, you'll never be safe again. Also, while I might be loose on a lot of my ethics, I do actually give a fuck what happens to this planet, and I am one of the few people who can put forth the money needed on research to get real results for climate change. The Russian mafia isn't something I want to fuck with, but they've given me no choice. I can't give in to their threats, which means I have to take them out. You're the potential collateral damage, and I can't have that. If I have to keep you somewhat locked down to keep you safe, that's what I'll do."

I let out a groan but don't have much to say. This is all too much to think about when my mind is still slushy from medication. I need to think this through before I know what my next step is.

"That reminds me," Asher says, looking a little hesitant. "You are also not to contact Lucy until this is all over."

"Excuse me?" *What in the actual fuck?*

"Lucy is a Morozov, a cousin of the Antonovs."

I bristle. "Lucy would never hurt me."

"I know that, Ella, I do. But regardless of Lucy's intentions, if the Antonovs learn about the connection between the two of you, they will try to exploit it."

"She would *never* help them or hurt me."

"She probably wouldn't even know it's happening. They would use her in ways she wouldn't realize."

"She is not stupid or naïve, she would see right through them."

"Okay, maybe they don't use her. Maybe they just hurt her to get to you, which would get them to me. They might be her family, but they are ruthless. This is hundreds of billions of dollars on the line when you look at the long-term effects of cutting out significant portions of oil in everyday life. They're not going to risk that, and if they have to use one of their own to prevent that loss? They won't hesitate. For them it will be well worth the cost."

I press the heels of my hands into my eyes, groaning. "So,

this means I'm cut off from one of my best friends, my work, and a lot of the outside world."

"Until I have a handle on this, yes."

Fucking hell. "And how long will that take?"

"I don't know. But I'm coming for them with everything I have. I'm sorry, Ella. This is exactly why I've kept people at arm's length my entire life. It wasn't merely selfishness at wanting to live a carefree bachelor life; it was this. My life is complicated, and my status can make it dangerous. I'm sorry you've been dragged into this. You deserve better."

"It sounds like you're trying to say goodbye."

"I'm not, although you'd be better off in the long run if I did."

"Don't say that."

"It's the truth."

"I think that ship has sailed. Even if you did say goodbye, people will still know who I am. Your idea that I'll just fade into anonymity and have a normal life is something that could take years to accomplish."

"Which is why keeping you close is what's best."

"Is that the only reason you're keeping me close?" My stomach sinks. This conversation is starting to taste strongly of regret.

"Of course not. But the situation you're in is my *worst fear* come to life, and I hate it."

I reach my hand up and cup his face. "I hate it too. But if this is what it means to be with you, then I accept it. I accepted it from the beginning. I meant what I said when you were eavesdropping on my call with my mother and Maya. You're worth it. All the craziness that comes with your life, I'll take it if it means I get to be with you."

Asher swallows and leans his forehead down to mine. "I love you, Ella. And I'll spend every day of the rest of my life proving that to you." His lips meet mine, and he kisses me tenderly, with so much love and affection that tears prickle in the backs of my eyes. I hold on to the moment—trying to memorize it—since I have a feeling that I'll need these types of memories to help me deal with the uncertainty ahead of us.

Because without these small moments, without the reminder of who he is without all the outside pressures bearing down on him, I don't know if I could survive Asher's world.

33

ELLA

Declan: Are you ready for your prison break?

YES!

I'm almost there, little sis.

After three weeks of being stuck up in Asher's penthouse with only a few outings for charity work, Declan and I are finally enacting our plan. Thank the lord. It's been a long three weeks, and with the hefty security protocols in place, I've been practically climbing the walls the last few days. But today, Asher is busy with back-to-back meetings, so Declan and I are going rogue.

Asher will probably have an aneurysm when he finds out, but I can live with that if it means I get to do something productive for a change.

"Asher's going to have my balls in a vice," Declan says as he strolls through the front door of the penthouse.

"I won't let him." I say with a wink.

He chuckles. "If anyone can keep him from killing me, it's you. I'll just use you as a human shield."

"Don't worry, I'll protect you."

"I'm going to hold you to that."

After what happened at the office and hospital, Asher completely pivoted on the idea of showcasing Greenspan. No matter how much I've pestered him, he's vehemently turned down my involvement in sharing Greenspan with the world. Not because he doesn't like the idea, but because he's paranoid about my safety. And I get it. But no one has made a move in the last three weeks, so if we're going to do this, it needs to be now. I can't stay locked up in the penthouse forever, and putting Greenspan on the public map can go a long way to protecting it. Asher's just being unreasonable.

Jenkins and Marie Flores, my new female bodyguard, look like they're going to puke when I tell them the news that we're leaving with Declan. They know they can't say no to me, not unless Asher has specifically given them orders to, and he hasn't. So I'm using that loophole and making a jail break.

Declan's security joins mine, and the lot of us makes our way down to the garage. As I look around at the group of people, it hits me how strange it is that any time I go anywhere now I have at least two people with me, if not more. There is no longer such a thing as running a quick errand by myself, and I still can't wrap my mind around it most of the time.

The drive to Greenspan is quiet and tense, as far as the security officers are concerned. Jenkins informed Robert that we left the penthouse, but we timed our departure with a very important meeting of Asher's so that we could make it to Greenspan before he would be informed.

As soon as we pull up to Greenspan's research facility on the outskirts of the city, Declan pulls out his phone and types out a text.

"It's better if I let Asher know what we did directly, rather than having Robert deliver the news."

I snort. "You're acting like we broke the law."

"Well, in the eyes of Asher's law, we did."

"He doesn't own me; I can go where I want to."

Declan's face vacillates between amusement and hesitation. "Yeah, sure. We'll go with that."

"Just text him. If he has a problem, he can take it up with me."

"Oh I know, and I'm counting on that. You're the only one who can calm his wrath."

I roll my eyes.

"Okay, I've got the text ready to go. Hold my hand while I send it, Ella." Declan reaches out, and I laugh again as I take his hand. He presses send on his phone. When he's done, he slips his phone in the inner breast pocket of his suit jacket just as security opens the car door. "Well, let's get this over with. If he does kill me, it was fun knowing you."

"Just get out of the car, you big baby."

It's hilarious to watch a six-foot-five-man squirm with unease, but I get it. Asher's wrath is not something most people fuck around with. For instance, Kyle is realizing just how much he fucked up by threatening me with a gun. I already knew he'd been denied bail to get out of jail while he awaits trial, but I just learned this morning that he's been moved to a more secure facility than what his crimes justify, and he's been given a state-appointed attorney whose case wins number at zero— all while the prosecutor and the judge are friends of Asher's. It's looking more and more like it will be a miracle if Kyle makes it out of prison by the time he's fifty. Asher may not be quick to anger, but once he's angered, he's ruthless, cunning, and carries so much power and influence it's almost scary.

I pat Declan on the shoulder to give him a little boost.

"Don't worry, Asher won't hurt you, you're his brother. Plus, you have two inches on him. Who would win in a fight?"

Declan smirks. "It would probably be a draw, because while I'm bigger and more athletic, Asher's meaner and a sneaky fucker when he wants to be."

"Okay, but he wouldn't actually hurt you."

"You obviously haven't heard many tales from our child-hood if you think that. The number of brawls that happened in the Langford home is ridiculously high. My mom finally put a doctor on retainer to come to our house for stitches and minor wounds so she could stop taking us into the ER and attracting attention."

"But you were kids then. You're all grown up now."

"Since when does that stop men from hitting each other?"

I snort. "Good point. But I pinky promise that I won't let him hurt you."

I reach out, and Declan takes my pinky in his. We sort of cemented our partnership with a pinky promise the day Lucy stormed into Declan's office and demanded that Asher compensate me with more money because the media attention I was receiving was so much worse than what we initially expected. Pinky promises have been our little inside joke ever since.

"All right, let's do this," Declan says, stepping out of the car.

I follow him inside the building, and we're met by a film crew from a big news outlet. Declan welcomes them, intro-duces me, and thanks them for coming. He explains how important Greenspan is to their family, and what a pet project it's been for the Langfords for over three decades.

As we're waiting for the research floor to clear out so we can start the tour, my phone buzzes with a text from Asher.

I thought I was clear that this tour wasn't
happening.

I SMIRK AND TEXT BACK.

> And I thought I was clear that I know more
> about PR and marketing than you do and
> giving Greenspan attention will help protect it.
> I'm only looking out for everyone's best
> interests.

And what about your best interest? What
happens when Yegor and Sergei see this news
special with your face all over it?

> I'm already on their list, and they've already
> come for me, this won't change anything.

I'm on my way. You and my idiot of a brother
had better prepare. I am not a happy man
right now.

> You can take it out on me in the bedroom.

MATTHEW TEXTS ME.

Well, you did it. He's about to burst a blood
vessel. I hope you have a plan.

> My plan is sexual favors, the old tried and true.
> It can't possibly fail.

> Normally I would tell someone to try again with
> how angry Asher is right now, but I can't deny
> you hold some sort of sexual spell over him.
> Maybe you're a witch.

> I'm definitely a witch. A sex witch.

> Prepare to cast your spell then, witch. You're
> going to need a good one.

TRUE TO HIS WORD, Asher arrives thirty minutes later with fire raging in his eyes. As soon as Declan spots him marching toward us, he grabs me by my shoulders and hauls me in front of him.

"Okay, little human shield, do your duty and protect me."

A laugh bursts out of me, and Asher's eyes are near searing as he and Matthew come to a stop before us.

"What's up, Brother?" Declan says too casually. "I thought you had meetings today."

"I'll deal with you later," Asher growls.

"No, you won't," I snap. "Because you'll have to go through me."

Asher blinks as he lowers his head to look at me. An almost smirk tugs at the corner of his mouth as he notes the fact that I'm standing between him and Declan. Even with heels on, Asher is at least five inches taller than me, so I'm obviously not much of a threat. But that doesn't stop me from squaring my shoulders and doing my best to look intimidating.

He looks at Declan, then back down at me. "I knew the two of you becoming chummy with each other would cause me problems."

"Well, too bad for you. We're besties."

Asher's nostrils flare slightly. "You already have three best friends."

"You're right, and Declan is one of them."

"I meant Maya, Zahra, and Lucy."

"Maya is technically my sister, so she doesn't count as a best friend anymore. Lucky Declan here now gets to claim the third spot."

"That's me, lucky number three," Declan says from behind, but also above me, since my head is somewhere under his chin.

Asher lets out a long, slow, annoyed breath. "My brother is not one of your besties." He spits the last word like it's poisonous.

"He is so, and there's nothing you can do about it."

"I can when he goes against my orders and puts you in jeopardy."

I cluck my tongue. "No one is in jeopardy. We're just having a nice little tour with the news outlet, and we have plenty of security with us. You can join us on the tour if you'd like."

He gives me an unamused look. "How thoughtful of you to invite me along."

I step forward and snake my arms around his waist. "I know, right? And just think, when we get home, we can do whatever you'd like to alleviate your stress."

"Ew, I did not need to hear that," Declan says.

Asher shoots a glare at him over my head, but I take his chin in my hand and turn his focus back down to me. "Consider this an IOU. Although technically, I am a free person to go where I want when I want, so I don't actually owe you anything. But I'm willing to owe you because I like you."

He snorts. "You *like* me?"

"Definitely. And I'll like you an extra amount tonight after we do this tour."

A low growl escapes his throat. "Fine, you win. But only because I don't want to make a scene, which is undoubtedly why you and this asshole planned it this way."

"Glad you're on board."

Asher leans down to whisper in my ear. "But you'd better be prepared for me, Ms. Hale, because I am far from happy right now. And I plan to repay you for this little stunt."

I swallow hard as lust burns through me. Asher and I have never had angry sex before, and I find I'm highly anticipating it. My panties are already damp just thinking about it.

"Let's go," Asher says, waving his hand in the direction of the camera crew and journalists waiting down the hallway from us. "This is your show. Let's get it over with."

Well done, Matthew mouths to me behind Asher's back with a wink and a thumbs up.

Declan notices and laughs, and Asher turns back around to glare at the three of us.

"What's so funny?"

"Nothing," I say with a sweet smile. I link my arm with his and raise on my toes to plant a kiss on his cheek. "I'm glad you're here. I missed you this morning."

It's not a lie. Asher left early and didn't wake me, so this is the first time I've seen him today. My words seem to calm him some, and he slaps on a fake smile as we head toward the news crew.

Matthew hangs back slightly as Asher, Declan, and I take the news team on a guided tour through Greenspan's facility along with Akio Kobayashi, the head researcher, who now uses a wheelchair after his horrible accident. No one divulges that the accident in question happened here at the facility, and the sabotage and "accidents" are kept quiet as well. The point of this tour is to simply introduce Greenspan to the world and let it be known that Greenspan is on the brink of some major green energy solutions for the future.

While we tour, I take to social media, documenting the experience to get word out sooner. The story won't air for two weeks, so building buzz ahead of time is crucial. Asher stays near me the entire time, and I manage to get a few pictures and videos with him, which I include in my post. Like always, he fakes it for the camera, but I know he's still fuming inside. And he lets me know that as well, with the nipping kisses he sneaks in and the angry, dirty words he whispers in my ear.

After two hours, the tour ends, and Asher and Declan answer questions involving Greenspan, but the questions eventually turn away from Greenspan and toward Asher and me and our relationship.

"Mr. Langford, does the fact that you presented Ms. Hale with a famous Langford pendant mean there is to be a formal engagement in the near future?" a female reporter asks.

"That is typically the case in my family. The world will know whenever it is official."

"So, you plan to marry Ms. Hale?"

Asher lets out a long quiet breath. Only Declan and I can sense the unease beneath his façade, but it's there. Admitting to something like this publicly is a risk. He pulls me into his side, practically pinning me to him.

"Yes."

His voice is almost a growl.

"No more questions. I have work to get back to."

With that, he tugs me alongside him as we leave the news crew behind. He pulls me through the building, up a flight of stairs, and into an office. I yelp in surprise as he picks me up and sets me on the desk, rougher than normal.

"Whose office is this?" I ask, taking in the desk I'm sitting on, the computer, and shelves along the wall.

"Mine."

"You have an office at Greenspan?"

"No. But I own everything inside this building, including this office."

Asher flicks the lock on the door and gives me an appraising look filled with heat and scorching anger.

"You lied to me, Ella," he growls. "You went behind my back and defied me. And you roped my brother into your scheme."

"I did it to protect you and Greenspan."

"I don't need you to protect me."

"But you protect me. Am I not allowed to do the same for you?"

Asher prowls toward me, leaning down in my space until I'm pressed back against the desk, propped on my elbows.

"No. I don't care if it's toxic or sexist or misogynistic or all the above. You are mine to protect, not the other way around. And I will not have you putting yourself in harm's way."

I scoff. "I wasn't in harm's way. It was a simple tour and interview. Security was present as well as you and Declan. I was more than safe."

"But the fallout could put you in danger."

"We've already covered this. I'm on Yegor's and Sergei's radar. This interview isn't going to change that."

"But it will anger them more than they already are."

"But it will also make them think twice about their actions. With the public's eyes on Greenspan, they can no longer work in the shadows to try to destroy it."

"You're lucky you have a good fucking point," he growls, nipping at my earlobe. "But as it stands, I'm still furious."

"And what are you going to do about it, Mr. Langford?" My voice is breathy and full of need. Daring him to take what he wants in retribution.

"I'm going to fuck that defiance right out of you. But only after I make you choke on my cock. On your knees, Ella."

I hide my excitement and do as he says, slipping off the desk and lowering myself to my knees before him. For anyone else, I would take his harsh words as an insult and would refuse to obey his commands. But for Asher, fuck if I can keep myself from complying. Just as he said, I don't care if it's toxic or sexist,

I'll gladly get on my knees for this man, even if it's for punishment.

Without preamble, he undoes his belt and unzips his pants.

"Open up, pretty girl."

I do, and without mercy, he shoves his massive cock into my mouth, hissing and groaning as soon as it's inside. He rocks his hips, furiously fucking my mouth as promised. I take him in, using my hand to palm his base, since there's no way I can fit all of him inside me. I suck him with everything I have, gagging when he hits the back of my throat. But I don't care about the tears that track their way down my cheeks from my watering eyes or the punishing way Asher slams into my mouth. This man is hot as sin, and even hotter when he's angry.

Abruptly, he pulls out of my mouth and hauls me to my feet. Then he picks me up and sets me on the desk again, pressing me down until my back is flush with the surface. He leans over me and shoves my skirt up over my hips.

"I'm not coming down your throat. Not today. I'm going to come by punishing this pussy. And when I'm inside you, I want you to remember who you belong to. And I want you to promise me that you'll never defy me again."

He grabs my panties and a *tear* rips through the air as he shreds them in his hands. He lines his cock up with my entrance, but before he can slide in, I close my knees as much as I'm able with my legs wrapped around him.

"Wait," I say.

Asher arches a dangerous brow. "Wait?"

"You have to promise me something first."

"You are not in the position to ask for promises, Ella."

"You can't hurt Declan," I blurt out. "This was my idea, and I made him go through with it."

"You're defending my brother while your legs are spread open for me?"

I swallow hard and nod.

"What I do or don't do to my brother is my business."

"He's kind of like a brother to me now, and I promised him I wouldn't let you hurt him."

Asher's eyes narrow almost to slits.

"Please. You can take your anger out on me all you want but leave Declan out of it."

"He is a big boy; he doesn't need you defending him."

"Well, he has it whether he needs it or not."

"I shouldn't have to reiterate the fact that I don't like you talking about my brother while we're fucking."

"And I shouldn't have to reiterate the fact that there's literally no threat there. As I said, he's like a *brother* to me. And as such, he's my family, and I'll protect him. Just like I wanted to protect you. So, just give me your promise that you won't take your anger out on him, and we can get back to you punish fucking me."

"I don't have to promise anything."

"You do if you want inside me."

Asher's eyes flash with challenge, and his fingers trace my entrance. "Who does this pussy belong to, Ella?" He plunges two fingers inside me. "This pussy is *mine*. It's mine to fuck, to punish, to eat, to *live* inside. You know that as well as I do."

I whimper at his delicious touch but hold firm. "Promise me."

"You want my promise, then you make one in return. Promise me you'll never defy me like this again. You'll never go behind my back, even if you think you're protecting me."

"I . . ."

"Promise me."

Is that something I can promise? I'm not sure, but I'm sincerely hoping there's no need for me to do that in the future, so I sigh and give him what he wants.

"Okay, I promise."

"And I promise not to kill my brother."

"Or hurt or punish him."

"That too."

Without another word, he yanks my legs open and slams inside me. I cry out from both pleasure and pain, relishing in the feel of him inside me. Asher sets a relentless pace, fucking me hard, fast, and without mercy. I gasp as he lifts my shirt up and yanks my bra down and bites down on my breast, sucking hard on my nipple.

"Oh god, Asher," I moan, already floating on a high. I'm going to feel him between my legs for the next few days, but I can't be mad about it. Not when it feels this damn good. Not when his punishing kisses and bites light my skin on fire and set my pulse thrumming with heady excitement and lust.

"That's right, baby. Moan my name. And tell me you're sorry. Beg for my forgiveness for defying me."

"I'm sorry," I gasp. "I'll never go behind your back again."

"Beg."

"Please forgive me, Asher."

"I forgive you, but only because you're you. If you were anyone else, you'd be in so much trouble."

"I like being in trouble with you."

I mewl and gasp, unable to quiet myself at the sensations Asher rings from me. I cry out as my orgasm shoots through me. My ears pop and ring, and I yell Asher's name as he pounds into me, and then he finds his own release, gritting his teeth as he comes.

When he stills, Asher leans his forehead down against mine. "I could never stay mad at you, but that doesn't mean I'm not still furious at the situation." He gently bites at my bottom lip. "This is only the beginning. You wait until I'm home tonight. You'll get your full punishment then."

I fight back a smile.

Yes, please.

34

ELLA

A week later, the story hits the air. It's a week earlier than I expected, but the network couldn't wait, not when they had footage of Asher and me together, as well as with Declan. It's the first interview of our relationship to hit television, and even though it's not an official relationship type of interview, it's content the network has that no one else does so they decided to put it out as quickly as possible. Some banter Declan and I shared at the beginning of the tour is highlighted, and the head journalist comments on how integrated into the family I must be if I already share such an easy-going relationship with Asher's younger brother. The spotlight focuses less on Greenspan than I would have liked and more on Asher's and my relationship, but I still take it as a win.

After the story hits, interest in Greenspan spikes, and I breathe a sigh of relief. If Yegor and Sergei make a move, it's now more likely to be seen and heard by the public. I'm under no delusion that this will stop them, but it might just pause them long enough to give Asher the edge he needs to take them down.

And we're all anxious for that to happen.

Life with extensive security is stifling, and I still only leave the penthouse here and there. I was able to help at the school district's summer pantry program to give kids with food insecurity a free lunch on a Friday, but I had to skip on another charity event when Robert was worried that he couldn't secure the location well enough. The sooner we end this threat, the sooner we can all get back to our lives, and I can't wait.

As it is, I'm at my photo shoot with Lennox Rose, and I have a veritable fleet of security with me, along with my mom, who flew in to spend time with me since I'm bored out of my mind most days. Unfortunately, she has to get back to her life, and she's leaving for the airport directly after the shoot.

"These are gorgeous, Ella," my mom gushes, looking at the photo monitor as Carlos, my photographer, flips through the photos I just finished modeling for. These photos are for their luxury coat fall line and won't come out for a couple of months, but it was so fun to shoot. I've never modeled before, so it took me some time to get comfortable, but in the end, I'm pleased with the results.

"You were made to be in front of the camera. Why you spent your time in a corporate office, I will not understand," Carlos says in his strong Spanish accent as he starts to pack up his camera. "You should be modeling, not pushing papers. Is that what they say?"

I giggle. "Yes, pushing papers. But I never thought modeling was an option; I'm not tall enough."

"You are too short for a catwalk, not the camera. But no worries, we will make you a model from here on out."

"That's kind of you to say. And thank you, I really enjoyed the shoot."

"You are welcome, hermosa." He gives me a quick kiss on both of my cheeks. "I look forward to working with you again."

"You really were wonderful," my mother says as we head

out to the black town car, flanked by Flores and Jenkins. "I always knew you were beautiful enough to model."

I snort. "You have to say that; you're my mom."

"I'm serious, sweetie. When you were born, I had several nurses visit my room to look at you. Our nurse told them that you were the most beautiful baby she'd ever seen, and all the other nurses had to see for themselves. They all agreed, and they were right. You've always been stunningly beautiful. I was just too scared of the modeling industry to let you try."

"That's okay. Modeling like this is fun, but it's more on own terms, you know? I don't know if I would have had the spine to claw and fight my way through the modeling industry when I was younger. It wasn't exactly my passion, plus there was too much going on . . ."

My mother sighs, linking her arm with mine. "I know. We were all just trying to survive losing your father. I'm still impressed you and Maya made it through college with the grief you carried. None of us had much to give back then."

I nod in agreement. The years after my father's death are both viscerally clear and a blur. The three of us really were just trying to make it through each day.

"I feel like I cheated with this, though," I say as we climb in the car and get settled. "I *didn't* claw and fight my way to make it in the modeling world—to work with these high-end brands. I started dating my boss." I half laugh at the ridiculousness of it.

"You worked hard at your job, which is how you met your boss in the first place. You didn't cheat in any of that, and you can't help it that your boss is one of the most famous men on the planet and that dating him put you in the spotlight. Once that spotlight was on you, people couldn't ignore your beauty."

I laugh again. Trust my mom to humblebrag about me to me.

"I still think you're a bit biased, but I appreciate it nonetheless."

"And besides, this is good for you. You aren't working in your old job anymore, and it's looking more and more like it will be difficult for you to hold a normal job. Not when you have security trailing your every step and everyone knows your name and your face."

"That wasn't a problem at Langford Holdings since that's normal for Asher, but things definitely shifted with the office environment once Asher and I became official."

My mom looks contemplative. "Maybe you could switch to another department at Langford Holdings and get some space from Asher at work. What if you went back to marketing?"

I shrug. "Part of me would love that. I've been thinking about this a lot these last few weeks since I haven't been working, but I think you're right in the sense that it's hard for me to work a normal job. Everyone treats me differently now. I'm not Ella Hale the marketing rep, I'm Asher Langford's girlfriend. Like it or not, his reputation has sort of enveloped and consumed mine, so it's hard to be taken seriously as I am."

"So, what is it you'd like to do?"

"Honestly? I think charity work is what feels right to me. I don't need to work anymore with all the money Asher transferred into my account." I nearly had a heart-attack when I opened my banking app and saw the insane deposit Asher made to it, and when I approached him about it, he adamantly refused to take even a penny back. "I've been throwing the idea around in my head of starting a foundation. Asher has so much money it's kind of fun to spend it where it's needed. Between that and modeling occasionally, I should be able to keep busy and feel fulfilled."

"That sounds wonderful."

I nod.

My mom scrunches her nose, the same way I do sometimes, as her eyes roam over me. "You seem a little sad."

I sigh. "I have some mixed feelings about all the changes in my life."

"Oh, sweetie. I'm sorry. It's hard to move into new chapters."

"I really am excited by what's to come, but I think I'm kind of mourning what was. Being a marketing and PR rep wasn't glamorous, but I still really enjoyed it. I was part of a team and had colleagues. Now, I'm on the outside. Asher's world is big in some ways, but it's incredibly small in others. I'm lonely when Asher's not around."

And confined. But I don't tell my mom that part. She only knows a portion of what's going on. She thinks the poison on the stalker letter came from the stalker. I haven't had the heart to tell her about any of the other threats.

"What about Zahra? Are you spending time with her?"

"As much as I'm able. She's busy with her job at the restaurant. Her new boss is an asshole, apparently, so she's just trying to keep her head above water at work. Then when she's home, she spends her time with Alec, since he's in residency and he's also always working. I don't want to take away their time together."

"Well, you have Asher. And once Maya's back, maybe she can live nearby. Asher could probably get her a job at a big fancy museum in New York."

I also don't have the heart to tell her that Maya doesn't want to come back to New York.

"Yeah, maybe."

"But you're good?" she asks, her eyes imploring me. "You know I like Asher, but I still worry about you."

"I'm good. Really. Things have just been a little crazy and we're all adjusting to a new normal. I just have to figure out what my future looks like now that everything has changed."

"Well, you know I'm always here for you. I'm a phone call or a plan ride away."

"Thank you."

She gives me a hug. "I love you, Ella Bella."

"Love you too, Mom."

"Ma'am?" Jenkins says as Andrew pulls up to the airport curb. "I just got confirmation that your new security officers have arrived at your home."

"How many are there?" she asks, her eyes a little wide.

"There are three now, ma'am."

"Isn't that excessive?"

"Mr. Langford has some big dealings going on right now, so we are being cautious."

I sigh. It's the same for Maya. She called me yesterday complaining that Sterling has been a verifiable ogre since I was in the hospital. He's almost worse than Asher, from the sounds of it. I have no idea why she would be a target since she's across the ocean, but Asher and Sterling are taking no chances. Asher even has security watching Zahra's apartment and hired extra security at the hospital Alec works at.

"Please say your goodbyes inside the car," Jenkins says. "You must stay inside the vehicle, Ms. Hale."

I take a calming breath to keep from rolling my eyes or snapping at him. I know he's just doing his job.

"I love you," my mom says, hugging me goodbye as we're both still seated in the car. "I'll call you when I'm home."

"I love you, too. Be safe."

Two security officers meet her outside the car. They're flying with her and won't leave her side until she's delivered to her front door where her new security officers will take over.

What the hell is my and my family's life now?

LATER THAT NIGHT, I freeze just outside Asher's office. He doesn't know I'm here yet; doesn't know that I'm watching him through the glass door. He's bent over his desk, running his hands through his hair, and knocking back whiskey like it's a sport. His tie is loose, with a few buttons of his shirt undone. But I'm not ogling him. I'm pulled up short because of the strain I can see on his face, in the posture of his body. We're meant to be headed to a charity event right now, but Asher was caught late at work, so I'm meeting him at the office on the way there. But it looks like the event is a million miles from his mind.

He picks up a remote on his desk and points it at the TV. I discreetly crack the door open and crane my neck, curious as to what Asher is watching while he's clearly stressed. At this angle I can see about half the screen.

"TDC Oil stocks have plummeted in the last four weeks," the reporter announces as stock prices flash along the bottom of the broadcast screen. "Insiders aren't sure what's caused such a ripple in the company, but some assert that it may be connected to Sergei Antonov, TDC's CEO, being taken into custody for questioning in connection to the death of Alan Hoffman, a former executive of Langford Holdings. Mr. Antonov vehemently denies the accusations and has made assurances TDC Oil is under control and that the company will recover and return to its normal stock prices soon."

Asher gives a small, wry smile of satisfaction before turning the TV off and slumping back in his chair, whiskey in hand. He closes his eyes and loosens his tie further. Dark circles rim beneath his eyes, and his jaw is clenched so tightly that I'm worried he'll crack his teeth. I've known Asher's been stressed this last month. He hasn't been the same since the poisoning incident, but now that I see him raw and unguarded, thinking he's alone, I realize how much he's been keeping from me.

My heart tightens at the thought of him carrying so much alone.

Jenkins walks up behind me, and the movement catches

Asher's attention. He looks at me and immediately tries to straighten up and wash the stress and fatigue from his face.

"Can you wait for us for a bit?" I ask Jenkins. "It looks like Asher still needs to change into his tux."

"Of course."

I enter the office and hit the switch that turns the glass of his door and wall of windows opaque.

"How are you?" I ask, standing above Asher, who's still seated at his desk.

"I'm fine. The time got away from me, sorry," he says, eyeing my silver floor-length gown. "I'll hurry and change so we aren't late."

"Don't apologize. Who cares if we're late?"

"Emily and Matthew would very much care. Entrances must be grand and all."

"We're not playing that game anymore. Who gives a shit about our entrance? We're going to this event because we were already committed, but the motives behind that have changed. This isn't a PR stunt; this is just a charity event."

He blows out a breath, and my heart breaks as I watch him try to collect himself. He squares his shoulders, sets down his whiskey, and fights the look of exasperation on his face. But he's not fooling me.

"What's wrong, Asher?"

"Nothing you need to worry about."

"Don't do that."

"Do what?"

"Shut me out."

"I have to right now."

"Why?"

"Because I can't trust that you won't do something rash, like organize a news interview and a tour of one of my companies behind my back."

I sigh. "I'm sorry I went behind your back, but we got what

we wanted out of it. Greenspan's stocks are up, and you said you had a lot of new investors interested. That must go a long way in convincing the board that Greenspan is worth keeping, right?"

Asher pinches his nose. "It does. But you've now connected yourself personally with Greenspan, and that is something my enemies will have taken notice of. You put yourself at risk, Ella. And I can't have that."

He takes a long draw of his whiskey.

"What else is going on? I can tell you're upset by something. I know you've been stressed since . . . the incident. I can see it, but I didn't realize it was this bad. I'm sorry."

"There's nothing for you to be sorry about. This is my responsibility to take care of."

I lean down and run my hand along his jaw, brushing my thumb over his stubbled cheek. "Asher, you don't have to carry the world by yourself. We're in this together. If you just let go of your worries for one minute, you'll see that I can help you. Let me shoulder some of this burden."

"No."

His eyes meet mine, and though he's still fighting like hell, I can see the fear and resignation in them.

"I know something else is going on and you need to tell me. Keeping me in the dark doesn't help. If anything, it puts me at more risk."

Those words seem to do the trick. His jaw ticks, and he lets out a long sigh.

"Yegor has disappeared."

My brows rise. "I thought he was in Moscow."

His jaw ticks again. "He was. And now it's like he's disappeared off the face of the planet. Sterling can't find him anywhere. Which means we can't keep any tabs on his movements, and whatever he has planned, we are blind to it. Sergei is licking his wounds very publicly with the chaos Sterling is causing in his company and with the murder suspicion, so we're able to keep an eye on him. But Yegor is now a mystery."

"Let's not go to the event," I say, pulling his head toward me. He leans forward and rests his head on my stomach, and his hands come to rest on either side of my hips, holding onto me like a lifeline. I skim my nails through his hair, trying to give him any comfort I can. "Let's just head home and call it a night. You're not in any state to go."

"I'm fine."

I gently lift his head and look down into his eyes. Those beautiful blue eyes that are creased with worry and exhaustion. "You're not fine, and that's okay."

"We've committed to the event. If we don't go, it will spark whispers and rumors."

"So? Who cares?"

"We have to keep up appearances."

"Fuck appearances."

Asher gives a wry chuckle. "Says the woman from my PR team."

"I'm not on your PR team anymore. Now I'm just on your team. And as your teammate, I can tell when you're not doing well. And tonight, you're not doing well."

"You'd give up a night of glitz and glamor and elite socializing because I'm not doing well?"

I roll my eyes. "Of course. You know I don't care about the glitz and glamor, and the socializing is practically hive-inducing. It's something I pluck my way through because it's necessary, not because it's something I particularly enjoy. You're what I care about."

A ghost of a smile flickers across his face. "Fuck if I wasn't right."

I crinkle my brows. "What does that mean?"

"It means that any heiress or socialite would be saying the exact opposite thing to me right now. They'd be pressuring me to get dressed, and they'd be worried over the fact that we're going to be late and how that will look and what they'd miss out on. They would not be suggesting skipping the event for a night in. Especially after they went through all the trouble of getting ready. Picking you was the best thing I've ever done."

"Saying yes to you was the best thing I've ever done."

Heat shines in Asher's eyes, and the air between us shifts.

"Do you still want to go? Or would you be open to . . . other activities?" I ask.

"Fuck," he hisses, running his hands from his hips to my ass, giving it a squeeze. "Don't tempt me."

"Oh, I will shamelessly tempt you."

He groans. "We really do need to go. I have questions for Senator Sanders, and I want them to be inconspicuous, so they need to be asked on neutral ground. Like a charity event."

"You're sure?"

"Yes. I don't want to go, but we have to."

"Fine. But on one condition."

"What's that?"

"You need a little TLC first."

I drop to my knees and reach for his belt.

"What are you doing?" Asher's hands grip the arms of his chair.

"I'm helping you relax after a stressful day and before we have to go to a stressful event." I slowly unbuckle his belt and undo his pants, feeling his cock harden beneath my hands. "And I just realized something now that I no longer work in this building."

"What's that?" Asher rasps out.

"We barely took advantage of our close proximity at work." I free his cock and stroke it, looking up at him. "We worked on the same floor for months and only had two filthy office encounters. It's a shame, really."

I wrap my lips around him and take him all the way to the

back of my throat. He's so big I have to focus to fight my gag reflex as best I can, but I don't care if my eyes water and my makeup runs. All I want is to give Asher some relief. If we have to go to this god-forsaken event, at least we can go on our own terms.

"Oh god, Ella," Asher says, threading a hand through my hair, guiding my head up and down as I take him in my mouth. I wrap my hand around his base and work my hand and mouth in tandem, taking him harder and faster. Asher lets out a string of hissed curses and his hips buck involuntarily.

A moment later, Asher's hands are on me, and he yanks me up. His cock leaves my mouth with a pop, and before I know what's happening, he lifts me up and sets me on his desk.

"I wasn't finished," I complain.

Asher's eyes gleam with lust. "You made a valid point, Ms. Hale. You reminded me that I never did taste you on top of my desk. It's time I remedy that."

Asher lowers me onto my back as he sits in his chair, then he hikes my dress up to my hips. He slips my panties down, yanking on them in annoyance when they get caught on the stiletto heels of my shoes. Once they're off, he tosses them aside and pulls my hips toward his mouth, then lifts my legs over his shoulders.

"Do you know how many times I wanted to pull you out of your office and spread you wide on my desk?" he says, and his breath blows across my pussy as he speaks. He runs his tongue down my slit. "Do you have any idea what your little business skirts did to me? How I couldn't keep my eyes off you? Do you know how many times I found myself trying to look down your shirt while we were in this building? I miss having you around, but I'll admit, I'm a lot more productive when I'm not fighting the temptation to fuck you the entire day."

He sucks on my clit and slips two fingers inside me.

"Were you always this soaking for me at work?" he growls as

his fingers sliding in and out of my pussy make a filthy, wet sound.

"Yes," I admit breathlessly. "I'm always wet for you, Asher."

"Good girl."

He slips his tongue inside me and feasts on me, gripping my hips with his forearms. I thread my fingers through his hair and shamelessly ride his face. Just as I'm about to come, he pulls away, and I whimper. He stands up and lines his cock up, then slides inside of me. I wrap my legs around his waist, and my eyes practically roll into the back of my head as soon as he's inside me.

Asher ruthlessly fucks me. Hard and fast. Tension coils in my core with every thrust as he hits that perfect spot over and over again.

"Come for me, Ella," Asher growls as I'm close. And I do. I shatter around him just as he cries out, and we come together. He lowers his head to mine, our ragged breaths mingling as he stills inside me. He kisses me like a starved man, tasting like whiskey . . . and home.

"Let me get changed," he says, regret in his tone. "Before I change my mind and take you home to fuck you into oblivion."

"I like that option a lot better than a charity event."

Asher chuckles. "And that's one reason I love you so much."

35

ASHER

"Let's get the fuck out of here," I say to Robert, knocking back the last of my drink. "This night has been a waste." Despite my best efforts, I couldn't get Senator Sanders alone. He's clearly avoiding me, and if I can't speak to him, there's no reason to stay.

I set my glass on a passing waiter's tray as Robert speaks into his cuff to alert Andrew to pull the car around. I nod at Jenkins across the room, and he mirrors Robert, speaking into his own comms to alert the rest of the security officers that we're ready to go.

"You're exhausting so many resources on something so fleeting," a female voice says behind me. A voice I unfortunately know too well.

I turn. "Charlotte," I say in a clipped tone.

Charlotte Fucking Edwards. One of the last people I want to see tonight. Especially when all I want to do is get out of here.

She brushes her hair back from her ear, tilting her head and smiling at me.

"It's good to see you, Asher."

It's good to see me? Is this woman for real?

"I was just headed out."

"So soon?" Her hand darts out, grabbing me by the wrist. "The event organizer still needs to give a speech."

"I'm not interested in staying for it."

As I yank my arm away from her, her eyes move away from my face and scan to the corner of the room before she squares her attention back on me.

"I'd love to catch up."

"*Catch up?* Are you fucking kidding me, Charlotte?"

"So much has changed in such a short amount of time." She nods her head in Ella's direction. "Rumor has it there's a dozen security officers here tonight. You don't think that's a little excessive?"

Ella is speaking to Declan and my mother, and they're surrounded by four security guards while seven others are scattered throughout the ballroom, patrolling.

"I'm sure you're privy to what happened to Ella, so no, it's not even close to excessive."

Her brows rise, but she quickly hides her surprise behind a smirk. "You'd spend that kind of money and attention on someone who's merely a PR stunt?"

"Shut your fucking mouth," I growl.

Now Charlotte can't hide her surprise. Her eyes widen, and she sucks in a breath.

"I should bring down my legal team and crucify your husband for breaking his NDA. You shouldn't know a damn thing about Ella except what you read in gossip magazines."

"You know what pillow talk can wring from someone." She winks.

I almost shudder. *What the fuck did I ever see in this woman?* "Then you had better keep it all to yourself if you value your luxurious life. Because if you don't, I'll come for both you and Henry, and I won't hesitate to burn your lives to the ground."

After a breath of what seems like worry on her face, her coy smile fights for a reappearance. "So threatening, Asher. One would think you actually have feelings for your little employee."

"Ella is no longer my employee. She's my girlfriend, and I plan to make her my fiancée soon. And then my *wife*—as quickly as she and my mother will allow it. Our wedding will be expected to be a big affair, after all."

She blinks at me. "I thought you weren't the marrying type."

"What do you care? You're married, not that you divulged that little detail with me when we were together. Nor who your husband was."

Her annoying coy smile is back fully now. I want to tell her it's nowhere nearly as effective as she thinks it is. *How did I ever fall for it?* I was an idiot, that's how. Thank god those days are behind me and that I have Ella now.

"If I had told you, we wouldn't have had our fun."

"Then I guess I should thank you."

She puffs up her breasts and steps closer to me, a glint of victory shining in her eyes.

How wrong her assumption is.

"Not for the fun. That was fine." I shrug. "Something to pass the time. I should thank you because it's what brought me to Ella. Without our affair, the board wouldn't have forced my hand. And in . . . a twist of fate, shall we say, that forced situation brought me true happiness."

Charlotte's eyes narrow. "So the board gets its happily ever after story, how sweet. I'll give you this, you're much better at pretending now, Asher."

I let out a humorless laugh. "I'm not pretending, and this isn't a story for the fucking board. The PR contract was terminated, or didn't your husband divulge that to you with his *pillow talk*? I am with Ella because I want to be and because she's the only woman who's ever made me happy. The only woman worthy of being the future Mrs. Langford. Good night, Char-lotte. Have the life you deserve."

I brush past her shocked face and head straight for Ella. I've pledged my money, and I've made my appearance. I had to force my way through a conversation with Charlotte. I'm done. I just want to get Ella home and in our bed so that I can worship her like the future Mrs. Langford she is.

"Hey, you, what's wrong?" Ella asks as I march up to her. She's getting good at reading me; she can clearly see the tension I feel after my conversation with Charlotte.

I tug her to me and surprise her with a kiss. Declan chuckles beside us and my mom clears her throat after a moment.

"We're in public, Asher," my mom reminds me under her breath.

"I don't give a fuck," I mumble as I reluctantly pull away from Ella's lips. It's probably becoming unhealthy, but I feel like Ella is the only thing that grounds me anymore. She's the only person and place that truly makes me feel at ease. I need her like a drug, and I have no intention of getting clean. "We're leaving."

"There's still two hours left," my mom admonishes.

"Asher needs some downtime," Ella says, curling up to my side. "I'd better get him home before he starts a riot."

My mom sighs. "You're probably right. Goodnight, darling." She gives me a peck on my cheek. "And goodnight, Ella."

We say the rest of our quick goodbyes as we make our way outside. The relief I feel when we're in the car is palpable. I don't like being exposed like this with Yegor on the loose and with the wildcard of Sergei. His feelings toward me must be beyond volatile. His son is dead, his daughter was publicly humiliated, he was brought in by the NYPD and questioned about Alan's murder, and his company is failing by the minute. It's only a matter of time before he strikes back.

But I want to forget about all of that tonight. I want to get Ella home and just spend time with her. I want to pretend we're normal for one goddamn minute.

"Do you picture yourself having kids?" I blurt out to Ella just after the car pulls away from the event. "I know I've mentioned it, but we haven't actually talked about it."

She flashes me a quizzical look and a half smile as she buckles her seatbelt. "What's brought on that question?"

I take her hand in mine. "Because I'm curious what our future looks like."

"And . . . you want to have kids with me?" Her voice is low and cautious.

"Of course I do—if you're willing. I sure as fuck don't want to have them with anyone else."

She bites her lip, hiding a smile. "Yes, I want to have kids. I can't say how many, though. I don't think I'll know that until I start having them. You seem even more upset than you were earlier, is everything okay, Asher?"

"I just ran into Charlotte Edwards, and it got me thinking." Ella seems to curl in on herself. "Not anything like that. Stop thinking so little of yourself." I lift her hand to my lips and give it a little chastising nip, then a kiss. I hate that she immediately assumes that my seeing Charlotte means I want anything to do with her.

"There's no other woman on this planet, or any other, who holds any interest for me. You're it, Ella. But seeing Charlotte got me thinking that I'm happy to leave my old life behind. For the first time, I'm excited for the next chapter. For marriage, children, all of it. I'm not trying to rush you, I know this is a lot to throw at you, and we'll take things as fast or as slow as you want. I just want . . . more. I want all the things, and I want them with you."

Ella's lower lip trembles. "I want that too," she whispers.

I lean in to kiss her, but before I can, the car swerves sharply, and I'm thrown back in my seat.

"What the fuck was that?" I demand of Andrew.

Robert, Jenkins, Flores, and Wilkins all shift to alert, looking out the windows.

"We have a tail," Andrew says. "Fuck," he curses a second later. "We have three tails."

I glance out the window. The second car with the rest of our security detail trails us closely, but three large black cars just like ours flank behind and on either side of them. The one to our right swerves toward us again. Andrew pulls out of the way just in time, but we nearly crash into the black car to our left.

With the traffic, there's nowhere to go and no way to lose them. And yet, there's much less traffic than there should be. It's normally bumper to bumper, but instead, there's only about a third of the typical cars on the road.

"Goddammit," Robert says, his hand at his ear, communicating with the rest of the team. "They've surrounded the apartment building. Eight cars full of men—waiting for us."

"Get the fucking NYPD there, now!" I bark. I grab my phone and dial Chief Olsen.

"What do you need, Langford?" he answers in a clipped tone.

"I'm being fucking ambushed. My car is being tailed by three black SUVs, and there are another eight cars full of men waiting outside my penthouse."

Olsen curses. "You know who it is?"

"My best guess is he Russian fucking mafia."

"What the hell are you doing messing with them?"

The car to our right swerves for us, and Andrew barely manages to avoid the collision.

"I want air support for my vehicle, immediately," I growl.

"I'm on it. Don't die in the meantime." The line clicks dead, and I look over at Ella. Her face is ashen, and her hands are shaking. "It's going to be okay," I say, taking her hand in mine again. I tell that to myself, willing myself to believe it.

"Brace!" Flores calls out as the car on our left slams into us. Then the car on our right hits us, and we ping pong back and forth, hitting each of the cars, two, three, four times. The image of a speeding car, of my grandfather's lifeless body sprawled on the floor of his black limousine, flashes through my mind. *This is not that*, I say to myself, fighting to keep my wits about me.

A bus speeds up and slams into the security car behind us. Ella screams as the car rearends us. I turn and watch as the bus hits the car from another angle, causing it to flip over three times.

"We've lost our backup!" I shout.

The bus now speeds toward us from behind. Andrew swerves just in time to miss the impact, but we slam into the car to our right again. We're caged in.

"Head for the four ninety-five!" I shout at Andrew. "We need to go to the estate!"

Andrew speeds, slows, swerves, and does his best to maneuver the car to avoid hits. Every impact and almost impact bring back the moment of the crash from my childhood in my mind. The way time seemed to slow. The way the glass shattered from the windows and sparkled as it flew. The way the air rushed from my lungs as I was thrown forward so hard that I'm not sure how the lap belt kept me from flying through the car. The way my neck snapped and popped. And worse, the way my grandfather's body flew, slamming into the partition between the front and back of the limousine. The pain.

This is not that, I remind myself again.

I hold onto Ella, forcing the images and memories away. I must keep her safe. I will not let her be hurt. This will not be a repeat of that night.

"We're almost to the four ninety-five!" Andrew announces.

"We have to take out the cars on either side of us before we enter the interstate," I say to Robert. He nods, and we both unholster our Glocks. Flores and Wilkins follow suit. "Jenkins, cover Ella."

Jenkins moves across the car into the middle of the back seat and covers Ella's body with his own as we roll the windows down just enough to fit the short barrels of our guns through. Robert and I fire, aiming for the tires. Flores and Wilkins do the same on the opposite side. Return fire ricochets off the bulletproof windows, and Robert and I duck out of the way before firing again.

"Fuck!" Wilkins shouts. "I've been hit!"

I turn and see blood splattered along his neck.

"I can't shoot; they got my shoulder!"

"Trade places with me!" Jenkins yells.

A second later, Jenkins is firing out the window with Flores, and Wilkins is covering Ella's body.

"Are you okay?" Ella shouts.

"Fine, nothing vital," Wilkins says through gritted teeth.

Finally, just as my clip is about empty, Robert and I both hit the front and back tires, and the car whips around and crashes into the barrier leading to the interstate. Seconds later, Flores and Jenkins take out the second car. But the bus still follows, ramming into us as we enter the on-ramp.

We roll the windows up just as we hear the whirring of a helicopter above us.

"Air support is here!" Andrew calls from the front.

Jenkins pulls Wilkins to the opposite seat and takes off his jacket, assessing the wound. "It's a clean exit. You're lucky, man."

"Where is the bullet, then?" Robert asks, and then his eyes go wide as he sees it buried in the wall of the car, right next to his head. Three inches to the left and that bullet would have killed him.

"Get on the phone with the police force in Long Island," I

say to Jenkins. "We can't go back to the penthouse. We've got to go to the estate."

The bus rams us again, and the car swivels dangerously before Andrew regains control. "I don't know how much more damage we can take!" he calls back.

Sirens wail from behind us. A call comes through my cell. Olsen. "My chopper is on your route, and we're setting up a spike trap six miles ahead. It's the only way we're going to take down that bus without bystander casualties. But be aware, the bus is following too close to wait until after your car is over to engage it. Both vehicles will hit the spikes; there's no other option. Make sure you're all buckled and that your driver slows down right before the spikes. Hang on until then."

He hangs up, and I relay the message to Andrew and move next to Ella again. I triple check her seatbelt, then make sure I'm buckled.

"We're going to make it through this," I promise her, choking back my panic.

She nods with pools of tears gathered in her green eyes. "You survived a car crash once; you can do it again."

"*We* will survive."

Two tears escape and paint lines down her cheeks. "We will. No matter what happens, I love you, Asher."

I can't say the words back; they feel too much like a preemptive goodbye. Instead, I hold onto her. Six miles feels like a lifetime and like a second all at once. I fight to stay present, but my mind doesn't cooperate. It plays through the images of the car crash over and over again. Grandfather's body sprawled at an unnatural angle on the floor of the car. His blue eyes open and glazed over in death. The high speed causing the world to race by too fast. My shaking fingers fumbling to buckle my seatbelt with bound hands. The blood from my head dripping into my eyes. The relief from the click of the seatbelt. The *boom* of impact. Shattered glass. Flying shards. Pain. Then nothing.

This is not that.
This is not that.
This is not that.

I take Ella's hands into my shaking ones. It takes every ounce of control I have to not lose myself to fear. To not succumb to the past.

This is not that.

"I love you," I shout, giving in to the words as Andrew shouts for us to brace for impact.

Before we can, the bus slams into us from behind, but this time, with more purpose. When the bus hit us before, it was to slow the car or push it off course and get it to stop. This is not that. This is the bus ramming into our car as fast as it can to take us out.

I fly forward in my seat as the *crunch* from the crash hits from behind. A second later, I'm jostled up and back as the car hits the spikes in the road.

The world stills.

I float but am still tethered by my seatbelt.

Glass shatters.

Shards fly.

Nothing feels real as the car spins in circles, then swerves back and forth.

A second and a lifetime later, we come to a crashing halt. I gasp for air and look over at Ella. She lies against the side of the car, still buckled, but limp. Her head hangs down onto her chest. Her eyes are closed. Blood runs in rivulets down the side of her face.

My worst nightmare has come to life.

36

ASHER

"You killed him, you fucking idiot!" *One of the men in the ski masks yells at the other—his voice strikes me.* There's something familiar about it.

"*We were ordered to break him until he gave us information, not kill him in the process!*" *another masked man shouts, panicked.* "*We have to make it look like an accident! No one can know!*"

"*What about the kid?*" *the third masked man shouts.* "*He has to go. No one can know what happened here!*"

Grandpa's limp, dead body is hauled from the ground by the first two masked men. They shove him into the back of his car. The third man picks me up and throws me over his shoulder. I fight, kick, scream, but he punches me in the ribs to shut me up and keep me still. My breath is knocked out of my chest.

I'm thrown into the back of the car on top of Grandpa's body. I roll off him, screaming, panicking. What's happening? Where are we going? Why hasn't someone come for us? *Grandpa pressed his alert button when the masked men pulled us from the car. That was a long time ago.* Where is security? Why didn't they come?

The door shuts, and the car darts away, tires squealing. Only one of the masked men is in the car. He's driving grandpa's long limo recklessly. The faint lights outside the dark window blur by faster than I've ever seen them as the driver speeds up, swerving, and I fly off the seat, landing on the floor next to Grandpa.

"You must always wear a seatbelt, young Mr. Langford," *my security guard's words ring through my mind. Mr. Henley is always pushy about my seatbelt.*

In a haze, I wriggle my way back up to the seat with my bound hands. I can't reach the over the shoulder seat belts, but the center seat only has a lap belt. I shimmy onto the seat, grab the lap belt, and toss it, trying to throw it over my lap. I try one, two, three, four times before it works. I turn my body and grasp for the buckle with my bound hands, but the driver veers, knocking me onto my side.

I inch my way back up to sitting, frantic. Too fast. We're driving too fast. I look behind me, over my shoulder, trying to get the lap belt into the buckle. My hands shake as I try to fit the buckle together. The two pieces clink against one another, but don't connect. I try again, and again. Each time I'm close, the car hits a bump or swerves. Clink, clink, clink. *No connection, just the two pieces hitting against each other.*

The car engine revs, and we pick up more speed.

The driver begins to shout out a Catholic prayer in a hysterical, manic voice.

I try again. Finally, click. *The seatbelt is fastened! I use my teeth to grab the excess length, and pull it as far as I can, tightening the belt.*

The fabric of the belt barely leaves my mouth before the boom *of the crash.*

Everything goes dark.

THE SCENE REWINDS. I watch as it all moves backward until we're back at the beginning.

. . .

THE UNFAMILIAR SCENT *of strong cologne from the front seat hits me. Grandfather notices it, but not before we're already driving.*

"Who are you?" he demands.

I stop playing with my action figures and look at grandfather. His face is full of anger . . . and fear.

Then I realize what he's asking. This isn't Grandpa's driver. Grandpa's driver is older, and he doesn't wear this sour cologne I can smell all the way in the back of the limo.

The car swerves around and drives in the opposite direction.

"Get down, Asher," Grandpa commands me.

I see him hit the panic button hidden in his watch. He nods at me, and I do the same. I'm so scared I start to cry, but I know I have to be quiet. I've been trained on this. My security guards have gone over the protocol with me many times. Stay down, stay quiet, hit my panic button.

The limo pulls into an old warehouse. The door to the limo opens, and a large man in a ski mask lifts me out. Three more throw Grandpa to the ground.

The man holds me, and I thrash against him. He hits me on the head with the handle of his gun. A pop rings through my ears, and black spots pepper my vision. The man sets me down, and I teeter on my feet, still seeing stars. The man shoves fabric into my mouth from behind, then pulls it tight. He binds my hands and holds me tightly to him. I can do nothing as I watch the other men shout at Grandpa and tie him to a chair. I can't hear what they say. All I can hear is my heart beating in my ears.

The men hit and punch Grandpa, then point a gun at his head. They kick in his knees. They yell and shout and threaten. I cry and scream and try to get free, but the man holding me is too large, too strong. My shouts are muffled by the gag in my mouth.

Finally, one signals to the man holding me, and he carries me toward Grandpa and the other men. The man holding me hits me with his gun again, slicing my skin open near the corner of my eye. Blood dribbles down my face. He shoves the gun to my forehead.

One of the men leans down toward Grandpa. "We can make this easy, or we can make this hurt."

"Asher," a voice says.

I thrash in bed, my mind pulling from my dream.

"Asher!" Now I recognize Ella's voice, pulling me up, up, up, and out.

I sit up, gasping for breath. Ella's hands are on my shoulders. Her face appears before mine.

"It's okay, baby. It was just a dream." I can hear her words, but they're distant, an echo. I vaguely feel her hands skate up to my jaw, and she holds my face in them. She kisses my lips.

"We can make this easy, or we can make this hurt."

Why is that phrase so familiar?

"Asher, look at me."

Ella climbs onto my lap. She wraps her arms around me.

"We can make this easy, or we can make this hurt."

My mind drifts back to earlier this year. A rainy day in late winter. Charlotte in my apartment, taking it in.

"Your penthouse is so impressive, Asher. I'd love to live in a place like this," she says as I hand her a glass of wine.

I'm annoyed with her, but I like the fling we have going on, so I bite my tongue. I don't want her here. I don't bring women back to my penthouse, and this is exactly why. Women know I'm wealthy, but when they are in my home surrounded by the grandeur of it, that point seems to hit on a more profound level. I always insist on meeting women at hotels. Hotels keep the lines clear, and it keeps women out of my personal space. Charlotte showed up unexpectedly, and I was busy finishing up work, so I let her up.

I'm regretting it now.

"Let's go," I say.

"*Go where?*"

"*To the Plaza, as planned.*"

"*Why would we go to the Plaza? I'm already here.*"

"*I don't fuck women in my home,*" I snap, my patience waning.

She gives me an incredulous look. "*Why not?*"

"*I just prefer hotels.*"

"*Your home is nicer than a hotel.*" *She sets her glass of wine down and runs her hand over my cock and pants.* "*I'll make it worth your while.*"

I groan as she starts to unbuckle my belt. I step back, and her face is incredulous.

"*You'd really hold off on sex just to go to a hotel?*"

"*I told you; I don't mix these things with my home life.*"

She smirks at me, unbuttoning her blouse. She tosses it aside. Then her bra follows. "*We can make it quick today, if you prefer.*"

And when she's successful at getting my fly open and her hand down my briefs, my resolve starts to crumble. But I still pull away. She grips me tighter, and my traitorous cock hardens. Another groan slips past my lips. Fuck. She knows she has the upper hand.

She suddenly removes her hand. "We can make this easy, or we can make this hurt, Asher."

Her skirt hits the floor, and she stands before me in nothing but her panties.

"Fine," *I growl.* "But upstairs in one of the guest rooms. Final offer."

"Fuck," I hiss to myself.

"What is it?" Ella asks. "Asher, talk to me."

Another memory.

A BOARD MEETING. *Everyone is arguing. Conrad and Henry are pushing to sell Greenspan.*

"It's a fucking suck on resources!" Henry shouts. "We lose twenty-five million dollars per year on Greenspan."

"And for the fifty-millionth time," I yell, "fossil fuel energy will eventually run its course and another source of energy will be needed. If we're not investing in it now, we'll lose billions in the future by not being prepared. Technology comes at a cost, yes, but when that technology lands in the everyday lives of the citizens of the globe, that cost will be recouped and more."

"We're not budging on this, Asher," Conrad grinds out. "You agree to the sale, and the buyer will agree to let us keep what we have of Greenspan's IP as it stands now. Or, we can go over your head and sell to any other buyer who will insist on taking all previous Greenspan IP and wiping our servers clean. You'll lose all the research you've paid for."

"Why the fuck would we sell and keep the IP? We'd need to find another company to take that IP and keep developing that technology."

"But we could find a smaller company to do it, and we could negotiate pay at a much smaller scale and cut our losses in half each year."

"And risk having less brilliant minds working on this IP? That's not worth it. This is a technology race, so I will have the best and the brightest working on it. I'm not willing to sell and get some second-rate scientists just to save a few bucks."

"Twenty-five million isn't a few bucks."

"To you it isn't," I say with a smirk.

"You're so goddamn arrogant that you're going to ruin this company!"

"I've made this company more money in five years than you've made it in thirty. So, tell me again how I'm ruining this company."

"I want this sell!" Conrad says.

"We have the agreement of the majority of the board." Henry puffs out his chest. "So, we can make this easy, or we can make this hurt."

"Is that a threat?" I say, in a deathly quiet voice.

"It can be if it needs to be," Henry sneers.

Conrad cuts in. "No one is making threats."

"This discussion is over. I hold the majority shares, and I say no. So, fuck off. And Henry? Threaten me again and see what happens."

"Are you okay?" Ella asks again.

I let out a shaky breath. "I am, but I need to talk to Sterling and Declan. Now. Stay here. I'm not sure when I'll be back. Just go back to sleep, baby."

I pull on shorts and a T-shirt and head out of the room and down the hallway. We're at my house on Long Island. The house my grandfather left me. Once I knew we couldn't go back to the penthouse, I had Andrew head here. It was the only safe option. It's five a.m., and I only fell asleep an hour ago, but that doesn't matter. I need to speak to my brothers. I dial them both.

"What the fuck?" Declan grumbles sleepily.

"Is everything okay?" Sterling asks. "How is Ella holding up?"

"She's fine. We finally got to sleep an hour ago." Between the crash, the fires, and the hospital to make sure neither of us had any serious injuries, we didn't make it to the house until after three a.m. "I'm calling because I had a dream."

"And what, you want us to tuck you back in?" Declan says through a yawn.

"He was just in a car accident, you dumb fuck," Sterling snaps.

"I know. I can still give him shit. Otherwise, life isn't worth living."

"Listen, asshole," I growl. "The crash last night jarred some old memories. The dream I had was about the night Grandpa died. And something that was *said* that night. I know who was working TDC at that time, and it wasn't just Alan."

"Who?" Sterling demands.

"Henry Edwards."

"No fucking way," Declan says.

"Yes, fucking way."

"How do you know?"

"Because I'm pretty fucking sure he was there that night. He was one of the men in ski masks."

They're both quiet for a moment.

"Was he the one who swung the hammer?" Declan demands.

"No, that was the man next to him. Henry was the one yelling at the idiot for doing it. They weren't supposed to kill Grandpa, just beat him until he agreed to their terms and answered their questions. Now I'm thinking the terms must have been the sale of Greenspan."

"What year did Henry start working for Langford Holdings?" I ask Sterling.

A moment later I hear the *clacking* of the keys on his laptop.

"How do you know he was there that night?" Declan asks.

"Because of a phrase one of the men said to Grandpa. The man said, *'We can make this easy, or we can make this hurt.'* I had a fucking gun to my head, and I was ten, so it's no wonder I'd forgotten until now. But I've heard that same exact phrase more recently. Then probably six years ago or so, Henry said the same thing to me during an argument in the board room. The only reason it stuck with me was because he had never been so aggressive before. It was close enough to a threat that I didn't brush it aside.

"And a few months ago, when I was sleeping with Charlotte, she said the same phrase. I didn't know she was Henry's wife at the time, but now I'm starting to think we didn't accidentally 'meet' at that charity auction. I think Henry sent her to get close to me. Looking back, we didn't just have sex. We talked about my work a lot. She asked questions that I didn't really think much of at the time. But now? Yeah, she asked what seemed like innocuous questions that often lead to something about Greenspan or musings about all the companies we have under us that are developing technologies of some sort. Charlotte was never just a fling; she was a spy for her husband."

"1994," Sterling says, answering my earlier question. "Four years before Grandpa's death. And mother fucking hell, he worked in Albert's secondary division, Operations Management. That's why I couldn't find him. I was looking into R&D. So, we have to assume that Uncle Albert was involved."

"And you think Henry was there, in person, the night Grandpa died?"

"Yes. Now that I can remember it clearly, I recognize Henry's voice, even if it was a younger version of it. He must use that phrase quite a bit since he said it to me in the boardroom twice that I can remember, and it's rubbed off on Charlotte."

"Conrad has pushed selling Greenspan for years. Do we think he could be working with Henry? Or does he simply see a company that loses money each year?" Declan asks.

"No way to know yet. But we're going to find out."

"Do you think your affair with Charlotte being leaked to the press was a coincidence?" Declan asks. "Because it was Henry and Janet that spearheaded this little ultimatum that threatened your majority share. No one thought twice about it because we understood that Henry was furious at finding out you were fucking his wife. But now I wonder if he thought you wouldn't be able to follow the terms of the ultimatum and that you'd lose your majority stake in the company. Then he could push to sell Greenspan, and you wouldn't have been able to stop it. And other board members would go along because almost all of them hate Greenspan, and that would have been just enough to push the sale forward even with Dad, Sterling, and me voting no."

"What the fuck is TDC offering him that has him putting so much at risk?" Sterling muses.

"Whatever it is, he's a fool for taking it. Because now he's a dead man," I say. Rage burns in my veins. But an eerie calm also settles over me. Now that the questions are answered, at least most of them, there's nothing left but action.

"I want to know if Conrad is involved, and I want Janet off the board and out of our company. Leave Henry to me."

I hang up and head back into the bedroom. Ella is fast asleep again, thank god. She needs rest. I stand at the edge of the bed and take her in in the early dawn light that creeps into the room, highlighting her sleeping form. Even after a car accident and a bandaged head, she's the most beautiful thing in the world. But I can't find any peace at admiring her. Because the bandage on her head is bloody, and scratches crisscross the skin up and down her arms.

She very easily could have died tonight.

And that is unacceptable.

I lean down and brush her hair back from her bandage and place a soft kiss on the top of her head. She is everything to me. And yet, she's lying here injured because she's with me.

I need to make sure she's safe. There is nothing more important than that.

I'll make Sergei and Yegor pay, but it won't be easy. And it won't be clean. It's clear now that if I'm going to be successful in taking them down, I will have to focus all my energy on it.

My heart stutters as I place another kiss on her head. I hate myself for what I need to do. But I have no other choice.

I can't have any distractions.

37

ELLA

I grunt and hiss in pain as I climb out of bed. I refused pain meds at the hospital, not wanting to be knocked out for the next day, so I'm feeling every bit of damage my body went through during the crash.

I keep replaying it in my mind.

I've never felt fear like that before.

Not just for me, but for Asher. For what he must have been going through. He hid it well, but I could still see the ghosts of his past haunting his eyes. My heart nearly cracked in two, right down the middle, dreading the reality that it could have been the end for one or both of us.

I still can't take a full breath.

I wander out onto the luxurious balcony that overlooks the estate's massive grounds. The golden sunlight of late morning casts a glow over the perfectly manicured lawn and gardens, and under different circumstances, I would sit here in silence and admire the view. This house, the house Asher's grandfather left him, is breathtaking and feels as if it was plucked straight out of *The Great Gatsby* novel.

But today, there are much more pressing things on my mind.

"Any word?" I ask Asher as I slowly take a seat in the chair next to him, doing my best to hide a wince of pain. I'm in one of his T-shirts and a pair of boxers that he keeps at the house for when he visits, and as I cross my legs, I notice scrapes and bruises along my skin. I have more on my arms and a hell of a goose egg above my temple. But I count myself fortunate. Things could have been so much worse. And I'm so grateful they weren't.

He shakes his head. "The two men in the bus killed themselves after the crash." He doesn't look at me as he speaks, he just stares ahead, seemingly numb. "The men in the other cars got away, and the cars and the bus were taken care of before the police got to them."

"Taken care of?"

"The men dumped a canister of gas inside their vehicles then set them on fire. Basically, nothing is left of the cars or the bus, and there's no DNA to extract from them."

"What about the cars that surrounded the apartment?"

"They fled before the police got there, but it looks like they had help from within the police force."

"Olsen?"

"I don't think so. But Senator Sanders is a powerful man. He could have some dirty cops on his payroll."

"But even without DNA, you still know who's behind all this."

He nods and finally looks at me. "I can't rest until they're both eliminated."

"And what happens after that?"

He's back to staring aimlessly at the grounds. "That should send the message that I'm not to be fucked with. But to drive it home, I have Sterling working on something behind the scenes. Once Sergei and Yegor are finished, there will be nothing left of their empires, and I'll take them over and gain exponentially more wealth and power."

"More?" Asher is already one of the most powerful men on earth.

"More."

"Why?"

"Because the elite like to consolidate power and wealth by whatever means necessary. And someone within their league needs to keep them in check. I can't do that if I'm not at the top of the food chain."

"And who keeps you in check?"

He looks at me again. "You. My family. The ethics my parents drilled into me."

"It's easy to let those things go with that kind of wealth and power."

He rubs a hand over his tired face. "I already have that kind of wealth and power. More at this point is just more."

"And you'll use that wealth and power to keep the elite in check?"

"I already do. But yes, I'll continue."

We slip into silence, and fear slithers inside me. Last night was a disaster, and the insanity of it is bleeding into today. I don't know what to do, how to help. I woke in the hospital after the crash and as soon as I was cleared, a fleet of security arrived to bring us here.

Asher has hardly spoken to me since the accident. He was out of bed at dawn and since then he's been on the phone almost nonstop with Chief Olsen, security, his brothers, and who knows who else. He's completely contained and stoic. It's scaring me. He's not spiraling into anxiety like he normally does. He's cold and caged and so distant he hardly seems human.

I've never seen Asher like this, and I'm not sure what to do or how to help him.

I stand and move over to him. I sit on his lap and force him to look at me as I run my fingers through his hair.

"We should have just stayed in last night," I joke, smirking at him. "It would have saved us a lot of hassle."

He gives me an unamused look. "I can't argue there. If I had listened to you and gone back to our penthouse, we wouldn't have been chased after the event. However, the eight cars of men that showed up there might have overpowered the building's security, so we may have been attacked in our own home."

"All that matters is that we made it out safe."

Asher lets out a long sigh. "This time."

"And we're safe here?" This estate is like a fortress, but with such large grounds, I wonder if people could sneak in if they really wanted to.

"We're as safe as we can be."

"That doesn't sound reassuring."

"It's not."

"What do we do now?"

"We get you safe."

"What does that mean?"

Asher blinks and forces a smile that I know he means to be reassuring. "Let's not worry about that just now. Let's eat, and I'll show you around the house."

I know there's so much more he's not saying, but with Asher, I can't force it out of him. He'll tell me when he's ready.

"Okay."

Asher takes me by the hand and leads me to the dining room. The house is so old there isn't a traditional kitchen and dining area. The main kitchen is in the basement as is a separate room where only the staff would have worked, and Asher's family would have eaten only in a vast formal dining room. But Asher points out that forty years ago, a remodel allowed for a smaller dining area and kitchen to be installed on the main floor, and that's where Asher usually eats when he's here, unless his family is with him.

The house is a mix of dark, almost black, wood and cream stone and tiling. There are ornate patterns in the stone floors, luxurious trim around the windows and doorways, and large windows that provide breathtaking views of the grounds and the ocean. Every inch of the mansion is a master class in luxury, beauty, and wealth. It almost takes my breath away as I admire it.

"This home is incredible," I say, as we exit the massive, two-storied library on the first floor.

"Thank you. It was built in the 1850s by my great-great-grandfather, and it's been in our family ever since. It's always passed down to the oldest male heir of the Langford family."

"Has there always been a male heir?"

"Surprisingly, yes. I don't know what it is about our genes, but most of our family members are male. My mother wanted a girl so badly and ended up with three boys. Each generation, there are usually only two to three girls in total. My cousin Celeste is the only girl in our age range. But then, my grandparents only had two sons, an heir and a spare, so the options were limited. My father's second cousin had six kids before they finally got a girl."

"Five boys? That sounds like a mini circus."

"It was. They're all younger than I am. The girl is only, like, twelve years old now; she was at the luncheon over Memorial Day. No one else tried that many times to get a girl, most give up after two or three unruly Langford boys."

I laugh. "I don't blame them. I still say your mother deserves a medal for raising the three of you."

"I agree."

"Mr. Langford?" the housekeeper says, walking toward us. "Breakfast is served in the small dining room."

"Thank you, Darla."

Asher grows quiet again as we eat.

"What are you thinking?" I ask, picking at my food. Asher's aloof demeanor is making me nervous.

He smiles his false smile again. "I'm wishing you weren't seeing this house for the first time under these circumstances. I wanted to bring you out here for a little vacation later this summer. I'm disappointed that the first time I brought you here was because we were running for our safety."

I run a comforting hand over his. "I'm sorry. But either way, I'm thrilled to be here. I can't believe this is your house. It's insane that someone owns a home like this. It's like a fancy hotel."

"My father wasn't interested in it, with the other house he lives in, so my grandfather had it pass straight to me. I have been on the deed as the owner since I was ten years old."

Neither of us mention the reason for the young age of ownership, and a heavy silence settles over us.

I take a sip of coffee and set down my mug. I don't know what to say. I don't know how to make it better. But I know Asher is reeling, I can see it in the line of his jaw, in the hardness of his eyes.

The circle of events is too much.

Asher was supposed to be headed to this very house the night he and his grandfather were taken hostage—and now we're here because of a car chase involving the same people who not only murdered his grandfather, but who tried to use a car crash to murder him as a child.

Asher's phone *dings* with a text, and his face stills as he reads it. His eyes close for a brief second, and the line of his mouth pulls into a resolute grimace.

"Is everything okay?"

"It will be. Are you finished?" He nods at my plate.

"Yes, my stomach is too upset to eat much."

"Come. Flores and Jenkins are here."

He grabs my hand and leads me to the grand foyer where Flores and Jenkins stand beneath a massive, glittering chandelier that looks old-fashioned and modern at the same time.

"Good to see you up and about, Ms. Hale," Jenkins says, patting my shoulder.

"Thanks. How are you two holding up?"

"We're all good. No need to worry about us."

"Of course I worry about you."

"What he's trying to say, is that other than a little soreness from the accident, we're fine," Flores says in a snarky tone I've never heard from her. I like it.

"And how is Wilkins doing?" I know his gunshot wound wasn't fatal, but it still freaks me out.

"He's stitched up and home resting. We're all thankful the bullet didn't hit anything and just passed through the muscle."

They're so nonchalant about a bullet wound, but I guess that sort of comes with the territory, even if it's crazy to me.

Asher clears his throat.

"We'll just be outside, then," Flores says to Asher.

"What comes next?" I ask as soon as they leave. "Are we staying here for a while, or are we going back to the penthouse?"

"Neither."

"Then what's the plan?"

"To get you to safety."

I still. "That's the second time you've said it that way. Get *me* to safety. What about you?"

"I need to take care of this."

"What does that mean?"

He's silent and his gaze seems to be looking anywhere but at me.

"Asher, what are you saying?" I demand.

"I need to take care of Sergei and Yegor once and for all, and I need you safe while I do what needs to be done."

My stomach sinks, understanding all too well everything he's not saying.

"I'm not going anywhere without you." My tone is hard and leaves no room for argument.

Asher's eyes are filled with regret as he takes my face in his hands. He brushes his thumb along my lower lip. "I love you," he whispers.

"I . . . I love you too," I choke out. "But I don't like this. Whatever it is you're doing, whatever you have planned . . . please, Asher. Don't push me away."

Asher's lips meet mine, and he kisses me hard. His hands thread through my hair, and he pulls me so close there's not an inch of space between us. I wrap my arms around his neck and hold him tight.

The kiss turns almost manic, and panic rises inside me as I can practically feel the resignation and anxiety pouring off Asher. I latch onto him harder, praying I'm wrong. Hoping I'm making this all up.

I gasp as a bitter tang hits my tongue, shocking me. I pull away. *What is that?*

A moment later, I blink as stars form in front of my eyes, and I grow light-headed.

Asher pulls away and wipes his mouth with the back of his hand, then he takes a napkin out of his pocket and wipes his mouth again.

"What did you do?" I ask, and the words are slightly garbled in my mouth. My tongue is heavy, and my face is starting to prickle with numbness.

"I did what needed to be done."

"No!" I rasp out, clutching his arms. I start to sway on my feet. Asher wraps his arms around me and holds me tight, and the last minute of his actions clicks into place. He brushed something onto my lips . . . then kissed me to make sure it got into my mouth. "You . . . drugged . . . me."

"I'm sorry, Ella. I wish it hadn't come to this."

"How . . . why?"

"I love you. That's why."

"No, Asher. I . . . don't want . . . to be . . . with-without you."

"I'm sorry."

"No. Please."

"I love you."

The world turns black.

38

ELLA

My body feels heavy, as if it's been compressed beneath the weight of something I can't actually feel, but that something holds me down anyway. My eyes flutter. My fingers twitch. I can't connect my mind to my body to force it do what I want it to, and it's frustrating bordering on maddening. Before I can fight the exhaustion inside me, I fall back down into oblivion.

At some point later, I hear low murmurs of voices I faintly recognize. I'm jostled and carried, but I can't form the questions to ask where I am or what's going on. And again, I slip into darkness before I can find answers.

Finally, after what feels like too much time and no time at all, my eyes manage to open. They're so heavy it takes all my concentration to force them to stay that way. My mouth is raw and dry, my lips are chapped, and I'm so thirsty it's almost painful. Slowly, I push myself to sitting. It takes my brain too long to register my surroundings, and then a moment longer to believe them. I rub my heavy eyes and look around again.

The room I'm in is light and airy, lined with large windows, cream colored furniture, and wooden accents throughout. But what I see *outside* the windows is what has me shaking my head in disbelief. Outside is a tropical paradise of lush green plants and vibrant flowers in all shapes and colors. I would think myself crazy if I wasn't certain I was hearing the twittering of exotic birds and breathing in warm, humid air.

Where the hell am I?

I slide out of bed and wobble on shaking legs as I head out of the bedroom. I find myself in an indoor-outdoor loft area with a large balcony overlooking a literal tropical forest. There is a hammock in one corner of the loft and an indoor-outdoor tub sits in another. There is a sitting area in the center, and a bar against the wall across from the couch. I cross the loft to a staircase on the other side. The answers I need are obviously downstairs, so I hold tight to the railing, and head downstairs on shaking, weak legs.

The bottom of the staircase opens to a large kitchen and living room, and seated at the dining room table playing cards, are Flores and Jenkins.

"Oh, you're awake," Flores says in surprise. She's ditched her typical navy suit and wears a white button-down blouse and tan suit pants. Jenkins is the same, although both still have their holsters with guns strapped to either side of their torsos.

"Where the hell are we?" I demand, my voice hoarse.

"I'm afraid we can't tell you," Jenkins says, looking uncomfortable.

"You'd better rethink that answer, Jenkins."

He sighs. "I'm sorry, Ms. Hale. But we really can't tell you."

"Then answer this: what are we doing here?"

"Keeping you safe and out of the action," Flores says.

"How long are we going to be here?"

"As long as it takes."

Anger burns through me. "I was drugged and brought here against my will. Stop with the vague answers and give me some real fucking information." I know my anger is misplaced, I know this is all Asher's doing, but I can't help it.

Now Flores sighs. "We've been ordered to only give you so much."

"Why?"

"To keep you safe."

"What—" I don't finish my question as I sway on my feet, a dizzy spell hitting me hard.

"Let's get you seated," Flores says, standing and hurrying over to me.

She helps me to the table, and I plop down into a seat.

"Would the lady like some food?" an older woman with tanned skin and gray hair asks, walking with a limp into the kitchen. "The lady must be hungry. She has been sleeping for many hours." She sets a glass of water down in front of me.

I snatch it up and drink the entire thing in a matter of seconds.

"Yes, dinner would be nice, Camila," Flores says. "Thank you."

"Mr. Langford has ordered us to remain in this safe house until he authorizes us to leave," Jenkins says in a calm, reassuring tone. "He is taking care of the problems back home with his brothers, but he couldn't do that with you and your safety as a constant distraction."

"I'm a distraction?" I growl.

"When he's constantly worried that you're going to be taken hostage or killed, you are."

"So, where are we?"

"Somewhere in South America."

"That's helpful."

"That's all the information we can give you. There is no internet for you to use, and no way to trace where we are."

"What the hell? No internet for me to use? But there is internet for someone else to use?"

"Jenkins and I have to stay connected, but for your safety, you're not."

"For my safety? What the hell am I going to do with the internet to jeopardize my safety?"

"If you're logged on somewhere or contact someone, you could be traced. The Ghost is one of the best hackers in the world, and he's worked for Sergei and Yegor in the past. We can't risk him getting a lock on you."

"This is insane! Where's my phone?"

"You won't need it while you're here."

"Are you fucking kidding me? You can't just take my phone from me!"

"We already did."

"I want it back!"

"You'll get it back when we go back to New York."

"Mother*fucker*," I hiss. "So, I'm in what, like, a tropical prison for the foreseeable future?"

Jenkins grimaces. "Basically." His face morphs, trying for a hopeful expression. "But it's a very nice tropical prison."

I roll my eyes.

"And no one knows we're here." It's a statement, not a question.

"Except Camila and Asher, no," Flores responds.

"Has Asher contacted my mother, my coworkers? I know I wasn't working much lately, but people are going to ask questions if I just disappear."

"He's contacted them. The story is that you're on a much-needed tropical vacation and Asher works in New York Monday through Friday and joins you here on the weekends."

"*Is* Asher going to fly here on the weekends?"

"No," Jenkins answers. "It was risky enough taking the jet to the next country over and driving our way here. We can't leave any trails."

"We flew to a different country and then drove here? How long have I been asleep?"

"Two days."

"What the hell?" I glance down at my hand and notice a bandage on the back. I rip the bandage off to find a tiny red scab. "Did I have an IV with drugs to keep me asleep?"

Now Flores looks uneasy. "The IV also kept you hydrated and nourished with vitamins."

"You fucking assholes!"

"Mr. Langford is the one who arranged it. We just carted you here."

"Why didn't he just ask me to leave? Why drug me?"

"Would you have complied?" Jenkins asks. When I don't answer, he gives a small, self-satisfied smile. "You would have refused. This was the only way."

Damn Asher and his *act now and ask for permission later* ways. "I'm going to kill him."

Flores snorts. "Good luck with that."

"And you two are okay with this? You agreed to this?"

"It's not our place to agree or disagree. This is our assignment," Jenkins says.

"And this really is to keep you safe," Flores adds. "Now you're out of harm's way until Asher settles everything."

"I want to speak to him."

"Can't just yet. He'll contact us first. Although I did text him to let him know you're awake. He's relieved, by the way."

"Relieved? That prick. You know what? Actually, I don't want to talk to him. Why don't you text him and tell him I said he can go fuck himself."

Jenkins chuckles as Camila sets a bowl of some kind of potato soup in front of me. I eat it and then a second helping, famished, as Flores and Jenkins give me more useless information. It's all I can do not to stab either of them with my butter knife.

After dinner, I walk through the house, taking everything in. If I was here with Asher on a vacation and he hadn't drugged me and flown me across the world without my permission, I might be able to appreciate how stunning the property is. The house is large, but not massive, and is beautifully decorated. The grounds are a tropical paradise with a pool and a small lawn out back. Beyond the normal rooms for a house, there's a gym, a sauna, a small library, a theater room, and a game room. Not to mention the loft upstairs that's an indoor/outdoor haven. I couldn't ask to be in a more beautiful environment if I have to be stuck somewhere for an extended period, but I'm beyond pissed that I'm here. And I'm furious that Asher made that decision for me without my consent. If I didn't love him, I'd want to strangle him.

Even loving him, I still kind of do.

After my tour, my body is heavy and tired again, still working through the drugs in my system. I'm just about to go lie down when Jenkins' phone rings.

"It's Asher," he says, passing me the phone.

I practically rip it out of his hands. "How dare you do this to me," I hiss as soon as I bring the phone to my ear. It seems the dinner, a house tour, and the three hours it's been since I woke have done nothing to quell my rage.

"I'm sorry, Ella. It was necessary."

"Says who?" I huff, walking up the stairs to my bedroom for privacy.

"Says me."

"You don't get to make these kinds of decisions for me, Asher! That is not how relationships work!"

"I told you I would do anything to keep you safe. I meant it."

"Drugging me and shipping me across the goddamn globe like a human package is a little over the line, don't you think?"

"You weren't shipped. You flew on a private plane. With two bodyguards. And a flight attendant that doubled as a nurse."

If I weren't so mad, I would smirk at his sarcasm. Under normal circumstances I would give him those concessions. Under normal circumstances I don't overly mind his possessive ways. But this time, he went too far.

"You arrogant asshole. Like any of that justifies your actions."

"When it comes to keeping you safe, nothing is over the line."

"Yes, Asher. Some things are over the line. This was over the line!"

"I'd do it again if it means keeping you safe."

"You would push me out of the way, out of your life, to keep me safe."

Asher pauses so long I'm not sure if he's still on the line. "Possibly, yes."

"What do you mean possibly? You already did. At least for the time being, I was told."

Asher is silent again.

My heart stammers in my chest. "Unless you mean push me *fully* out of your life."

"I . . ."

"Oh my god."

The silence between us is deafening, and my head swims as the reality of what he is and isn't saying sinks in.

"I'm so stupid," I whisper.

"No, Ella . . . I wouldn't."

"Yes, you would. You've been honest all along, Asher, I was just too caught up in you to listen. The situation with Sergei and Yegor is exactly the thing you're terrified of, and it's happened. You'd rather push me away than live with the fear of what might happen to me, and you're not entirely sure you wouldn't push me away permanently if you thought it was safer for me."

He takes a long time to answer. "I don't want to push you away."

"And yet you did."

"Just until I have things handled."

"So you say. But what happens when the next thing comes along? You'll do this again until the next thing is handled."

"It's my responsibility to keep you safe. I dragged you into all of this."

"And in the future? What if we have those kids you asked me about? Are you going to drug them and ship them to *somewhere in South America*, too?"

"Ella . . . I . . ."

"You can't even give me a straight answer!"

"I don't know what you want me to say."

"I want you to say that you understand that you went too far and that this will never happen again."

"Everything I did, I did to keep you safe."

"Your fear is ruling you, Asher! I told you I understood the risk of getting involved with you. At first, I thought it was just the paparazzi, but as time has gone on, I obviously know it's more than that. You're a powerful man, and that brings along powerful enemies. But I made peace with that. I accepted that. I agreed to go along with your security to stay safe because I understood that it is not an idle threat. I've tried to go along with all the things you needed.

"I've made some mistakes along the way, but for the most part, I have done everything you've asked. I flipped my life upside down to be with you. I gave in to your demands and compromised for you, but you refuse to do that with me. As soon as the threats got real, you shipped me off without my consent. That isn't balance. That isn't how healthy relationships work."

Asher starts to cut in, but I practically snarl at him. "I'm not done! I can handle your possessiveness and your aggressive tactics because so far, you've done them while also treating me with dignity and respect. But this . . . this isn't respect. And now you're all but admitting that one day you might get pushed to the point that you remove me from your life completely because you think it's what's best for me. You don't get to make those kinds of decisions on my behalf!

"I don't care about your rule over trivial things like the clothes or the security officers or working on the executive floor. I can be flexible. I'm secure enough as a person to not be too bothered by a lot of your behaviors, especially since I understand where they come from. But this? I don't know how to move forward knowing that you might pull the rug out from under me one day because your fear overrides your judgment. I don't want to sit around waiting for you to decide it's too dangerous and end things forever. That's not love, Asher. And that's not a life I can accept."

"What are you saying?"

"I'm asking you to promise me that you'll never do something like this again. And I'm asking you to promise that you won't break up with me because you think that's what's best for me or for my safety. If you fall out of love with me, that's one thing. I would be heartbroken, but at least I can understand something like that. But pushing me away because you're afraid for my safety? I can't tolerate that one. Promise me both of those things, and I can promise to work on forgiving you."

Another loaded silence. "I can't promise that."

Tears that have been pooling in my eyes spill down my cheeks. My stomach hollows as if it's been run through with a blade.

"Then I can't be with you," I whisper. I almost don't believe the words as they leave my mouth. But I can't take them back. Not if he can't meet me on this.

"Don't do this, Ella," he pleads.

"Then *promise me*."

"I *can't*." His voice breaks on the last word.

My pulse pounds in my ears as disbelief courses through me. It's all I can do to make my voice speak. "Then that's all I needed to hear. I love you, Asher. I've never loved anyone like I love you, and I know I never will again. But I can't be with you if I can't have those guarantees."

"Please, Ella."

"I'm sorry."

The phone slips through my fingers, clattering on the wood floor, and I follow suit, crumpling next to it. This isn't the way it was supposed to be. This can't be real. But it is, and that realization almost shreds me from the inside out.

A wave of dizziness hits me as my breaths come in gasping, choked pants, and a sob rips from my chest as my heart shatters into a million pieces.

39

ASHER

I flick the lighter and give it a toss. The puddle of gas beneath the front door of the mansion bursts into flames. Seconds later, a plume of fire engulfs the entirety of the lavish porch, and I watch with hollow satisfaction as the flames grow, trailing their way up and inside the house. Consuming, raging. Much like the fury that now seems to permanently reside in my soul.

The fire and destruction before me only partially assuage it.

Maybe I might feel more satisfied if Henry and Charlotte were here so I could see not only the looks on their faces as their house goes up in flames, but their reactions to the fact that before I sparked those flames, I sent my men inside their house to loot and raid it like common thieves. They removed everything of worth, and it's all been donated or sold off. An almost smile tugs at my mouth as I think of the profits I'll make from his valuables and how I'm going to give them to the "poors" Henry so despises.

Not that he'll ever know.

Henry realized I knew he was Sergei's main accomplice within Langford Holdings and that he had been betraying my family for decades. Alan was just Henry's little bitch boy. He hadn't known half of what Henry was up to; he'd just followed orders like a good little foot soldier. Once Henry realized that I was onto him, he took Charlotte and ran to Europe.

But he didn't get far.

I got the call an hour ago.

He and Charlotte were picked up by my men in Portugal. Henry tried to run and was killed in the process. Charlotte is currently pissing herself as she's being flown back here. I don't have anything on her legally, and I haven't ordered her death, even though I should. Not only did she use me for information to put me in jeopardy with my own board, but she knew about the car chase that took place almost six weeks ago. The night of the charity event, she didn't come to speak to me out of a sense of nostalgia. She was tailing me and heard me tell Robert that we were leaving early. She only approached me to delay me so the cars could get into position. It's not sentimentality or kindness that keeps me from killing her, I simply think that what awaits will be far worse for her in the end.

The life insurance she should have received at Henry's death has been collected and distributed to his and Charlotte's least favored charitable causes. Homelessness and drug addiction centers. I also convinced the insurance company to drop the homeowner's insurance on the house that's burning in front of my eyes.

She has nothing left—and she won't be able to get even a shred of it back. I've blacklisted her from ever working in the state of New York or with any company that wants to remain in my favor. And since there are so few companies that I don't have the potential to use my influence over, she'll never work for anything more than a small business again. There will be no more high society lifestyle for her. I've stripped her of every dime, every connection, and destroyed her home. I can't decide if she or Henry is the lucky one in this scenario.

No matter. They've both gotten what they deserve, along with Janet and Senator Sanders. Janet was not directly involved with Henry, but with everything that happened, I convinced the rest of the board to vote her out, so she's now one less thorn in my side. Unfortunately, I could never prove that Conrad worked with her, so he and his idiot son are still kicking around Langford Holdings.

The good senator was arrested a week ago on multiple counts of fraud, espionage, and so many other charges that I can't keep track of them. He certainly got around. But fortunately, or unfortunately, someone in his circle decided he was better silenced than dragged through court, potentially outing accomplices, and he was murdered in his prison cell. His funeral is in two days.

"We're almost done," Declan says, stepping up behind me. He's been instrumental in all this. I couldn't have accomplished everything I did these last weeks without him and without Sterling working his hacking skills from London. "TDC Oil is all but finished. I just got a notification that their COO is considering our offer."

I nod. "Good."

It's a shame that several of TDC's oil sights and refineries have had such tragic accidents one after another of late. It's also a shame that the FBI is investigating them for their involvement with the Russian mafia. Langford Holdings is now in negotiation to buy TDC Oil since its stock prices are at an all-time low, and funny enough, the sabotage to their refineries and oil sights won't stop until we own them.

Irony is a real bitch.

"Any word on Yegor?" I ask.

"Nothing yet. He's still a slippery bastard, and the Russian government is protecting him."

"Sergei?"

"Rumor has it that he's getting ready to jump ship. He's

spooked by the death of his friend Senator Sanders. His wife is already in the Caribbean, and Katrina is set to meet her there soon."

"They can stay there, but I want Sergei dead."

"We'll make it happen."

"I want it done as quickly as possible. Grandfather's memorial is in a week. I'd like to bring everyone responsible for his death to justice by then."

"And when it's all over?" Declan asks, clapping his hand on my shoulder. "What then?"

I turn away from the inferno and head for my car. "Then it's done, and I can move on."

"And does moving on involve Ella?"

I stop at my car, my hand frozen on the handle. These past weeks have been hell. I can hardly sleep, hardly eat since Ella ended things. *Again.* The only thing that has given me any reprieve from my hell has been finally making headway in taking down my enemies. I just wish I could have realized Henry's involvement without the car accident. That night may have spurred my memories, but it also showed me that no matter how much I plan, I will always be vulnerable. Ella will always be vulnerable. The sight of her passed out and bleeding from her head still haunts me. It's why I can't give in to her demands. I want to. But . . . I just can't. I can't promise her that if her life is in danger that I won't do questionable things to protect her.

"We both want things neither of us can give." I hate the words as they leave my lips. I don't want them to be real. But unfortunately, they are.

"Come on, man. Don't do this."

"Do what?"

"Punish yourself. Punish her. Your stubbornness is what makes you so goddamn successful, but sometimes it's your downfall, Asher. Don't give up on the best thing that ever happened to you. I've never seen you as happy as you were with Ella. And you've been a miserable fuck ever since things ended. You don't want to spend the rest of your life like this. And no one else wants you to, either. You're a nightmare to be around."

I clench my jaw. "Thanks."

"Just giving my loving, brotherly opinion."

Declan reaches inside his jacket and pulls out a glossy magazine, then holds it out toward me.

I take it from him. "What's this?"

"Just look at it."

My chest pinches as I look at the cover. It's Ella. Her fall line shoot. She's so fucking beautiful it takes my breath away. But it's not just her beauty that does me in. It's the happy, mischievous glint in her eye that does it. Even posed for a cover shoot, Ella's soul shines through. Her goodness. Her optimism. Her carefree spirit. It's so apparent, even in a photo.

She's my opposite in so many ways, and I didn't realize until now how good that was for me. My rigid, domineering nature was balanced by her easy-going joyfulness. And her spice—I loved watching her sassy, take no shit side come out and own my ass when she needed to. I miss it. I miss her. It's fucking killing me to be separated from her.

"Tell me you don't want her back," Declan says, his voice uncharacteristically soft.

"Of course I want her back."

"Then when this is all over, you need to fight for her. Give her what she wants. What she's asking for is not even unreasonable, you dumb fuck." And there's the normal Declan back.

"I want to, but you know I can't promise that I won't do something like this in the future if it's necessary. And without that promise, I don't know if she'll have me."

"Then convince her. She's in love with you. If you can pull your head out of your ass, you can get her back."

"I'll try."

Declan is halfway in his car but pauses to look at me. "And Asher? Go to therapy. I know this whole situation has brought up a lot of shit for you, but you need to get past it. Don't hold your life hostage because of Grandpa's death. He wouldn't want that."

His words pierce my chest. I stand frozen and can only watch as he shuts his door and starts his car. I'm still rooted to the spot as he drives off. I don't look to Declan for wisdom often, but I can't deny the truth in his words.

Grandpa wouldn't want this.

He would be disappointed if he knew I was wasting my life because of my fears. His death was tragic, but it shouldn't be the thing that keeps me from happiness. When I think of Ella's absence and the hole in my life it's caused, I think *maybe* I finally understand that. But can I move beyond it? Can I breathe freely, knowing Ella will always be at risk? I don't know. I want to. But I'm still not sure if I can.

Maybe I am just a dumb fuck.

40

ELLA

W hy so many socialites aspire to this lifestyle, I'll never know. Don't get me wrong, swimming and sitting by the pool most of the day and doing yoga on the balcony surrounded by tropical plants as the sun rises is a dream. But after doing it for six weeks straight? I'm bored as hell and going crazy.

Well, not a full six weeks. I spent a week in bed after I ended things with Asher. I cried and cried until I was sick. Until my eyes and nose were so red and raw that I could hardly touch them. Five weeks later, I'm still a mess. I still cry over everything and nothing, but it's hard to get past it when I'm stuck in this limbo. No amount of negotiating has convinced Flores and Jenkins to let me go. I've insisted time and again that since I'm no longer with Asher that I shouldn't be kept here against my will. They've insisted that their orders are to bring me back to New York only when Asher gives the word that it's safe.

So, I've been here for six weeks, slowly going crazy. It doesn't help that I've been cut off from the world. There is no phone or internet. There's only a TV, and it's not hooked up to any internet, streaming services, or even cable. All I can watch are the blue-ray disks in the house. If not for the books, I'd have gone batshit by now.

My days consist mostly of stupid amounts of yoga and Pilates, self-defense training, reading, sitting by the pool, and watching whatever movie I can stomach each night. I do take a few short strolls around the property with Flores or Jenkins, and that helps suppress the cabin fever a bit, but it only does so much. I'm still in a prison. It's a luxurious, tropical paradise, but it's still a form of prison.

My other saving grace is that Flores and Jenkins feed me updates on what's going on back home any time they get an update from Asher. I'll give Asher one thing: he's definitely following through on all his threats. To a scary degree.

Almost everything Asher wanted to accomplish is done. Jenkins let me know that Sergei's untimely demise happened yesterday, so the only thing we're waiting on is for Yegor to be brought to justice. And then I can get the hell out of here and go home. But as I think about it, my heart sinks, and for the thousandth time, I cry. Because . . . *where is home now?* I went from Kyle's apartment to Asher's, and now that things have ended, I'll have to find my own place.

All the dreams I had begun to let myself have deflate in a puddle of fresh tears. The night of the car chase, Asher had asked me if I wanted to have kids with him. I'd meant it when I'd said yes. Then we had ended up at his estate on Long Island, and even though we had been in danger and there was so much going on, and even though the house is ridiculously big, I couldn't help but picture it —a life there with Asher. A wedding on the vast grounds. Children eating at the table in the sun-filled dining room and hiding in all the nooks and corners, causing chaos in the pristine manor. I couldn't help but picture it and want it.

I still want it.

But how can I trust it? How can I trust that Asher won't do this to me again someday? Is that a risk I'm willing to take?

I don't know.

But being away from him feels like torture. And I don't know if I can take a lifetime of this. I'm still so mad at him, but I can't stop loving and wanting him despite it. When this is all over and I'm back in New York, I don't know if I'll be able to stay away from him. I don't know if I can just let those visions, those dreams of our future, go. But I also can't trust him.

It's all a mess.

"Emily just emailed me," Flores says, sitting down on the pool chair next to me. "The breakup will be formally announced a week after Edward Langford's memorial, which is in three days. They don't want the news to overshadow the event."

I swipe away my tears and nod.

Clearly Asher doesn't feel the same as I do. If he's ready to release a PR statement, it seems he's okay with our breakup and is ready to move forward with his life. Without me.

"Can I go home then?"

Flores winces. "No. Mr. Langford thinks it would be best for you to be out of the media spotlight when the news hits. For your safety and privacy. Plus, Yegor is still proving to be difficult to get a lock on. You're not leaving until that changes."

"If Asher doesn't want to be with me, why does he care?" I hiss, wiping snot from my nose.

God, will I ever be done crying?

"If you think Mr. Langford doesn't want to be with you, you're a fool. You're the one who broke up with him, remember?"

I shoot her a glare. "He drugged me, had me brought here, and is keeping me here against my will."

"To keep you safe."

"I'm a prisoner. Yes, I know, it's a luxurious prison," I say for the millionth time, rolling my tear-filled eyes, "but it's all been done without my input or consent. Why does no one seem to understand how violating that is?"

Flores gives me a pitying look. "I get it. He did a shitty thing. He shouldn't have drugged you, and he should have talked to you about his plans. But you also wouldn't have agreed to come, so in some ways, you forced his hand. Even now, you still aren't willing to see how dangerous Yegor is. He's one of the heads of the Russian mafia for Christ's sake. He's a very dangerous man, and if he got a hold of you, you don't want to even *imagine* what he'd do to you.

"So, if you can't understand why that might make Mr. Langford a little paranoid, a little overreactive, then you're not helping matters. Your life is in *very real danger*, Ms. Hale. Especially now that Mr. Langford has thrown down the gauntlet. He's destroyed everyone but Yegor, and Yegor is aware of that and won't go down without a fight. The last thing any of us want is to hear that he's taken you hostage. Death may very well be a mercy in that scenario. So, get over your tantrum, enjoy your tropical paradise, and stop calling it a prison. It's for your protection."

She stands and leaves without another word.

JENKINS BEAR hugs me from behind and roughly hauls me into his chest.

"What are your options to break my hold?" he asks, his arms gripping me so tightly they might leave bruises.

The warm, humid air coats my skin, making it slick with sweat as we work through our self-defense session on the grass behind the house.

"I could head-butt you if I have the angle to hit your nose."

"Only do that if it's your last resort, don't forget that a head-butt, even using the back of your head, could hurt you. What are other vulnerable parts of my body you could reach without hurting yourself?"

"Your instep." I lift my foot and pretend to stomp down on Jenkins's right foot.

"Good. What else?"

"I could use my elbow." I twist and shift my weight and pretend to elbow him in the stomach.

We go through the motions again and again until we're both dripping with sweat and out of breath. When Jenkins is satisfied with my progress, we end our session and head into the blessedly air-conditioned house.

As I shake out my exhausted limbs, I bitterly wonder why I'm even continuing with the sessions since I can't help but think that my need for self-defense is about to become obsolete. No one cared who I was before I dated Asher, and I presume that after some time, people will forget about me. It's not that I care about the notoriety, it's that I still can't believe that our relationship is over.

"The breakup will be formally announced a week after Edward Langford's memorial."

Flores's statement, no matter how gently she delivered it, still rakes across my mind like jagged glass. I know I asked for this, I know I ended things, but that doesn't mean it's not killing me inside.

I wonder again what my life will look like once this is all over. Where will I live? Where will I work? Will Lennox Rose still want me as a brand ambassador? There are a million unknowns, a million unanswered questions, and the thought of facing them fills me with dread.

The only thing I'm sure of is the fact that I'll stay safely hidden away until the fallout over the breakup is over. Because I have no choice. Fucking overprotective Asher.

I'm also dreading the moment I re-enter society. According

to Flores, Emily is already barely keeping her head above water with the rumors and questions about my current absence, and that's without a breakup. A very public breakup where one member of the relationship is hidden out of sight. People will only buy the "she's on a much-needed vacation" excuse for so long before it becomes suspicious, and a suspicious public does not make for a quiet life—PR wise.

But most of all, I'm dreading a life without Asher.

"Hey," Flores says, sitting down on the couch next to me that night after dinner.

I pause my movie that I'm not really paying attention to. "Hey."

"I was probably a little harsh with you yesterday, but I wasn't wrong."

I raise my brow. *Where is she going with this?*

"I have the intel Sterling gave Asher on Volkov regarding his past crimes and victims. I think it's high time it was shared with you. But be warned, what I'm about to show you is graphic, so if it's too much, just tell me. I'd rather you not lose your dinner."

What the hell?

She pulls out a tablet and holds it between us.

"These are the crimes we know are connected to Volkov. He's never pictured, he's very good at staying hidden, but that doesn't mean the blood you're about to see is not on his hands. He either performed these acts himself or they were performed by his men on his orders."

She swipes her finger and pulls up an image.

A shock pierces through me, and my breath catches in my chest.

The image is of a man lying in a pool of blood. His open eyes stare blankly into space. But it's not the death you can see in his eyes, or the blood, that has me reeling. It's the mutilation of his body. His body was carved and sliced and broken a hundred different ways, presumably before he died.

I swallow hard.

Flores swipes again.

Another image, this time of a much-younger man. A late-aged teenager, probably. Shot through the head and chest at least dozen times.

Another image. Several men dead on a warehouse floor, shell casings surround their bodies, littering the ground like confetti, shimmering among a sea of red.

Another image. More blood.

Another image. More death.

Another image. More carnage.

Swipe after swipe of heinous, graphic, violence, all at the hands of Yegor Volkov.

Another image.

This time of a woman. She's beautiful, with long golden hair and big blue eyes. Her naked body is covered in blood, mutilated, almost beyond recognition in some places.

"That was the wife of a man who betrayed Volkov," Flores murmurs. "She was . . . raped by six men before they ended her. He ordered the same thing to be done to the man's daughter." She pauses and takes a long breath. "The girl was barely sixteen."

Tears spring to my eyes as bile creeps up my throat.

I race to the bathroom and hurl up my dinner, just like Flores predicted I might.

A moment later, Flores is there, holding my hair and running a soothing hand down my spine. When there's nothing left inside me, I flush the toilet and slump down next to it.

"There are at least twenty more pictures I could show you," Flores says, sliding down the wall to sit next to me.

I turn my head and look at her. Her brown eyes are sad but

fervent. "I agree with you that Mr. Langford went about this the wrong way. But as we discussed yesterday, you wouldn't have left willingly. You know you would have put up a fight. I want you to ask yourself, if you were him and you saw those pictures, what would you do? Yegor and Sergei made it clear they would come for you to hurt Mr. Langford. If you knew someone was capable of what you saw in those pictures, would you take that risk? Or would you do everything in your power to keep the person you love safe from that kind of fate?

"You don't know the conversations we have had as a security team. You haven't seen the absolute terror on Mr. Langford's face when we discussed all the things Volkov is capable of. He has looked at every one of those pictures and imagined what it would be like if *you* were the victim of those heinous acts. I know this situation is hard and confusing, and yes, I agree with you that it is violating. But Volkov would do a *hell* of a lot more than violate you. The reason Jenkins and I went along with this plan is because we care about you, and we agree with Mr. Langford that this is the only way we can guarantee your safety.

"Mr. Langford is not a regular man, and his enemies are not regular men. These threats against you are the worst of the worst. Whether you believe or not, whether you agree with it or not—it doesn't change that reality. You are in danger. Full stop. If Volkov gets a hold of you, you may end up as one of those pictures. Do you really want to live through the pain, the terror, and the trauma he would inflict on you before he killed you? Think about it, Ella. Think about what it would be like to live through that. You'd be *begging* for death. Mr. Langford and the rest of us are doing everything we can to prevent that."

She stands and exits the bathroom, leaving me alone with my shocked and splintered thoughts.

41

ELLA

The weight of the mattress shifts beneath me. A body presses against mine. Fingertips skim down my cheekbone. My mind whirrs with worry before a sense of calm settles over me.

"I've missed you," Asher whispers against my skin where a sliver of it peeks out between my silk pajama top and shorts. His lips trace their way up my stomach as he pushes my top up with his rough, calloused hands. My eyes flutter open as the night air brushes across my exposed breasts.

"What are you doing here?" I gasp, taking in Asher's beautiful, shadowed face.

"I had to see you."

I hiss as his tongue traces my hardened nipple, and then I groan when he takes it in his mouth.

"Asher," I whimper, threading my hands through his hair. I can't believe he's here. His touch, his scent, his voice, the press of his large body against mine brings a sense of giddy relief. "I missed you, too," I confess. "Nothing feels right without you."

"I need you," he growls, tearing my shirt over my head then

stripping my shorts and underwear off in one desperate yank. Before I can respond, his tongue traces my center, and my hips buck off the bed. Sparks of pleasure burst through me at the feel of his mouth on me, of the scratch of his five-o'clock shadow grazing the sensitive skin of my inner thighs.

"*Fuck,* I missed the taste of this pussy."

He eats me like a starved man, then slides one, then two fingers inside me as he sucks on my clit.

"Yes, oh god," I moan, reveling in the feel of him.

I wrap my legs around his back as he pumps his fingers in and out of me, hitting that perfect spot. Tingles race down my spine as Asher, who knows every inch, every secret of my body, works it as if he's worshipping it. A second later I cry out as a flood of pleasure, relief, and unadulterated happiness surges through me.

"That's right, come for me, baby."

My orgasm has barely subsided when Asher lines up his cock to my entrance and shoves it inside me in a single thrust.

"*Ella,*" he hisses. "*Fuck, fuck, fuck.*" He grits his teeth as we both adjust to our connection, then he starts moving, thrusting in and out of me harder than he ever has before. It's both pleasure and pain, and so all-consuming that I can't even think. I can only feel.

Our lips collide and I can taste myself on his tongue. He kisses me like he fucks me, like a crazed, starved man barely hanging onto his sanity.

I meet his hips thrust for thrust and our hands and arms are a frenzied mess of bruising touches as we frantically cling to one another.

"I missed you," he rasps against my mouth. "I love you. Never leave me again."

"I didn't leave you." I pull my mouth away and kiss my way up the side of his throat. "You sent me away."

"I had to keep you safe."

"I'm safe."

He pulls back, his eyes meeting mine in the dark. "I had to keep you safe."

I reach up to grasp his cheek with my hand, but he tenses, his whole body turning rigid. He climbs off me, then off the bed and out of sight.

"Asher?" I call out, sitting up. I scramble off the bed behind him, but I can't see anything in the dark.

Where did he go?

"Asher?" I yell again as I step out onto the indoor/outdoor loft.

A light breeze rustles the leaves of the trees and the sound of insects chirping and buzzing fills the air.

"Asher, where are you?"

I make my way toward the stairs, but trip over something in the middle of the floor. I right myself and look down. As I do, a scream tears from my throat.

It's the woman. The one from the image Flores showed me. She lies sprawled and naked on my balcony. Her dead eyes are somehow still filled with fear and pain. Her mouth is pulled open, as if stuck in a gasp. Her beautiful skin is marred and mangled. Her blood puddles, flowing away from her. It spills down the stairs with a steady *drip, drip, drip.*

"No," I wheeze. "No!"

"I have to keep you safe!" Asher's voice booms from everywhere and nowhere, all at once.

I jerk awake with another scream.

I pant and sob and my hands shake as they swipe away the tears trailing down my cheeks.

It's not real. It's not real. It's not real.

She's not here.

But neither is Asher.

My heart plummets in my chest. I thought it was real. I

thought he was here, and everything inside me felt whole again. The echoes of his voice, of his touches, whisper across my skin and my mind—the bliss of it is almost euphoric.

Then the pain at the loss of him carves into me like the edge of a blade.

"Asher," I whimper, my voice quivering.

How can the pain of losing dream Asher feel as devastating as when I lost the real one weeks ago?

I don't know, and yet, it does.

I run my hands through my hair. I hug my knees to my chest. I can't get that dream out of my head. It felt so real—until it turned into a nightmare.

The vision of the dead woman flashes across my mind.

I take a deep, steadying breath, but it does nothing to calm my racing heart. A cacophony of thoughts slam into me, confusing the hell out of me. I miss Asher. I want Asher. I'm mad at Asher. I'm terrified of his enemies and what they're capable of.

The image of the woman is all I see when I blink.

I climb off the bed and open a window, one on the opposite side of the room as the indoor/outdoor balcony. I take in a long, shuddering breath, and force my thundering heartbeat to quiet as I listen to the soft calls of birds and the hum of insects. This place is beautiful. This place is safe.

And now I understand, at least to a degree, why Asher did what he did.

Part of me is still furious. He let his fear rule him, and he made an insane choice to drug me and haul me across the globe without my consent. The anger I feel from that is valid . . . but if Asher was under that same threat, if my choices became keeping him safe and keeping him from being one of Volkov's victims—I would hide him away, too. I would do questionable things to keep him safe. I know I would. I can't lie to myself and say that I wouldn't.

Because nothing matters more to me than his life.

And I know he feels the same about me.

"You okay?" Flores asks me over a late breakfast the next morning. Her eyes are slightly concerned as they take in my appearance.

I'm sure I look like shit.

"Had trouble sleeping."

She nods in acknowledgment and nothing more needs to be said. She hasn't been with me for as long as Jenkins has, but in the time we've had together, she's become good at reading my moods and tells—and I'm sure she's filled in the blank as to why I had a shit night of sleep last night.

"I've just had a message come through," Jenkins says, coming into the kitchen. "I missed the call, but I got a voicemail from Mr. Langford. He wants you at the memorial for his grandfather tomorrow."

The fork freezes mid-air toward my mouth. "He does?"

"He said the press is hounding him about your absence, and his family thinks it will be in their best interest to have you there. Your absence will cause such a media circus they're afraid it will distract from the event."

"And after the memorial? Am I to come back here? Or will I stay in New York?"

"The message didn't say anything about that. You'll probably have to take that up with Mr. Langford after the event."

Hope blooms inside me. No matter my confused feelings about Asher, one thing is undeniable, and that's how much I miss him. I want to see him. And I want him to hold me and tell me everything is going to be okay.

After hours of restless thoughts last night, something inside me shifted. Even though I'm still hurt by the situation, I can't help but want Asher. And I want to know if the visions of our future that I pictured are still possible—because despite everything, I want them to be.

"The Langford jet isn't able to come get us because it's en route with Sterling from London," Jenkins goes on, "but Mr. Langford sent another jet. I've done the calculations, and we need to leave within the next two hours to make it to the airport in time. The jet is set to take off in fifteen hours, since we have such a long travel time to get to the airport, which means, by the time we take off and fly to New York, we'll be arriving just in time for the memorial. So, Ella, you're going to need to pack whatever clothes and makeup and hair stuff you need to be photo ready the minute we land. We'll go straight from the airport to the memorial."

"Got it."

I breathe a sigh of relief at the fact that the house came stocked with an entire wardrobe, not that I've worn a fraction of it. How, when, and why Asher had it filled with not only casual clothes (the only things I've worn since I've been here) but with work-appropriate attire and formal clothes including gowns and dresses, I don't know—but right now I'm glad for the fact that he's always thorough with details in everything he does. I think there's a black dress that will work perfectly, and I cross my fingers that it fits.

"And, Ms. Hale, as we travel, we're trusting that you don't divulge where you've been to anyone."

"How would I do that? I don't even know where I'm at."

"I'm sure you'll pick up some clues along the way, even if you don't know any definitive locations."

I snort. "My sense of direction is as hopeless as my cooking. I'd get lost with GPS *and* a map; you don't need to worry about me giving up your secrets."

"Be that as it may, remember, the official story is that you've been on a much-needed vacation, and you can leave it at that."

"Understood. I'll go get ready and pack."

The hope inside me grows until it's a dizzying level of excitement. After six long, emotionally draining weeks, I finally get to be back with Asher. I ache to see him, to touch him. My world is just not right when he's not in it, and the thought of this torture coming to an end is the sweetest kind of relief.

I just hope it's the kind of relief that lasts.

42

ELLA

"We're nearly there," the driver says from the front of the car, and my anxiety is barely appeased. I'm exhausted from nearly twenty hours of travel. We're running late with a small flight delay, traffic has been terrible, and the memorial is about to start.

Everything about our travel has been more difficult than usual. We had a different jet and flight crew, and we have a different driver with us today since all of Asher's staff is at the memorial. It's all been made worse by the fact that both Jenkins's and Flores's phones have had terrible, basically non-existent service, so we haven't been able to get any updates or information about the memorial. All I know is that the memorial celebration is inside the venue, and then there's an outside procession leading to a statue of Edward that will be revealed. At least that was the itinerary the last time I checked in on the plans for the event, which was over two months ago.

Needless to say, we've been scrambling since we got Asher's orders, and we aren't running like the well-oiled machine we usually are.

It's stressing me the hell out.

I'm already in knots over seeing Asher. What will I say? What will he say? Will we be able to talk after the memorial and figure things out? All these thoughts are overwhelming enough, and running late is only making it worse.

Finally, we pull up to the venue and hurry out of the car. Jenkins and Flores stay practically pinned to my side as we walk inside. A sign in the entrance announces the tribute of Edward Alexander Xavier Langford and designates the way to the ballroom, but before we follow the directions, Flores breaks away.

"I'm going to see if I can find Waters and get a rundown of the plans for the procession," she says. "I don't like the idea of walking in that crowd without knowing what the plan is first."

Waters usually patrols outside main event spaces, so he's typically the easiest security officer to find.

Jenkins nods. "See if he has some extra comms while you're at it. I'll be near Ms. Hale's table."

Both Jenkins and Flores are uneasy since they don't have their usual equipment, and I know they'll both breathe a sigh of relief when they're back up and running like normal.

"You got it."

Jenkins and I turn from her and hurry down a long hallway, but just before we enter the ballroom, a burly security officer stops us.

"You'll both need to step in here for a briefing," he says in a brusque tone.

"What briefing?" Jenkins asks. "I wasn't told of any briefings."

"We've had some last-minute changes this morning."

"Remind me of your name," Jenkins says, eyeing the man as we follow him into a small room just off the ballroom.

"Can we hurry with this?" I snap. "I can hear the event starting. I don't want to stroll in late and disrupt it."

"Taylor," the security officer says, answering Jenkins. "Mr. Langford hired extra security for the event."

"What's the new briefing then, Taylor?" Jenkins asks in a clipped tone.

"Nothing."

Taylor raises a gun with a suppressor on the end of it and shoots Jenkins between the eyes before Jenkins can respond.

I scream as Jenkins's body hits the floor.

"Scream again, and I'll put the next bullet through you," Taylor, if that's really his name, says, rushing for me and shoving his gun into my side. "You do as I say and keep quiet, or you'll regret it."

My chest seizes and I can't draw a full breath. Stars swim across my vision and I furiously try to blink them away. I stand frozen, disbelief swirling inside me as my eyes dart from Jenkins's lifeless body to the man holding a gun to my side.

This can't be happening.

This isn't real.

That isn't Jenkins on the ground.

Taylor pulls a cloth out of his pocket, and I flinch as he swipes it over the side of my face.

To wipe off the blood, I realize.

Jenkins's blood.

Some survival instinct buried in the back of my mind reminds me that I need to calm down. I blink and take a long breath, choking back the scream of terror that wants nothing more than to erupt from me. I force down the panic roaring inside me just enough to function. I push all thoughts of Jenkins aside. I can't think about him, not yet. If I do, I'll break, and I can't afford to do that with the hulking man gripping my arm and holding a gun to me.

Taylor yanks me to him and traps me against his chest. Again, panic threatens to overwhelm me, but Water's voice echoes in the back of my mind about what to do if I'm held in this exact position. I stomp down Taylor's foot with my heel, and when he flinches, I manage to break his grip. I whirl out of his grasp and race for the door, but as soon as I'm out of the room a man holding tight to Flores blocks my escape. Taylor is behind me a second later, his gun presses to my side again, just like the man before me has a gun jutting into Flores's ribs.

She's not dead, I think with relief. But she's not safe, either.

"Follow me, or she'll be lying next to your other security guard," Taylor growls, his disgusting breath skittering across my cheek.

If you can't escape, comply with your attacker's demands until we can get to you.

It's the protocol Robert, Jenkins, Waters, and Flores all drilled into me.

With Flores's life on the line, it's my only option.

I don't fight as Taylor pulls me after him toward the ballroom. When we enter, he tucks me into his side as if he's simply helping me along—as if he doesn't have a gun shoved against my ribcage.

A round of applause begins for whatever speaker is taking the stage, but the eyes of every attendee turn toward Taylor and me as we cross the room. But it's not the eyes of the guests that has my stomach in knots, it's Asher's eyes when they meet mine.

They aren't happy or welcoming.

No, they're filled with shock and confusion. He subtly shakes his head, and it hits me.

I'm not meant to be here.

He isn't expecting me.

Whatever voicemail Jenkins got, it wasn't Asher that left it. It wasn't Asher who sent the jet to pick us up.

Fuck.

"Mr. Langford," Taylor says as we arrive at his table. "I have a delivery for you." Taylor pushes me into an empty seat next to

Asher; the place card says it's meant to be Asher's grandmother's seat.

Taylor stands between the two of us and leans down so that both Asher and I can hear him as he speaks.

"Yegor sends his regards. You shouldn't be surprised to know that the new security you hired for the event works for him. Since he hasn't been able to get you on speaking terms, he's brought those speaking terms to you. There are snipers stationed in this room and outside along the procession, and they are ordered to keep their rifles aimed at Ms. Hale. If you don't cooperate, if either of you breathe in a way Yegor disapproves of, Ms. Hale here will be taken care of swiftly."

Asher says nothing, but he nods curtly in understanding.

"Good. Enjoy the program. Yegor will speak to you at some point so that the two of you can come to an agreement. If you don't accept his terms, Ms. Hale will pay the price."

Taylor stalks off, and I reach for my watch and hit the panic button three times in quick succession. I don't know if it will help at this point, but I don't know what else to do.

With the eyes of the guests on us, Asher kisses me quickly on the cheek and turns his attention forward, pretending to pay attention to the Master of Ceremony who welcomes the guests.

"How did you get here?" he asks in a low voice, not looking at me.

"Jenkins said he got a voicemail from you ordering us here."

"I didn't call Jenkins, and I sure as hell didn't leave him a voicemail."

"I know that now. It was a different jet and crew that met us at the airport, but they seemed to follow all the typical protocol and said the Langford jet was flying Sterling, so we didn't think anything of it. He's . . . oh god, he's dead now. Jenkins." I swallow hard and take a breath to keep from hyperventilating. I can't keep from replaying the scene in my mind. Jenkins's look of annoyance that flashed into fear and surprise when he saw the gun. The bullet piercing his flesh. The blood. "That man, T-Taylor, killed him as soon as we got here. And another man has Flores. She's in danger."

"I'll let Robert know," he whispers back. "But our priority is figuring out what the hell is going on."

The audience claps, and it pulls me back to our surroundings. Asher and I clap as well, and I force a smile as I fight back tears and try to keep my panic at bay.

"What are we going to do, Asher?" I ask when the next speaker begins.

"I won't let anything happen to you."

"How many new security officers did you hire?"

"Fifty."

"How many of your regular men are here?"

"Twenty."

Shit.

Asher and I do our best to smile and fake it through the program. Neither of us touches our food or drink, and no matter how much I try, I can't stop my hands from shaking. It's clear from the rigid postures of Declan, Sterling, Harrington, and Catherine, that they know something is going on. I do my best to look like I'm paying attention, though, I only hear bits and pieces of what's said.

Edward seems to have been an incredible man; the man that changed the way the Langford family operates. The first man in over a century to admit that their family's wealth had been created by exploiting the poor and working class. He was the visionary who wanted to give back and right wrongs. I can't fully digest what's being said, not with the constant fear churning inside me. Not while knowing there are sniper rifles aimed at me, ready to fire on Yegor's command if I do something out of turn or if Asher doesn't comply.

The program passes in a blur, and soon we're outside in the procession. Asher grips my hand and holds me so close that there's hardly any space between us. We walk behind Harrington and Catherine, but Declan, Sterling, and all of Asher's extended family are cut off from us since the two of us have been surrounded by our security—five officers I've never seen before.

Asher's eyes scan the buildings, clearly looking for snipers, as we walk the two-block procession. The road has been closed, and there are hundreds of people walking behind the Langfords. Distributed among the crowd are more security officers I don't recognize. God, everyone here is in danger, and most of them have no idea.

We've barely begun to walk when a cold voice speaks from behind us, sending chills up my spine.

"You have been busy, Mr. Langford," the voice says. The voice is male, deep, and has a heavy Russian accent. "But our games are done, and your time is up."

43

ASHER

"Eyes forward, Ms. Hale," Volkov says. "Remember, there are television cameras pointed at you, watching your every move. And there are . . . other things pointed at you as well, so do behave."

Bastard. It takes every ounce of my self-control not to turn around and kill him. But I can't risk Ella.

Declan and Sterling are right outside our ring of fake security, and without looking, I know their gazes are turned on us. I know they've realized who is walking behind Ella and me. Who threatens us quietly, using the public nature of the memorial to keep us from reacting as his men keep guns trained on us. I shift my attention to Sterling out of the corner of my eye. He gives a subtle shake of his head. Dammit.

"I must confess, I am displeased by your actions toward TDC, Langford. My cousin Sergei and I worked tirelessly to build our oil empire."

"I am not the one who started this war, Volkov. You and Sergei did. I am merely intent on winning it."

Volkov laughs. "I like you, Langford. Your spirit and fire are commendable. It is a shame we are enemies. We could have been great allies. Alas, that can never be, not when we want such different things.

"I tried to get what I wanted without much bloodshed, but you decided to be difficult. At first, I thought about killing you to take a powerful enemy out of my way, but then I did a little research on you. If you die, it won't help my cause. Your shares in Langford Holdings will go to your brothers, who always agree with your desires, and now they'll also go to Ms. Hale, who would no doubt go along with whatever your brothers say. So, instead of killing you, I tried to speak to you in Singapore. But you got the upper hand. I'm here to rectify that and to help you understand that I intend to get what I want. I may not be able to kill you yet, but I can kill Ms. Hale. I have my terms for you, and if you do not agree and cooperate, I will signal for one of my men to put a bullet through your pretty girlfriend's head."

Ella flinches, and her hand trembles in mine. I give it a squeeze. Nothing and no one will hurt her. I won't fucking allow it.

"Here are my terms, Langford. First, you will call off your dogs and stop the destruction of our refineries and digging sights. Second, you will sign over fifty percent of your Langford Holdings shares to me. This will put you far below the mark of the highest shareholder in Langford Holdings and should help me recoup the losses you've caused. You will agree to sell Greenspan to me for pennies of what it's worth. And last, you will stop the clean energy legislation you're pushing."

Fury lights inside me, but I don't react.

"We have all the paperwork drawn up. I even have a notary and lawyer on standby. As soon as this little memorial service is over, you will sign, and then you and Ms. Hale can walk away intact."

The procession ends as we arrive at the statue of my grandfather, which is still covered by a large gray canvas cloth. Once the crowd is settled, my father and Uncle Conrad grab the cloth and pull it off, revealing the statue. More applause surrounds me. I remember to clap.

My father steps up to a podium on a small, erected stage to the side of the statue. I don't hear his speech. But my father's eyes meet mine several times, communicating to me that he sees Yegor behind me.

I continue to check in with Sterling.

Too soon, it's my turn. My speech. I try to pull Ella with me, but Volkov grabs onto her elbow.

"I don't think so, Langford. She will stay here where I can keep a close watch on her."

Again, I fight every instinct inside me and step away from her. Her life depends on me doing so. I climb the stage.

"How bad is it?" my father whispers as we give a quick hug while exchanging places.

"Bad. But as long as I cooperate, we should make it through."

I step to the podium, and it takes me a few seconds to compose myself. To the outside world, hopefully it looks like I'm simply overcome with emotion due to this being a celebration of my grandfather's legacy on the anniversary of his death. Under normal circumstances, it would be. But my mind hardly registers the words as I speak, addressing the crowd. All my thoughts are on keeping Ella safe.

Volkov watches me with satisfaction. He stands too close behind Ella, and she's ringed in by five fake security guards. All I can think about is how I'll kill Volkov for this. Slowly.

As I'm nearing the end of my speech, Sterling catches my eye, subtly nodding at me.

"Snipers down." Sterling's voice comes from my earpiece. Fucking finally.

"We're not here celebrating my grandfather because of his business pursuits and successes, but because of what he gave back to the world," I say, my voice gaining a little strength with the relief that the snipers have been taken care of. "We celebrate how his views changed the fabric of the Langford family, and what our legacy is to be. In observance of my grandfather's legacy, I am honored to announce that from this year forward, twenty-five percent of my annual income will be donated to organizations whose goals are to improve the lives of everyday Americans." The crowd erupts in shocked applause.

Volkov narrows his eyes, knowing full well that if I sign over fifty percent of my shares to him, there is no way I'd agree to also part with twenty-five percent of my income. He places a threatening hand on Ella's shoulder.

"I will work with charities who focus on fighting homelessness and food insecurity. Organizations who seek to improve impoverished neighborhoods and schools. And I will fight to find ways to incentivize the companies owned by Langford Holdings to pay their employees livable wages, provide more affordable healthcare, and more flexibility. My grandfather understood that our family's legacy was not simply built by our forebears, but by the everyday people who worked for them.

"I recognize their contribution today. I honor those who work for Langford Holdings and our subsidiaries, and I am committed to helping improve their lives. We all deserve to live in comfort and dignity. I hope to lead by example, proving to those in power that the world will function better, and our society as a whole will improve, if we can create better living conditions for everyone. The Langfords have always been trailblazers, and we don't intend to stop that anytime soon."

Applause erupts again, and I can see the shock on my uncle's face, as well as my cousins' and the faces of the remaining members of the board. But I'm not focused on them. I'm focused on Volkov, who is shifting, wavering. He doesn't want to order Ella's public death, not when he's standing behind her, knowing it would inevitably be caught on camera.

Little does he know that he can't order that hit anymore anyway, now that Sterling and Robert got the snipers taken care of.

Ella flinches, arching her back, and I can tell by how Volkov holds onto her that he has a gun pressed to her. He shakes his head at me as I end my speech and thank the audience.

I nod and give the signal.

The five security officers surrounding Ella turn. Yegor's eyes widen, and he brandishes his gun. Everything slows as I watch Declan dive in the circle of guards and grab Ella's arm, but as he pulls her away, a shot rings out.

My heart stops and panic seizes me as I watch Declan and Ella fall to the ground.

The crowd shouts. Everyone starts panicking and running.

The security officers descend on Volkov, and he's tackled to the ground.

Sterling reaches inside his suit jacket pocket and presses a button. Twenty men in security officer clothing start to convulse and collapse.

Another shot rings out.

I run off the stage and into the circle.

Declan lies atop Ella, and I roll him off her. Red blood pools across his white shirt.

"Declan!" Ella shouts, crawling toward him.

"I'm . . . okay," he rasps out. Ella untucks his shirt and lifts it. A gunshot wound gushes blood on the side of his abdomen. "At least, I hope so."

I crouch down beside him and haul Ella into my arms as a security officer hovers over Declan, putting pressure on the wound.

"Are you hurt?" I demand, scanning her from head to toe.

She shakes her head as tears freely flow down her cheeks. "I'm okay. But Declan . . . when he grabbed me, Yegor pulled the trigger. The bullet hit Declan instead of me."

"Shit, Dec," I fumble for words, taking in the blood covering his abdomen.

"Nice to know where I fall as far as your priorities go," he rasps out, somehow smirking at me through his pained grimace.

"Paramedics are already here," Sterling says, kneeling beside us. "I had them on standby."

My mother and father rush to us, and my mother cries out as she kneels next to Declan.

Police officers and paramedics descend on us. We stand and move out of the way as Declan is hauled onto a stretcher and wheeled over to an ambulance. I hold fast to Ella as the police move in to arrest Volkov, but that proves to be pointless. He lies with blank, open eyes, in a pool of blood, surrounded by security officers he thought worked for him.

"I don't understand," Ella says, her voice quivering. "I thought they were his. I thought he had tricked you and surrounded us with his men."

"He *thought* he had. And some of the men here were his, but Sterling took care of them." I nod to one of the security officers passed out on the ground. The ones who shook and convulsed just a moment ago.

"All of them need to be taken into custody," Sterling orders the police officers. "They all work for the Russian mafia."

The officers' eyes go wide, but they get to work locating the men in suits who lie unconscious, scattered throughout the street.

"What the hell happened?" Ella asks. Her entire body is shaking, and I know if I'm not careful, she might just pass out.

I pull her close, inhaling her scent and nearly crying from relief. That was close. Too fucking close.

"Let's get you home, baby. Then I'll explain everything."

44

ELLA

"Goddammit, Ella!" Lucy shrieks the moment we step foot in Asher's penthouse. "What are you doing in New York?"

She practically tackles me in a hug, sobbing.

"What are *you* doing here, Lucy? Would someone please tell me what the hell is happening?" I gasp while crying into Lucy's shoulder.

We move into Asher's living room as a group. I sit between Asher and Lucy, and Sterling sits on the ottoman, facing us. It's hard not to note Declan's absence, as well as Asher's parents, who are with him at the hospital.

"We knew about Volkov's plan," Sterling says, running his hand over his jaw, a trait very similar to his older brother's. "At least most of it, but he still surprised us in the end. And that surprise, god, that surprise could have cost us you."

Asher pulls me into his side and runs a comforting hand down my back.

"I intercepted Volkov's plans three weeks ago," Sterling explains, "and at first, we thought we'd try to intervene, but he had been so good at evading us, that we decided to let him enact his plan so that we could draw him out. Because we had that intel, I knew the general idea of what would happen today, and we had everything in place to keep Asher safe and to stop Yegor." Sterling sighs. "But he had two tricks up his sleeve that we didn't know about. The snipers and *you*. You weren't supposed to be here. You were supposed to stay at the safe house until this was all over and the fallout was taken care of."

"We were tricked," I say, leaning my head on Asher's shoulder. The shock and adrenaline are starting to wear off, and my body is a weak mess. "Jenkins got a voicemail from Asher telling him that he wanted me back in New York for the memorial. There was even a private jet that picked us up and flew us back."

"I never called Jenkins or left him a voicemail," Asher growls.

"I know that now. But I heard the voicemail, it was your voice. I don't know how, but it was."

"It must have been AI," Sterling hisses. "There are enough recordings of Asher's voice that Volkov could have had a voicemail created with it. Fuck, I should have been prepared for something like that."

"There's no way you could have predicted that, Sterling," I say. "The thought of the voicemail being fake didn't occur to any of us who heard it. Not until we got here and realized things were off."

"Regardless, that was a huge oversight on my part," he insists. "But as far as today goes, we were prepared for Yegor— until you showed up. We knew he had decided to use the public nature of the memorial to corner Asher by surrounding him with fake security, and we knew he also planned to take Asher and force him to sign the contract right after the statue unveiling and the speeches."

"But they didn't end up being Volkov's men," I point out. "I thought they were until they grabbed him at the end."

"They were mine," Lucy says, taking a hold of my hand. "I have to tell you something." She hesitates for a moment, shifting uncomfortably. "My family . . . I don't speak about them often because they're . . ."

"In the mafia? I know," I say, gently.

Lucy swallows. "Yes. I know you all probably guessed something to that nature, but I never wanted to come out and admit it. I love my family, but it's not easy to be a part of them sometimes. But in this case, it was beneficial. The Morozovs heard whispers of Yegor's plans since we're distantly related. I knew anything that impacted Asher, impacted you, so I couldn't sit idly by.

"I forced my father to investigate and help Sterling gather intel. And when we heard about the plan to send in decoy men, I had my father reach out to Yegor and offer his services. Yegor's men are mostly in Russia, and what's left of Sergei's are busy putting out a thousand fires of Asher's making, so he needed men. My father offered his in a deal, and Yegor happily accepted. Our men pretended to do Yegor's bidding, but they were really following *our* orders. And our orders were that Asher and the other Langfords were to be protected at all costs. The men would act as if they worked for Yegor until he was ensnared, and then at a signal, they'd turn on him."

"Who were the men that collapsed? And how and why did they all collapse?" I ask.

"Those were Yegor's true men," Sterling answers. "With Lucy's help, I was able to identify all of them. I have some side projects I work on with Langford Holdings, and one technology we've created is a small taser the size of a microchip. It works a little differently, but as you saw today, it's highly effective. Lucy's men made sure to plant them on Volkov's men. Once the shit started to hit the fan, I activated the chips, and essentially tased them on the spot. The chip is powerful enough to knock someone unconscious for about thirty minutes.

"But what we were worried about was the snipers," Sterling continues. "We had no intel on that beforehand. If Volkov's man hadn't gloated and disclosed the snipers' presence to you and Asher, we would have gone in blind. Luckily, I had Asher, myself, Declan, and my dad fit with earpieces and microphones today, so we heard everything the security guard and Volkov said to Asher. As soon as I found out, I sent word to our security, and they got to work tracking them down. That's why our normal men were nowhere to be seen. I sent them all off to hunt down the snipers. It took a full hour to find and dispatch all of them, so our hands were tied until that point. As soon as I got word that they were taken care of, I let Asher know, and he gave the signal. We're all just upset that you were a part of it. All of this was supposed to be aimed at Asher, not you."

"I still hate the idea of any of it being aimed at Asher," I grind out, furious with the lot of them. No matter how prepared they were, the plan was still too damn risky.

"Then you understand a fraction of how I feel when you're in danger," Asher whispers in my ear.

"I don't feel a fraction, I feel the same amount of fear you do," I hiss, wanting to strangle him and kiss him all at the same time. But there's no time for either of those things right now.

"Has anyone heard anything about Declan?" I ask. "I'm so worried about him."

"He'll be okay," Sterling says. "I just got a text from my mom. Nothing vital was hit. He just came out of surgery, and everything went well."

"Thank god. Why did he do that?" I groan, livid with Declan for putting himself in danger.

"Because Volkov knew he was done for at that point and was about to shoot you just out of spite," Sterling answers. "None of us could stand by and watch that happen. You're family, Ella."

My eyes widen, and I swallow hard. I haven't interacted

with Sterling nearly as much as I have with Declan, and to hear him call me family has my already frail emotions ready to overflow.

"And Flores? I never saw her after I was hauled into the ballroom."

"She's okay," Sterling reassures. "She's a little worse for the wear, they roughed her up a bit, but the men holding her were tased with the rest, so she got away."

I let out a long sigh of relief, but my anxiety is still ricocheting inside me.

Asher must sense that I'm about near my end because he takes me by the hand and hauls me off the couch. "Can everyone give us a minute?" he says, before leading me to his bedroom.

The moment the door shuts, he pulls me to him and buries his face in my hair. He lets out a devastating, shuddering breath that I mirror.

"Ella," he whispers, his voice trembling. He runs his hands down my back and pulls me in tighter, as if he's afraid I'll disappear.

"It's okay. I'm okay," I reassure him. "It's over, Asher. Yegor's gone. We're safe."

"I thought I might lose you. Just let me hold you for a minute, please?"

We sway softly, as if we're dancing without music. It's been weeks since I touched him. And every day was agony. Weeks since we broke up and my heart shattered and my world crumbled beneath my feet. All the pain of those weeks bleeds between us, and all either of us can do is cling to the other for any form of comfort.

"I'm so sorry, baby," Asher says, over and over again.

Soon, I'm sobbing into his shoulder. He bends down, picks me up, and carries me to his bed. He sets me down gently, then peels off his suit jacket. The holsters with guns strapped to either side of him remind me of the realities of Asher's life, and it hits me again just how dangerous today was. How Asher knew he was walking into a trap set by Yegor, and yet he did it anyway. How he was prepared for that trap until I showed up unexpectedly and changed everything.

"It's okay, baby," he says as he carefully takes out each gun, then unloading them, before setting them in his nightstand drawer. "You're safe, and I'll never let anything like this happen again." Once he's free of his holsters, he lies down next to me and draws me to him. My sobbing intensifies as the fear of today and the sorrow of the last month hit me with a force I can't withstand.

Asher kisses my hair, my temples, and runs soothing hands down my back. "I'm here, love," he whispers. "I'll always be here."

A SOFT THUD stirs me from sleep. I blink, but the room is mostly dark. I must have drifted off after I cried until my tears dried up. I roll over and push myself to sit up.

Asher is sitting next to me in bed.

"Once again, it's good to see your eyes open, Ms. Hale."

I let out a ghost of a chuckle.

Asher reaches over and turns on the bedside lamp, then reaches into the drawer of his nightstand and pulls something out of it. A deep blue jewelry box shines under the soft lighting. He scoots next to me and places the box on my lap before opening it. My breath catches.

The Langford pendant sits inside.

"I know I fucked up," Asher says, his voice catching. "And you were right. It was wrong to drug you and force you away, but I honestly didn't know what else to do. Every day you were in danger, and we couldn't track down Yegor. Letting you stay was too much of a risk, and your life is not a risk I will ever gamble with."

"You should have talked to me."

He lets out a long sigh. "I know. And I'm sorry. I panicked. Plain and simple. I just fucking panicked. I guess I'm hoping you can understand why, and that you can try to forgive me for it."

"I'm still mad that you went behind my back . . . but I know why you felt you had to. It took me a while to realize that sometimes I can be just as stubborn as you." It stings my pride and my sense of self to admit that, but Flores's words ring through me, and I know I need to be honest with myself. I would have fought Asher tooth and nail if he'd suggested I leave. And maybe leaving wasn't the answer, but maybe it was. Who's to know? It's not like there's a manual that we could have consulted to know the best way to deal with a situation like this. I hate that Asher did what he did, but I can certainly understand that he panicked and did what he thought was best.

"This has all been a bit of uncharted waters, so if you promise to never do that to me again, I promise to really listen when you are worried about safety and to cooperate with what needs to be done."

Asher laces his fingers through mine and rubs his thumb along the back of my hand. "I promise. I learned my lesson. I won't let my past, or my fear, rule me anymore. My life will always come with risk and danger, and I'll always be possessive and arrogant and crazy about security, I can't help that, but I promise I won't let it overtake me again. And I promise to communicate with you and consult you on things. I won't keep you in the dark and make decisions on your behalf."

"Thank you," I whisper.

"You're my *home*, Ella—my everything. I will do anything, promise you anything, if you'll give me another chance. I can't imagine my life without you. I've lived that life for six weeks, and I can't do it for another second." He lets out a long breath and his blue eyes shimmer with unshed emotion as he levels me with a look of raw want and need that takes my breath away. "I never expected to love anyone, and I *definitely* never expected to love someone the way I love you. You changed my life. You changed *me*. And you own me— completely." He lifts the pendant from the box. "Can you accept this again?"

I run my fingertips over it.

"This seems to be a pattern with us, doesn't it?" I can't help but tease. "You fucking up and then apologizing and presenting me with jewelry."

Asher lets out a half laugh, then clears his throat. "It does. Luckily for me, I have a vast amount of jewelry at my disposal, so I have lots of wiggle room for future apologies."

I shake my head. "You're shameless."

"Always."

He nudges the box, eyeing me expectantly. "So, will you?"

"I'm not sure."

Asher startles, blinking at me in surprise.

"But maybe if it was an official dare, I could."

Asher's eyes flash with relief and then narrow. He pinches my side and leans in to nip at my earlobe, his favorite little form of correction.

"Ella Hale, I solemnly dare you to accept this Langford pendant, and to be mine in every way possible. For forever."

I smile at him, and it takes me no time to decide. "Yes."

Asher crashes his lips to mine.

A moment later he pulls away, and I almost whimper at the loss. He smirks as he clasps the necklace around my neck. The pendant settles on my chest, and Asher runs his hand along the chain and stops his fingers on the pendant, admiring it almost as if he's in awe at seeing it back on me. His eyes meet mine, and just like that, everything settles back into place, as it should be. As if the last six weeks hadn't happened. As if there's nothing that can keep our future from us.

Asher takes my face in his hands and kisses me again. Slowly, reverently at first, but within seconds, the kiss evolves. The weight of all we've been through these last few weeks lifts, and that consuming need blooms between us. The kiss turns frantic, and soon his hands are in my hair, on my back, skimming all over me, as if he can't touch me enough.

Our hands clash and tangle with each other as clothes go flying between our gasps and panting breaths. Asher kisses down my neck and chest and takes my breast in his mouth with a groan. A second later he slides inside me with one thrust, and now it's my turn to groan. We both still for a moment, reveling at the feel of it. At the rightness of him inside me.

I run my hand along his jaw, and he keeps his eyes locked on mine as he trails his fingertips over the pendant around my throat again. "You're mine," he whispers as he starts to move. "Forever."

"I'm yours. And you're mine."

"Always."

As we move together, all our hurt and fear crumble away. And once again, there is nothing that exists beyond him and me and our love. He rests his forehead on mine, and my fingertips cling to his back as he threads his fingers through my hair. This is more than just making love. This is an apology. This is an admission. This is a vow of life to come—a promise of our future as one.

"Mine," he whispers again.

I look into those beautiful blue eyes that once intimidated me. And then everything changed. Now all I see is home.

"Yours."

EPILOGUE

ELLA
SEVEN MONTHS LATER

"Why is the party being held at Langford Holdings?" I ask as we pull up to the building.

Asher takes my hand just as he used to when we worked here together and leads me to the elevator.

"A change of pace. This isn't a party for the entire company, it's a small affair. Why go through the fuss of a big ballroom?"

"And what's this for again?"

"A celebration. We're having a fantastic first quarter, and we decided to throw our management a thank-you party."

"It will be nice to see everyone. I haven't seen anyone but Emily and Matthew in ages."

I haven't been back as an employee of Langford Holdings since the poisoning incident. I don't miss the work per se, since PR wasn't really my thing, but I do miss the people from time to time. I should make time to come visit them, but I'm so busy lately that I haven't even thought of it.

After his grandfather's memorial, Asher and I launched Langford Charities, and I've been the head of it since. I love the work, I truly do. Sometimes I laugh at how on brand it is to be that stereotypical rich bitch who runs a charity, but then I remind myself that this is something I've truly grown a passion for, and I get to use my marketing skills more often than not, so it's a really good fit for me. Plus, with the literal hundred million dollars Asher transferred into my bank account, and the fact that I live in Asher's world where everything is provided for me, I never have to work a day in my life again. I know how stupidly fortunate that is, and I want to give back. Between Langford Charities and my brand ambassadorship with Lennox Rose, I'm busier than I've ever been. And with Asher, I'm happier than I've ever been.

I'm still learning to navigate the attention from the paparazzi, which has let up some but is still very much a part of my life. And I'm still getting used to people recognizing me and publishing all sorts of news and stories about me—most of which are false—but it is what it is. With my focus on charity work and the opportunity to interact with amazing people working to help those in need every day, my perspective remains clear. At the end of the day, I'm incredibly lucky, and I don't take it for granted.

But it's not just the money and lifestyle that make me so damn lucky. It's Asher. Those things are secondary to him. Without him, all of that would be meaningless. Since I met him a year ago, life has been crazy, but it's also been heaven on earth. We still argue about his overly protective ways, and he still often acts first and asks for forgiveness later. But it's okay, I secretly love that about him. He's been much better at communicating with me since the memorial, so I take it as a win.

"Why aren't we heading to the east lobby?" I ask, confused at the direction he's leading me in.

"Emily wanted to show me something quickly before the party. It's in her office, and I don't want to make her bring it up, so I told her we'd meet her there first."

"My old marketing floor," I say as we take the elevator up.

"Feeling nostalgic, Ms. Hale?" He quirks a brow.

"Maybe I am. Maybe you can fuck me on my old desk."

Asher chokes and covers it with a cough.

I smile despite myself as Asher pushes open the glass doors that lead to the marketing and PR floor. I can't help but think of how intimidated I was by him in our PR meetings and how he hated me at first. I chuckle to myself. How times have changed.

"What are you laughing about?"

"I was just thinking about how mad you were the first time we met. And how you seriously thought about firing me on more than one occasion."

Asher grins. "Good thing I didn't."

Asher heads left, and I furrow my brows. "I thought you said we were meeting Emily in her office. It's the other way."

"Did I say her office? I meant the conference room."

Asher pushes open the doors to the conference room, and as I follow him through, I gasp. The lights are off, but the room is lit with hundreds of candles that are spread across the floor and the table that has been pushed against the wall. Rose petals cover every inch of the floor, and the ceiling has been draped in cream tuille. It's beautiful, decadent—romantic. But the best part is that standing in the center of the room, holding more candles, are the people we love most. My mom, Maya, Zahra, Lucy, Declan, Sterling, Alec, Harrington, Catherine, Emily, and Matthew.

Asher leads me to them and kneels in front of me.

I immediately start to cry.

"One year ago today, you stumbled into this office in the most god-awful clothes, late to our meeting."

I let out a small laugh through my tears.

"I was so angry about being forced into that meeting that your disruption almost made my temper boil over. But it didn't. Because one second after seeing you, something inside me shifted. I didn't realize it at the time. I hardly recognized it. But it happened, nonetheless. Something about you immediately drew my attention and intrigued me, and by the next day, I knew you were something remarkable. I could see it in your clever mind and work ethic, and of course, I couldn't help but be awed by your beauty.

"I wanted you long before I admitted it to myself. And then once I had you, you were like an addiction I couldn't get enough of. No matter how hard I tried to stay professional, to keep boundaries, I couldn't. Something deep inside me wanted you—all of you. And once we decided to drop all pretense and be together, I realized I'd never known true happiness before in my life.

"Ella, you're my world, my everything, and I can't live without you. Will you make the happiest man on earth? Will you marry me?"

Tears spill freely down my cheeks. "Yes," I squeak, barely able to speak.

"The ring, idiot," Declan stage whispers.

"Oh, right." Asher reaches into his suit pocket. He pulls out a dark blue velvet jewelry case. A Langford jewelry case. He opens the box and a ring I've seen before sits inside. A ring I've worn before. But I keep that bit of information to myself. No need to explain to his parents that I wore a *lot* of Langford jewelry once upon a time. But Asher remembers. He winks and smirks at me as he slides it onto my finger.

The diamond ring is oval shaped, and such an ungodly size that it can possibly be seen from space, and it's set into a gorgeous gold band with more diamonds. The ring is simple but stunning, and most importantly, it links Asher and me together forever.

Asher stands and lifts me off my feet, kissing me.

Our families and friends cheer, and I hear Matthew and Emily already discussing the engagement announcement set to go out as soon as possible.

"You'd best get planning, Ms. Hale," Asher says in his bossy CEO voice as he sets me on my feet. "I expect to be calling you Mrs. Langford by the end of summer."

God, that CEO voice does things to me. I fight the flush in my cheeks and remind myself that we're not alone. I lean in and whisper in his ear. "As long as you sometimes call me Ms. Hale in the bedroom to make sure I'm still your good little employee, I'll do whatever you want."

Asher makes a growl in the back of his throat and leans down and whispers roughly in my ear. "Keep talking like that, Ms. Hale, and I'll throw you on that table and fuck you like my good little employee in front of our families."

I blush.

Then I laugh as I brush away my tears of happiness. Asher lifts my left hand to his mouth and kisses my knuckle above my ring.

"Thank you for loving me," he says.

"Thank you for choosing me."

He smirks and shakes his head slightly. "It wasn't a choice. It was an inevitability."

New tears spring up as Asher kisses me again and our loved ones circle around us.

"Mine," he says, brushing his thumb over my bottom lip.

"Yours."

ACKNOWLEDGMENTS

First off, I want to say thank you to **you**, my dear reader! Without you, none of this is possible. Thank you for your support, your time, your reviews, and your willingness to share these characters with the world and with your book besties—it makes all the difference in the world to an indie author like me! I hope you loved these characters as much as I do, and I hope we find ourselves back in this same place book after book, for years to come.

Thank you to my Blush and Burn Book Club besties!!! Laura Eakin and Annie Baxter, thank you for all you do! Joining your book club has given me so much confidence and having a gaggle of amazing women champion my writing and my books is something I'm so grateful for. To my beta readers: Annie, Annie 2 or Innocent Annie, whom we've all happily corrupted, Alexis, Amy, Brooke, Emily, and Mikala, thank you for your awesome feedback, it truly helped me to make the story so much stronger!

Thank you to Ailene Kubricky for your editing prowess and your patience. Your enthusiasm for this story and these characters helped me get through the hard days. And thank you to Artscandare for the beautiful cover.

And finally, thank you to my family! Your love and support mean everything to me. Without you, none of this would be possible. Thank you for staying on this ride with me for all the years it's taken me to get here. You believed in me every step of the way and that is a gift I don't take lightly. To my girls: you inspire me every day. Being your mother is the light of my life, and loving you made me brave enough to become my true self and dare to share that person with the world. You are my everything, and I love you more than words can express. To my doodles, thank you for always staying by my side. Writing can be a lonesome endeavor, but having my little shadows with me makes it a lot less lonely!

ABOUT THE AUTHOR

A.V. Archer is a romance author who loves a good book boyfriend, no matter their shade of gray, and loves to write about them and the strong heroine counterparts they lose their minds over. A.V. Archer spends her days writing, homeschooling, and being followed around incessantly by two golden doodles. She has a TBR list a mile high, has no self-control and reads far too late into the nights, and lives for a good iced latte. You can connect with her at:

facebook.com/avarcherauthor

instagram.com/@avarcherauthor

tiktok.com/@avarcherauthor